THE TWO HEROINES OF PLUMPLINGTON
AND OTHER STORIES

ANTHONY TROLLOPE

THE TWO HEROINES OF PLUMPLINGTON AND OTHER STORIES

INTRODUCED BY
JULIAN SYMONS

DRAWINGS BY
PETER REDDICK

THE FOLIO SOCIETY
LONDON 1981

SET IN TEN POINT SCOTCH ROMAN LEADED ONE POINT
AND PRINTED BY BUTLER & TANNER LTD, FROME
ON FINE BOOK WOVE PAPER
BOUND BY BUTLER & TANNER LTD
IN SCHOLCO BRILLIANTA CLOTH
WITH PRINTED PAPER SIDES
DESIGNED BY SALLY LOU SMITH

Printed in Great Britain

CONTENTS

INTRODUCTION

In the great resurgence of Anthony Trollope's reputation that brought back to fame and popularity first the Barchester stories, then the Palliser series, and then such late and masterly works as *The Way We Live Now* and *Mr Scarborough's Family*, his short stories have been ignored. Michael Sadleir, who was more responsible than any other single person for the Trollope revival, gave them a single page in *Trollope: A Commentary*, observing that such a story as 'John Bull on the Guadalquivir' had its origins in an occasion when the author mistook a duke for a torero, and adding with a touch of condescension that some of the European tales show Trollope laughing a little heavily at his own heaviness. No critic since Sadleir has considered the short stories seriously, yet Trollope published five collections of them, and although they are of minor importance in the body of his work, their writing and publication show him at his most ruthlessly practical. A novel for Trollope was something to be planned, with preliminary attention paid to characters and plot. For short stories he often used incidents that had occurred on his travels, surrounding them with a coating of fiction.

One of his earliest extant letters, to the publisher Richard Bentley, mentions his own projected work after dealing with the printer's dilatoriness in relation to a book of his mother's. 'Is it in your power to lend me any assistance in procuring the insertions of lucubrations of my own in any of the periodical magazines &c which come out in such monthly swarms?' he asks. This was twelve years before the appearance of his first novel, and although stories were presumably written, none appeared in print. At the end of the eighteen fifties, however, he began work on a series of stories 'to be called when completed, "Tales of All Countries",' he told *Harper's New Monthly Magazine*, adding that each would refer to some different nation or people, and that he would like to see a story published every month. The idea was important to him, for although the first three Barchester books had appeared, and the amounts he received had steadily increased, the largest sums he had received at this time in 1859 were £400 each for *Doctor Thorne* and *The Bertrams*. He got £20 a story from *Harper's* (who, however, published only four) and hoped for a further £50 a story in England, reserving the right to publish in book form after six months.

There was thus the possibility of doing very well out of the stories, although his hopes were not fully realised, for he got only £20 in several cases where he had asked for £50. In the meantime, however, the financial importance of the stories was diminished by the offer of £1,000 to write a novel for the *Cornhill Magazine* (this was *Framley Parsonage*). The eighteen sixties was the most prolific and the most profitable decade of Trollope's writing life. *Tales of All Countries* duly appeared in book form, eight stories in the first volume published in 1861, nine in the second which came out two years later, but whatever may have been the author's original intention they were now no more than by-products of his career as a highly successful novelist.

If these remarks seem strongly preoccupied with questions of money, they reflect Trollope's own concern to strike the best possible bargain, whether negotiating with *Harper's*, with Thackeray for the *Cornhill*, with the manager of the newly-founded *London Review*, or with George Smith of Smith, Elder, who objected to the indelicacy of one story. 'The Banks of the Jordan', later renamed 'A Ride Across Palestine', told of how the narrator travelled across the desert in the company of a young woman dressed as a man, without identifying her sex. At one point the narrator got hold of his companion by the calf to demonstrate that it would be better to have an English rather than a Turkish saddle, and this scene in particular disturbed the publisher. 'The affair of the saddle, and that other affair of the leg (I think I said leg –) could be arranged,' Trollope said, but Smith had also asked for cuts, and these he refused. His reply is typical in its down-to-earth candour and its good humour:

'Did you ever buy your own meat? That cutting down of thirty pages to twenty, is what you proposed to the butcher when you asked him to take off the bony bit at this end, & the skinny bit at the other. You must remember that the butcher told you that nature had produced the joint bone & skin as you saw it, & that it behoved him to sell what nature had thus produced. Besides one cannot shorten a story. Little passages are sure to hang on what is taken out.'

When this story appeared in another magazine, readers wrote to complain of its low moral tone, and Trollope had similar trouble with another tale in the series, 'Mrs General Talboys', which was rejected by Thackeray for the *Cornhill*. This is a little comedy about an innocent but incurably flirtatious matron on holiday in Rome, whose extravagant language is misunderstood by an Irish artist. He suggests that she should accompany him to Naples, and is given 'a knock in the ribs that nearly sent me backwards' for his impertinence. The story seems harmless enough by any standards, but Trollope mentioned in passing the fact that another member of this artistic-literary set was living in Rome with his mistress and two illegitimate children, something viewed without disapprobation by Mrs General Talboys, who said that he was seeking 'such comfort in another love as the hard cruel world will allow him'. Trollope said that he felt no annoyance at Thackeray's rejection of this story. 'Pure morals must be supplied, and the owner of the responsible name must be the Judge of the purity,' he wrote with perhaps a touch of irony, but he strongly rejected the idea that his work was indecent, and remarked on the illegitimacies and naughtiness to be found in Scott, Charlotte Brontë, George Eliot, Dickens and Thackeray himself. 'I have mentioned our five greatest names & feel that I do not approach them in naughtiness any more than I do in genius.'

In spite of this firm defence, Trollope cannot have been pleased by such criticisms, nor with financial returns smaller than he had hoped. However, he still wrote short stories, occasionally, publishing nine of them in *Lotta Schmidt* (1867) and another five in the collection *Why Frau Frohmann Raised Her Prices* which appeared in the year of his death, as well as *An Editor's Tales* (1870) which had their origins in his editorial work for *St Paul's Magazine*. The extent to which he felt himself to be a workman, entitled to a fair return for his labour but also with a duty to give value for money, is emphasised by a letter to the publisher Alexander Strahan, who proposed to bring out *Lotta Schmidt* in two volumes. This Trollope positively refused to permit, adding that 'I have always endeavored to give good measure to the public – The pages, as you propose to publish them, are so thin and desolated, and contain such a poor rate of type meandering thro' a desert of margin, as to make me ashamed of putting my name to the book.' He ended by offering to share the expense involved 'on condition that you break up the type and print the stories afresh,' and *Lotta Schmidt* duly appeared as a single volume.

Three of the stories republished here, 'John Bull on the Guadalquivir', 'Aaron Trow' and 'The Man Who Kept His Money in a Box' come from the *Tales of All Countries* collections. 'Lotta Schmidt' appeared first in 1866, and 'Why Frau Frohmann Raised Her Prices' and 'Christmas at Thompson Hall' belong to the late eighteen seventies. The short stories as a whole reflect the astonishing extent of Trollope's travels. Many of his journeys were carried out on behalf of the Post Office, for whom he went to Egypt, Malta and Gibraltar, made a journey to the West Indies, and looked in on Cuba and Panama, 'thence across Central America, through Costa Rica, and down the Nicaraguan rivers to the Musquito coast, and after that home by Bermuda and New York.' Wherever he went (and those official journeys are less than half of his travels) he accepted what happened with gusty enjoyment, looked with endless curiosity through his little spectacles at the people he met and, as passages like that in 'John Bull' about Seville cathedral show, was more perceptive about what he looked at than might be expected.

The selection made here is an excellent reflection of his scope as a short story writer, ranging from the legendary action story 'Aaron Trow' (very likely based on a tale he heard when visiting Bermuda) to the French farce of 'Christmas at Thompson Hall', from the comedy of errors of 'The Man Who Kept His Money in a Box', the central incident of which seems to anticipate the puzzle of Mr Crawley's cheque, to the homely economics of 'Frau Frohmann'. The novels are full of irony both sharp and delicate, but their humour is often of the disastrously clodhopping kind found in *The Struggles of Brown, Jones and Robinson*. The comic short stories often seem to come off better, perhaps just because they are short, perhaps because the John Bullish narrator who appears in several of them is seen as a figure of fun.

'The Two Heroines of Plumplington' stands rather apart from the rest of the collection. It is a novella rather than a short story, and it is set in England, even nominally in Barsetshire. It was written to appear in a Christmas Annual for 1882, but on December 6 of that year Trollope died. The story remained almost unknown until a hard-cover edition was published in 1953.

I say that the story is set only nominally in Barsetshire in part because none of the old characters appear, although Hiram's Hospital is mentioned, and in part because Plumplington, although said to be the second town in the county, was previously unknown to readers of the six Barset chronicles. It does not appear on Trollope's map of Barsetshire, nor on those drawn by Father Ronald Knox, Mr Spencer van Bokkelen Nichols or the Folio Society's cartographer. John Hampden's claim that the story is 'one more chronicle of Barsetshire' cannot really be maintained. The style and character of the Barset novels is missing, but that is not to call the story negligible, as Mr Hampden seems to think it.

On the contrary, below the sugared surface of goodwill and play-fulness obligatory for a Victorian Christmas story, the tale is concerned with the levels of social snobbery that occupied Trollope more and more in his old age. *The Way We Live Now* excoriates a whole group of characters whose snobbery wars continually against their love of money. 'The Two Heroines' has no such serious purpose, but Trollope sees with an amused eye the indignation of Mr Greenmantle the bank manager, when Dr Freeborn the rector equates his paternal problems with those of the artisan Hickory Peppercorn. 'Your papa and my father are not the same,' Polly Peppercorn says to Emily Greenmantle. 'One is a gentleman, and the other isn't.'

To Dr Freeborn, however, neither a bank manager nor a sawyer can be a gentleman. He regards it as ridiculous that Greenmantle should hope to have 'some young county swell for his son-in-law'. Yet in the next paragraph Trollope lets us know that the rector's daughters 'had taken husbands nearly as old as their father, because Dr Freeborn and his wife had thought much of "blood".' A quarter of a century earlier Trollope might have supported such distinc-tions, regarding them as a necessary part of the social fabric. Now he points out their absurdity in a gentle social fable. This graceful little story is a minor work, of course, but it still shows the hand of a master.

JULIAN SYMONS

THE TWO HEROINES
OF PLUMPLINGTON

1: THE TWO GIRLS

In the little town of Plumplington last year, just about this time
of the year – it was in November – the ladies and gentlemen forming
the Plumplington Society were much exercised as to the affairs of
two young ladies. They were both the only daughters of two elderly
gentlemen, well known and greatly respected in Plumplington.
All the world may not know that Plumplington is the second town
in Barsetshire, and though it sends no member to Parliament, as
does Silverbridge, it has a population of over 20,000 souls, and
three separate banks. Of one of these Mr Greenmantle is the manager,
and is reputed to have shares in the bank. At any rate he is known
to be a warm man. His daughter Emily is supposed to be the heiress
of all he possesses, and has been regarded as a fitting match by
many of the sons of the country gentlemen around. It was rumoured
a short time since that young Harry Gresham was likely to ask
her hand in marriage, and Mr Greenmantle was supposed at the
time to have been very willing to entertain the idea. Whether Mr
Gresham has ever asked or not, Emily Greenmantle did not in-
cline her ear that way, and it came out while the affair was being
discussed in Plumplington circles that the young lady much preferred one Mr Philip Hughes. Now Philip Hughes was a very
promising young man, but was at the time no more than a cashier
in her father's bank. It became known at once that Mr Greenmantle
was very angry. Mr Greenmantle was a man who carried himself
with a dignified and handsome demeanour, but he was one of
whom those who knew him used to declare that it would be found
very difficult to turn him from his purpose. It might not be possible
that he should succeed with Harry Gresham, but it was considered
out of the question that he should give his girl and his money to
such a man as Philip Hughes.

The other of these elderly gentlemen is Mr Hickory Peppercorn.
It cannot be said that Mr Hickory Peppercorn had ever been put
on a par with Mr Greenmantle. No one could suppose that Mr
Peppercorn had ever sat down to dinner in company with Mr and

Miss Greenmantle. Neither did Mr or Miss Peppercorn expect to
be asked on the festive occasion of one of Mr Greenmantle's dinners.
But Miss Peppercorn was not unfrequently made welcome to Miss
Greenmantle's five o'clock tea-table; and in many of the affairs of
the town the two young ladies were seen associated together. They
were very active in the schools, and stood nearly equal in the good
graces of old Dr Freeborn. There was, perhaps, a little jealousy on
this account in the bosom of Mr Greenmantle, who was pervaded
perhaps by an idea that Dr Freeborn thought too much of himself.
There never was a quarrel, as Mr Greenmantle was a good church-
man; but there was a jealousy. Mr Greenmantle's family sank into
insignificance if you looked beyond his grandfather; but Dr Freeborn could talk glibly of his ancestors in the time of Charles I. And
it certainly was the fact that Dr Freeborn would speak of the two
young ladies in one and the same breath.

Now Mr Hickory Peppercorn was in truth nearly as warm a man
as his neighbour, and he was one who was specially proud of being
warm. He was a foreman - or rather more than a foreman - a kind
of top sawyer in the brewery establishment of Messrs Du Boung and
Co., a firm which has an establishment also in the town of Silverbridge. His position in the world may be described by declaring
that he always wears a dark coloured tweed coat and trousers, and
a chimney-pot hat. It is almost impossible to say too much that is
good of Mr Peppercorn. His one great fault has been already
designated. He was and still is very fond of his money. He does not
talk much about it; but it is to be feared that it dwells too constantly
on his mind. As a servant to the firm he is honesty and constancy
itself. He is a man of such a nature that by means of his very presence
all the partners can be allowed to go to bed if they wish it. And
there is not a man in the establishment who does not know him to
be good and true. He understands all the systems of brewing, and
his very existence in the brewery is a proof that Messrs Du Boung
and Co. are prosperous.

He has one daughter, Polly, to whom he is so thoroughly devoted
that all the other girls in Plumplington envy her. If anything is
to be done Polly is asked to go to her father, and if Polly does go to
her father the thing is done. As far as money is concerned it is not
known that Mr Peppercorn ever refused Polly anything. It is the
pride of his heart that Polly shall be, at any rate, as well dressed as
Emily Greenmantle. In truth nearly double as much is spent on
her clothes, all of which Polly accepts without a word to show her
pride. Her father does not say much, but now and again a sigh does
escape him. Then it came out, as a blow to Plumplington, that Polly

way, afraid of Polly. Polly could order the things, in and about the house, very much after her own fashion. To tell the truth Polly had but slight fear but that she would have her own way, and when she laid by her best silks she did not do it as a person does bid farewell to those treasures which are not to be seen again. They could be made to do very well for the future Mrs Hollycombe. At any rate, like a Marlborough or a Wellington, she went into the battle thinking of victory and not of defeat. But Wellington was a long time before he had beaten the French, and Polly thought that there might be some trouble also for her. With Emily there was no prospect of ultimate victory.

Mr Greenmantle was a very stern man, who could look at his daughter as though he never meant to give way. And, without saying a word, he could make all Plumplington understand that such was to be the case. 'Poor Emily,' said the old doctor to his old wife; 'I'm afraid there's a bad time coming for her.' 'He's a nasty cross old man,' said the old woman. 'It always does take three generations to make a "gentleman". ' For Mrs Freeborn's ancestors had come from the time of James I.

'You and I had better understand each other,' said Mr Greenmantle, standing up with his back to the fireplace, and looking as though he were all poker from the top of his head to the heels of his boots. 'You cannot marry Mr Philip Hughes.' Emily said nothing but turned her eyes down upon the ground. 'I don't suppose he thinks of doing so without money.'

'He has never thought about money at all.'

'Then what are you to live upon? Can you tell me that? He has £220 from the bank. Can you live upon that? Can you bring up a family?' Emily blushed as she still looked upon the ground. 'I tell you fairly that he shall never have the spending of my money. If you mean to desert me in my old age – go.'

'Papa, you shouldn't say that.'

'You shouldn't think it.' Then Mr Greenmantle looked as though he had uttered a clenching argument. 'You shouldn't think it. Now go away, Emily, and turn in your mind what I have said to you.'

2: 'DOWN I SHALL GO'

Then there came about a conversation between the two young ladies which was in itself very interesting. They had not met each other for about a fortnight when Emily Greenmantle came to Mr Peppercorn's house. She had been thoroughly unhappy, and among her causes for sorrow had been the severance which seemed to have taken place between her and her friend. She had discussed all her troubles with Dr Freeborn, and Dr Freeborn had advised her to see Polly. 'Here's Christmas-time coming on and you are all going to quarrel among yourselves. I won't have any such nonsense. Go and see her.'

'It's not me, Dr Freeborn,' said Emily. 'I don't want to quarrel with anybody; and there is nobody I like better than Polly.' Thereupon Emily went to Mr Peppercorn's house when Peppercorn would be certainly at the brewery, and there she found Polly at home.

Polly was dressed very plainly. It was manifest to all eyes that the Polly Peppercorn of today was not the same Polly Peppercorn that had been seen about Plumplington for the last twelve months. It was equally manifest that Polly intended that everybody should see the difference. She had not meekly put on her poorer dress so that people should see that she was no more than her father's child; but it was done with some ostentation. 'If father says that Jack and I are not to have his money, I must begin to reduce myself by times.' That was what Polly intended to say to all Plumplington. She was sure that her father would have to give way under such shots as she could fire at him.

'Polly, I have not seen you, oh, for such a long time.'

Polly did not look like quarrelling at all. Nothing could be more pleasant than the tone of her voice. But yet there was something in her mode of address which at once excited Emily Greenmantle's attention. In bidding her visitor welcome she called her Miss Greenmantle. Now on that matter there had been some little trouble heretofore, in which the banker's daughter had succeeded in getting the better of the banker. He had suggested that Miss Peppercorn was safer than Polly; but Emily had replied that Polly was a nice dear girl, very much in Dr Freeborn's good favours, and in point of fact that Dr Freeborn wouldn't allow it. Mr Greenmantle had frowned, but had felt himself unable to stand against Dr Freeborn in such a matter. 'What's the meaning of the Miss Greenmantle?' said Emily sorrowfully.

'It's what I'm come to,' said Polly, without any show of sorrow, 'and it's what I mean to stick to as being my proper place. You have heard all about Jack Hollycombe. I suppose I ought to call him John as I'm speaking to you.'

'I don't see what difference it will make.'

'Not much in the long run; but yet it will make a difference. It isn't that I should not like to be just the same to you as I have been, but father means to put me down in the world, and I don't mean to quarrel with him about that. Down I shall go.'

'And therefore I'm to be called Miss Greenmantle.'

'Exactly. Perhaps it ought to have been always so as I'm so poorly minded as to go back to such a one as Jack Hollycombe. Of course it is going back. Of course Jack is as good as father was at his age. But father has put himself up since that and has put me up. I'm such poor stuff that I wouldn't stay up. A girl has to begin where her husband begins; and as I mean to be Jack's wife I have to fit myself for the place.'

'I suppose it's the same with me, Polly.'

'Not quite. You're a lady bred and born, and Mr Hughes is a gentleman. Father tells me that a man who goes about the country selling malt isn't a gentleman. I suppose father is right. But Jack is a good enough gentleman to my thinking. If he had a share of father's money he would break out in quite a new place.'

'Mr Peppercorn won't give it to him?'

'Well! That's what I don't know. I do think the governor loves me. He is the best fellow anywhere for downright kindness. I mean to try him. And if he won't help me I shall go down as I say. You may be sure of this – that I shall not give up Jack.'

'You wouldn't marry him against your father's wishes?'

Here Polly wasn't quite ready with her answer. 'I don't know that father has a right to destroy all my happiness,' she said at last. 'I shall wait a long time first at any rate. Then if I find that Jack can remain constant – I don't know what I shall do.'

'What does he say?'

'Jack? He's all sugar and promises. They always are for a time. It takes a deal of learning to know whether a young man can be true. There is not above one in twenty that do come out true when they are tried.'

'I suppose not,' said Emily sorrowfully.

'I shall tell Mr Jack that he's got to go through the ordeal. Of course he wants me to say that I'll marry him right off the reel and that he'll earn money enough for both of us. I told him only this morning –'

'Did you see him?'

'I wrote him – out quite plainly. And I told him that there were other people had hearts in their bodies besides him and me. I'm not going to break father's heart – not if I can help it. It would go very hard with him if I were to walk out of this house and marry Jack Hollycombe, quite plain like.'

'I would never do it,' said Emily with energy.

'You are a little different from me, Miss Greenmantle. I suppose my mother didn't think much about such things, and as long as she got herself married decent, didn't trouble herself much what her people said.'

'Didn't she?'

'I fancy not. These sort of cares and bothers always come with money. Look at the two girls in this house. I take it they only act just like their mothers, and if they're good girls, which they are, they get their mothers' consent. But the marriage goes on as a matter of course. It's where money is wanted that parents become stern and their children become dutiful. I mean to be dutiful for a time. But I'd rather have Jack than father's money.'

'Dr Freeborn says that you and I are not to quarrel. I am sure I don't see why we should.'

'What Dr Freeborn says is very well.' It was thus that Polly carried on the conversation after thinking over the matter for a moment or two. 'Dr Freeborn is a great man in Plumplington, and has his own way in everything. I'm not saying a word against Dr Freeborn, and goodness knows I don't want to quarrel with you, Miss Greenmantle.'

'I hope not.'

'But I do mean to go down if father makes me, and if Jack proves himself a true man.'

'I suppose he'll do that,' said Miss Greenmantle. 'Of course you think he will.'

'Well, upon the whole I do,' said Polly. 'And though I think father will have to give up, he won't do it just at present, and I shall have to remain just as I am for a time.'

'And wear –' Miss Greenmantle had intended to inquire whether it was Polly's purpose to go about in her second-rate clothes, but had hesitated, not quite liking to ask the question.

'Just that,' said Polly. 'I mean to wear such clothes as shall be suitable for Jack's wife. And I mean to give up all my airs. I've been thinking a deal about it, and they're wrong. Your papa and my father are not the same.'

'They are not the same, of course,' said Emily.

'One is a gentleman, and the other isn't. That's the long and the short of it. I oughtn't to have gone to your house drinking tea and the rest of it; and I oughtn't to have called you Emily. That's the long and short of that,' said she, repeating herself.

'Dr Freeborn thinks –'

'Dr Freeborn mustn't quite have it all his own way. Of course

Dr Freeborn is everything in Plumplington; and when I'm Jack's wife I'll do what he tells me again.'

'I suppose you'll do what Jack tells you then.'

'Well, yes; not exactly. If Jack were to tell me not to go to church – which he won't – I shouldn't do what he told me. If he said he'd like to have a leg of mutton boiled, I should boil it. Only legs of mutton wouldn't be very common with us, unless father comes round.'

'I don't see why all that should make a difference between you and me.'

'It will have to do so,' said Polly with perfect self-assurance. 'Father has told me that he doesn't mean to find money to buy legs of mutton for Jack Hollycombe. Those were his very words. I'm determined I'll never ask him. And he said he wasn't going to find clothes for Jack Hollycombe's brats. I'll never go to him to find a pair of shoes for Jack Hollycombe or one of his brats. I've told Jack as much, and Jack says that I'm right. But there's no knowing what's inside a young man till you've tried him. Jack may fall off, and if so there's an end of him. I shall come round in time, and wear my fine clothes again when I settle down as an old maid. But father will never make me wear them, and I shall never call you anything but Miss Greenmantle, unless he consent to my marrying Jack.'

Such was the eloquence of Polly Peppercorn as spoken on that occasion. And she certainly did fill Miss Greenmantle's mind with a strong idea of her persistency. When Polly's last speech was finished the banker's daughter got up, and kissed her friend, and took her leave. 'You shouldn't do that,' said Polly with a smile. But on this one occasion she returned the caress; and then Miss Greenmantle went her way thinking over all that had been said to her.

'I'll do it too, let him persuade me ever so.' This was Polly's soliloquy to herself when she was left alone, and the 'him' spoken of on this occasion was her father. She had made up her own mind as to the line of action she would follow, and she was quite resolved never again to ask her father's permission for her marriage. Her father and Jack might fight that out among themselves, as best they could. There had already been one scene on the subject between herself and her father in which the brewer's foreman had acted the part of stern parent with considerable violence. He had not beaten his girl, nor used bad words to her, nor, to tell the truth, had he threatened her with any deprivation of those luxuries to which she had been accustomed; but he had sworn by all the oaths which

he knew by heart that if she chose to marry Jack Hollycombe she should go 'bare as a tinker's brat'. 'I don't want anything better,' Polly had said. 'He'll want something else though,' Peppercorn had replied, and had bounced out of the room and banged the door.

Miss Greenmantle, in whose nature there was perhaps something of the lugubrious tendencies which her father exhibited, walked away home from Mr Peppercorn's house with a sad heart. She was very sorry for Polly Peppercorn's grief, and she was very sorry also for her own. But she had not that amount of high spirits which sustained Polly in her troubles. To tell the truth Polly had some hope that she might get the better of her father, and thereby do a good turn both to him and to herself. But Emily Greenmantle had but little hope. Her father had not sworn at her, nor had he banged the door, but he had pressed his lips together till there was no lip really visible. And he had raised his forehead on high till it looked as though one continuous poker descended from the crown of his head passing down through his entire body. 'Emily, it is out of the question. You had better leave me.' From that day to this not a word had been spoken on the 'subject'. Young Gresham had been once asked to dine at the bank, but that had been the only effort made by Mr Greenmantle in the matter.

Emily had felt as she walked home that she had not at her

command weapons so powerful as those which Polly intended to use against her father. No change in her dress would be suitable to her, and were she to make any it would be altogether inefficacious. Nor would her father be tempted by his passion to throw in her teeth the lack of either boots or legs of mutton which might be the consequence of her marriage with a poor man. There was something almost vulgar in these allusions which made Emily feel that there had been some reason for her papa's exclusiveness – but she let that go by. Polly was a dear girl, though she had found herself able to speak of the brats' feet without even a blush. 'I suppose there will be brats, and why shouldn't she – when she's talking only to me. It must be so I suppose.' So Emily had argued to herself, making the excuse altogether on behalf of her friend. But she was sure that if her father had heard Polly he would have been offended.

But what was Emily to do on her own behalf? Harry Gresham had come to dinner, but his coming had been altogether without effect. She was quite sure that she could never care for Harry Gresham, and she did not quite believe that Harry Gresham cared very much for her. There was a rumour about in the country that Harry Gresham wanted money, and she knew well that Harry Gresham's father and her own papa had been closeted together. She did not care to be married after such a fashion as that. In truth Philip Hughes was the only young man for whom she did care.

She had always felt her father to be the most impregnable of men – but now on this subject of her marriage he was more impregnable than ever. He had never yet entirely digested that poker which he had swallowed when he had gone so far as to tell his daughter that it was 'entirely out of the question'. From that hour her home had been terrible to her as a home, and had not been in the least enlivened by the presence of Harry Gresham. And now how was she to carry on the battle? Polly had her plans all drawn out, and was preparing herself for the combat seriously. But for Emily, there was no means left for fighting.

And she felt that though a battle with her father might be very proper for Polly, it would be highly unbecoming for herself. There was a difference in rank between herself and Polly of which Polly clearly understood the strength. Polly would put on her poor clothes, and go into the kitchen, and break her father's heart by preparing for a descent into regions which would be fitting for her were she to marry her young man without a fortune. But to Miss Greenmantle this would be impossible. Any marriage, made now or later, without her father's leave, seemed to her out of the question. She would only ruin her 'young man' were she to attempt it, and the attempt would be altogether inefficacious. She could only be unhappy, melancholy – and perhaps morose; but she could not be so unhappy and melancholy – or morose, as was her father. At such weapons he could certainly beat her. Since that unhappy word had been spoken, the poker within him had not been for a moment lessened in vigour. And she feared even to appeal to Dr Freeborn. Dr Freeborn could do much – almost everything in Plumplington – but there was a point at which her father would turn even against Dr Freeborn. She did not think that the doctor would ever dare to take up the cudgels against her father on behalf of Philip Hughes. She felt that it would be more becoming for her to abstain and to suffer in silence than to apply to any human being for assistance. But she could be miserable – outwardly miserable as well as inwardly – and very miserable she was determined that she would be! Her father no doubt would be miserable too; but she was sad at heart as she bethought herself that her father would rather like it. Though he could not easily digest a poker when he had swallowed it, it never seemed to disagree with him. A state of misery in which he would speak to no one seemed to be almost to his taste. In this way poor Emily Greenmantle did not see her way to the enjoyment of a happy Christmas.

3: MR GREENMANTLE IS MUCH PERPLEXED

That evening Mr Greenmantle and his daughter sat down to dinner together in a very unhappy humour. They always dined at half-past seven; not that Mr Greenmantle liked to have his dinner at that hour better than any other, but because it was considered to be fashionable. Old Mr Gresham, Harry's father, always dined at half-past seven, and Mr Greenmantle rather followed the habits of a county gentleman's life. He used to dine at this hour when there was a dinner-party, but of late he had adopted it for the family meal. To tell the truth there had been a few words between him and Dr Freeborn while Emily had been talking over matters with Polly Peppercorn. Dr Freeborn had not ventured to say a word as to Emily's love affairs; but had so discussed those of Jack Hollycombe and Polly as to leave a strong impression on the mind of Mr Greenmantle. He had quite understood that the doctor had been talking at himself, and that when Jack's name had been mentioned, or Polly's, the doctor had intended that the wisdom spoken should be intended to apply to Emily and to Philip Hughes. 'It's only because he can give her a lot of money,' the doctor had said. 'The young man is a good man, and steady. What is Peppercorn that he should want anything better for his child? Young Hollycombe has taken her fancy, and why shouldn't she have him?'

'I suppose Mr Peppercorn may have his own views,' Mr Greenmantle had answered.

'Bother his views,' the doctor had said. 'He has no one else to think of but the girl and his views should be confined to making her happy. Of course he'll have to give way at last, and will only make himself ridiculous. I shouldn't say a word about it only that the young man is all that he ought to be.'

Now in this there was not a word which did not apply to Mr Greenmantle himself. And the worst of it was the fact that Mr Greenmantle felt that the doctor intended it.

But as he had taken his constitutional walk before dinner, a walk which he took every day of his life after bank hours, he had sworn to himself that he would not be guided, or in the least affected, by Dr Freeborn's opinion in the matter. There had been an under-lying bitterness in the doctor's words which had much aggravated the banker's ill-humour. The doctor would not so have spoken of the marriage of one of his own daughters – before they had all been married. Birth would have been considered by him almost before anything. The Peppercorns and the Greenmantles were looked down upon almost from an equal height. Now Mr Greenmantle considered himself to be infinitely superior to Mr Peppercorn, and to be almost, if not altogether, equal to Dr Freeborn. He was much the richer man of the two, and his money was quite sufficient to outweigh a century or two of blood.

Peppercorn might do as he pleased. What became of Peppercorn's money was an affair of no matter. The doctor's argument was no doubt good as far as Peppercorn was concerned. Peppercorn was not a gentleman. It was that which Mr Greenmantle felt so acutely. The one great line of demarcation in the world was that which separated gentlemen from non-gentlemen. Mr Greenmantle assured himself that he was a gentleman, acknowledged to be so by all the county. The old Duke of Omnium had customarily asked him to dine at his annual dinner at Gatherum Castle. He had been in the habit of staying occasionally at Greshambury, Mr Gresham's county seat, and Mr Gresham had been quite willing to forward the match between Emily and his younger son. There could be no doubt that he was on the right side of the line of demarcation. He was therefore quite determined that his daughter should not marry the cashier in his own bank.

As he sat down to dinner he looked sternly at his daughter, and thought with wonder at the viciousness of her taste. She looked at him almost as sternly as she thought with awe of his cruelty. In her eyes Philip Hughes was quite as good a gentleman as her father. He was the son of a clergyman who was now dead, but had been intimate with Dr Freeborn. And in the natural course of events might succeed her father as manager of the bank. To be manager of the bank at Plumplington was not very much in the eyes of the world; but it was the position which her father filled. Emily vowed to herself as she looked across the table into her father's face, that she would be Mrs Philip Hughes – or remain unmarried all her life. 'Emily, shall I help you to a mutton cutlet?' said her father with solemnity.

'No thank you, papa,' she replied with equal gravity.

'On what then do you intend to dine?' There had been a sole of which she had also declined to partake. 'There is nothing else, unless you will dine off rice pudding.'

'I am not hungry, papa.' She could not decline to wear her customary clothes as did her friend Polly, but she could at any rate go without her dinner. Even a father so stern as was Mr Greenmantle could not make her eat. Then there came a vision across her eyes of a long sickness, produced chiefly by inanition, in which she might wear her father's heart out. And then she felt that she might too probably lack the courage. She did not care much for her dinner; but she feared that she could not persevere to the breaking of her father's heart. She and her father were alone together in the world, and he in other respects had always been good to her. And now a tear trickled from her eye down her nose as she gazed upon the empty plate. He ate his two cutlets one after another in solemn silence and so the dinner was ended.

He, too, had felt uneasy qualms during the meal. 'What shall I do if she takes to starving herself and going to bed, all along of that young rascal in the outer bank?' It was thus that he had thought of it, and he too for a moment had begun to tell himself that were she to be perverse she must win the battle. He knew himself to be strong in purpose, but he doubted whether he would be strong enough to stand by and see his daughter starve herself. A week's starvation or a fortnight's he might bear, and it was possible that she might give way before that time had come.

Then he retired to a little room inside the bank, a room that was half private and half official, to which he would betake himself to spend his evening whenever some especially gloomy fit would fall upon him. Here, within his own bosom, he turned over all the circumstances of the case. No doubt he had with him all the laws of God and man. He was not bound to give his money to any such interloper as was Philip Hughes. On that point he was quite clear. But what step had he better take to prevent the evil? Should he resign his position at the bank, and take his daughter away to live in the south of France? It would be a terrible step to which to be driven by his own cashier. He was as efficacious to do the work of the bank as ever he had been, and he would leave this enemy to occupy his place. The enemy would then be in a condition to marry a wife without a fortune; and who could tell whether he might not show his power in such a crisis by marrying Emily! How terrible in such a case would be his defeat! At any rate he might go for three months on sick leave. He had been for nearly forty years in the bank, and had never yet been absent for a day on sick leave. Thinking of all this he remained alone till it was time for him to go to bed.

On the next morning he was dumb and stiff as ever, and after breakfast sat dumb and stiff in his official room behind the bank counter, thinking over his great trouble. He had not spoken a word to Emily since yesterday's dinner beyond asking her whether she would take a bit of fried bacon. 'No thank you, papa,' she had said; and then Mr Greenmantle had made up his mind that he must take her away somewhere at once, lest she should be starved to death. Then he went into the bank and sat there signing his name, and meditating the terrible catastrophe which was to fall upon him. Hughes, the cashier, had become Mr Hughes, and if any young man could be frightened out of his love by the stern look and sterner voice of a parent, Mr Hughes would have been so frightened.

Then there came a knock at the door, and Mr Peppercorn having been summoned to come in, entered the room. He had expressed a desire to see Mr Greenmantle personally, and having proved his eagerness by a double request, had been allowed to have his way. It was quite a common affair for him to visit the bank on matters referring to the brewery; but now it was evident to any one with half an eye that such at present was not Mr Peppercorn's business. He had on the clothes in which he habitually went to church instead of the light-coloured pepper and salt tweed jacket in which he was accustomed to go about among the malt and barrels. 'What can I do for you, Mr Peppercorn?' said the banker. But the aspect was the aspect of a man who had a poker still fixed within his head and gullet.

"Tis nothing about the brewery, sir, or I shouldn't have troubled you. Mr Hughes is very good at all that kind of thing.' A further frown came over Mr Greenmantle's face, but he said nothing. 'You know my daughter Polly, Mr Greenmantle?'

'I am aware that there is a Miss Peppercorn,' said the other. Peppercorn felt that an offence was intended. Mr Greenmantle was of course aware. 'What can I do on behalf of Miss Peppercorn?'

'She's as good a girl as ever lived.'

'I do not in the least doubt it. If it be necessary that you should speak to me respecting Miss Peppercorn, will it not be well that you should take a chair?'

Then Mr Peppercorn sat down, feeling that he had been snubbed. 'I may say that my only object in life is to do every mortal thing to make my girl happy.' Here Mr Greenmantle simply bowed. 'We sit close to you in church, where, however, she comes much more reg'lar than me, and you must have observed her scores of times.'

'I am not in the habit of looking about among young ladies at church time, but I have occasionally been aware that Miss Peppercorn has been there.'

'Of course you have. You couldn't help it. Well, now, you know the sort of appearance she has made.'

'I can assure you, Mr Peppercorn, that I have not observed Miss Peppercorn's dress in particular. I do not look much at the raiment worn by young ladies even in the outer world – much less in church. I have a daughter of my own –'

'It's her as I'm coming to.' Then Mr Greenmantle frowned more severely than ever. But the brewer did not at the moment say a word about the banker's daughter, but reverted to his own. 'You'll see next Sunday that my girl won't look at all like herself.'

'I really cannot promise –'

'You cannot help yourself, Mr Greenmantle. I'll go bail that every one in church will see it. Polly is not to be passed over in a crowd – at least she didn't used to be. Now it all comes of her wanting to get herself married to a young man who is altogether – beneath her. Not as I mean to say anything against John Hollycombe as regards his walk of life. He is an industrious young man, as can earn forty shillings a week, and he comes over here from Barchester selling malt and such like. He may rise himself to £3 some of these days if he looks sharp about it. But I can give my girl – well; what is quite unfit that he should think of looking for with a wife. And it's monstrous of Polly wanting to throw herself away in such a fashion. I don't believe in a young man being so covetous.'

'But what can I do, Mr Peppercorn?'

'I'm coming to that. If you'll see her next Sunday you'll think of what my feelings must be. She's a-doing of it all just because she wants to show me that she thinks herself fit for nothing better than to be John Hollycombe's wife. When I tell her that I won't have it – this sudden changing of her toggery, she says it's only fitting. It ain't fitting at all. I've got the money to buy things for her, and I'm willing to pay for it. Is she to go poor just to break her father's heart?'

'But what can I do, Mr Peppercorn?'

'I'm coming to that. The world does say, Mr Greenmantle, that your young lady means to serve you in the same fashion.'

Hereupon Mr Greenmantle waxed very wroth. It was terrible to his ideas that his daughter's affairs should be talked of at all by the people at Plumplington at large. It was worse again that his daughter and the brewer's girl should be lumped together in the scandal of the town. But it was worse, much worse, that this man Peppercorn should have dared to come to him, and tell him all about it. Did the man really expect that he, Mr Greenmantle, should talk unreservedly as to the love affairs of his Emily? 'The world, Mr Peppercorn, is very impertinent in its usual scandalous conversations as to its betters. You must forgive me if I do not intend on this occasion to follow the example of the world. Good morning, Mr Peppercorn.'

'It's Dr Freeborn as has coupled the two girls together.'

'I cannot believe it.'

'You ask him. It's he who has said that you and I are in a boat together.'

'I'm not in a boat with any man.'

'Well – in a difficulty. It's the same thing. The doctor seems to think that young ladies are to have their way in everything. I don't see it. When a man has made a tidy bit of money, as have you and I, he has a right to have a word to say as to who shall have the spending of it. A girl hasn't the right to say that she'll give it all to this man or to that. Of course, it's natural that my money should go to Polly. I'm not saying anything against it. But I don't mean that John Hollycombe shall have it. Now if you and I can put our heads together, I think we may be able to see our way out of the wood.'

'Mr Peppercorn, I cannot consent to discuss with you the affairs of Miss Greenmantle.'

'But they're both alike. You must admit that.'

'I will admit nothing, Mr Peppercorn.'

'I do think, you know, that we oughtn't to be done by our own daughters.'

'Really, Mr Peppercorn –'

'Dr Freeborn was saying that you and I would have to give way at last.'

'Dr Freeborn knows nothing about it. If Dr Freeborn coupled the two young ladies together he was I must say very impertinent; but I don't think he ever did so. Good morning, Mr Peppercorn. I am fully engaged at present and cannot spare time for a longer interview.' Then he rose up from his chair, and leant upon the table with his hands by way of giving a certain signal that he was to be left alone. Mr Peppercorn, after pausing a moment, searching for an opportunity for another word, was overcome at last by the rigid erectness of Mr Greenmantle and withdrew.

4: JACK HOLLYCOMBE

Mr Peppercorn's visit to the bank had been no doubt inspired by Dr Freeborn. The doctor had not actually sent him to the bank, but had filled his mind with the idea that such a visit might be made with good effect. 'There are you two fathers going to make two fools of yourselves,' the doctor had said. 'You have each of you got a daughter as good as gold, and are determined to break their hearts because you won't give your money to a young man who happens to want it.'

'Now, doctor, do you mean to tell me that you would have married your young ladies to the first young man that came and asked for them?'

'I never had much money to give my girls, and the men who came happened to have means of their own.'

'But if you'd had it, and if they hadn't, do you mean to tell me you'd never have asked a question?'

'A man should never boast that in any circumstances of his life he would have done just what he ought to do – much less when he has never been tried. But if the lover be what he ought to be in morals and all that kind of thing, the girl's father ought not to refuse to help them. You may be sure of this – that Polly means to have her own way. Providence has blessed you with a girl that knows her own mind.' On receipt of this compliment Mr Peppercorn scratched his head. 'I wish I could say as much for my friend Greenmantle. You two are in a boat together, and ought to make up your mind as to what you should do.' Peppercorn resolved that he would remember the phrase about the boat, and began to think that it might be good that he should see Mr Greenmantle. 'What on earth is it you two want? It is not as though you were dukes, and looking for proper alliances for two ducal spinsters.'

Now there had no doubt been a certain amount of intended venom in this. Dr Freeborn knew well the weak points in Mr Greenmantle's character, and was determined to hit him where he was weakest. He did not see the difference between the banker and the brewer nearly so clearly as did Mr Greenmantle. He would probably have said that the line of demarcation came just below himself. At any rate, he thought that he would be doing best for Emily's interest if he made her father feel that all the world was on her side. Therefore it was that he so contrived that Mr Peppercorn should pay his visit to the bank.

On his return to the brewery the first person that Peppercorn saw standing in the doorway of his own little sanctum was Jack Hollycombe. 'What is it you're wanting?' he asked gruffly.

'I was just desirous of saying a few words to yourself, Mr Peppercorn.'

'Well, here I am!' There were two or three brewers and porters about the place, and Jack did not feel that he could plead his cause well in their presence. 'What is it you've got to say – because I'm busy? There ain't no malt wanted for the next week; but you know that, and as we stand at present you can send it in without any more words, as it's needed.'

'It ain't about malt or anything of that kind.'

'Then I don't know what you've got to say. I'm very busy just at present, as I told you.'

'You can spare me five minutes inside.'

'No, I can't.' But then Peppercorn resolved that neither would it suit him to carry on the conversation respecting his daughter in the presence of the workmen, and he thought that he perceived that Jack Hollycombe would be prepared to do so if he were driven. 'Come in if you will,' he said; 'we might as well have it out.' Then he led the way into the room, and shut the door as soon as Jack had followed him. 'Now what is it you have got to say? I suppose it's about that young woman down at my house.'

'It is, Mr Peppercorn.'

'Then let me tell you that the least said will be soonest mended. She's not for you – with my consent. And to tell you the truth I think that you have a mortal deal of brass coming to ask for her. You've no edication suited to her edication – and what's wus, no money.' Jack had shown symptoms of anger when his deficient education had been thrown in his teeth, but had cheered up somewhat when the lack of money had been insisted upon. 'Them two things are so against you that you haven't a leg to stand on. My word! what do you expect that I should say when such a one as you comes-a-courting to a girl like that?'

'I did, perhaps, think more of what she might say.'

'I daresay – because you knew her to be a fool like yourself. I suppose you think yourself to be a very handsome young man.'

'I think she's a very handsome young woman. As to myself I never asked the question.'

'That's all very well. A man can always say as much as that for himself. The fact is you're not going to have her.'

'That's just what I want to speak to you about, Mr Peppercorn.'

'You're not going to have her. Now I've spoken my intentions, and you may as well take one word as a thousand. I'm not a man as was ever known to change my mind when I'd made it up in such a matter as this.'

'She's got a mind too, Mr Peppercorn.'

'She have, no doubt. She have a mind and so have you. But you haven't either of you got the money. The money is here,' and Mr Peppercorn slapped his breeches pocket. 'I've had to do with earning it, and I mean to have to do with giving it away. To me there is no idea of honesty at all in a chap like you coming and asking a girl to marry you just because you know that she's to have a fortune.'

'That's not my reason.'

'It's uncommon like it. Now you see there's somebody else that's got to be asked. You think I'm a good-natured fellow. So I am, but I'm not soft like that.'

'I never thought anything of the kind, Mr Peppercorn.'

'Polly told you so, I don't doubt. She's right in thinking so, because I'd give Polly anything in reason. Or out of reason for the matter of that, because she is the apple of my eye.' This was indiscreet on the part of Mr Peppercorn, as it taught the young man to think that he himself must be in reason or out of reason, and that in either case Polly ought to be allowed to have him. 'But there's one thing I stop at; and that is a young man who hasn't got either edication, or money – nor yet manners.'

'There's nothing against my manner, I hope, Mr Peppercorn.'

'Yes; there is. You come a-interfering with me in the most delicate affair in the world. You come into my family, and want to take away my girl. That I take it is the worst of manners.'

'How is any young lady to get married unless some young fellow comes after her?'

'There'll be plenty to come after Polly. You leave Polly alone, and you'll find that she'll get a young man suited to her. It's like your impudence to suppose that there's no other young man in the world so good as you. Why – dash my wig; who are you? What are you? You're merely acting for them corn-factors over at Barsester.'

'And you're acting for them brewers here at Plumplington. What's the difference?'

'But I've got the money in my pocket, and you've got none. That's the difference. Put that in your pipe and smoke it. Now if you'll please to remember that I'm very busy, you'll walk yourself off. You've had it out with me, which I didn't intend; and I've explained my mind very fully. She's not for you – at any rate my money's not.'

'Look here, Mr Peppercorn.'

'Well?'

'I don't care a farthing for your money.'

'Don't you, now?'

'Not in the way of comparing it with Polly herself. Of course money is a very comfortable thing. If Polly's to be my wife –'

'Which she ain't.'

'I should like her to have everything that a lady can desire.'

'How kind you are.'

'But in regard to money for myself I don't value it that.' Here Jack Hollycombe snapped his fingers. 'My meaning is to get the girl I love.'

'Then you won't.'

'And, if she's satisfied to come to me without a shilling, I'm satisfied to take her in the same fashion. I don't know how much you've got, Mr Peppercorn, but you can go and found a Hiram's Hospital with every penny of it.' At this moment a discussion was going on respecting a certain charitable institution in Barchester – and had been going on for the last forty years – as to which Mr Hollycombe was here expressing the popular opinion of the day. 'That's the kind of thing a man should do who don't choose to leave his money to his own child.' Jack was now angry, having had his deficient education twice thrown in his teeth by one whom he conceived to be so much less educated than himself. 'What I've got to say to you, Mr Peppercorn, is that Polly means to have me, and she's got to wait – why, I'm so minded that I'll wait for her as long as ever she'll wait for me.' So saying Jack Hollycombe left the room.

Mr Peppercorn thrust his hat back upon his head, and stood with his back to the fire, with the tails of his coat appearing over his hands in his breeches pockets, glaring out of his eyes with anger which he did not care to suppress. This man represented to him a picture of his future life which was most unalluring. There was

nothing he desired less than to give his money to such an abominable institution as Hiram's Hospital. Polly, his own dear daughter
Polly, was intended to be the recipient of all his savings. As he
went about among the beer barrels, he had been a happy man as he
thought of Polly bright with the sheen which his money had provided
for her. But it was of Polly married to some gentleman that he

thought at these moments – of Polly surrounded by a large family
of little gentlemen and little ladies. They would all call him grand-
papa; and in the evenings of his days he would sit by the fire in
that gentleman's parlour, a welcome guest because of the means
which he had provided; and the little gentlemen and the little
ladies would surround him with their prattle and their noises and
caresses. He was not a man whom his intimates would have supposed to be gifted with a strong imagination, but there was the
picture firmly set before his mind's eye. 'Edication,' however, in the
intended son-in-law was essential. And the son-in-law must be a
gentleman. Now Jack Hollycombe was not a gentleman, and was
not educated up to that pitch which was necessary for Polly's
husband.

But Mr Peppercorn, as he thought of it all, was well aware that Polly had a decided will of her own. And he knew of himself that his own will was less strong than his daughter's. In spite of all the severe things which he had just said to Jack Hollycombe, there was present to him a dreadful weight upon his heart, as he thought that Polly would certainly get the better of him. At this moment he hated Jack Hollycombe with most un-Christian rancour. No misfortune that could happen to Jack, either sudden death, or forgery with flight to the antipodes, or loss of his good looks – which Mr Peppercorn most unjustly thought would be equally efficacious with Polly – would at the present moment of his wrath be received otherwise than as a special mark of good-fortune. And yet he was well aware that if Polly were to come and tell him that she had by some secret means turned herself into Mrs Jack Hollycombe, he knew very well that for Polly's sake he would have to take Jack with all his faults, and turn him into the dearest son-in-law that the world could have provided for him. This was a very trying position, and justified him in standing there for a quarter of an hour with his back to the fire, and his coat-tails over his arms, as they were thrust into his trousers pockets.

In the meantime Jack had succeeded in obtaining a few minutes' talk with Polly – or rather the success had been on Polly's side, for she had managed the business. On coming out from the brewery Jack had met her in the street, and had been taken home by her. 'You might as well come in, Jack,' she had said, 'and have a few words with me. You have been talking to father about it, I suppose.'

'Well; I have. He says I am not sufficiently educated. I suppose he wants to get some young man from the colleges.'

'Don't you be stupid, Jack. You want to have your own way, I suppose.'

'I don't want him to tell me I'm uneducated. Other men that I've heard of ain't any better off than I am.'

'You mean himself – which isn't respectful.'

'I'm educated up to doing what I've got to do. If you don't want more, I don't see what he's got to do with it.'

'As the times go of course a man should learn more and more. You are not to compare him to yourself; and it isn't respectful. If you want to say sharp things against him, Jack, you had better give it all up – for I won't bear it.'

'I don't want to say anything sharp.'

'Why can't you put up with him? He's not going to have his own way. And he is older than you. And it is he that has got the money. If you care about it –'

'You know I care.'

'Very well. Suppose I do know, and suppose I don't. I hear you say you do, and that's all I've got to act upon. Do you bide your time if you've got the patience, and all will come right, I shan't at all think so much of you if you can't bear a few sharp words from him.'

'He may say whatever he pleases.'

'You ain't educated – not like Dr Freeborn, and men of that class.'

'What do I want with it?' said he.

'I don't know that you do want it. At any rate I don't want it; and that's what you've got to think about at present. You just go on, and let things be as they are. You don't want to be married in a week's time.'

'Why not?' he asked.

'At any rate I don't; and I don't mean to. This time five years will do very well.'

'Five years! You'll be an old woman.'

'The fitter for you, who'll still be three years older. If you've patience to wait leave it to me.'

'I haven't over much patience.'

'Then go your own way and suit yourself elsewhere.'

'Polly, you're enough to break a man's heart. You know that I can't go and suit myself elsewhere. You are all the world to me, Polly.'

'Not half so much as a quarter of malt if you could get your own price for it. A young woman is all very well just as a play-thing; but business is business – isn't it, Jack?'

'Five years! Fancy telling a fellow that he must wait five years.'

'That'll do for the present, Jack. I'm not going to keep you here idle all the day. Father will be angry when I tell him that you've been here at all.'

'It was you that brought me.'

'Yes, I did. But you're not to take advantage of that. Now I say, Jack, hands off. I tell you I won't. I'm not going to be kissed once a week for five years. Well. Mark my words, this is the last time I ever ask you in here. No; I won't have it. Go away.' Then she succeeded in turning him out of the room and closing the house door behind his back. 'I think he's the best young man I see about anywhere. Father twits him about his education. It's my belief there's nothing he can't do that he's wanted for. That's the kind of education a man ought to have. Father says it's because he's hand-some I like him. It does go a long way, and he is handsome. Father has got ideas of fashion into his head which will send him crazy before he has done with them.' Such was the soliloquy in which Miss Peppercorn indulged as soon as she had been left by her lover.

'Educated! Of course I'm not educated. I can't talk Latin and Greek as some of those fellows pretend to – though for the matter of that I never heard it. But two and two make four, and ten and ten make twenty. And if a fellow says that it don't he is trying on some dishonest game. If a fellow understands that, and sticks to it, he has education enough for my business – or for Peppercorn's either.' Then he walked back to the inn yard where he had left his horse and trap.

As he drove back to Barchester he made up his mind that Polly Peppercorn would be worth waiting for. There was the memory of that kiss upon his lips which had not been made less sweet by the severity of the words which had accompanied it. The words indeed had been severe; but there had been an intention and a purpose about the kiss which had altogether redeemed the words. 'She is just one in a thousand, that's about the truth. And as for waiting for her – I'll wait like grim death, only I hope it won't be necessary!' It was thus he spoke of the lady of his love as he drove himself into town under Barchester Towers.

5: DR FREEBORN AND PHILIP HUGHES

Things went on at Plumplington without any change for a fort-night – that is without any change for the better. But in truth the ill-humour both of Mr Greenmantle and of Mr Peppercorn had increased to such a pitch as to add an additional blackness to the general haziness and drizzle and gloom of the November weather. It was now the end of November, and Dr Freeborn was becoming a little uneasy because the Christmas attributes for which he was desirous were still altogether out of sight. He was a man specially anxious for the mundane happiness of his parishioners and who would take any amount of personal trouble to insure it; but he was in fault perhaps in this, that he considered that everybody ought to be happy just because he told them to be so. He belonged to the Church of England certainly, but he had no dislike to Papists or Presbyterians, or dissenters in general, as long as they would arrange themselves under his banner as 'Freebornites'. And he had such force of character that in Plumplington – beyond which he was not ambitious that his influence should extend – he did in general prevail. But at the present moment he was aware that

Mr Greenmantle was in open mutiny. That Peppercorn would yield he had strong hope. Peppercorn he knew to be a weak, good fellow, whose affection for his daughter would keep him right at last. But until he could extract that poker from Mr Greenmantle's throat, he knew that nothing could be done with him.

At the end of the fortnight Mr Greenmantle called at the Rectory about half an hour before dinner time, when he knew that the doctor would be found in his study before going up to dress for dinner. 'I hope I am not intruding, Dr Freeborn,' he said. But the rust of the poker was audible in every syllable as it fell from his mouth.

'Not in the least. I've a quarter of an hour before I go and wash my hands.'

'It will be ample. In a quarter of an hour I shall be able sufficiently to explain my plans.' Then there was a pause, as though Mr Greenmantle had expected that the explanation was to begin with the doctor. 'I am thinking,' the banker continued after a while, 'of taking my family abroad to some foreign residence.' Now it was well known to Dr Freeborn that Mr Greenmantle's family consisted exclusively of Emily.

'Going to take Emily away?' he said.

'Such is my purpose – and myself also.'

'What are they to do at the bank?'

'That will be the worst of it, Dr Freeborn. The bank will be the great difficulty.'

'But you don't mean that you are going for good?'

'Only for a prolonged foreign residence – that is to say for six months. For forty years I have given but very little trouble to the directors. For forty years I have been at my post and have never suggested any prolonged absence. If the directors cannot bear with me after forty years I shall think them unreasonable men.' Now in truth Mr Greenmantle knew that the directors would make no opposition to anything that he might propose; but he always thought it well to be armed with some premonitory grievance. 'In fact my pecuniary matters are so arranged that should the directors refuse I shall go all the same.'

'You mean that you don't care a straw for the directors.'

'I do not mean to postpone my comfort to their views – or my daughter's.'

'But why does your daughter's comfort depend on your going away? I should have thought that she would have preferred Plumplington at present.'

That was true, no doubt. And Mr Greenmantle felt – well; that he was not exactly telling the truth in putting the burden of his departure upon Emily's comfort. If Emily, at the present crisis of affairs, were carried away from Plumplington for six months, her comfort would certainly not be increased. She had already been told that she was to go, and she had clearly understood why. 'I mean as to her future welfare,' said Mr Greenmantle very solemnly.

Dr Freeborn did not care to hear about the future welfare of young people. What had to be said as to their eternal welfare he thought himself quite able to say. After all there was something of benevolent paganism in his disposition. He liked better to deal with their present happiness – so that there was nothing immoral in it. As to the world to come he thought that the fathers and mothers of his younger flock might safely leave that consideration to him. 'Emily is a remarkably good girl. That's my idea of her.'

Mr Greenmantle was offended even at this. Dr Freeborn had no right, just at present, to tell him that his daughter was a good girl. Her goodness had been greatly lessened by the fact that in regard to her marriage she was anxious to run counter to her father.

'She is a good girl. At least I hope so.'

'Do you doubt it?'

'Well no – or rather yes. Perhaps I ought to say no as to her life in general.'

'I should think so. I don't know what a father may want – but I should think so. I never knew her miss church yet – either morning or evening.'

'As far as that goes she does not neglect her duties.'

'What is the matter with her that she is to be taken off to some foreign climate for prolonged residence?' The doctor among his other idiosyncrasies entertained an idea that England was the proper place for all Englishmen and Englishwomen who were not driven out of it by stress of pecuniary circumstances. 'Has she got a bad throat or a weak chest?'

'It is not on the score of her own health that I propose to move her,' said Mr Greenmantle.

'You did say her comfort. Of course that may mean that she likes the French way of living. I did hear that we were to lose your services for a time, because you could not trust your own health.'

'It is failing me a little, Dr Freeborn. I am already very near sixty.'

'Ten years my junior,' said the doctor.

'We cannot all hope to have such perfect health as you possess.'

'I have never frittered it away,' said the doctor, 'by prolonged residence in foreign parts.' This quotation of his own words was most harassing to Mr Greenmantle, and made him more than once inclined to bounce in anger out of the doctor's study. 'I suppose the truth is that Miss Emily is disposed to run counter to your wishes in regard to her marriage, and that she is to be taken away not from consumption or a weak throat, but from a dangerous lover.' Here Mr Greenmantle's face became black as thunder. 'You see, Greenmantle, there is no good in our talking about this matter unless we understand each other.'

'I do not intend to give my girl to the young man upon whom she thinks that her affections rest.'

'I suppose she knows.'

'No, Dr Freeborn. It is often the case that a young lady does not know; she only fancies, and where that is the case absence is the best remedy. You have said that Emily is a good girl.'

'A very good girl.'

'I am delighted to hear you so express yourself. But obedience to parents is a trait in character which is generally much thought of. I have put by a little money, Dr Freeborn.'

'All Plumplington knows that.'

'And I shall choose that it shall go somewhat in accordance with my wishes. The young man of whom she is thinking –'

'Philip Hughes, an excellent fellow. I've known him all my life. He doesn't come to church quite so regularly as he ought, but that will be mended when he's married.'

'Hasn't got a shilling in the world,' continued Mr Greenmantle, finishing his sentence. 'Nor is he – just – just – just what I should choose for the husband of my daughter. I think that when I have said so he should take my word for it.'

'That's not the way of the world, you know.'

'It's the way of my world, Dr Freeborn. It isn't often that I speak out, but when I do it's about something that I've a right to speak of. I've heard this affair of my daughter talked about all over the town. There was one Mr Peppercorn came to me –'

'One Mr Peppercorn? Why, Hickory Peppercorn is as well known in Plumplington as the church steeple.'

'I beg your pardon, Dr Freeborn; but I don't find any reason in that for his interfering about my daughter. I must say that I took it as a great piece of impertinence. Goodness gracious me! If a man's own daughter isn't to be considered peculiar to himself I don't know what is. If he'd asked you about your daughters – before they were married?' Dr Freeborn did not answer this, but declared to himself that neither Mr Peppercorn nor Mr Greenmantle could have taken such a liberty. Mr Greenmantle evidently was not aware of it. but in truth Dr Freeborn and his family belonged

altogether to another set. So at least Dr Freeborn told himself.
'I've come to you now, Dr Freeborn, because I have not liked to
leave Plumplington for a prolonged residence in foreign parts
without acquainting you.'

'I should have thought that unkind.'

'You are very good. And as my daughter will of course go with
me, and as this idea of a marriage on her part must be entirely
given up – ' the emphasis was here placed with much weight on the
word entirely – 'I should take it as a great kindness if you would
let my feelings on the subject be generally known. I will own that
I should not have cared to have my daughter talked about, only
that the mischief has been done.'

'In a little place like this,' said the doctor, 'a young lady's marriage
will always be talked about.'

'But the young lady in this case isn't going to be married.'

'What does she say about it herself?'

'I haven't asked her, Dr Freeborn. I don't mean to ask her. I
shan't ask her.'

'If I understand her feelings, Greenmantle, she is very much set
upon it.'

'I cannot help it.'

'You mean to say then that you intend to condemn her to unhappiness merely because this young man hasn't got as much
money at the beginning of his life as you have at the end of yours?'

'He hasn't got a shilling,' said Mr Greenmantle.

'Then why can't you give him a shilling? What do you mean to
do with your money?' Here Mr Greenmantle again looked offended.
'You come and ask me, and I am bound to give you my opinion for
what it's worth. What do you mean to do with your money? You're
not the man to found a Hiram's Hospital with it. As sure as you
are sitting there your girl will have it when you're dead. Don't
you know that she will have it?'

'I hope so.'

'And because she's to have it, she's to be made wretched about
it all her life. She's to remain an old maid, or else to be married to
some well-born pauper, in order that you may talk about your
son-in-law. Don't get into a passion, Greenmantle, but only think
whether I'm not telling you the truth. Hughes isn't a spendthrift.'

'I have made no accusation against him.'

'Nor a gambler, nor a drunkard, nor is he the sort of man to
treat a wife badly. He's there at the bank so that you may keep him
under your own eye. What more on earth can a man want in a
son-in-law?'

Blood, thought Mr Greenmantle to himself; an old family name; county associations, and a certain something which he felt quite sure Philip Hughes did not possess. And he knew well enough that Dr Freeborn had married his own daughters to husbands who possessed these gifts; but he could not throw the fact back into the rector's teeth. He was in some way conscious that the rector had been entitled to expect so much for his girls, and that he, the banker, was not so entitled. The same idea passed through the rector's mind. But the rector knew how far the banker's courage would carry him. 'Good night, Dr Freeborn,' said Mr Greenmantle suddenly.

'Good night, Greenmantle. Shan't I see you again before you go?' To this the banker made no direct answer, but at once took his leave.

'That man is the greatest ass in all Plumplington,' the doctor said to his wife within five minutes of the time of which the hall door was closed behind the banker's back. 'He's got an idea into his head about having some young county swell for his son-in-law.'

'Harry Gresham. Harry is too idle to earn money by a profession and therefore wants Greenmantle's money to live upon. There's Peppercorn wants something of the same kind for Polly. People are such fools.' But Mrs Freeborn's two daughters had been married much after the same fashion. They had taken husbands nearly as old as their father, because Dr Freeborn and his wife had thought much of 'blood'.

On the next morning Philip Hughes was summoned by the banker into the more official of the two back parlours. Since he had presumed to signify his love for Emily, he had never been asked to enjoy the familiarity of the other chamber. 'Mr Hughes, you may probably have heard it asserted that I am about to leave Plumplington for a prolonged residence in foreign parts.' Mr Hughes had heard it and so declared. 'Yes, Mr Hughes, I am about to proceed to the south of France. My daughter's health requires attention – and indeed on my own behalf I am in need of some change as well. I have not as yet officially made known my views to the directors.'

'There will be, I should think, no impediment with them.'

'I cannot say. But at any rate I shall go. After forty years of service in the bank I cannot think of allowing the peculiar views of men who are all younger than myself to interfere with my comfort. I shall go.'

'I suppose so, Mr Greenmantle.'

'I shall go. I say it without the slightest disrespect for the board. But I shall go.'

'Will it be permanent, Mr Greenmantle?'

'That is a question which I am not prepared to answer at a

moment's notice. I do not propose to move my furniture for six months. It would not, I believe, be within the legal power of the directors to take possession of the bank house for that period.'

'I am quite sure they would not wish it.'

'Perhaps my assurance on that subject may be of more avail. At any rate they will not remove me. I should not have troubled you on this subject were it not that your position in the bank must be affected more or less.'

'I suppose that I could do the work for six months,' said Philip Hughes.

But this was a view of the case which did not at all suit Mr Greenmantle's mind. His own duties at Plumplington had been, to his thinking, the most important ever confided to a bank manager. There was a peculiarity about Plumplington of which no one knew the intricate details but himself. The man did not exist who could do the work as he had done it. But still he had determined to go, and the work must be intrusted to some man of lesser competence. 'I should think it probable,' he said, 'that some confidential clerk will be sent over from Barchester. Your youth, Mr Hughes, is against you. It is not for me to say what line the directors may determine to take.'

'I know the people better than any one can do in Barchester.'

'Just so. But you will excuse me if I say you may for that reason be the less efficient. I have thought it expedient, however, to tell you of my views. If you have any steps that you wish to take you can now take them.'

Then Mr Greenmantle paused, and had apparently brought the meeting to an end. But there was still something which he wished to say. He did think that by a word spoken in due season – by a strong determined word, he might succeed in putting an end to this young man's vain and ambitious hopes. He did not wish to talk to the young man about his daughter; but, if the strong word might avail here was the opportunity. 'Mr Hughes,' he began.

'Yes, sir.'

'There is a subject on which perhaps it would be well that I should be silent.' Philip, who knew the manager thoroughly, was now aware of what was coming, and thought it wise that he should say nothing at the moment. 'I do not know that any good can be done by speaking of it.' Philip still held his tongue. 'It is a matter no doubt of extreme delicacy – of the most extreme delicacy I may say. If I go abroad as I intend, I shall as a matter of course take with me – Miss Greenmantle.'

'I suppose so.'

'I shall take with me – Miss Greenmantle. It is not to be supposed that when I go abroad for a prolonged sojourn in foreign parts, that I should leave – Miss Greenmantle behind me.'

'No doubt she will accompany you.'

'Miss Greenmantle will accompany me. And it is not improbable that my prolonged residence may in her case be – still further prolonged. It may be possible that she should link her lot in life to some gentleman whom she may meet in those realms.'

'I hope not,' said Philip.

'I do not think that you are justified, Mr Hughes, in hoping anything in reference to my daughter's fate in life.'

'All the same, I do.'

'It is very – very – ! I do not wish to use strong language, and therefore I will not say impertinent.'

'What am I to do when you tell me that she is to marry a foreigner?'

'I never said so. I never thought so. A foreigner! Good heavens! I spoke of a gentleman whom she might chance to meet in those realms. Of course I meant an English gentleman.'

'The truth is, Mr Greenmantle, I don't want your daughter to marry anyone unless she can marry me.'

'A most selfish proposition.'

'It's a sort of matter in which a man is apt to be selfish, and it's my belief that if she were asked she'd say the same thing. Of course you can take her abroad and you can keep her there as long as you please.'

'I can – and I mean to do it.'

'I am utterly powerless to prevent you, and so is she. In this contention between us I have only one point in my favour.'

'You have no point in your favour, sir.'

'The young lady's good wishes. If she be not on my side – why then I am nowhere. In that case you needn't trouble yourself to take her out of Plumplington. But if –'

'You may withdraw, Mr Hughes,' said the banker. 'The interview is over.' Then Philip Hughes withdrew, but as he went he shut the door after him in a very confident manner.

6: THE YOUNG LADIES ARE TO BE TAKEN ABROAD

How should Philip Hughes see Emily before she had been carried away to 'foreign parts' by her stern father? As he regarded the matter it was absolutely imperative that he should do so. If she should be made to go, in her father's present state of mind, without having reiterated her vows, she might be persuaded by that foreign-living English gentleman whom she would find abroad, to give him her hand. Emily had no doubt confessed her love to Philip, but she had not done so in that bold unshrinking manner which had been natural to Polly Peppercorn. And her lover felt it to be incumbent upon him to receive some renewal of her assurance before she was taken away for a prolonged residence abroad. But there was a difficulty as to this. If he were to knock at the door of the private house and ask for Miss Greenmantle, the servant, though she was in truth Philip's friend in the matter, would not dare to show him up. The whole household was afraid of Mr Greenmantle, and would receive any hint that his will was to be set aside with absolute dismay. So Philip at last determined to take the bull by the horns and force his way into the drawing-room. Mr Greenmantle could not be made more hostile than he was; and then it was quite on the cards, that he might be kept in ignorance of the intrusion. When therefore the banker was sitting in his own more private room, Philip passed through from the bank into the house and made his way upstairs with no one to announce him.

With no one to announce him he passed straight through into the drawing-room, and found Emily sitting very melancholy over a half-knitted stocking. It had been commenced with an idea that it might perhaps be given to Philip, but as her father's stern severity had been announced she had given up that fond idea, and had increased the size, so as to fit them for the paternal feet. 'Good gracious, Philip,' she exclaimed, 'how on earth did you get here?'

'I came upstairs from the bank.'

'Oh, yes; of course. But did you not tell Mary that you were coming?'

'I should never have been let up had I done so. Mary has orders not to let me put my foot within the house.'

'You ought not to have come; indeed you ought not.'

'And I was to let you go abroad without seeing you! Was that what I ought to have done? It might be that I should never see you again. Only think of what my condition must be.'

'Is not mine twice worse?'

'I do not know. If it be twice worse than mine then I am the happiest man in all the world.'

'Oh, Philip, what do you mean?'

'If you will assure me of your love –'

'I have assured you.'

'Give me another assurance, Emily,' he said, sitting down beside her on the sofa. But she started up quickly to her feet. 'When you gave me the assurance before, then – then –'

'One assurance such as that ought to be quite enough.'

'But you are going abroad.'

'That can make no difference.'

'Your father says, that you will meet there some Englishman who will –'

'My father knows nothing about it. I shall meet no Englishman, and no foreigner; at least none that I shall care about. You oughtn't to get such an idea into your head.'

'That's all very well, but how am I to keep such ideas out? Of course there will be men over there; and if you come across some idle young fellow who has not his bread to earn as I do, won't it be natural that you should listen to him?'

'No, it won't be natural.'

'It seems to me to be so. What have I got that you should continue to care for me?'

'You have my word, Philip. Is that nothing?' She had now seated herself on a chair away from the sofa, and he, feeling at the time some special anxiety to get her into his arms, threw himself down on his knees before her, and seized her by both her hands. At that moment the door of the drawing-room was opened, and Mr Green-mantle appeared within the room. Philip Hughes could not get upon his feet quick enough to return the furious anger of the look which was thrown on him. There was a difficulty even in disem-barrassing himself of poor Emily's hands; so that she, to her father, seemed to be almost equally a culprit with the young man. She uttered a slight scream, and then he very gradually rose to his legs.

'Emily,' said the angry father, 'retire at once to your chamber.'

'But, papa, I must explain.'

'Retire at once to your chamber, miss. As for this young man, I do not know whether the laws of his country will not punish him for this intrusion.'

Emily was terribly frightened by this allusion to her country's laws. 'He has done nothing, papa; indeed he has done nothing.'

'His very presence here, and on his knees! Is that nothing? Mr Hughes, I desire that you will retire. Your presence in the bank is required. I lay upon you my strict order never again to presume to come through that door. Where is the servant who announced you?'

'No servant announced me.'

'And did you dare to force your way into my private house, and into my daughter's presence unannounced? It is indeed time that I should take her abroad to undergo a prolonged residence in some foreign parts. But the laws of the country which you have outraged will punish you. In the meantime why do you not withdraw? Am I to be obeyed?'

'I have just one word which I wish to say to Miss Greenmantle.'

'Not a word. Withdraw! I tell you, sir, withdraw to the bank. There your presence is required. Here it will never be needed.'

'Goodbye, Emily,' he said, putting out his hand in his vain attempt to take hers.

'Withdraw, I tell you.' And Mr Greenmantle, with all the stiffness of the poker apparent about him, backed poor young Philip Hughes through the doorway on to the staircase, and then banged the door behind him. Having done this, he threw himself on to the sofa, and hid his face with his hands. He wished it to be understood that the honour of his family had been altogether disgraced by the lightness of his daughter's conduct.

But his daughter did not see the matter quite in the same light. Though she lacked something of that firmness of manner which Polly Peppercorn was prepared to exhibit, she did not intend to be altogether trodden on. 'Papa,' she said, 'why do you do that?'

'Good heavens!'

'Why do you cover up your face?'

'That a daughter of mine should have behaved so disgracefully!'
'I haven't behaved disgracefully, papa.'
'Admitting a young man surreptitiously to my drawing-room!'
'I didn't admit him; he walked in.'
'And on his knees! I found him on his knees.'
'I didn't put him there. Of course he came – because – because –'
'Because what?' he demanded.
'Because he is my lover. I didn't tell him to come; but of course he wanted to see me before we went away.'
'He shall see you no more.'
'Why shouldn't he see me? He's a very good young man, and I am very fond of him. That's just the truth.'
'You shall be taken away for a prolonged residence in foreign parts before another week has passed over your head.'
'Dr Freeborn quite approves of Mr Hughes,' pleaded Emily. But the plea at the present moment was of no avail. Mr Greenmantle in his present frame of mind was almost as angry with Dr Freeborn as with Emily or Philip Hughes. Dr Freeborn was joined in this frightful conspiracy against him.
'I do not know,' said he grandiloquently, 'that Dr Freeborn has any right to interfere with the private affairs of my family. Dr Freeborn is simply the Rector of Plumplington – nothing more.'
'He wants to see the people around him all happy,' said Emily.
'He won't see me happy,' said Mr Greenmantle with awful pride.
'He always wishes to have family quarrels settled before Christmas.'
'He shan't settle anything for me.' Mr Greenmantle, as he so expressed himself, determined to maintain his own independence. 'Why is he to interfere with my family quarrels because he's the Rector of Plumplington? I never heard of such a thing. When I shall have taken up my residence in foreign parts he will have no right to interfere with me.'
'But, papa, he will be my clergyman all the same.'
'He won't be mine, I can tell him that. And as for settling things by Christmas, it is all nonsense. Christmas, except for going to church and taking the Sacrament, is no more than any other day.'
'Oh papa!'
'Well, my dear, I don't quite mean that. What I do mean is that Dr Freeborn has no more right to interfere with my family at this time of the year than at any other. And when you're abroad, which you will be before Christmas, you'll find that Dr Freeborn will have nothing to say to you there.' 'You had better begin to pack up at once,' he said on the following day.

'Pack up?'

'Yes, pack up. I shall take you first to London, where you will stay for a day or two. You will go by the afternoon train tomorrow.'

'Tomorrow!'

'I will write and order beds today.'

'But where are we to go?'

'That will be made known to you in due time,' said Mr Greenmantle.

'But I've got no clothes,' said Emily.

'France is a land in which ladies delight to buy their dresses.'

'But I shall want all manner of things – boots and underclothing – and – and linen, papa.'

'They have all those things in France.'

'But they won't fit me. I always have my things made to fit me. And I haven't got any boxes.'

'Boxes! what boxes? work-boxes?'

'To put my things in. I can't pack up unless I've got something to pack them in. As to going tomorrow, papa, it's quite impossible. Of course there are people I must say goodbye to. The Freeborns –'

'Not the slightest necessity,' said Mr Greenmantle. 'Dr Freeborn will quite understand the reason. As to boxes, you won't want the boxes till you've bought the things to put in them.'

'But, papa, I can't go without taking a quantity of things with me. I can't get everything new; and then I must have my dresses made to fit me.' She was very lachrymose, very piteous and full of entreaties; but still she knew what she was about. As the result of the interview, Mr Greenmantle did almost acknowledge that they could not depart for a prolonged residence abroad on the morrow.

Early on the following morning Polly Peppercorn came to call. For the last month she had stuck to her resolution – that she and Miss Greenmantle belonged to different sets in society, and could not be brought together, as Polly had determined to wear her second-rate dresses in preparation for a second-rate marriage – and this visit was supposed to be something altogether out of the way. It was clearly a visit with a cause, as it was made at eleven o'clock in the morning. 'Oh, Miss Greenmantle,' she said, 'I hear that you're going away to France – you and your papa, quite at once.'

'Who has told you?'

'Well, I can't quite say; but it has come round through Dr Freeborn.' Dr Freeborn had in truth told Mr Peppercorn, with the express view of exercising what influence he possessed so as to prevent the rapid emigration of Mr Greenmantle. And Mr Peppercorn had told his daughter, threatening her that something of the same kind would have to happen in his own family if she proved obstinate about her lover. 'It's the best thing going,' said Mr Peppercorn, 'when a girl is upsetting and determined to have her own way.' To this Polly made no reply, but came away early on the following morning, so as to converse with her late friend, Miss Greenmantle.

'Papa says so; but you know it's quite impossible.'

'What is Mr Hughes to do?' asked Polly in a whisper.

'I don't know what anybody is to do. It's dreadful, the idea of going away from home in this sudden manner.'

'Indeed it is.'

'I can't do it. Only think, Polly, when I talk to him about clothes he tells me I'm to buy dresses in some foreign town. He knows nothing about a woman's clothes – nor yet a man's for the matter of that. Fancy starting tomorrow for six months. It's the sort of thing that Ida Pfeiffer used to do.'

'I didn't know her,' said Polly.

'She was a great traveller, and went about everywhere almost without anything. I don't know how she managed it, but I'm sure that I can't.'

'Dr Freeborn says that he thinks it's all nonsense.' As Polly said this she shook her head and looked uncommonly wise. Emily, however, made no immediate answer. Could it be true that Dr Freeborn had thus spoken of her father? Emily did think it was all nonsense, but she had not yet brought herself to express her thoughts openly. 'To tell the truth, Miss Greenmantle,' continued Polly, 'Dr Freeborn thinks that Mr Hughes ought to be allowed to have his own way.' In answer to this Emily could bring herself to say nothing; but she declared to herself that since the beginning of things Dr Freeborn had always been as near an angel as any old gentleman could be. 'And he says that it's quite out of the question that you should be carried off in this way.'

'I suppose I must do what papa tells me.'

'Well; yes. I don't know quite about that. I'm all for doing everything that papa likes, but when he talks of taking me to France, I know I'm not going. Lord love you, he couldn't talk to anybody there.' Emily began to remember that her father's proficiency in the French language was not very great. 'Neither could I for the matter of that,' continued Polly. 'Of course, I learned it at school, but when one can only read words very slowly one can't talk them at all. I've tried it, and I know it. A precious figure father and I would make finding our way about France.'

'Does Mr Peppercorn think of going?' asked Emily.

'He says so – if I won't drop Jack Hollycombe. Now I don't mean to drop Jack Hollycombe; not for father nor for anyone. It's only Jack himself can make me do that.'

'He won't, I suppose.'

'I don't think he will. Now it's absurd, you know, the idea of our papas both carrying us off to France because we've got lovers in Plumplington. How all the world would laugh at them! You tell your papa what my papa is saying, and Dr Freeborn thinks that that will prevent him. At any rate, if I were you, I wouldn't go and buy anything in a hurry. Of course, you've got to think of what would do for married life.'

'Oh, dear no!' exclaimed Emily.

'At any rate I should keep my mind fixed upon it. Dr Freeborn says that there's no knowing how things may turn out.' Having finished the purport of her embassy, Polly took her leave without even having offered one kiss to her friend.

Dr Freeborn had certainly been very sly in instigating Mr Peppercorn to proclaim his intention of following the example of his neighbour the banker. 'Papa,' said Emily when her father came in to luncheon, 'Mr Peppercorn is going to take his daughter to foreign parts.'

'What for?'

'I believe he means to reside there for a time.'

'What nonsense! He reside in France! He wouldn't know what to do with himself for an hour. I never heard anything like it. Because I am going to France is all Plumplington to follow me? What is Mr Peppercorn's reason for going to France?' Emily hesitated; but Mr Greenmantle pressed the question, 'What object can such a man have?'

'I suppose it's about his daughter,' said Emily. Then the truth flashed upon Mr Greenmantle's mind, and he became aware that he must at any rate for the present abandon the idea. Then, too, there came across him some vague notion that Dr Freeborn had instigated Mr Peppercorn and an idea of the object with which he had done so.

'Papa,' said Emily that afternoon, 'am I to get the trunks I spoke about?'

'What trunks?'

'To put my things in, papa. I must have trunks if I am to go abroad for any length of time. And you will want a large portmanteau. You would get it much better in London than you would at Plumplington.' But here Mr Greenmantle told his daughter that she need not at present trouble her mind about either his travelling gear or her own.

A few days afterwards Dr Freeborn sauntered into the bank, and spoke a few words to the cashier across the counter. 'So Mr Greenmantle, I'm told, is not going abroad,' said the rector.

'I've heard nothing more about it,' said Philip Hughes.

'I think he has abandoned the idea. There was Hickory Pepper-corn thinking of going too, but he has abandoned it. What do they want to go travelling about France for?'

'What indeed, Dr Freeborn – unless the two young ladies have something to say to it.'

'I don't think they wish it, if you mean that.'

'I think their fathers thought of taking them out of harm's way.'

'No doubt. But when the harm's way consists of a lover it's very hard to tear a young lady away from it.' This was said so that Philip only could hear it. The two lads who attended the bank were away at their desks in distant parts of the office. 'Do you keep your eyes open, Philip,' said the rector, 'and things will run smoother yet than you expected.'

'He is frightfully angry with me, Dr Freeborn. I made my way up into the drawing-room the other day, and he found me there.'

'What business had you to do that?'

'Well, I was wrong, I suppose. But if Emily was to be taken away suddenly I had to see her before she went. Think, doctor, what a prolonged residence in a foreign country means. I mightn't see her again for years.'

'And so he found you up in the drawing-room. It was very improper; that's all I can say. Nevertheless, if you behave yourself, I shouldn't be surprised if things were to run smoother before Christmas.' Then the doctor took his leave.

'Now, father,' said Polly, 'you're not going to carry me off to foreign parts.'

'Yes, I am. As you're so wilful it's the only thing for you.'

'What's to become of the brewery?'

'The brewery may take care of itself. As you won't want the money for your husband there'll be plenty for me. I'll give it up. I ain't going to slave and slave all my life and nothing come of it. If you won't oblige me in this the brewery may go and take care of itself.'

'If you're like that, father, I must take care of myself. Mr Green-mantle isn't going to take his daughter over.'

'Yes; he is.'

'Not a bit of it. He's as much as told Emily that she's not to get her things ready.' Then there was a pause, during which Mr Peppercorn showed that he was much disturbed. 'Now, father, why don't you give way, and show yourself what you always were – the kindest father that ever a girl had.'

'There's no kindness in you, Polly. Kindness ought to be reciprocal.'

'Isn't it natural that a girl should like her young man?'

'He's not your young man.'

'He's going to be. What have you got to say against him? You ask Dr Freeborn.'

'Dr Freeborn, indeed! He isn't your father!'

'He's not my father, but he's my friend. And he's yours, if you only knew it. You think of it, just for another day, and then say that you'll be good to your girl.' Then she kissed him, and as she left him she felt that she was about to prevail.

7: THE YOUNG LADIES ARE TO REMAIN AT HOME

Miss Emily Greenmantle had always possessed a certain character for delicacy. We do not mean delicacy of sentiment. That of course belonged to her as a young lady – but delicacy of health. She was not strong and robust, as her friend Polly Peppercorn. When we say that she possessed that character, we intend to imply that she perhaps made a little use of it. There had never been much the matter with her, but she had always been a little delicate. It seemed to suit her, and prevented the necessity of over-exertion. Whereas Polly, who had never been delicate, felt herself always called upon to 'run round', as the Americans say. 'Running round' on the part of a young lady implies a readiness and a willingness to do everything that has to be done in domestic life. If a father wants his slippers or a mother her thimble, or the cook a further supply of sauces, the active young lady has to 'run round'. Polly did run round; but Emily was delicate and did not. Therefore when she did not get up one morning, and complained of a headache, the doctor was sent for. 'She's not very strong, you know,' the doctor said to her father. 'Miss Emily always was delicate.'

'I hope it isn't much,' said Mr Greenmantle.

'There is something I fear disturbing the even tenor of her thoughts,' said the doctor, who had probably heard of the hopes entertained by Mr Philip Hughes and favoured them. 'She should be kept quite quiet. I wouldn't prescribe much medicine, but I'll

tell Mixet to send her in a little draught. As for diet she can have pretty nearly what she pleases. She never had a great appetite.' And so the doctor went his way. The reader is not to suppose that Emily Greenmantle intended to deceive her father, and play the old soldier. Such an idea would have been repugnant to her nature. But when her father told her that she was to be taken abroad for a prolonged residence, and when it of course followed that her lover was to be left behind, there came upon her a natural feeling that the best thing for her would be to lie in bed, and so to avoid all the troubles of life for the present moment.

'I am very sorry to hear that Emily is so ill,' said Dr Freeborn, calling on the banker further on in the day.

'I don't think it's much, Dr Freeborn.'

'I hope not; but I just saw Miller, who shook his head. Miller never shakes his head quite for nothing.'

In the evening Mr Greenmantle got a little note from Mrs Freeborn. 'I am *so unhappy* to hear about *dear* Emily. The poor child always is *delicate*. *Pray* take care of her. She must see Dr Miller twice every day. Changes do take place so *frequently*. If you think she would be better here, we would be *delighted* to have her. There is so much in having the attention of a *lady*.'

'Of course I am nervous,' said Mr Philip Hughes next morning to the banker. 'I hope you will excuse me, if I venture to ask for one word as to Miss Greenmantle's health.'

'I am very sorry to hear that Miss Greenmantle has been taken so poorly,' said Mr Peppercorn, who met Mr Greenmantle in the street. 'It is not very much, I have reason to hope,' said the father, with a look of anger. Why should Mr Peppercorn be solicitous as to his daughter?

'I am told that Dr Miller is rather alarmed.' Then Polly called at the front door to make special inquiry after Miss Greenmantle's health.

Mr Greenmantle wrote to Mrs Freeborn thanking her for the offer, and expressing a hope that it might not be necessary to move Emily from her own bed. And he thanked all his other neighbours for the pertinacity of their inquiries – feeling however all the while that there was something of a conspiracy being hatched against him. He did not quite think his daughter guilty, but in his answer made to the inquiry of Philip Hughes, he spoke as though he believed that the young man had been the instigator of it. When on the third day his daughter could not get up, and Dr Miller had ordered a more potent draught, Mr Greenmantle almost owned to himself that he had been beaten. He took a walk by himself and meditated on it. It was a cruel case. The money was his money, and the girl was his girl, and the young man was his clerk. He ought according to the rules of justice in the world to have had plenary power over them all. But it had come to pass that his power was nothing. What is a father to do when a young lady goes to bed and remains there? And how is a soft-hearted father to make any use of his own money when all his neighbours turn against him?

'Miss Greenmantle is to have her own way, father,' Polly said to Mr Peppercorn on one of these days. It was now the second week in December, and the whole ground was hard with frost. 'Dr Freeborn will be right after all. He never is much wrong. He declared that Emily would be given to Philip Hughes as a Christmas box.'

'I don't believe it a bit,' said Mr Peppercorn.

'It is so all the same. I knew that when she became ill her father wouldn't be able to stand his ground. There is no knowing what these delicate young ladies can do in that way. I wish I were delicate.'

'You don't wish anything of the kind. It would be very wicked to wish yourself to be sickly. What should I do if you were running up a doctor's bill?'

'Pay it – as Mr Greenmantle does. You've never had to pay half-a-crown for a doctor for me, I don't know when.'

'And now you want to be poorly.'

'I don't think you ought to have it both ways, you know. How am I to frighten you into letting me have my own lover? Do you think that I am not as unhappy about him as Emily Greenmantle? There he is now going down to the brewery. You go after him and tell him that he shall have what he wants.'

Mr Peppercorn turned round and looked at her. 'Not if I know,' he said.

'Then I shall go to bed,' said Polly, 'and send for Dr Miller tomorrow. I don't see why I'm not to have the same advantage as other girls. But, father, I wouldn't make you unhappy, and I wouldn't cost you a shilling I could help, and I wouldn't not wait upon you for anything. I wouldn't pretend to be ill – not for Jack Hollycombe.'

'I should find you out if you did.'

'I wouldn't fight my battle except on the square for any earthly consideration. But, father –'

'What do you want of me?'

'I am broken-hearted about him. Though I look red in the face, and fat, and all that, I suffer quite as much as Emily Greenmantle. When I tell him to wait perhaps for years, I know I'm unreasonable. When a young man wants a wife, he wants one. He has made up his mind to settle down, and he doesn't expect a girl to bid him remain as he is for another four or five years.'

'You've no business to tell him anything of the kind.'

'When he asks me I have a business – if it's true. Father!'

'Well!'

'It is true. I don't know whether it ought to be so, but it is true. I'm very fond of you.'

'You don't show it.'

'Yes, I am. And I think I do show it, for I do whatever you tell me. But I like him the best.'

'What has he done for you?'

'Nothing – not half so much as I have done for him. But I do like him the best. It's human nature. I don't take on to tell him so – only once. Once I told him that I loved him better than all the rest – and that if he chose to take my word for it, once spoken, he might have it. He did choose, and I'm not going to repeat it, till I tell him when I can be his own.'

'He'll have to take you just as you stand.'

'May be; but it will be worth while for him to wait just a little, till he shall see what you mean to do. What do you mean to do with it, father? We don't want it at once.'

'He's not edicated as a gentleman should be.'

'Are you?'

'No; but I didn't try to get a young woman with money. I made the money, and I've a right to choose the sort of son-in-law my daughter shall marry.'

'No; never!' she said.

'Then he must take you just as you are; and I'll make ducks and drakes of the money after my own fashion. If you were married tomorrow what do you mean to live upon?'

'Forty shillings a week. I've got it all down in black and white.'

'And when children come – one after another, year by year.'

'Do as others do. I'll go bail my children won't starve – or his. I'd work for them down to my bare bones. But would you look on the while, making ducks and drakes of your money, or spending it at the pot-house, just to break the heart of your own child? It's not in you to do it. You'd have to alter your nature first. You speak of yourself as though you were strong as iron. There isn't a bit of iron about you – but there's something a deal better. You are one of those men, father, who are troubled with a heart.'

'You're one of those women,' said he, 'who trouble the world by their tongues.' Then he bounced out of the house and banged the door.

He had seen Jack Hollycombe through the window going down to the brewery, and he now slowly followed the young man's steps. He went very slowly as he got to the entrance to the brewery yard, and there he paused for a while thinking over the condition of things. 'Hang the fellow,' he said to himself; 'what on earth has he done that he should have it all his own way. I never had it all my way. I had to work for it – and precious hard too. My wife had to cook the dinner with only just a slip of a girl to help make the bed. If he'd been a gentleman there'd have been something in it. A gentleman expects to have things ready to his hand. But he's to walk into all my money just because he's good-looking. And then Polly tells me, that I can't help myself because I'm good-natured. I'll let her know whether I'm good-natured! If he wants a wife he must support a wife – and he shall.' But though Mr Peppercorn stood in the doorway murmuring after this fashion he knew very well that he was about to lose the battle. He had come down the street on purpose to signify to Jack Hollycombe that he might go up and settle the day with Polly; and he himself in the midst of all his objurgations was picturing to himself the delight with which he would see Polly restored to her former mode of dressing. 'Well, Mr Hollycombe, are you here?'

'Yes, Mr Peppercorn, I am here.'

'So I perceive – as large as life. I don't know what on earth you're doing over here so often. You're wasting your employer's time, I believe.'

'I came over to see Messrs Grist and Grindall's young man.'

'I don't believe you came to see any young man at all.'

'It wasn't any young woman, as I haven't been to your house, Mr Peppercorn.'

'What's the good of going to my house? There isn't any young woman there can do you any good.' Then Mr Peppercorn looked round and saw that there were others within hearing to whom the conversation might be attractive. 'Do you come in here. I've got something to say to you.' Then he led the way into his own little parlour, and shut the door. 'Now Mr Hollycombe, I've got something to communicate.'

'Out with it, Mr Peppercorn.'

'There's that girl of mine up there is the biggest fool that ever was since the world began.'

'It's astonishing,' said Jack, 'what different opinions different people have about the same thing.'

'I daresay. That's all very well for you; but I say she's a fool. What on earth can she see in you to make her want to give you all my money?'

'She can't do that unless you're so pleased.'

'And she won't neither. If you like to take her, there she is.'

'Mr Peppercorn, you make me the happiest man in the world.'

'I don't make you the richest – and you're going to make yourself about the poorest. To marry a wife upon forty shillings a week! I did it myself, however – upon thirty-five, and I hadn't any stupid old father-in-law to help me out. I'm not going to see her break her heart; and so you may go and tell her. But you needn't tell her as I'm going to make her any regular allowance. Only tell her to put on some decent kind of gown, before I come home to tea. Since all this came up the slut has worn the same dress she bought three winters ago. She thinks I didn't know it.'

And so Mr Peppercorn had given way; and Polly was to be allowed to flaunt it again this Christmas in silks and satins. 'Now you'll give me a kiss,' said Jack when he had told his tale.

'I've only got it on your bare word,' she answered, turning away from him.

'Why; he sent me here himself; and says you're to put on a proper frock to give him his tea in.'

'No.'

'But he did.'

'Then, Jack, you shall have a kiss. I am sure the message about the frock must have come from himself. Jack, are you not the happiest young man in all Plumplington?'

'How about the happiest young woman,' said Jack.

'Well, I don't mind owning up. I am. But it's for your sake. I could have waited, and not have been a bit impatient. But it's so different with a man. Did he say, Jack, what he meant to do for you?'

'He swore that he would not give us a penny.'

'But that's rubbish. I am not going to let you marry till I know what's fixed. Nor yet will I put on my silk frock.'

'You must. He'll be sure to go back if you don't do that. I should risk it all now, if I were you.'

'And so make a beggar of you. My husband shall not be dependent on any man – not even on father. I shall keep my clothes on as I've got 'em till something is settled.'

'I wouldn't anger him if I were you,' said Jack cautiously.

'One has got to anger him sometimes, and all for his own good. There's the frock hanging upstairs, and I'm as fond of a bit of finery as any girl. Well – I'll put it on tonight because he has made something of a promise; but I'll not continue it till I know what he means to do for you. When I'm married my husband will have to pay for my clothes, and not father.'

'I guess you'll pay for them yourself.'

'No, I shan't. It's not the way of the world in this part of England. One of you must do it, and I won't have it done by father – not regular. As I begin so I must go on. Let him tell me what he means to do and then we shall know how we're to live. I'm not a bit afraid of you and your forty shillings.'

'My girl!' Here was some little attempt at embracing, which, however, Polly checked.

'There's no good in all that when we're talking business. I look upon it now that we're to be married as soon as I please. Father has given way as to that, and I don't want to put you off.'

'Why no! You ought not to do that when you think what I have had to endure.'

'If you had known the picture which father drew just now of what we should have to suffer on your forty shillings a week!'

'What did he say, Polly?'

'Never mind what he said. Dry bread would be the best of it. I don't care about the dry bread – but if there is to be anything better it must be all fixed. You must have the money for your own.'

'I don't suppose he'll do that.'

'Then you must take me without the money. I'm not going to have him giving you a five-pound note at the time and your having to ask for it. Nor yet am I going to ask for it. I don't mind it now. And to give him his due, I never asked him for a sovereign but what he gave me two. He's very generous.'

'Is he now?'

'But he likes to have the opportunity. I won't live in the want of any man's generosity – only my husband's. If he chooses to do anything extra that'll be as he likes it. But what we have to live upon – to pay for meat and coals and such like – that must be your own. I'll put on the dress tonight because I won't vex him. But before he goes to bed he must be made to understand all that. And you must understand it too, Jack. As we mean to go on so must we begin!' The interview ended, however, in an invitation given to Jack to stay in Plumplington and eat his supper. He knew the road so well that he could drive himself home in the dark.

'I suppose I'd better let them have two hundred a year to begin with,' said Peppercorn to himself, sitting alone in his little parlour.

'But I'll keep it in my own hands. I'm not going to trust that fellow further than I can see him.'

But on this point he had to change his mind before he went to bed. He was gracious enough to Jack as they were eating their supper, and insisted on having a hot glass of brandy and water afterwards – all in honour of Polly's altered dress. But as soon as Jack was gone Polly explained her views of the case, and spoke such undoubted wisdom as she sat on her father's knee, that he was forced to yield. 'I'll speak to Mr Scribble about having it all properly settled.' Now Mr Scribble was the Plumplington attorney.

'Two hundred a year, father, which is to be Jack's own – for ever. I won't marry him for less – not to live as you propose.'

'When I say a thing I mean it,' said Peppercorn. Then Polly retired, having given him a final kiss.

About a fortnight after this Mr Greenmantle came to the Rectory and desired to see Dr Freeborn. Since Emily had been taken ill there had not been many signs of friendship between the Greenmantle and the Freeborn houses. But now there he was in the Rectory hall, and within five minutes had followed the Rectory footman into Dr Freeborn's study. 'Well, Greenmantle, I'm delighted to see you. How's Emily?'

Mr Greenmantle might have been delighted to see the doctor but he didn't look it. 'I trust that she is somewhat better. She has risen from her bed today.'

'I'm glad to hear that,' said the doctor.

'Yes; she got up yesterday, and today she seems to be restored to her usual health.'

'That's good news. You should be careful with her and not let her trust too much to her strength. Miller said that she was very weak, you know.'

'Yes; Miller has said so all through,' said the father; 'but I'm not quite sure that Miller has understood the case.'

'He hasn't known all the ins and outs you mean – about Philip Hughes.' Here the doctor smiled, but Mr Greenmantle moved about uneasily as though the poker were at work. 'I suppose Philip Hughes had something to do with her malady.'

'The truth is –,' began Mr Greenmantle.

'What's the truth?' asked the doctor. But Mr Greenmantle looked as though he could not tell his tale without many efforts. 'You heard what old Peppercorn has done with his daughter? – Settled £250 a year on her for ever, and has come to me asking me whether I can't marry them on Christmas Day. Why if they were to be married by banns there would not be time.'

'I don't see why they shouldn't be married by banns,' said Mr Greenmantle, who amidst all these difficulties disliked nothing so much as that he should be put into the category with Mr Pepper-corn, or Emily with Polly Peppercorn.

'I say nothing about that. I wish everybody was married by banns. Why shouldn't they? But that's not to be. Polly came to me the next day, and said that her father didn't know what he was talking about.'

'I suppose she expects a special licence like the rest of them,' said Mr Greenmantle.

'What the girls think mostly of is their clothes. Polly wouldn't mind the banns the least in the world; but she says she can't have her things ready. When a young lady talks about her things a man has to give up. Polly says that February is a very good month to be married in.'

Mr Greenmantle was again annoyed, and showed it by the knit-ting of his brow, and the increased stiffness of his head and shoulders. The truth may as well be told. Emily's illness had prevailed with him and he too had yielded. When she had absolutely refused to look at her chicken-broth for three consecutive days her father's heart had been stirred. For Mr Greenmantle's character will not have been adequately described unless it be explained that the stiffness lay rather in the neck and shoulders than in the organism by which his feelings were conducted. He was in truth very like Mr Peppercorn, though he would have been infuriated had he been told so. When he found himself alone after his defeat – which took place at once when the chicken-broth had gone down untasted for the third time – he was ungainly and ill-natured to look at. But he went to work at once to make excuses for Philip Hughes, and ended by assuring himself that he was a manly honest sort of fellow, who was sure to do well in his profession; and ended by assuring himself that it would be very comfortable to have his married daughter and her husband living with him. He at once saw Philip, and explained to him that he had certainly done very wrong in coming up to his drawing-room without leave. 'There is an etiquette in those things which no doubt you will learn as you grow older.' Philip thought that the etiquette wouldn't much matter as soon as he had married his wife. And he was wise enough to do no more than beg Mr Green-mantle's pardon for the fault which he had committed. 'But as I am informed by my daughter,' continued Mr Greenmantle, 'that her affections are irrevocably settled upon you' – here Philip could only bow – 'I am prepared to withdraw my opposition, which has only been entertained as long as I thought it necessary for my daughter's happiness. There need be no words now,' he continued, seeing that Philip was about to speak, 'but when I shall have made up my mind as to what it may be fitting that I shall do in regard to money, then I will see you again. In the meantime you're welcome to come into my drawing-room when it may suit you to pay your respects to Miss Greenmantle.' It was speedily settled that the marriage should take place in February, and Mr Greenmantle was now informed that Polly Peppercorn and Mr Hollycombe were to be married in the same month!

He had resolved, however, after much consideration, that he would himself inform Dr Freeborn that he had given way, and had now come for this purpose. There would be less of triumph to the enemy, and less of disgrace to himself, if he were to declare the truth. And there no longer existed any possibility of a permanent quarrel with the doctor. The prolonged residence abroad had altogether gone to the winds. 'I think I will just step over and tell the doctor of this alteration in our plans.' This he had said to Emily, and Emily had thanked him and kissed him, and once again had called him 'her own dear papa'. He had suffered greatly during the period of his embittered feelings, and now had his reward. For it is not to be supposed that when a man has swallowed a poker the evil results will fall only upon his companions. The process is painful also to himself. He cannot breathe in comfort so long as the poker is there.

'And so Emily too is to have her lover. I am delighted to hear it. Believe me she hasn't chosen badly. Philip Hughes is an excellent young fellow. And so we shall have the double marriage coming after all.' Here the poker was very visible. 'My wife will go and see her at once and congratulate her; and so will I as soon as I have heard that she's got herself properly dressed for drawing-room visitors. Of course I may congratulate Philip.'

'Yes, you may do that,' said Mr Greenmantle very stiffly.

'All the town will know all about it before it goes to bed tonight. It is better so. There should never be a mystery about such matters. Goodbye, Greenmantle, I congratulate you with all my heart.'

8: CHRISTMAS DAY

'Now I'll tell you what we'll do,' said the doctor to his wife a few days after the two marriages had been arranged in the manner thus described. It yet wanted ten days to Christmas, and it was known to all Plumplington that the doctor intended to be more than ordinarily blithe during the present Christmas holidays. 'We'll have these young people to dinner on Christmas Day, and their fathers shall come with them.'

'Will that do, doctor?' said his wife.

'Why should it not do?'

'I don't think that Mr Greenmantle will care about meeting Mr Peppercorn.'

'If Mr Peppercorn dines at my table,' said the doctor with a certain amount of arrogance, 'any gentleman in England may meet him. What! not meet a fellow townsman on Christmas Day and on such an occasion as this!'

'I don't think he'll like it,' said Mrs Freeborn.

'Then he may lump it. You'll see he'll come. He'll not like to refuse to bring Emily here, especially as she is to meet her betrothed. And the Peppercorns and Jack Hollycombe will be sure to come. Those sort of vagaries as to meeting this man and not that, in sitting next to one woman and objecting to another, don't prevail on Christmas Day, thank God. They've met already at the Lord's Supper, or ought to have met; and they surely can meet afterwards at the parson's table. And we'll have Harry Gresham to show that there is no ill will. I hear that Harry is already making up to the dean's daughter at Barchester.'

'He won't care whom he meets,' said Mrs Freeborn. 'He has got a position of his own and can afford to meet anybody. It isn't quite so with Mr Greenmantle. But of course you can have it as you please. I shall be delighted to have Polly and her husband at dinner with us.'

So it was settled and the invitations were sent out. That to the Peppercorns was despatched first, so that Mr Greenmantle might be informed whom he would have to meet. It was conveyed in a note from Mrs Freeborn to Polly, and came in the shape of an order rather than a request. 'Dr Freeborn hopes that your papa and Mr Hollycombe will bring you to dine with us on Christmas Day at six o'clock. We'll try and get Emily Greenmantle and her lover to meet you. You must come because the doctor has set his heart upon it.'

'That's very civil,' said Mr Peppercorn. 'Shan't I get any dinner till six o'clock?'

'You can have lunch, father, of course. You must go.'

'A bit of bread and cheese when I come out of church – just when I'm most famished! Of course, I'll go. I never dined with the doctor before.'

'Nor did I; but I've drunk tea there. You'll find he'll make himself very pleasant. But what are we to do about Jack?'

'He'll come of course.'

'But what are we to do about his clothes?' said Polly. 'I don't think he's got a dress coat; and I'm sure he hasn't a white tie. Let him come just as he pleases, they won't mind on Christmas Day as long as he's clean. He'd better come over and go to church with us; and then I'll see as to making him up tidy.' Word was sent to say that Polly and her father and her lover would come, and the necessary order was at once despatched to Barchester.

'I really do not know what to say about it,' said Mr Greenmantle when the invitation was read to him. 'You will meet Polly Peppercorn and her husband as is to be,' Mrs Freeborn had written in her note; 'for we look on you and Polly as the two heroines of Plumplington for this occasion.' Mr Greenmantle had been struck with dismay as he read the words. Could he bring himself to sit down to dinner with Hickory Peppercorn and Jack Hollycombe; and ought he to do so? Or could he refuse the doctor's invitation on such an occasion? He suggested at first that a letter should be prepared declaring that he did not like to take his Christmas dinner away from his own house. But to this Emily would by no means consent. She had plucked up her spirits greatly since the days of the chicken broth, and was determined at the present moment to rule both her future husband and her father. 'You must go, papa. I wouldn't not go for all the world.'

'I don't see it, my dear; indeed I don't.'

'The doctor has been so kind. What's your objection, papa?'

'There are differences, my dear.'

'But Dr Freeborn likes to have them.'

'A clergyman is very peculiar. The rector of a parish can always meet his own flock. But rank is rank you know, and it behoves me to be careful with whom I shall associate. I shall have Mr Peppercorn slapping my back and poking me in the ribs some of these days. And moreover they have joined your name with that of the young lady in a manner that I do not quite approve. Though you each of you may be a heroine in your own way, you are not the two heroines of Plumplington. I do not choose that you shall appear together in that light.'

'That is only his joke,' said Emily.

'It is a joke to which I do not wish to be a party. The two heroines of Plumplington! It sounds like a vulgar farce.'

Then there was a pause, during which Mr Greenmantle was thinking how to frame the letter of excuse by which he would avoid the difficulty. But at last Emily said a word which settled him. 'Oh, papa, they'll say that you were too proud, and then they'll laugh at

you.' Mr Greenmantle looked very angry at this, and was preparing himself to use some severe language to his daughter. But he remembered how recently she had become engaged to be married, and he abstained. 'As you wish it, we will go,' he said. 'At the present crisis of your life I would not desire to disappoint you in anything.' So it happened that the doctor's proposed guests all accepted; for Harry Gresham too expressed himself as quite delighted to meet Emily Greenmantle on the auspicious occasion.

'I shall be delighted also to meet Jack Hollycombe,' Harry had said. 'I have known him ever so long and have just given him an order for twenty quarters of oats.'

They were all to be seen at the parish church of Plumplington on that Christmas morning – except Harry Gresham who, if he did so at all, went to church at Greshamsbury – and the Plumplington world all looked at them with admiring eyes. As it happened the Peppercorns sat just behind the Greenmantles and on this occasion Jack Hollycombe and Polly were exactly in the rear of Philip Hughes and Emily. Mr Greenmantle as he took his seat observed that it was so, and his devotions were, we fear, disturbed by the fact. He walked up proudly to the altar among the earliest and most aristocratic recipients, and as he did so could not keep himself from turning round to see whether Hickory Peppercorn was treading on his kibes. But on the present occasion Hickory Peppercorn was very modest and remained with his future son-in-law nearly to the last.

At six o'clock they all met in the Rectory drawing-room. 'Our two heroines,' said the doctor as they walked in, one just after the other, each leaning on her lover's arm. Mr Greenmantle looked as though he did not like it. In truth he was displeased, but he could not help himself. Of the two young ladies Polly was by far the most self-possessed. As long as she had got the husband of her choice she did not care whether she were or were not called a heroine. And her father had behaved very well on that morning as to money. 'If you come out like that, father,' she had said, 'I shall have to wear a silk dress every day.' 'So you ought,' he said with true Christmas generosity. But the income then promised had been a solid assurance, and Polly was the best contented young woman in all Plumplington.

They all sat down to dinner, the doctor with a bride on each side of him, the place of honour to his right having been of course accorded to Emily Greenmantle; and next to each young lady was her lover. Miss Greenmantle as was her nature was very quiet, but Philip Hughes made an effort and carried on, as best he could, a conversation with the doctor. Jack Hollycombe till after pudding-time said not a word and Polly tried to console herself through his silence by remembering that the happiness of the world did not depend upon loquacity. She herself said a little word now and again, always with a slight effort to bring Jack into notice. But the doctor with his keen power of observation understood them all, and told himself that Jack was to be a happy man. At the other end of the table Mr Greenmantle and Mr Peppercorn sat opposite to each other, and they too, till after pudding-time, were very quiet. Mr Peppercorn felt himself to be placed a little above his proper position, and could not at once throw off the burden. And Mr Greenmantle would not make the attempt. He felt that an injury had been done him in that he had been made to sit opposite to Hickory Peppercorn. And in truth the dinner party as a dinner party would have been a failure, had it not been for Harry Gresham, who, seated in the middle between Philip and Mr Peppercorn, felt it incumbent upon him in his present position to keep up the rattle of the conversation. He said a good deal about the 'two heroines', and the two heroes, till Polly felt herself bound to quiet him by saying that it was a pity that there was not another heroine also for him.

'I'm an unfortunate fellow,' said Harry, 'and am always left out in the cold. But perhaps I may be a hero too some of these days.'

Then when the cloth had been removed – for the doctor always had the cloth taken off his table – the jollity of the evening really began. The doctor delighted to be on his legs on such an occasion and to make a little speech. He said that he had on his right and on his left two young ladies both of whom he had known and had loved throughout their entire lives, and now they were to be delivered over by their fathers, whom he delighted to welcome this Christmas Day at his modest board, each to the man who for the future was to be her lord and her husband. He did not know any occasion on which he, as a pastor of the church, could take greater delight, seeing that in both cases he had ample reason to be satisfied with the choice which the young ladies had made. The bridegrooms were in both instances of such a nature and had made for themselves such characters in the estimation of their friends and neighbours as to give all assurance of the happiness prepared for their wives. There was much more of it, but this was the gist of the doctor's eloquence. And then he ended by saying that he would ask the two fathers to say a word in acknowledgement of the toast.

This he had done out of affection to Polly, whom he did not wish to distress by calling upon Jack Hollycombe to take a share in the speech-making of the evening. He felt that Jack would require a little practice before he could achieve comfort during such an operation; but the immediate effect was to plunge Mr Greenmantle into a cold bath. What was he to say on such an opportunity? But he did blunder through, and gave occasion to none of that sorrow which Polly would have felt had Jack Hollycombe got upon his legs, and then been reduced to silence. Mr Peppercorn in his turn made a better speech than could have been expected from him. He said that he was very proud of his position that day, which was due to his girl's manner and education. He was not entitled to be there by anything that he had done himself. Here – the doctor cried, 'Yes, yes, yes, certainly.' But Peppercorn shook his head. He wasn't specially proud of himself, he said, but he was awfully proud of his girl. And he thought that Jack Hollycombe was about the most fortunate young man of whom he had ever heard. Here Jack declared that he was quite aware of it.

After that the jollity of the evening commenced; and they were very jolly till the doctor began to feel that it might be difficult to restrain the spirits which he had raised. But they were broken up before a very late hour by the necessity that Harry Gresham should return to Greshamsbury. Here we must bid farewell to the 'two heroines of Plumplington', and to their young men, wishing them many joys in their new capacities. One little scene however must be described, which took place as the brides were putting on their hats in the doctor's study. 'Now I can call you Emily again,' said Polly, 'and now I can kiss you; though I know I ought to do neither the one nor the other.'

'Yes, both, both, always do both,' said Emily. Then Polly walked home with her father, who, however well satisfied he might have been in his heart, had not many words to say on that evening.

WHY FRAU FROHMANN
RAISED HER PRICES

1: THE BRUNNENTHAL PEACOCK

If ever there was a Tory upon earth, the Frau Frohmann was a
Tory; for I hold that landed possessions, gentle blood, a gray-
haired butler behind one's chair, and adherence to the Church of
England, are not necessarily the distinguishing marks of Toryism.
The Frau Frohmann was a woman who loved power, but who loved
to use it for the benefit of those around her – or at any rate to think
that she so used it. She believed in the principles of despotism and
paternal government – but always on the understanding that she
was to be the despot. In her heart of hearts she disliked education,
thinking that it unfitted the minds of her humbler brethren for the
duties of their lives. She hated, indeed, all changes – changes in
costume, changes in hours, changes in cookery, and changes in
furniture; but of all changes she perhaps hated changes in prices
the most. Gradually there had come over her a melancholy conviction that the world cannot go on altogether unaltered. There was,
she felt, a fate in things – a necessity which, in some dark way within
her own mind, she connected with the fall of Adam and the general
imperfection of humanity – which demanded changes, but they
were always changes for the worse; and therefore, though to those
around her she was mostly silent on this matter, she was afflicted by
a general idea that the world was going on towards ruin. That all
things throve with herself was not sufficient for her comfort; for,
being a good woman with a large heart, she was anxious for the
welfare not only of herself and of her children, but for that of all
who might come after her, at any rate in her own locality. Thus,
when she found that there was a tendency to dine at one instead of
twelve, to wear the same clothes on week days as on Sundays, to
desire easy chairs, and linen that should be bleached absolutely
white, thoughts as to the failing condition of the world would get
the better of her and make her melancholy.

These traits are perhaps the evidences of the weakness of Toryism
– but then Frau Frohmann also had all its strength. She was
thoroughly pervaded by a determination that, in as far as in her lay,

all that had aught to do with herself should be 'well-to-do' in the world. It was a grand ambition in her mind that every creature connected with her establishment, from the oldest and most time-honoured guest down to the last stray cat that had taken refuge under her roof, should always have enough to eat. Hunger, unsatisfied hunger, disagreeable hunger, on the part of any dependent of hers, would have been a reproach to her. Her own eating troubled her little or not at all, but the cooking of the establishment generally was a great care to her mind. In bargaining she was perhaps hard, but hard only in getting what she believed to be her own right. Aristides was not more just. Of bonds, written bonds, her neighbours knew not much; but her word for twenty miles round was as good as any bond. And though she was perhaps a little apt to domineer in her bargains – to expect that she should fix the prices and to resent opposition – it was only to the strong that she was tyrannical. The poor sick widow and the little orphan could generally deal with her at their own rates; on which occasions she would endeavour to hide her dealings from her own people, and would give injunctions to the favoured ones that the details of the transaction should not be made public. And then, though the Frau was, I regret to say, no better than a Papist, she was a thoroughly religious woman, believing in real truth what she professed to believe, and complying, as far as she knew how, with the ordinances of her creed.

Therefore I say that if ever there was a Tory, the Frau Frohmann was one.

And now it will be well that the reader should see the residence of the Frau, and learn something of her condition in life. In one of the districts of the Tyrol, lying some miles south of Innsbruck, between that town and Brixen, there is a valley called the Brunnenthal, a most charming spot, in which all the delights of scenery may be found without the necessity of climbing up heart-rending mountains, or sitting in oily steamboats, or paying for greedy guides, or riding upon ill-conditioned ponies. In this valley Frau Frohmann kept an hotel called the Peacock, which however, though it was known as an inn, and was called by that name, could hardly be regarded as a house of common public entertainment. Its purpose was to afford recreation and comfort to a certain class of customers during the summer months – persons well enough to do in the world to escape from their town work and their town residences for a short holiday, and desirous during that time of enjoying picturesque scenery, good living, moderate comfort, and some amount of society. Such institutions have now become so common that there is hardly any one who has not visited or at any rate seen such a place. They are to be found in every country in Europe, and are very common in America. Our own Scotland is full of them. But when the Peacock was first opened in Brunnenthal they were not so general.

Of the husband of the Frau there are not many records in the neighbourhood. The widow has been a widow for the last twenty years at least, and her children – for she has a son and daughter – have no vivid memories of their father. The house and everything in it, and the adjacent farm, and the right of cutting timber in the forests, and the neighbouring quarry, are all the undoubted property of the Frau, who has a reputation for great wealth. Though her son is perhaps nearly thirty, and is very diligent in the affairs of the establishment, he has no real authority. He is only, as it were, the out-of-doors right hand of his mother, as his sister, who is perhaps five years younger, is an in-doors right hand. But they are only hands. The brain, the intelligence, the mind, the will by which the Brunnenthal Peacock is conducted and managed, come all from the Frau Frohmann herself. To this day she can hardly endure a suggestion either from Peter her son or from her daughter Amalia, who is known among her friends as Malchen, but is called 'the fraulein' by the Brunnenthal world at large. A suggestion as to the purchase of things new in their nature she will not stand at all, though she is liberal enough in maintaining the appurtenances of the house generally.

But the Peacock is more than a house. It is almost a village; and yet every shed, cottage, or barn at or near the place forms a part of the Frau's establishment. The centre or main building is a large ordinary house of three stories – to the lower of which there is an ascent by some half-dozen stone steps – covered with red tiles, and with gable ends crowded with innumerable windows. The ground floor is devoted to kitchens, offices, the Frau's own uses, and the needs of the servants. On the first story are the two living rooms of the guests, the greater and by far the more important being devoted to eating and drinking. Here, at certain hours, are collected all the forces of the establishment – and especially at one o'clock, when, with many ringing of bells and great struggles in the culinary department, the dinner is served. For to the adoption of this hour has the Frau at last been driven by the increasing infirmities of the world around her. The scenery of the locality is lovely; the air is considered to be peculiarly health-compelling; the gossipings during the untrammelled idleness of the day are very grateful to those whose lives are generally laborious; the love-makings are frequent and no doubt sweet; skittles and bowls and draughts and dominoes have their devotees; and the smoking of many pipes fills up the vacant hours of the men.

But, at the Brunnenthal, dinner is the great glory of the day. It would be vain for any aesthetical guest, who might conceive himself to be superior to the allurements of the table, to make little of the Frau's dinner. Such a one had better seek other quarters for his summer's holiday. At the Brunnenthal Peacock it is necessary that you should believe in the paramount importance of dinner. Not to come to it at the appointed time would create, first marvel, in the Frau's mind, then pity – as to the state of your health – and at last hot anger should it be found that such neglect arose from contempt. What muse will assist me to describe these dinners in a few words? They were commenced of course by soup – real soup, not barley broth with a strong prevalence of the barley. Then would follow the boiled meats, from which the soup was supposed to have been made – but such boiled meat, so good, that the supposition must have contained a falsehood. With this there would be always potatoes and pickled cabbages and various relishes. Then there would be two other kinds of meat, generally with accompaniment of stewed fruit; after that fish – trout from the neighbouring stream, for the preservation of which great tanks had been made. Vegetables with unknown sauces would follow – and then would come the roast, which consisted always of poultry, and was accompanied of course by salad. But it was after this that were made the efforts on which the Frau's fame most depended. The puddings, I think, were the subject of her greatest struggles, and most complete success. Two puddings daily were, by the rules of the house, required to be eaten; not two puddings brought together so that you might choose with careless haste either one or the other; but two separate courses of puddings, with an interval between for appreciation, for thought, and for digestion. Either one or both can, no doubt, be declined. No absolute punishment – such as notice to leave the house – follows such abstention. But the Frau is displeased, and when dressed in her best on Sundays does not smile on those who abstain. After the puddings there is dessert, and there are little cakes to nibble if you will. They are nibbled very freely. But the heat of the battle is over with the second pudding.

They have a great fame, these banquets; so that ladies and gentlemen from Innsbruck have themselves driven out here to enjoy them. The distance each way is from two to three hours, so that a pleasant holiday is made by a visit to the Frau's establishment. There is a ramble up to the waterfall and a smoking of pipes among the rocks and pleasant opportunities for secret whispers among

young people – but the Frau would not be well pleased if it were
presumed that the great inducement for the visit were not to be
found in the dinner which she provides. In this way, though the
guests at the house may not exceed perhaps thirty in number, it
will sometimes be the case that nearly twice as many are seated
at the board. That the Frau has an eye to profit cannot be doubted.
Fond of money she is certainly – fond of prosperity generally. But,
judging merely from what comes beneath his eye, the observer
will be led to suppose that her sole ambition on these occasions is
to see the food which she has provided devoured by her guests. A
weak stomach, a halting appetite, conscientious scruples as to the
over-enjoyment of victuals, restraint in reference to subsequent
excesses or subsequent eatings – all these things are a scandal to
her. If you can't, or won't, or don't eat your dinner when you get
it, you ought not to go to the Brunnenthal Peacock.

This banqueting hall, or Speise Saal, occupies a great part of the
first floor; but here also is the drawing room, or reading room, as it
is called, having over the door 'Lese Saal' painted so that its purpose
may not be doubted. But the reading room is not much, and the
guests generally spend their time chiefly out of doors or in their
bedrooms when they are not banqueting. There are two other banquets, breakfast and supper, which need not be specially described
– but of the latter it may be said that it is a curtailed dinner, having
limited courses of hot meat, and only one pudding.

On this floor there is a bedroom or two, and a nest of others above;
but the accommodation is chiefly afforded in other buildings, of
which the one opposite is longer, though not so high, as the central
house; and there is another, a little down the road, near the mill, and
another as far up the stream, where the baths have been built – an
innovation to which Frau Frohmann did not lend herself without
much inward suffering. And there are huge barns and many stables;
for the Frau keeps a posting establishment, and a diligence passes
the door three times each way in the course of the day and night,
and the horses are changed at the Peacock – or it was so, at any
rate, in the days of which I am speaking, not very long ago. And
there is the blacksmith's forge, and the great carpenter's shed, in
which not only are the carts and carriages mended, but very much
of the house furniture is made. And there is the mill, as has been
said before, in which the corn is ground, and three or four cottages
for married men, and a pretty little chapel, built by the Frau herself,
in which mass is performed by her favourite priest once a month –
for the parish chapel is nearly three miles distant if you walk by
the mountain path, but is fully five if you have yourself carried

round by the coach road. It must, I think, be many years since the Frau can have walked there, for she is a dame of portly dimensions.

Whether the buildings are in themselves picturesque I will not pretend to say. I doubt whether there has been an attempt that way in regard to any one except the chapel. But chance has so grouped them, and nature has so surrounded them, that you can hardly find anywhere a prettier spot. Behind the house, so as to leave only space for a little meadow which is always as green as irrigation can make it, a hill rises, not high enough to be called a mountain, which is pine-clad from the foot to the summit. In front and around the ground is broken, but immediately before the door there is a way up to a lateral valley, down which comes a nameless stream which, just below the house, makes its way into the Ivil, the little river which runs from the mountain to the inn, taking its course through that meadow which lies between the hill and the house. It is here, a quarter of a mile perhaps up this little stream, at a spot which is hidden by many turnings from the road, that visitors come upon the waterfall – the waterfall which at Innsbruck is so often made to be the excuse of these outings which are in truth performed in quest of Frau Frohmann's dinners. Below the Peacock, where the mill is placed, the valley is closely confined, as the sombre pine-forests rise abruptly on each side; and here, or very little lower, is that gloomy or ghost-like pass through the rocks, which is called the Höllenthor; a name which I will not translate. But it is a narrow ravine, very dark in dark weather, and at night as black as pitch. Among the superstitious people of the valley the spot is regarded with the awe which belonged to it in past ages. To visitors of the present day it is simply picturesque and sublime. Above the house the valley spreads itself, rising, however, rapidly; and here modern engineering has carried the road in various curves and turns round knolls of hills and spurs of mountains, till the traveller as he ascends hardly knows which way he is going. From one or two points among these curves the view down upon the Peacock with its various appendages, with its dark-red roofs, and many windows glittering in the sun, is so charming, that the tourist is almost led to think that they must all have been placed as they are with a view to effect.

The Frau herself is what used to be called a personable woman. To say that she is handsome would hardly convey a proper idea. Let the reader suppose a woman of about fifty, very tall and of large dimensions. It would be unjust to call her fat, because though very large she is still symmetrical. When she is dressed in her full Tyrolese costume – which is always the case at a certain hour on Sunday, and on other stated and by no means unfrequent days as to which I was never quite able to learn the exact rule – when she is so dressed her arms are bare down from her shoulders, and such arms I never saw on any human being. Her back is very broad and her bust expansive. But her head stands erect upon it as the head of some old Juno, and in all her motions – though I doubt whether she could climb by the mountain path to her parish church – she displays a certain stately alertness which forbids one to call her fat. Her smile – when she really means to smile and to show thereby her goodwill and to be gracious – is as sweet as Hebe's. Then it is that you see that in her prime she must in truth have been a lovely woman. There is at these moments a kindness in her eyes and a playfulness about her mouth which is apt to make you think that you can do what you like with the Frau. Who has not at times been charmed by the frolic playfulness of the tiger? Not that Frau Frohmann has aught of the tiger in her nature but its power. But the power is all there, and not unfrequently the signs of power. If she be thwarted, contradicted, counselled by unauthorised counsellors – above all if she be censured – then the signs of power are shown. Then the Frau does not smile. At such times she is wont to speak her mind very plainly, and to make those who hear her understand that, within the precincts and purlieus of the Brunnenthal Peacock, she is an irresponsible despot. There have been guests there rash enough to find some trifling faults with the comforts provided for them – whose beds perhaps have been too hard, or their towels too limited, or perhaps their hours not agreeably arranged for them. Few, however, have ever done so twice, and they who have so sinned – and have then been told that the next diligence would take them quickly to Innsbruck if they were discontented – have rarely stuck to their complaints and gone. The comforts of the house, and the prices charged, and the general charms of the place have generally prevailed – so that the complainants, sometimes with spoken apologies, have in most cases sought permission to remain. In late years the Frau's certainty of victory has created a feeling that nothing is to be said against the arrangements of the Peacock. A displeased guest can exercise his displeasure best by taking himself away in silence.

The Frau of late years has had two counsellors; for though she is but ill inclined to admit advice from those who have received no authority to give it, she is not therefore so self-confident as to feel that she can live and thrive without listening to the wisdom of others. And those two counsellors may be regarded as representing – the first or elder her conscience, and the second and younger her worldly prudence. And in the matter of her conscience very much more is concerned than simple honesty. It is not against cheating or extortion that her counsellor is sharp to her; but rather in regard to those innovations which he and she think to be prejudicial to the manner and life of Brunnenthal, of Innsbruck, of the Tyrol, of the Austrian empire generally, and, indeed, of the world at large. To be as her father had been before her – for her father, too, had kept the Peacock; to let life be cheap and simple, but yet very plentiful as it had been in his days, this was the counsel given by Father Conolin the old priest, who always spent two nights in each month at the establishment, and was not unfrequently to be seen there on other occasions. He had been opposed to many things which had been effected – that alteration of the hour of dinner, the erection of the bath-house, the changing of plates at each course, and especially certain notifications and advertisements by which foreigners may have been induced to come to the Brunnenthal. The kaplan, or chaplain, as he was called, was particularly averse to strangers, seeming to think that the advantages of the place should be reserved, if not altogether for the Tyrolese, at any rate for the Germans of Southern Germany, and was probably of opinion that no real good could be obtained by harbouring Lutherans. But, of late, English also had come, to whom, though he was personally very courteous, he was much averse in his heart of hearts. Such had ever been the tendency of his advice, and it had always been received with willing, nay, with loving ears. But the fate of the kaplan had been as is the fate of all such counsellors. Let the toryism of the Tory be ever so strong, it is his destiny to carry out the purposes of his opponents. So it had been, and was, with the Frau. Though she was always in spirit antagonistic to the other counsellor, it was the other counsellor who prevailed with her.

At Innsbruck for many years there had lived a lawyer, or rather a family of lawyers, men always of good repute and moderate emans, named Schlessen; and in their hands had been reposed by the Frau that confidence as to business matters which almost every one in business must have in some lawyer. The first Schlessen whom the Frau had known in her youth, and who was then a very old man, had been almost as Conservative as the priest. Then had come his son, who had been less so, but still lived and died without much either of the light of progress or contamination of revolutionary ideas from the outer world. But about three years before the date of our tale he also had passed away, and now young Fritz Schlessen sat in the chair of his forefathers. It was the opinion of Innsbruck generally that the young lawyer was certainly equal, probably superior, in attainments and intellect to any of his predecessors. He had learned his business both at Munich and Vienna, and though he was only twenty-six when he was left to manage his clients himself, most of them adhered to him. Among others so did our Frau, and this she did knowing the nature of the man and of the counsel she might expect to receive from him. For though she loved the priest, and loved her old ways, and loved to be told that she could live and thrive on the rules by which her father had lived and thriven before her - still, there was always present to her mind the fact that she was engaged in trade, and that the first object of a tradesman must be to make money. No shoemaker can set himself to work to make shoes having as his first intention an ambition to make the feet of his customers comfortable. That may come second, and to him, as a conscientious man, may be essentially necessary. But he sets himself to work to make shoes in order that he may earn a living. That law - almost of nature we may say - had become so recognised by the Frau that she felt that it must be followed, even in spite of the priest if need were, and that, in order that it might be followed, it would be well that she should listen to the advice of Herr Schlessen. She heard, therefore, all that her kaplan would say to her with gracious smiles, and something of what her lawyer would say to her, not always very graciously; but in the long-run she would take her lawyer's advice.

It will have to be told in a following chapter how it was that Fritz Schlessen had a preponderating influence in the Brunnenthal, arising from other causes than his professional soundness and general prudence. It may, however, be as well to explain here that Peter Frohmann the son sided always with the priest, and attached himself altogether to the conservative interest. But he, though he was honest, diligent, and dutiful to his mother, was lumpy, uncouth, and slow both of speech and action. He understood the cutting of timber and the making of hay - something perhaps of the care of horses and of the nourishment of pigs; but in money matters he was not efficient. Amalia, or Malchen, the daughter, who was four or five years her brother's junior, was much brighter, and she was strong on the reforming side. British money was to her thinking as good as Austrian, or even Tyrolese. To thrive even better than her forefathers had thriven seemed to her to be desirable. She therefore, though by her brightness and feminine ways she was very dear to the priest, was generally opposed to him in the family conclaves. It was chiefly in consequence of her persistency that the table napkins at the Peacock were now changed twice a week.

2: THE BEGINNING OF TROUBLES

Of late days, and up to the time of which we are speaking, the chief contest between the Frau, with the kaplan and Peter on one side, and Malchen with Fritz Schlessen on the other, was on that most important question whether the whole rate of charges should not be raised at the establishment. The prices had been raised, no doubt, within the last twenty years, or the Frau could not have kept her house open - but this had been done indirectly. That the matter may not be complicated for our readers, we will assume that all charges are made at the Peacock in zwansigers and kreutzers, and that the zwansiger, containing twenty kreutzers, is worth eightpence of English money. Now it must be understood that the guests at the Peacock were entertained at the rate of six zwansigers, or four shillings, a day, and that this included everything necessary - a bed, breakfast, dinner, a cup of coffee after dinner, supper, as much fresh milk as anybody chose to drink when the cows were milked, and the use of everything in and about the establishment. Guests who required wine or beer, of course, were charged for what they had. Those who were rich enough to be taken about in carriages paid so much per job – each separate jaunt having been inserted in a tariff. No doubt there were other possible and probable extras: but an ordinary guest might live for his six zwansigers a day – and the bulk of them did so live with the addition of whatever allowance of beer each might think appropriate. From time to time a little had been added to the cost of luxuries. Wine had become dearer, and perhaps the carriages. A bath was an addition to the bill, and certain larger and more commodious rooms were supposed to be entitled to an extra zwansiger per week – but the main charge had always remained fixed. In the time of the Frau's father guests had been entertained at, let us say four shillings a head, and guests were so entertained now. All the world – at any rate all the Tyrolese world south of Innsbruck – knew that six zwansigers was the charge in the Brunnenthal. It would be like adding a new difficulty to the path of life to make a change. The Frau had always held her head high – had never been ashamed of looking her neighbour in the face, but when she was advised to rush at once up to seven zwansigers and a half (or five shillings a day) she felt that, should she do so, she would be overwhelmed with shame. Would not her customers then have cause of complaint? Would not they have such cause that they would in truth desert her? Did she not know that Herr Weiss, the magistrate from Brixen, with his wife, and his wife's sister, and the children, who came yearly to the Peacock, could not afford to bring his family at this increased rate of expenses? And the Fraulein Tendel with her sister would never come from Innsbruck if such an announcement was made to her. It was the pride of this woman's heart to give all that was necessary for good living, to those who would come and submit themselves to her, for four shillings a day. Among the 'extras' she could endure some alteration. She did not like extras, and if people would have luxuries they must be made to pay for them. But the Peacock had always been kept open for six zwansigers, and though Fritz Schlessen was very eloquent, she would not give way to him.

Fritz Schlessen simply told her that the good things which she provided for her guests cost at present more than six zwansigers, and could not therefore be sold by her at that price without a loss. She was rich, Fritz remarked, shrugging his shoulders, and having amassed property could if she pleased dispose of it gradually by entertaining her guests at a loss to herself – only let her know what she was doing. That might be charity, might be generosity, might be friendliness; but it was not trade. Everything else in the world had become dearer, and therefore living at the Peacock should be dearer. As to the Weisses and the Tendels, no doubt they might be shocked, and perhaps hindered from coming. But their places would surely be filled by others. Was not the house always full from the 1st of June till the end of September? Were not strangers refused admittance week after week from want of accommodation? If the new prices were found to be too high for the Tyrolese and Bavarians, they would not offend the Germans from the Rhine, or the Belgians or the English. Was it not plain to every one that people now came from greater distances than heretofore?

These were the arguments which Herr Schlessen used; and, though they were very disagreeable, they were not easily answered. The Frau repudiated altogether the idea of keeping open her house on other than true trade principles. When the young lawyer talked to her about generosity she waxed angry and accused him of laughing at her. 'Dearest Frau Frohmann,' he said, 'it is so necessary you should know the truth! Of course you intend to make a profit – but if you cannot do so at your present prices, and yet will not raise them, at any rate understand what it is that you are doing.' Now the last year had been a bad year, and she knew that she had not increased her store. This all took place in the month of April, when a proposition was being made as to the prices for the coming season. The lawyer had suggested that a circular should be issued, giving notice of an altered tariff.

Malchen was clearly in favour of the new idea. She could not see that the Weisses and Tendels, and other neighbours, should be entertained at a manifest loss; and, indeed, she had prepossessions in favour of foreigners, especially of the English, which, when expressed, brought down upon her head sundry hard words from her mother, who called her a 'pert hussey', and implied that if Fritz Schlessen wanted to pull the house down she, Malchen, would be willing that it should be done. 'Better do that, mother, than keep the roof on at a loss,' said Malchen; who upon that was turned at once out of the little inner room in which the conference was being held.

Peter, who was present on the occasion, was decidedly opposed to all innovations, partly because his conservative nature so prompted him, and partly because he did not regard Herr Schlessen with a friendship so warm as that entertained by his sister. He was, perhaps, a little jealous of the lawyer. And then he had an idea that as things were prosperous to the eye, they would certainly come right at last. The fortunes of the house had been made at the rate of six zwansigers a day, and there was, he thought, no wisdom more clear than that of adhering to a line of conduct which had proved itself to be advantageous.

The kaplan was clear against any change of prices; but then he burdened his advice on the question with a suggestion which was peculiarly disagreeable to the Frau. He acknowledged the truth of much that the lawyer had said. It appeared to him that the good things provided could not in truth be sold at the terms as they were now fixed. He was quite alive to the fact that it behoved the Frau as a wise woman to make a profit. Charity is one thing and business is another. The Frau did her charities like a Christian, generally using Father Conolin as her almoner in such matters. But, as a keeper of a house of public entertainment, it was necessary that she should live. The kaplan was as wide awake to this as was the Frau herself, or the lawyer. But he thought that the changes should not be in the direction indicated by Schlessen. The condition of the Weisses and the Tendels should be considered. How would it be if one of the 'meats' and one of the puddings were discontinued, and if the cup of coffee after dinner were made an extra? Would not that so reduce the expenditure as to leave a profit? And in that case the Weisses and the Tendels need not necessarily incur any increased charges.

When the kaplan had spoken the lawyer looked closely into the Frau's face. The proposition might no doubt for the present meet the difficulty, but he knew that it would be disagreeable. There came a cloud upon the old woman's brow, and she frowned even upon the priest.

'They'd want to be helped twice out of the one pudding, and you'd gain nothing,' said Peter.

'According to that,' said the lawyer, 'if there were only one course the dinner would cost the same. The fewer the dishes, the less the cost, no doubt.'

'I don't believe you know anything about it,' said the Frau.

'Perhaps not,' said the lawyer. 'On those little details no doubt you are the best judge. But I think I have shown that something should be done.'

'You might try the coffee, Frau Frohmann,' said the priest.

'They would not take any. You'd only save the coffee,' said the lawyer.

'And the sugar,' said the priest.

'But then they'd never ask for brandy,' suggested Peter.

The Frau on that occasion said not a word further, but after a little while got up from her chair and stood silent among them; which was known to be a sign that the conference was dismissed.

All this had taken place immediately after dinner, which at this period of the year was eaten at noon. It had simply been a family meal, at which the Frau had sat with her two children and her two friends. The kaplan on such occasions was always free. Nothing that he had in that house ever cost him a kreutzer. But the attorney paid his way like any one else. When called on for absolute work done – not exactly for advice given in conference – he made his charges. It might be that a time was coming in which no money would pass on either side, but that time had not arrived as yet. As soon as the Frau was left alone, she reseated herself in her accustomed arm-chair, and set herself to work in sober and almost solemn sadness to think over it all. It was a most perplexing question. There could be no doubt that all the wealth which she at present owned had been made by a business carried on at the present prices and after the existing fashion. Why should there be any change? She was told that she must make her customers pay more because she herself was made to pay more. But why should she pay more? She could understand that in the general prosperity of the Brunnenthal those about her should have somewhat higher wages. As she had prospered why should not they also prosper? The servants of the poor must, she thought, be poorer than the servants of the rich. But why should poultry be dearer, and meat? Some things she knew were cheaper, as tea and sugar and coffee. She had bought three horses during the winter and they certainly had been costly. Her father had not given such prices, nor, before this, had she. But that probably had been Peter's fault, who had too rashly acceded to the demands made upon him. And now she remembered with regret that, on the 1st of January, she had acceded to a petition from the carpenter for an addition of six zwansigers to his monthly wages. He had made the request on the plea of a sixth child, adding also, that journeymen carpenters both at Brixen and at Innsbruck were getting what he asked. She had granted to the coming of the additional baby that which she would probably have denied to the other argument; but it had never occurred to her that she was really paying the additional four shillings a month because carpenters were becoming dearer throughout the world. Malchen's clothes were certainly much more costly than her own had been, when she was young; but then Malchen was a foolish girl, fond of fashion from Munich, and just at this moment was in love. It could hardly be right that these poor Tendel females, with their small and fixed means, should be made to pay more for their necessary summer excursions because Malchen would dress herself in so-called French finery, instead of adhering, as she ought, to Tyrolese customs.

The Frau on this occasion spent an hour in solitude, thinking over it all. She had dismissed the conference but that could not be regarded as an end to the matter. Herr Schlessen had come out from Innsbruck with a written document in his pocket, which he was proposing to have printed and circulated, and which, if printed and circulated, would intimate to the world at large that the Frau Frohmann had raised her prices. Therein the new rates, seven zwansigers and a half a head, were inserted unblushingly at full length, as though such a disruption of old laws was the most natural thing in the world. There was a flippancy about it which disgusted the old woman. Malchen seemed to regard an act which would banish from the Peacock the old friends and well-known customers of the house as though it were an easy trifle; and almost desirable with that very object. The Frau's heart warmed to the well-known faces as she thought of this. Would she not have infinitely greater satisfaction in cooking good dinners for her simple Tyrolese neighbours, than for rich foreigners who, after all, were too often indifferent to what was done for them? By those Tendel ladies her puddings were recognised as real works of art. They thought of them, talked of them, ate them, and no doubt dreamed of them. And Herr Weiss – how he enjoyed her dinners, and how proud he always was as he encouraged his children around him to help themselves to every dish in succession! And the Frau Weiss – with all her cares and her narrow means – was she to be deprived of that cheap month's holiday which was so necessary for her, in order that the Peacock and the charms of the Brunnenthal generally might be devoted to Jews from Frankfurt, or rich shopkeepers from Hamburg, or, worse still, to proud and thankless Englishmen? At the end of the hour the Frau had determined that she would not raise her prices.

But yet something must be done. Had she resolved, even silently resolved, that she would carry on her business at a loss, she would have felt that she was worthy of restraint as a lunatic. To keep a house of public entertainment and to lose by it was, to her mind, a very sad idea! To work and be out of pocket by working! To her who knew little or nothing of modern speculation, such a catastrophe was most melancholy. But to work with the intention of losing could be the condition only of a lunatic. And Schlessen had made good his point as to the last season. The money spent had been absolutely more than the money received. Something must be done. And yet she would not raise her prices.

Then she considered the priest's proposition. Peter, she knew, had shown himself to be a fool. Though his feelings were good, he always was a fool. The expenses of the house no doubt might be much diminished in the manner suggested by Herr Conolin. Salt butter could be given instead of fresh at breakfast. Cheaper coffee could be procured. The courses at dinner might be reduced. The second pudding might be discontinued with economical results. But had not her success in these things been the pride of her life; and of what good would her life be to her if its pride were crushed? The Weisses no doubt would come all the same, but how would they whisper and talk of her among themselves when they found these parsimonious changes! The Tendel ladies would not complain. It was not likely that a breath of complaint would ever pass their humble lips; but she herself, she, Frau Frohmann, who was perhaps somewhat unduly proud of her character for wealth, would have to explain to them why it was that the second pudding had been abolished. She would be forced to declare that she could no longer afford to supply it, a declaration which to her would have in it something of meanness, something of degradation. No! she could not abandon the glory of her dinner. It was as though you should ask a Royal Academician to cease to exhibit his pictures, or an actor to consent to have his name withdrawn from the bills. Thus at last she came to that further resolve. The kaplan's advice must be rejected, as must that of the lawyer.

But something must be done. For a moment there came upon her a sad idea that she would leave the whole thing to others, and retire into obscurity at Schwatz, the village from whence the Frohmanns had originally come. There would be ample means for private comfort. But then who would carry on the Peacock, who would look after the farm, and the timber, and the posting, and the mill? Peter was certainly not efficient for all that. And Malchen's ambition lay elsewhere. There was, too, a cowardice in this idea of running away which was very displeasing to her.

Why need there be any raising of prices at all – either in one direction or in the other? – Had she herself never been persuaded into paying more to others, then she would not have been driven to demand more from others. And those higher payments on her part had, she thought, not been obligatory on her. She had been soft and good-natured, and therefore it was that she was now called upon to be exorbitant. There was something abominable to her in this general greed of the world for more money. At the moment she felt almost a hatred for poor Seppel the carpenter, and regarded that new baby of his as an impertinent intrusion. She would fall back upon the old wages, the old prices for everything. There would be a difficulty with that Innsbruck butcher; but unless he would give way she would try the man at Brixen. In that matter of fowls

she would not yield a kreutzer to the entreaties of her poor neighbours who brought them to her for sale.

Then she walked forth from the house to a little arbour or summer-
house which was close to the chapel opposite, in which she found
Schlessen smoking his pipe with a cup of coffee before him, and
Malchen by his side. 'I have made up my mind, Herr Schlessen,'
she said. It was only when she was angry with him that she called
him Herr Schlessen.

'And what shall I do?' asked the lawyer.

'Do nothing at all; but just destroy that bit of paper.' So saying,
the Frau walked back to the house, and Fritz Schlessen, looking
round at Malchen, did destroy that bit of paper.

3: THE QUESTION OF THE *MITGIFT*

About two months after the events described in the last chapter,
Malchen and Fritz Schlessen were sitting in the same little arbour,
and he was again smoking his pipe, and again drinking his coffee.
And they were again alone. When these two were seated together
in the arbour, at this early period of the season, they were usually
left alone, as they were known to be lovers by the guests who would
then be assembled at the Peacock. When the summer had grown into
autumn, and the strangers from a distance had come, and the place
was crowded, then the ordinary coffee-drinkers and smokers would
crowd round the arbour, regardless of the loves of Amalia and Fritz.

The whole family of the Weisses were now at the Peacock, and
the two Tendel ladies and three or four others, men with their
wives and daughters, from Botzen, Brunecken, and places around
at no great distance. It was now the end of June; but it is not till
July that the house becomes full, and it is in August that the real
crowd is gathered at Frau Frohmann's board. It is then that folk
from a distance cannot find beds, and the whole culinary resources
of the establishment are put to their greatest stress. It was now
Monday, and the lawyer had been making a holiday, having come
to the Brunnenthal on the previous Saturday. On the Sunday there
had been perhaps a dozen visitors from Innsbruck who had been
driven out after early mass for their dinner and Sunday holiday.
Everything had been done at the Peacock on the old style. There
had been no diminution either in the number or in the excellence
of the dishes, nor had there been any increase in the tariff. It had
been the first day of the season at which there had been a full table,
and the Frau had done her best. Everybody had known that the

sojourners in the house were to be entertained at the old rates; but it had been hoped by the lawyer and the priest and by Malchen – even by Peter himself – that a zwansiger would be added to the charge for dinner demanded from the townspeople. But at the last moment word had gone forth that there should be no increase. All the morning the old lady had been very gloomy. She had heard mass in her own chapel, and had then made herself very busy in the kitchen. She had spoken no word to any one till, at the moment before dinner, she gave her instructions to Malchen, who always made out the bills, and saw that the money was duly received. There was to be no increase. Then, when the last pudding had been sent in, she went, according to her custom, to her room and decorated herself in her grand costume. When the guests had left the dining-room and were clustering about in the passages and on the seats in front of the house, waiting for their coffee, she had come forth, very fine, with her grand cap on her head, with her gold and silver ornaments, with her arms bare, and radiant with smiles. She shook Madame Weiss very graciously by the hand and stooped down and

kissed the youngest child. To one fraulein after another she said a
civil word. And when, as it happened, Seppel the carpenter went
by, dressed in his Sunday best, with a child in each hand, she
stopped him and asked kindly after the baby. She had made up her
mind that, at any rate for a time, she would not submit to the
humiliation of acknowledging that she was driven to the necessity
of asking increased prices.

That had taken place on the Sunday, and it was on the following
day that the two lovers were in the arbour together. Now it must
be understood that all the world knew that these lovers were lovers,
and that all the world presumed that they were to become husband
and wife. There was not and never had been the least secrecy about
it. Malchen was four or five and twenty, and he was perhaps thirty.
They knew their own minds, and were, neither of them, likely to be
persuaded by others either to marry or not to marry. The Frau had
given her consent – not with that ecstasy of joy with which sons-
in-law are sometimes welcomed – but still without reserve. The
kaplan had given in his adhesion. The young lawyer was not quite
the man he liked – entertained some of the new ideas about religion,
and was given to innovations; but he was respectable and well-to-
do. He was a lover against whom he, as a friend of the family, could
not lift up his voice. Peter did not like the man, and Peter, in his
way, was fond of his sister. But he had not objected. Had he done
so, it would not have mattered much. Malchen was stronger at the
Brunnenthal than Peter. Thus it may be said that things generally
smiled upon the lovers. But yet no one had ever heard that a day
was fixed for their marriage. Madame Weiss had once asked Malchen,
and Malchen had told her – not exactly to mind her own business;
but that had been very nearly the meaning of what she had said.

There was, indeed, a difficulty; and this was the difficulty. The
Frau had assented – in a gradual fashion, rather by not dissenting
as the thing had gone on, so that it had come to be understood that
the thing was to be. But she had never said a word as to the young
lady's fortune – as to that 'mitgift' which in such a case would
certainly be necessary. Such a woman as the Frau in giving her
daughter would surely have to give something with her. But the
Frau was a woman who did not like parting with her money; and
was such a woman that even the lawyer did not like asking the
question. The fraulein had once inquired, but the mother had merely
raised her eyebrows and remained silent. Then the lawyer had
told the priest that in the performance of her moral duties the Frau
ought to settle something in her own mind. The priest had assented,
but had seemed to imply that in the performance of such a duty

an old lady ought not to be hurried. A year or two, he seemed to
think, would not be too much for consideration. And so the matter
stood at the present moment.

Perhaps it is that the Germans are a slow people. It may be that
the Tyrolese are especially so. Be that as it may, Herr Schlessen did
not seem to be driven into any agony of despair by these delays.
He was fondly attached to his Malchen; but as to offering to take
her without any *mitgift* – quite empty-handed, just as she stood –
that was out of the question. No young man who had anything,
ever among his acquaintances, did that kind of thing. Scales should
be somewhat equally balanced. He had a good income, and was
entitled to some substantial *mitgift*. He was quite ready to marry her
tomorrow, if only this important question could get itself settled.

Malchen was quite as well aware as was he that her mother should
be brought to do her duty in this matter; but, perhaps of the two,
she was a little the more impatient. If there should at last be a slip
between the cup and the lip, the effect to her would be so much
more disastrous than to him! He could very easily get another wife.
Young women were as plenty as blackberries. So the fraulein told
herself. But she might find it difficult to suit herself, if at last this
affair were to be broken off. She knew herself to be a fair, upstanding,
good-looking lass, with personal attractions sufficient to make such
a young man as Fritz Schlessen like her society; but she knew
also that her good looks, such as they were, would not be improved
by fretting. It might be possible that Fritz should change his mind
some day, if he were kept waiting till he saw her becoming day by
day more commonplace under his eyes. Malchen had good sense
enough not to overrate her own charms, and she knew the world
well enough to be aware that she would be wise to secure, if possible,
a comfortable home while she was at her best. It was not that she
suspected Fritz; but she did not think that she would be justified
in supposing him to be more angelic than other young men simply
because he was her lover. Therefore, Malchen was impatient, and
for the last month or two had been making up her mind to be very
'round' with her mother on the subject.

At the present moment, however, the lovers, as they were sitting
in the arbour, were discussing rather the Frau's affairs in regard to
the establishment than their own. Schlessen had, in truth, come to
the Brunnenthal on this present occasion to see what would be done,
thinking that if the thin edge of the wedge could have been got in
– if those people from the town could have been made to pay an
extra zwansiger each for their Sunday dinner – then, even yet, the
old lady might be induced to raise her prices in regard to the autumn

and more fashionable visitors. But she had been obstinate, and had gloried in her obstinacy, dressing herself up in her grandest ornaments and smiling her best smiles, as in triumph at her own victory.

'The fact is, you know, it won't do,' said the lawyer to his love. 'I don't know how I am to say any more, but anybody can see with half an eye she will simply go on losing money year after year. It is all very fine for the Weisses and Tendels, and very fine for old Trauss,' – old Trauss was a retired linen-draper from Vienna, who lived at Innsbruck, and was accustomed to eat many dinners at the Peacock; a man who could afford to pay a proper price, but who was well pleased to get a good dinner at a cheap rate – 'and very well for old Trauss,' continued the lawyer, becoming more energetic as he went on, 'to regale themselves at your mother's expense – but that's what it comes to. Everybody knows that everybody has raised the price of everything. Look at the Golden Lion.' The Golden Lion was the grand hotel in the town. 'Do you think they haven't raised their prices during the last twenty years?'

'Why is it, Fritz?'

'Everything goes up together, of course. If you'll look into old accounts you'll see that three hundred years ago you could buy a sheep at Salzburg for two florins and a half. I saw it somewhere in a book. If a lawyer's clerk then had eighty florins a year he was well off. That would not surprise her. She can understand that there should be an enormous change in three hundred years; but she can't make out why there should be a little change in thirty years.'

'But many things have got cheaper, Fritz.'

'Living altogether hasn't got cheaper. Look at wages!'

'I don't know why we should pay more. Everybody says that bread is lower than it used to be.'

'What sort of bread do the people eat now? Look at that man.' The man was Seppel, who was dragging a cart which he had just mended out of the shed which was close by – in which cart were seated his three eldest children, so that he might help their mother as assistant nurse even while he was at his work. 'Don't you think he gets more wheaten flour into his house in a week than his grandfather did in a year? His grandfather never saw white bread.'

'Why should he have it?'

'Because he likes it, and because he can get it. Do you think he'd have stayed here if his wages had not been raised?'

'I don't think Seppel ever would have moved out of the Brunnenthal, Fritz.'

'Then Seppel would have been more stupid than the cow, which knows very well on which side of the field it can find the best grass.

Everything gets dearer – and if one wants to live one has to swim with the stream. You might as well try to fight with bows and arrows, or with the old-fashioned flint rifles, as to live at the same rate as your grandfather.' The young lawyer, as he said this, rapped his pipe on the table to knock out the ashes, and threw himself back on his seat with a full conviction that he had spoken words of wisdom.

'What will it all come to, Fritz?' This Malchen asked with real anxiety in her voice. She was not slow to join two things together. It might well be that her mother should be induced by her pride to carry on the business for a while, so as to lose some of her money, but that she should, at last, be induced to see the error of her ways before serious damage had been done. Her financial position was too good to be brought to ruin by small losses. But during the period of her discomfiture she certainly would not be got to open her hand in that matter of the *mitgift*. Malchen's own little affair would never get itself settled till this other question should have arranged itself satisfactorily. There could be no *mitgift* from a failing business. And if the business were to continue to fail for the next year or two, where would Malchen be then? It was not, therefore, wonderful that she should be in earnest.

'Your mother is a very clever woman,' said the lover.

'It seems to me that she is very foolish about this,' said Malchen, whose feeling of filial reverence was not at the moment very strong.

'She is a clever woman, and has done uncommonly well in the world. The place is worth double as much as when she married your father. But it is that very success which makes her obstinate. She thinks that she can see her way. She fancies that she can compel people to work for her and deal with her at the old prices. It will take her, perhaps, a couple of years to find out that this is wrong. When she has lost three or four thousand florins she'll come round.'

Fritz, as he said this, seemed to be almost contented with this view of the case – as though it made no difference to him. But with the fraulein the matter was so essentially personal that she could not allow it to rest there. She had made up her mind to be round with her mother; but it seemed to her to be necessary, also, that something should be said to her lover. 'Won't all that be very bad for you, Fritz?'

'Her business with me will go on just the same.'

This was felt to be unkind and very unloverlike. But she could not afford at the present moment to quarrel with him. 'I mean about our settling,' she said.

'It ought not to make a difference.'

'I don't know about ought – but won't it? You don't see her as I do, but, of course, it puts her into a bad temper.'

'I suppose she means to give you some fixed sum. I don't doubt but she has it all arranged in her own mind.'

'Why doesn't she name it, then?'

'Ah, my dear – *mein schatz* – there is nobody who likes too well to part with his money.'

'But when is there to be an end of it?'

'You should find that out. You are her child, and she has only two. That she should hang back is a matter of course. When one has the money of his own one can do anything. It is all in her own hand. See what I bear. When I tell her this or that she turns upon me as if I were nobody. Do you think I should suffer it if she were only just a client? You must persuade her, and be gentle with her; but if she would name the sum it would be a comfort, of course.'

The fraulein herself did not in the least know what the sum ought to be; but she thought she did know that it was a matter which should be arranged between her lover and her parent. What she would have liked to have told him was this – that as there were only two children, and as her mother was at any rate an honest woman, he might be sure that a proper dowry would come at last. But she was well aware that he would think that a *mitgift* should be a *mitgift*. The bride should come with it in her hand, so that she might be a comfort to her husband's household. Schlessen would not be at all willing to wait patiently for the Frau's death, or even for some final settlement of her affairs when she might make up her mind to leave the Peacock and betake herself to Schwatz. 'You would not like to ask her yourself?' she said.

He was silent for a while, and then he answered her by another question. 'Are you afraid of her?'

'Not afraid. But she would just tell me I was impertinent. I am not a bit afraid, but it would do no good. It would be so reasonable for you to do it.'

'There is just the difference, Malchen. I am afraid of her.'

'She could not bite you.'

'No – but she might say something sharp, and then I might answer her sharply. And then there might be a quarrel. If she were to tell me that she did not want to see me any more in the Brunnenthal, where should we be then? *Mein schatz*, if you will take my advice, you will just say a word yourself, in your softest, sweetest way.' Then he got up and made his way across to the stable, where was the horse which was to take him back to Innsbruck. Malchen was not altogether well pleased with her lover, but she perceived that on the present occasion she must, perforce, follow his advice.

4: THE FRAU RETURNS TO THE SIMPLICITY OF THE OLD DAYS

Two or three weeks went by in the Brunnenthal without any special occurrence, and Malchen had not as yet spoken to her mother about her fortune. The Frau had during this time been in more than ordinary good humour with her own household. July had opened with lovely weather, and the house had become full earlier than usual. The Frau liked to have the house full, even though there might be no profit, and therefore she was in a good humour. But she had been exceptionally busy, and was trying experiments in her housekeeping, as to which she was still in hope that they would carry her through all her difficulties. She had been both to Brixen on one side of the mountain and to Innsbruck on the other, and had changed her butcher. Her old friend Hoff, at the latter place, had altogether declined to make any reduction in his prices. Of course they had been raised within the last five or six years. Who did not know that that had been the case with butchers' meat all over the world? As it was, he charged the Frau less than he charged the people at the Golden Lion. So at least he swore; and when she told him that unless an alteration was made she must take her custom elsewhere–he bade her go elsewhere. Therefore she did make a contract with the butcher at Brixen on lower terms, and seemed to think that she had got over her difficulty. But Brixen was further than Innsbruck, and the carriage was more costly. It was whispered also about the house that the meat was not equally good. Nobody, however, had as yet dared to say a word on that subject to the Frau. And she, though in the midst of her new efforts she was good-humoured herself – as is the case with many people while they have faith in the efforts they are making – had become the cause of much unhappiness among others. Butter, eggs, poultry, honey, fruit, and vegetables, she was in the habit of buying from her neighbours, and had been so excellent a customer that she was as good as a market to the valley in general. There had usually been some haggling; but that, I think, by such vendors is considered a necessary and almost an agreeable part of the operation. The produce had been bought and sold, and the Frau had, upon the whole, been regarded as a kind of providence to the Brunnenthal. But now there were sad tales told at many a cottage and small farmstead around. The Frau had

declared that she would give no more than three zwansigers a pair
for chickens, and had insisted on having both butter and eggs at a
lower price than she had paid last year. And she had succeeded,
after infinite clamours. She had been their one market, their providence, and they had no other immediate customers to whom to
betake themselves. The eggs and the butter, the raspberries and the
currants, must be sold. She had been imperious and had succeeded,
for a while. But there were deep murmurs, and already a feeling
was growing up in favour of Innsbruck and a market cart. It was
very dreadful. How were they to pay their taxes, how were they
to pay anything, if they were to be crimped and curtailed in this
way? One poor woman had already walked to Innsbruck with three
dozen eggs, and had got nearly twice the money which the Frau
had offered. The labour of the walk had been very hard upon her,
and the economy of the proceeding generally may have been doubtful; but it had been proved that the thing could be done.

Early in July there had come a letter, addressed to Peter, from
an English gentleman who, with his wife and daughter, had been
at the Brunnenthal on the preceding year. Mr Cartwright had now
written to say, that the same party would be glad to come again
early in August, and had asked what were the present prices. Now
the very question seemed to imply a conviction on the gentleman's
mind that the prices would be raised. Even Peter, when he took
the letter to his mother, thought that this would be a good opportunity for taking a step in advance. These were English people,
and entitled to no loving forbearance. The Cartwrights need know
nothing as to the demands made on the Weisses and Tendels. Peter
who had always been on his mother's side, Peter who hated changes,
even he suggested that he might write back word that seven zwansigers and a half was now the tariff. 'Don't you know I have settled
all that?' said the old woman, turning upon him fiercely. Then
he wrote to Mr Cartwright to say that the charge would be six
zwansigers a day, as before. It was certainly a throwing away of
money. Mr Cartwright was a Briton, and would, therefore, almost
have preferred to pay another zwansiger or two. So at least Peter
thought. And he, even an Englishman, with his wife and daughter,
was to be taken in and entertained at a loss! At a loss – unless, indeed,
the Frau could be successful in her new mode of keeping her house.
Father Conolin in these days kept away. The complaints made by
the neighbours around reached his ears – very sad complaints –
and he hardly knew how to speak of them to the Frau. It was becoming very serious with him. He had counselled her against any rise
in her own prices, but had certainly not intended that she should

make others lower. That had not been his plan; and now he did not know what advice to give.

But the Frau, resolute in her attempt, and proud of her success as far as it had gone, constantly adducing the conduct of these two rival butchers as evidence of her own wisdom, kept her ground like a Trojan. All the old courses were served, and the puddings and the fruit were at first as copious as ever. If the meat was inferior in quality - and it could not be so without her knowledge, for she had not reigned so long in the kitchen of the Peacock without having become a judge in such matters - she was willing to pass the fault over for a time. She tried to think that there was not much difference. She almost tried to believe that second-rate meat would do as well as first-rate. There should at least be no lack of anything in the cookery. And so she toiled and struggled, and was hopeful that she might have her own way and prove to all her advisers that she knew how to manage the house better than any of them.

There was great apparent good humour. Though she had frowned upon Peter when he had shown a disposition to spoil those Egyptians the Cartwrights, she had only done so in defence of her own resolute purpose, and soon returned to her kind looks. She was, too, very civil to Malchen, omitting for the time her usual gibes and jeers as to her daughter's taste for French finery and general rejection of Tyrolese customs. And she said nothing of the prolonged absence of her two counsellors, the priest and the lawyer. A great struggle was going on within her own bosom, as to which she in these days said not a word to anybody. One counsellor had told her to raise her prices; another had advised her to lessen the luxuries supplied. As both the one proposition and the other had gone against her spirit, she had looked about her to find some third way out of her embarrassments. She had found it, and the way was one which recommended itself to her own sense of abstract justice. The old prices should prevail in the valley everywhere. She would extort nothing from Mr Cartwright, but then neither should her neighbours extort anything from her. Seppel's wife was ill, and she had told him that in consequence of that misfortune the increased wages should be continued for three months, but that after that she must return to the old rate. In the softness of her heart she would have preferred to say six months, but that in doing so she would have seemed to herself to have departed from the necessary rigour of her new doctrine. But when Seppel stood before her, scratching his head, a picture of wretchedness and doubt, she was not comfortable in her mind. Seppel had a dim idea of his own rights, and did not like to be told that his extra zwansigers came to him from the Frau's charity. To go away from the Brunnenthal at the end of the summer, to go away at all, would be terrible to him; but to work for less than fair wages, would that not be more terrible? Of all which the Frau, as she looked at him, understood much.

And she understood much also of the discontent and almost despair which was filling the minds of the poor women all around her. All those poor women were dear to her. It was in her nature to love those around her, and especially those who were dependent on her. She knew the story of every household – what children each mother had reared and what she had lost, when each had been brought to affliction by a husband's illness or a son's misconduct. She had never been deaf to their troubles; and though she might have been heard in violent discussions, now with one and now with another, as to the selling value of this or that article, she had always been held by them to be a just woman and a constant friend. Now they were up in arms against her, to the extreme grief of her heart.

Nevertheless it was necessary that she should support herself by an outward appearance of tranquillity, so that the world around her might know that she was not troubled by doubts as to her own conduct. She had heard somewhere that no return can be made from

evil to good courses without temporary disruptions, and that all lovers of justice are subject to unreasonable odium. Things had gone astray because there had been unintentional lapses from justice. She herself had been the delinquent when she had allowed herself to be talked into higher payments than those which had been common in the valley in her young days. She had not understood, when she made these lapses gradually, how fatal would be their result. Now she understood, and was determined to plant her foot firmly down on the old figures. All this evil had come from a departure from the old ways. There must be sorrow and trouble, and perhaps some ill blood, in this return. That going back to simplicity is always so difficult! But it should be done. So she smiled, and refused to give more than three zwansigers a pair for her chickens.

One old woman came to her with the express purpose of arguing it all out. Suse Krapp was the wife of an old woodman who lived high up above the Peacock, among the pines, in a spot which could only be reached by a long and very steep ascent, and who being old and having a daughter and granddaughters whom she could send down with her eggs and wild fruit, did not very often make her appearance in the valley. But she had known the Frau well for many years, having been one of those to welcome her when she had arrived there as a bride, and had always been treated with exceptional courtesy. Suse Krapp was a woman who had brought up a large family, and had known troubles; but she had always been able to speak her own mind; and when she arrived at the house, empty-handed, with nothing to sell, declaring at once her purpose of remonstrating with the Frau, the Frau regarded her as a delegate from the commercial females of the valley generally; and she took the coming in good part, asking Suse into her own inner room.

After sundry inquiries on each side, respecting the children and the guests, and the state of things in the world at large, the real question was asked, 'Ah meine liebe Frau Frohmann – my very dear Mrs Frohmann, as one might say here – why are you dealing with us all in the Brunnenthal after this hard fashion?'

'What do you call a hard fashion, Suse?'

'Only giving half price for everything that you buy. Why should anything be cheaper this year than it was last? Ah, alas! does not everybody know that everything is dearer?'

'Why should anything be dearer, Suse? The people who come here are not charged more than they were twenty years ago.'

'Who can tell? How can an old woman say? It is all very bad. The world, I suppose, is getting worse. But it is so. Look at the taxes.'

The taxes, whether imperial or municipal, was a matter on which the Frau did not want to speak. She felt that they were altogether beyond her reach. No doubt there had been a very great increase in such demands during her time, and it was an increase against which nobody could make any stand at all. But, if that was all, there had been a rise in prices quite sufficient to answer that. She was willing to pay three zwansigers a pair for chickens, and yet she could remember when they were to be bought for a zwansiger each.

'Yes, taxes,' she said; 'they are an evil which we must all endure. It is no good grumbling at them. But we have had the roads made for us.'

This was an unfortunate admission, for it immediately gave Suse Krapp an easy way to her great argument. 'Roads, yes! and they are all saying that they must make use of them to send the things into market. Josephine Bull took her eggs into the city and got two kreutzers apiece for them.'

The Frau had already heard of that journey, and had also heard that poor Josephine Bull had been very much fatigued by her labours. It had afflicted her much, both that the poor woman should have been driven to such a task, and that such an innovation should have been attempted. She had never loved Innsbruck dearly, and now she was beginning to hate the place. 'What good did she get by that, Suse? None, I fear. She had better have given her eggs away in the valley.'

'But they will have a cart.'

'Do you think a cart won't cost money? There must be somebody to drive the cart, I suppose.' On this point the Frau spoke feelingly, as she was beginning to appreciate the inconvenience of sending twice a week all the way to Brixen for her meat. There was a diligence, but though the horses were kept in her own stables, she had not as yet been able to come to terms with the proprietor.

'There is all that to think of certainly,' said Suse. 'But — Wouldn't you come back, meine liebe Frau, to the prices you were paying last year? Do you not know that they would sooner sell to you than to any other human being in all the world, and they must live by their little earnings?'

But the Frau could not be persuaded. Indeed had she allowed herself to be persuaded, all her purpose would have been brought to an end. Of course there must be trouble, and her refusal of such a prayer as this was a part of her trouble. She sent for a glass of kirschwasser to mitigate the rigour of her denial, and as Suse drank the cordial she endeavoured to explain her system. There could be no happiness, no real prosperity in the valley, till they had returned

to their old ways. 'It makes me unhappy,' said the Frau, shaking
her head, 'when I see the girls making for themselves long petticoats.' Suse quite agreed with the Frau as to the long petticoats;
but, as she went, she declared that the butter and eggs must be
taken into Innsbruck, and another allusion to the cart was the
last word upon her tongue.

It was on the evening of that same day that Malchen, unaware
that her mother's feelings had just then been peculiarly stirred up
by an appeal from the women of the valley, came at last to the
determination of asking that something might be settled as to the
mitgift. 'Mother,' said she, 'Fritz Schlessen thinks that something
should be arranged.'

'Arranged as how?'

'I suppose he wants – to be married.'

'If he don't, I suppose somebody else does,' said the mother
smiling.

'Well, mother! Of course it is not pleasant to be as we are now.
You must feel that yourself. Fritz is a good young man, and there is
nothing about him that I have a right to complain of. But, of course,
like all the rest of 'em, he expects some money when he takes a wife.
Couldn't you tell him what you mean to give?'

'Not at present, Malchen.'

'And why not now? It has been going on two years.'

'Nina Cobard at Schwatz was ten years before her people would
let it come off. Just at present I am trying a great experiment, and
I can say nothing about money till the season is over.' With this
answer Malchen was obliged to be content, and was not slow in
perceiving that it almost contained a promise that the affairs should
be settled when the season was over.

5: A ZWANSIGER IS A ZWANSIGER

In the beginning of August, the Weisses and the Tendels and Herr
Trauss had all left the Brunnenthal, and our friend Frau Frohmann was left with a house full of guests who were less intimately
known to her, but who not the less demanded and received all
her care. But, as those departed whom she had taught herself to
regard as neighbours and who were therefore entitled to something
warmer and more generous than mere tavern hospitality, she
began to feel the hardness of her case in having to provide so sump-
tuously for all these strangers at a loss. There was a party of Americans in the house who had absolutely made no inquiry whatsoever

as to prices till they had shown themselves at her door. Peter had been very urgent with her to mulct the Americans, who were likely, he thought, to despise the house merely because it was cheap. But she would not give way. If the American gentleman should find out the fact and turn upon her, and ask her why he was charged more than others, how would she be able to answer him? She had never yet been so placed as not to be able to answer any complaints, boldly and even indignantly. It was hard upon her; but if the prices were to be raised to any, they must be raised to all.

The whole valley now was in a hubbub. In the matter of butter there had been so great a commotion that the Frau had absolutely gone back to the making of her own, a system which had been abandoned at the Peacock a few years since, with the express object of befriending the neighbours. There had been a dairy with all its appurtenances; but it had come to pass that the women around had got cows, and that the Frau had found that without damage to herself she could buy their supplies. And in this way her own dairy had gone out of use. She had kept her cows because there had grown into use a great drinking of milk at the Peacock, and as the establishment had gradually increased, the demand for cream, custards, and such luxuries had of course increased also. Now, when, remembering this, she conceived that she had a peculiar right to receive submission as to the price of butter, and yet found more strong rebellion here than on any other point, she at once took the bull by the horns, and threw not only her energies, but herself bodily into the dairy. It was repaired and whitewashed, and scoured and supplied with all necessary furniture in so marvellously short a time, that the owners of cows around could hardly believe their ears and their eyes. Of course there was a spending of money, but there had never been any slackness as to capital at the Peacock when good results might be expected from its expenditure. So the dairy was set agoing.

But there was annoyance, even shame, and to the old woman's feeling almost disgrace, arising from this. As you cannot eat your cake and have it, so neither can you make your butter and have your cream. The supply of new milk to the milk-drinkers was at first curtailed, and then altogether stopped. The guests were not entitled to the luxury by any contract, and were simply told that as the butter was now made at home, the milk was wanted for that purpose. And then there certainly was a deterioration in the puddings. There had hitherto been a rich plenty which was now wanting. No one complained; but the Frau herself felt the falling off. The puddings now were such as might be seen at other places – at the

Golden Lion for instance. Hitherto her puddings had been un-rivalled in the Tyrol.

Then there had suddenly appeared a huckster, a pedlar, an itinerant dealer in the valley who absolutely went round to the old women's houses and bought the butter at the prices which she had refused to give. And this was a man who had been in her own employ-ment, had been brought to the valley by herself, and had once driven her own horses! And it was reported to her that this man was simply an agent for a certain tradesman in Innsbruck. There was an ingratitude in all this which nearly broke her heart. It seemed to her that those to whom in their difficulties she had been most kind were now turning upon her in her difficulty. And she thought that there was no longer left among the people any faith, any feeling of decent economy, any principle. Disregarding right or wrong, they would all go where they could get half a zwansiger more! They knew what it was she was attempting to do; for had she not explained it all to Suse Krapp? And yet they turned against her.

The poor Frau knew nothing of that great principle of selling in the dearest market, however much the other lesson as to buying in the cheapest had been brought home to her. When a fixed price had become fixed, that, she thought, should not be altered. She was demanding no more than she had been used to demand, though to do so would have been so easy! But her neighbours, those to whom she had even been most friendly, refused to assist her in her efforts to re-establish the old and salutary simplicity. Of course when the butter was taken into Innsbruck, the chickens and the eggs went with the butter. When she learned how all this was she sent for Suse Krapp, and Suse Krapp again came down to her.

'They mean then to quarrel with me utterly?' said the Frau with her sternest frown.

'Meine liebe Frau Frohmann!' said the old woman, embracing the arm of her ancient friend.

'But they do mean it?'

'What can we do, poor wretches? We must live.'

'You lived well enough before,' said the Frau, raising her fist in the unpremeditated eloquence of her indignation. 'Will it be better for you now to deal with strangers who will rob you at every turn? Will Karl Muntz, the blackguard that he is, advance money to any of you at your need? Well; let it be so. I too can deal with strangers. But when once I have made arrangements in the town, I will not come back to the people of the valley. If we are to be severed, we will be severed. It goes sadly against the grain with me, as I have a heart in my bosom.'

'You have, you have, my dearest Frau Frohmann.'

'As for the cranberries, we can do without them.' Now it had been the case that Suse Krapp with her grandchildren had supplied the Peacock with wild fruits in plentiful abundance, which wild fruits, stewed as the Frau knew how to stew them, had been in great request among the guests at the Brunnenthal. Great bowls of cranberries and bilberries had always at this period of the year turned the Frau's modest suppers into luxurious banquets. But there must be an end to that now; not in any way because the price paid for the fruit was grudged, but because the quarrel, if quarrel there must be, should be internecine at all points. She had loved them all; but, if they turned against her, not the less because of her love would she punish them. Poor old Suse wiped her eyes and took her departure, without any kirsch-wasser on this occasion.

It all went on from bad to worse. Seppel the carpenter gave her notice that he would leave her service at the end of August. 'Why at the end of August?' she asked, remembering that she had promised to give him the higher rate of wages up to a later date than that. Then Seppel explained, that as he must do something for himself – that is, find another place – the sooner he did that the better. Now Seppel the carpenter was brother to that Anton who had most wickedly undertaken the huckstering business on the part of Karl Muntz, the dealer in Innsbruck, and it turned out that Seppel was to join him. There was an ingratitude in this which almost drove the old woman frantic. If any one in the valley was more bound to her by kindly ties than another it was Seppel, with his wife and six children. Wages! There had been no question of wages when Babette, Seppel's wife, had been ill; and Babette had always been ill. And when he had chopped his own foot with his own axe, and had gone into the hospital for six weeks, they had wanted nothing! That he should leave her for a matter of six zwansigers a month, and not only leave her, but become her active enemy, was dreadful to her. Nor was her anger at all modified when he explained it all to her. As a man, and as a carpenter who was bound to keep up his own respect among carpenters, he could not allow himself to work for less than the ordinary wages. The Frau had been very kind to him, and he and his wife and children were all grateful. But she would not therefore wish him – this was his argument – she would not on that account require him to work for less than his due. Seppel put his hand on his heart, and declared that his honour was concerned. As for his brother's cart and his huckstery trade and Karl

Muntz, he was simply lending a hand to that till he could get a settled place as carpenter. He was doing the Frau no harm. If he did not look after the cart, somebody else would. He was very submissive and most anxious to avoid her anger; but yet would not admit that he was doing wrong. But she towered in her wrath, and would listen to no reason. It was to her all wrong. It was innovation, a spirit of change coming from the source of all evil, bringing with it unkindness, absence of charity, ingratitude! It was flat mutiny, and rebellion against their betters. For some weeks it seemed to the Frau that all the world was going to pieces.

Her position was the more painful because at the time she was without counsellors. The kaplan came indeed as usual, and was as attentive and flattering to her as of yore; but he said nothing to her about her own affairs unless he was asked; and she did not ask him, knowing that he would not give her palatable counsel. The kaplan himself was not well versed in political economy or questions of money generally; but he had a vague idea that the price of a chicken ought to be higher now than it was thirty years ago. Then why not also the price of living to the guests at the Peacock? On that matter he argued with himself that the higher prices for the chickens had prevailed for some time, and that it was at any rate impossible to go back. And perhaps the lawyer had been right in recommending the Frau to rush at once to seven zwansigers and a half. His mind was vacillating and his ideas misty; but he did agree with Suse Krapp when she declared that the poor people must live. He could not, therefore, do the Frau any good by his advice.

As for Schlessen he had not been at the Brunnenthal for a month, and had told Malchen in Innsbruck that unless he were specially wanted, he would not go to the Peacock until something had been settled as to the *mitgift*. 'Of course she is going to lose a lot of money,' said Schlessen. 'Anybody can see that with half an eye. Everybody in the town is talking about it. But when I tell her so, she is only angry with me.'

Malchen of course could give no advice. Every step which her mother took seemed to her to be unwise. Of course the old women would do the best they could with their eggs. The idea that any one out of gratitude should sell cheaper to a friend than to an enemy was to her monstrous. But when she found that her mother was determined to swim against the stream, to wound herself by kicking against the pricks, to set at defiance all the common laws of trade, and that in this way money was to be lost, just at that very epoch of her own life in which it was so necessary that money should be forthcoming for her own advantage - then she became moody, unhappy and silent. What a pity it was that all this power should be vested in her mother's hands.

As for Peter, he had been altogether converted. When he found that a cart had to be sent twice a week to Brixen, and that the very poultry which had been carried from the valley to the town had to be brought back from the town to the valley, then his spirit of conservatism deserted him. He went so far as to advise his mother to give way. 'I don't see that you do any good by ruining yourself,' he said.

But she turned at him very fiercely. 'I suppose I may do as I like with my own,' she replied.

Yes; she could do what she liked with her own. But now it was declared by all those around her, by her neighbours in the valley, and by those in Innsbruck who knew anything about her, that it was a sad thing and a bad thing that an old woman should be left with the power of ruining all those who belonged to her, and that there should be none to restrain her! And yet for the last twenty-five years previous to this it had been the general opinion in these parts that nobody had ever managed such a house as well as the Frau Frohmann. As for being ruined – Schlessen, who was really acquainted with her affairs, knew better than that. She might lose a large sum of money, but there was no fear of ruin. Schlessen was inclined to think that all this trouble would end in the Frau retiring to Schwatz, and that the settlement of the *mitgift* might thus be accelerated. Perhaps he and the Frau herself were the only two persons who really knew how well she had thriven. He was not afraid, and, being naturally patient, was quite willing to let things take their course.

The worst of it to the Frau herself was that she knew so well what people were saying of her. She had enjoyed for many years all that delight which comes from success and domination. It had not been merely, nor even chiefly, the feeling that money was being made. It is not that which mainly produces the comfortable condition of mind which attends success. It is the sense of respect which it engenders. The Frau had held her head high, and felt herself inferior to none, because she had enjoyed to the full this conviction. Things had gone pleasantly with her. Nothing is so enfeebling as failure; but she, hitherto, had never failed. Now a new sensation had fallen upon her by which at certain periods she was almost prostrated. The woman was so brave that at her worst moments she would betake herself to solitude and shed her tears where no one could see her. Then she would come out and so carry herself that none should guess how she suffered. To no ears did she utter a word of complaint, unless her indignation to Seppel, to Suse, and the others might be called complaining. She asked for no sympathy. Even to the kaplan she was silent, feeling that the kaplan, too, was against her. It was natural that he should take part with the poor. She was now, for the first time in her life, driven, alas, to feel that the poor were against her.

The house was still full, but there had of late been a great falling off of the midday visitors. It had, indeed, almost come to pass that that custom had died away. She told herself, with bitter regret, that this was the natural consequence of her deteriorated dinners. The Brixen meat was not good. Sometimes she was absolutely without poultry. And in those matters of puddings, cream and custards, we know what a falling off there had been. I doubt, however, whether her old friends had been stopped by that cause. It may have been so with Herr Trauss, who in going to Brunnenthal, or elsewhere, cared for little else but what he might get to eat and drink. But with most of those concerned the feeling had been that things were generally going wrong in the valley, and that in existing circumstances the Peacock could not be pleasant. She at any rate felt herself to be deserted, and this feeling greatly aggravated her trouble.

'You are having beautiful weather,' Mr Cartwright said to her one day when in her full costume she came out among the coffee-drinkers in the front of the house. Mr Cartwright spoke German, and was on friendly terms with the old lady. She was perhaps a little in awe of him as being a rich man, an Englishman, and one with a white beard, and a general deportment of dignity.

'The weather is well enough, sir,' she said.

'I never saw the place all round look more lovely. I was up at Sustermann's sawmills this morning, and I and my daughter agreed that it is the most lovely spot we know.'

'The sawmill is a pretty spot, sir, no doubt.'

'It seems to me that the house becomes fuller and fuller every year, Frau Frohmann.'

'The house is full enough, sir; perhaps too full.' Then she hesitated as though she would say something further. But the words were wanting to her in which to explain her difficulties with sufficient clearness for the foreigner, and she retreated, therefore, back into her domains. He, of course, had heard something of the Frau's troubles, and had been willing enough to say a word to her about things in general if the occasion arose. But he had felt that the subject must be introduced by herself. She was too great a potentate to have advice thrust upon her uninvited.

A few days after this she asked Malchen whether Schlessen was ever coming out to the Brunnenthal again. This was almost tantamount to an order for his presence. 'He will come directly, mother, if you want to see him,' said Malchen. The Frau would do no more than grunt in answer to this. It was too much to expect that she should say positively that he must come. But Malchen understood her, and sent the necessary word to Innsbruck.

On the following day Schlessen was at the Peacock and took a walk up to the waterfall with Malchen before he saw the Frau. 'She won't ruin herself,' said Fritz. 'It would take a great deal to ruin her. What she is losing in the house she is making up in the forests and in the land.'

'Then it won't matter if it does go on like this?'

'It does matter because it makes her so fierce and unhappy, and because the more she is knocked about the more obstinate she will get. She has only to say the word, and all would be right to-morrow.'

'What word?' asked Malchen.

'Just to acknowledge that everything has got to be twenty-five per cent dearer than it was twenty-five years ago.'

'But she does not like paying more, Fritz. That's just the thing.'

'What does it matter what she pays?'

'I should think it mattered a great deal.'

'Not in the least. What does matter is whether she makes a profit out of the money she spends. Florins and zwansigers are but names. What you can manage to eat, and drink, and wear, and what sort of a house you can live in, and whether you can get other people to do for you what you don't like to do yourself – that is what you have got to look after.'

'But, Fritz – money is money.'

'Just so, but it is no more than money. If she could find out suddenly that what she has been thinking was a zwansiger was in truth only half a zwansiger, then she would not mind paying two where she had hitherto paid one, and would charge two where she now charges one – as a matter of course. That's about the truth.'

'But a zwansiger is a zwansiger.'

'No – not in her sense. A zwansiger now is not much more than half what it used to be. If the change had come all at once she could have understood it better.'

'But why is it changed?'

Here Schlessen scratched his head. He was not quite sure that he knew, and felt himself unable to explain clearly what he himself only conjectured dimly. 'At any rate it is so. That's what she has

got to be made to understand, or else she must give it up and go and
live quietly in private. It'll come to that, that she won't have a
servant about the place if she goes on like this. Her own grandfather
and grandmother were very good sort of people, but it is useless to
try and live like them. You might just as well go back further, and
give up knives and forks and cups and saucers.'

Such was the wisdom of Herr Schlessen; and when he had spoken
it he was ready to go back from the waterfall, near which they were
seated, to the house. But Malchen thought that there was another
subject as to which he ought to have something to say to her. 'It is
all very bad for us – isn't it, Fritz?'

'It will come right in time, my darling.'

'Your darling! I don't think you care for me a bit.' As she spoke
she moved herself a little further away from him. 'If you did, you
would not take it all so easily.'

'What can I do, Malchen?' She did not quite know what he could
do, but she was sure that when her lover, after a month's absence,
got an opportunity of sitting with her by a waterfall, he should not
confine his conversation to a discussion on the value of zwansigers.

'You never seem to think about anything except money now.'

'That is very unfair, Malchen. It was you asked me, and so I
endeavoured to explain it.'

'If you have said all that you've got to say, I suppose we may
go back again.'

'Of course, Malchen, I wish she'd settle what she means to do
about you. We have been engaged long enough.'

'Perhaps you'd like to break it off.'

'You never knew me to break off anything yet.' That was true.
She did know him to be a man of a constant, if not an enthusiastic
temperament. And now, as he helped her up from off the rock, and
contrived to snatch a kiss in the process, she was restored to her
good humour.

'What's the good of that?' she said, thumping him, but not with
much violence. 'I did speak to mother a little while ago, and asked
her what she meant to do.'

'Was she angry?'

'No – not angry; but she said that everything must remain as it is
till after the season. Oh, Fritz! I hope it won't go on for another
winter. I suppose she has got the money.'

'Oh, yes; she has got it; but, as I've told you before, people who
have got money do not like to part with it.' Then they returned to
the house; and Malchen, thinking of it all, felt reassured as to her
lover's constancy, but was more than ever certain that, though it

might be for five years, he would never marry her till the *mitgift* had been arranged.

Shortly afterwards he was summoned into the Frau's private room, and there had an interview with her alone. But it was very short; and, as he afterwards explained to Malchen, she gave him no opportunity of proffering any advice. She had asked him nothing about prices, and had made no allusion whatever to her troubles with her neighbours. She said not a word about the butcher, either at Innsbruck or at Brixen, although they were both at this moment very much on her mind. Nor did she tell him anything of the wickedness of Anton, nor of the ingratitude of Seppel. She had simply wanted so many hundred florins – for a purpose, as she said – and had asked him how she might get them with the least inconvenience. Hitherto the money coming in, which had always gone into her own hands, had sufficed for her expenditure, unless when some new building was required. But now a considerable sum was necessary. She simply communicated her desire, and said nothing of the purpose for which it was wanted. The lawyer told her that she could have the money very easily – at a day's notice, and without any peculiar damage to her circumstances. With that the interview was over, and Schlessen was allowed to return to his lady love – or to the amusements of the Peacock generally.

'What did she want of you?' asked Peter.

'Only a question about business.'

'I suppose it was about business. But what is she going to do?'

'You ought to know that, I should think. At any rate, she told me nothing.'

'It is getting very bad here,' said Peter, with a peculiarly gloomy countenance. 'I don't know where we are to get anything soon. We have not milk enough, and half the time the visitors can't have eggs if they want them. And as for fowls, they have to be bought for double what we used to give. I wonder the folk here put up with it without grumbling.'

'It'll come right after this season.'

'Such a name as the place is getting!' said Peter. 'And then I sometimes think it will drive her distracted. I told her yesterday we must buy more cows – and, oh, she did look at me!'

6: HOFF THE BUTCHER

The lawyer returned to town, and on the next day the money was sent out to the Brunnenthal. Frau Frohmann had not winced when she demanded the sum needed, nor had she shown by any contorted line in her countenance that she was suffering when she asked for it; but, in truth, the thing had not been done without great pain. Year by year she had always added something to her store, either by investing money, or by increasing her property in the valley, and it would generally be at this time of the year that some deposit was made; but now the stream, which had always run so easily and so prosperously in one direction, had begun to flow backwards. It was to her as though she were shedding her blood. But, as other heroes have shed their blood in causes that have been dear to them, so would she shed hers in this. If it were necessary that these veins of her heart should be opened, she would give them to the knife. She had scowled when Peter had told her that more cows must be bought; but before the week was over the cows were there. And she had given a large order at Innsbruck for poultry to be sent out to her, almost irrespective of price. All idea of profit was gone. It was pride now for which she was fighting. She would not give way, at any rate till the end of this season. Then – then – then! There had come upon her mind an idea that some deluge was about to flow over her; but also an idea that even among the roar of the waters she would hold her head high, and carry herself with dignity.

But there had come to her now a very trouble of troubles, a crushing blow, a misfortune which could not be got over, which could not even be endured, without the knowledge of all those around her. It was not only that she must suffer, but that her sufferings must be exposed to all the valley – to all Innsbruck. When Schlessen was closeted with her, at that very moment, she had in her pocket a letter from that traitorous butcher at Brixen, saying that after such and such a date he could not continue to supply her with meat at the prices fixed. And this was the answer which the man had sent to a remonstrance from her as to the quality of the article! After submitting for weeks to inferior meat she had told him that there must be some improvement, and he had replied by throwing her over altogether!

What was she to do? Of all the blows which had come to her this was the worst. She must have meat. She could, when driven to it by necessity, make her own butter; but she could not kill her own beef and mutton. She could send into the town for ducks and chickens, and feel that in doing so she was carrying out her own project – that, at any rate, she was encountering no public disgrace. But now she must own herself beaten, and must go back to Innsbruck.

And there came upon her dimly a conviction that she was bound, both by prudence and justice, to go back to her old friend Hoff. She had clearly been wrong in this matter of meat. Hoff had plainly told her that she was wrong, explaining to her that he had to give much more for his beasts and sheep than he did twenty years ago, to pay more wages to the men who killed them and cut them up, and also to make a greater profit himself, so as to satisfy the increased needs of his wife and daughters. Hoff had been outspoken, and had never wavered for a moment. But he had seemed to the Frau to be almost insolent; she would have said, too independent. When she had threatened to take away her custom he had shrugged his shoulders, and had simply remarked that he would endeavour to live without it. The words had been spoken with, perhaps, something of a jeer, and the Frau had left the shop in wrath. She had since repented herself of this, because Hoff had been an old friend, and had attended to all her wishes with friendly care. But there had been the quarrel, and her custom had been transferred to that wretch at Brixen. If it had been simply a matter of forgiving and forgetting she could have made it up with Hoff easily enough, an hour after her anger had shown itself. But now she must own herself to have been beaten. She must confess that she had been wrong. It was in that matter of meat, from that fallacious undertaking made by the traitor at Brixen, that she, in the first instance, had been led to think that she could triumph. Had she not been convinced of the truth of her own theory by that success, she would not have been led on to quarrel with all her neighbours, and to attempt to reduce Seppel's wages. But now, when this, her great foundation, was taken away from her, she had no ground on which to stand. She had the misery of failure all around her, and, added to that, the growing feeling that, in some step of her argument, she must have been wrong. One should be very sure of all the steps before one allows oneself to be guided in important matters by one's own theories!

But after some ten days' time the supply of meat from Brixen would cease, and something therefore must be done. The Brixen traitor demanded now exactly the price which Hoff had heretofore charged. And then there was the carriage! That was not to be thought of. She would not conceal her failure from the world by submission so disgraceful as that. With the Brixen man she certainly would deal no more. She took twenty-four hours to think of it, and then she made up her mind that she would herself go into the town and acknowledge her mistake to Hoff. As to the actual difference of price, she did not now care very much about it. When a deluge is coming, one does not fret oneself as to small details of cost; but even when a deluge is coming one's heart and pride, and perhaps one's courage, may remain unchanged.

On a certain morning it was known throughout the Peacock at an early hour that the Frau was going into town that day. But breakfast was over before any one was told when and how she was to go. Such journeyings, which were not made very often, had always about them something of ceremony. On such occasions her dress would be, not magnificent as when she was arrayed for festive occasions at home, but yet very carefully arranged and equally unlike her ordinary habiliments. When she was first seen on this day – after her early visit to the kitchen, which was not a full-dress affair – she was clad in what may be called the beginnings or substratum of her travelling gear. She wore a very full, rich-looking, dark-coloured merino gown, which came much lower to the ground than her usual dress, and which covered her up high round the throat. Whenever this was seen it was known as a certainty that the Frau was going to travel. Then there was the question of the carriage and the horses. It was generally Peter's duty and high privilege to drive her in to town; and as Peter seldom allowed himself a holiday, the occasion was to him always a welcome one. It was her custom to let him know what was to befall him at any rate the night before; but now not a word had been said. After breakfast, however, a message went out that the carriage and horses would be needed, and Peter prepared himself accordingly. 'I don't think I need take you,' said the Frau.

'Why not me? There is no one else to drive them. The men are all employed.' Then she remembered that when last she had dispensed with Peter's services Anton had driven her – that Anton who was now carrying the butter and eggs into market. She shook her head, and was silent for a while in her misery. Then she asked whether the boy, Jacob, could not take her. 'He would not be safe with those horses down the mountains,' said Peter. At last it was decided that Peter should go – but she yielded unwillingly, being very anxious that no one in the valley should be informed that she was about to visit Hoff. Of course it would be known at last. Everybody about the place would learn whence the meat came. But she could not bear to think that those around her should talk of her as having been beaten in the matter.

About ten they started, and on the whole road to Innsbruck hardly a word was spoken between the mother and son. She was quite resolved that she would not tell him whither she was going, and resolved also that she would pay the visit alone. But of course, his curiosity would be excited. If he chose to follow her about and watch her, there could be no help for that. Only he had better not speak to her on the subject, or she would pour out upon him all the vials of her wrath! In the town there was a little hostel called the Black Eagle, kept by a cousin of her late husband, which on these journeys she always frequented: there she and Peter ate their dinner. At table they sat, of course, close to each other; but still not a word was spoken as to her business. He made no inquiry, and when she rose from the table simply asked her whether there was anything for him to do. 'I am going – alone – to see a friend,' she said. No doubt he was curious, probably suspecting that Hoff the butcher might be the friend; but he asked no further question. She declared that she would be ready to start on the return journey at four, and then she went forth alone.

So great was her perturbation of spirit that she did not take the directest way to the butcher's house, which was not, indeed, above two hundred yards from the Black Eagle, but walked round slowly by the river, studying as she went the words with which she would announce her purpose to the man – studying, also, by what wiles and subtlety she might get the man all to herself – so that no other ears should hear her disgrace. When she entered the shop Hoff himself was there, conspicuous with the huge sharpening-steel which hung from his capacious girdle, as though it were the sword of his knighthood. But with him there was a crowd either of loungers or customers, in the midst of whom he stood, tall above all the others, laughing and talking. To our poor Frau it was terrible to be seen by so many eyes in that shop – for had not her quarrel with Hoff and her dealings at Brixen been so public that all would know why she had come? 'Ah, my friend, Frau Frohmann,' said the butcher, coming up to her with hand extended, 'this is good for sore eyes. I am delighted to see thee in the old town.' This was all very well, and she gave him her hand. As long as no public reference was made to that last visit of hers, she would still hold up her head. But she said nothing. She did not know how to speak as long as all those eyes were looking at her.

The butcher understood it all, being a tender-hearted man, and intelligent also. From the first moment of her entrance he knew that there was something to be said intended only for his own ears. 'Come in, come in, Frau Frohmann,' he said; 'we will sit down within, out of the noise of the street and the smell of the carcases.' With that he led the way into an inner room, and the Frau followed him. There were congregated three or four of his children, but he sent them away, bidding them join their mother in the kitchen. 'And now, my friend,' he said, again taking her hand, 'I am glad to see thee. Thirty years of good fellowship is not to be broken by a word.' By this time the Frau was endeavouring to hide with her handkerchief the tears which were running down her face. 'I was thinking I would go out to the valley one of these days, because my heart misgave me that there should be anything like a quarrel between me and thee. I should have gone, but that, day after day, there comes always something to be done. And now thou art come thyself. What, shall the price of a side of beef stand betwixt thee and me?'

Then she told her tale – quite otherwise than as she had intended to tell it. She had meant to be dignified and very short. She had meant to confess that the Brixen arrangement had broken down, and that she would resort to the old plan and the old prices. To the saying of this she had looked forward with an agony of apprehension, fearing that the man would be unable to abstain from some killing expression of triumph – fearing that, perhaps, he might decline her offer. For the butcher was a wealthy man, who could afford himself the luxury of nursing his enmity. But his manner with her had been so gracious that she was altogether unable to be either dignified or reticent. Before half an hour was over she had

poured out to him, with many tears, all her troubles – how she had
refused to raise her rate of charges, first out of consideration for
her poorer customers, and then because she did not like to demand
from one class more than from another. And she explained how
she had endeavoured to reduce her expenditure, and how she had
failed. She told him of Seppel and Anton, of Suse Krapp and
Josephine Bull – and, above all, of that traitor at Brixen. With
respect to the valley folk Hoff expressed himself with magnanimity
and kindness; but in regard to the rival tradesman at Brixen his
scorn was so great that he could not restrain himself from expressing
wonder that a woman of such experience should have trusted to so
poor a reed for support. In all other respects he heard her with
excellent patience, putting in a little word here and there to encourage her, running his great steel all the while through his fingers,
as he sat opposite to her on a side of the table.

'Thou must pay them for their ducks and chickens as before,' he
said.

'And you?'

'I will make all that straight. Do not trouble thyself about me.
Thy guests at the Peacock shall once again have a joint of meat
fit for the stomach of a Christian. But my friend – – !'

'My friend!' echoed the Frau, waiting to hear what further the
butcher would say to her.

'Let a man who has brought up five sons and five daughters, and
who has never owed a florin which he could not pay, tell thee something that shall be useful. Swim with the stream.' She looked up
into his face, feeling rather than understanding the truth of what he
was saying. 'Swim with the stream. It is the easiest and the most
useful.'

'You think I should raise my prices.'

'Is not everybody doing so? The Tendel ladies are very good, but
I cannot sell them meat at a loss. That is not selling; it is giving.
Swim with the stream. When other things are dearer, let the
Peacock be dearer also.'

'But why are other things dearer?'

'Nay – who shall say that. Young Schlessen is a clear-headed lad,
and he was right when he told thee of the price of sheep in the old
days. But why –? There I can say nothing. Nor is there reason why
I should trouble my head about it. There is a man who has brought
me sheep from the Achensee these thirty years – he and his father
before him. I have to pay him now – ay, more than a third above his
first prices.'

'Do you give always what he asks?'

'Certainly not that, or there would be no end to his asking. But we can generally come to terms without hard words. When I pay him more for sheep, then I charge more for mutton; and if people will not pay it, then they must go without. But I do sell my meat, and I live at any rate as well now as I did when the prices were lower.' Then he repeated his great advice, 'Swim with the stream, my friend; swim with the stream. If you turn your head the other way, the chances are you will go backwards. At any rate you will make no progress.'

Exactly at four o'clock she started on her return with her son, who, with admirable discretion, asked no question as to her employment during the day. The journey back took much longer than that coming, as the road was up hill all the way, so that she had ample time to think over the advice which had been given her as she leaned back in the carriage. She certainly was happier in her mind than she had been in the morning. She had made no step towards success in her system – had rather been made to feel that no such step was possible. But, nevertheless, she had been comforted. The immediate trouble as to the meat had been got over without offence to her feelings. Of course she must pay the old prices – but she had come to understand that the world around her was, in that matter, too strong for her. She knew now that she must give up the business, or else raise her own terms at the end of the season. She almost thought that she would retire to Schwatz and devote the remainder of her days to tranquillity and religion. But her immediate anxiety had reference to the next six weeks, so that when she should have gone to Schwatz it might be said of her that the house had not lost its reputation for good living up to the very last. At any rate, within a very few days, she would again have the pleasure of seeing good meat roasting in her oven.

Peter, as was his custom, had walked half the hill, and then, while the horses were slowly advancing, climbed up to his seat on the box. 'Peter,' she said, calling to him from the open carriage behind. Then Peter looked back. 'Peter, the meat is to come from Hoff again after next Thursday.'

He turned round quick on hearing the words. 'That's a good thing, mother.'

'It is a good thing. We were nearly poisoned by that scoundrel at Brixen.'

'Hoff is a good butcher,' said Peter.

'Hoff is a good man,' said the Frau. Then Peter pricked up, because he knew that his mother was happy in her mind, and became eloquent about the woods, and the quarry, and the farm.

7 : AND GOLD BECOMES CHEAP

'But if there is more money, sir, that ought to make us all more comfortable.' This was said by the Frau to Mr Cartwright a few days after her return from Innsbruck, and was a reply to a statement made by him. She had listened to advice from Hoff the butcher, and now she was listening to advice from her guest. He had told her that these troubles of hers had come from the fact that gold had become more plentiful in the world than heretofore, or rather from that other fact that she had refused to accommodate herself to this increased plenty of gold. Then had come her very natural suggestion, 'If there is more money that ought to make us all more comfortable.'

'Not at all, Frau Frohmann.'

'Well, sir!' Then she paused, not wishing to express an unrestrained praise of wealth, and so to appear too worldly-minded, but yet feeling that he certainly was wrong according to the clearly expressed opinion of the world.

'Not at all. Though you had your barn and your stores filled with gold, you could not make your guests comfortable with that. They could not eat it, nor drink it, nor sleep upon it, nor delight themselves with looking at it as we do at the waterfall, or at the mill up yonder.'

'But I could buy all those things for them.'

'Ah, if you could buy them! That's just the question. But if everybody had gold so common, if all the barns were full of it, then people would not care to take it for their meat and wine.'

'It never can be like that, surely.'

'There is no knowing; probably not. But it is a question of degree. When you have your hay-crop here very plentiful, don't you find that hay becomes cheap?'

'That's of course.'

'And gold becomes cheap. You just think it over, and you'll find how it is. When hay is plentiful, you can't get so much for a load because it becomes cheap. But you can feed more cows, and altogether you know that such plenty is a blessing. So it is with gold. When it is plentiful, you can't get so much meat for it as you used to do; but, as you can get the gold much easier, it will come to the same thing – if you will swim with the stream, as your friend in Innsbruck counselled you.'

Then the Frau again considered, and again found that she could not accept this doctrine as bearing upon her own case. 'I don't think it can be like that here, sir,' she said.

'Why not here as well as elsewhere?'

'Because we never see a bit of gold from one year's end to the other. Barns full of it! Why, it's so precious that you English people, and the French, and the Americans always change it for paper before you come here. If you mean that it is because bank-notes are so common –'

Then Mr Cartwright scratched his head, feeling that there would be a difficulty in making the Frau understand the increased use of an article which, common as it had become in the great marts of the world, had not as yet made its way into her valley. 'It is because bank-notes are less common.' The Frau gazed at him steadfastly, trying to understand something about it.

'You still use bank-notes at Innsbruck?'

'Nothing else,' she said. 'There is a little silver among the shops, but you never see a bit of gold.'

'And at Munich?'

'At Munich they tell me the French pieces have become – well, not common, but not so very scarce.'

'And at Dresden?'

'I do not know. Perhaps Dresden is the same.'

'And at Paris?'

'Ah, Paris! Do they have gold there?'

'When I was young it was all silver at Paris. Gold is now as plentiful as blackberries. And at Berlin it is nearly the same. Just here in Austria, you have not quite got through your difficulties.'

'I think we are doing very well in Austria – at any rate, in the Tyrol.'

'Very well, Frau Frohmann; very well indeed. Pray do not suppose that I mean anything to the contrary. But though you haven't got into the way of using gold money yourself, the world all around you has done so; and, of course, if meat is dear at Munich because gold won't buy so much there as it used to do, meat will be dearer also at Innsbruck, even though you continue to pay for it with bank-notes.'

'It is dearer, sir, no doubt,' said the Frau, shaking her head. She had endeavoured to contest that point gallantly, but had been beaten by the conduct of the two butchers. The higher prices of Hoff at Innsbruck had become at any rate better than the lower prices of that deceitful enemy at Brixen.

'It is dearer. For the world generally that may suffice. Your friend's doctrine is quite enough for the world at large. Swim with the stream. In buying and selling – what we call trade – things arrange themselves so subtly, that we are often driven to accept them without quite knowing why they are so. Then we can only swim with the stream. But, in this matter, if you want to find out the cause, if you cannot satisfy your mind without knowing why it is that you must pay more for everything, and must, therefore, charge more to other people, it is because the gold which your notes represent has become more common in the world during the last thirty years.'

She did want to know. She was not satisfied to swim with the stream as Hoff had done, not caring to inquire, but simply feeling sure that as things were so, so they must be. That such changes should take place had gone much against the grain of her conservative nature. She, in her own mind, had attributed these pestilently increased expenses to elongated petticoats, French bonnets, swallow-tailed coats, and a taste for sour wine. She had imagined that Josephine Bull might have been contented with the old price for her eggs if she would also be contented with the old raiment and the old food. Grounding her resolutions on that belief, she had endeavoured not only to resist further changes, but even to go back to the good old times. But she now was quite aware that in doing so she had endeavoured to swim against the stream. Whether it ought to be so or not, she was not as yet quite sure, but she was becoming sure that such was the fact, and that the fact was too strong for her to combat.

She did not at all like swimming with the stream. There was something conveyed by the idea which was repugnant to her sense of honour. Did it not mean that she was to increase her prices because other people increased theirs, whether it was wrong or right? She hated the doing of anything because other people did it. Was not that base propensity to imitation the cause of the long petticoats which all the girls were wearing? Was it not thus that all those vile changes were effected which she saw around her on every side? Had it not been her glory, her great resolve, to stand as fast as possible on the old ways? And now in her great attempt to do so, was she to be foiled thus easily?

It was clear to her that she must be foiled, if not in one way, then in another. She must either raise her prices, or else retire to Schwatz. She had been thoroughly beaten in her endeavour to make others carry on their trade in accordance with her theories. On every side she had been beaten. There was not a poor woman in the valley, not one of those who had wont to be so submissive and gracious to her, who had not deserted her. A proposed reduction of two kreutzers

on a dozen of eggs had changed the most constant of humble
friends into the bitterest foes. Seppel would have gone through
fire and water for her. Anything that a man's strength or courage
could do, he would have done. But a threat of going back to
the old wages had conquered even Seppel's gratitude. Concurrent
testimony had convinced her that she must either yield – or go.
But, when she came to think of it in her solitude, she did not wish
to go. Schwatz! oh yes; it would be very well to have a quiet place
ready chosen for retirement when retirement should be necessary.
But what did retirement mean? Would it not be to her simply a
beginning of dying? A man, or a woman, should retire when no
longer able to do the work of the world. But who in all the world
could keep the Brunnenthal Peacock as well as she? Was she fatigued
with her kitchen, or worn out with the charge of her guests, or
worried inwardly by the anxieties of her position? Not in the least,
not at all, but for this later misfortune which had come upon her, a
misfortune which she knew how to remedy at once if only she could
bring herself to apply the remedy. The kaplan had indiscreetly
suggested to her that as Malchen was about to marry and be taken
away into the town, it would be a good thing that Peter should take
a wife, so that there might be a future mistress of the establishment in readiness. The idea caused her to arm herself instantly
with renewed self-assertion. So – they were already preparing for
her departure to Schwatz! It was thus she communed with herself.
They had already made up their minds that she must succumb to
these difficulties and go! The idea had come simply from the kaplan
without consultation with any one, but to the Frau it seemed as
though the whole valley were already preparing for her departure.
No, she would not go! With her strength and her energy, why should
she shut herself up as ready for death? She would not go to Schwatz
yet awhile.

But if not, then she must raise her prices. To waste her substance,
to expend the success of her life in entertaining folk gratis who, after
all, would believe that they were paying for their entertainment,
would be worse even than going to Schwatz. 'I have been thinking
over what you were telling me,' she said to Mr Cartwright about a
week after their last interview, on the day before his departure
from the valley.

'I hope you do not find I was wrong, Frau Frohmann.'

'As for wrong and right, that is very difficult to get at in this
wicked world.'

'But one can acknowledge a necessity.'

'That is where it is, sir. One can see what is necessary; but if

one could only see that it were right also, one would be so much
more comfortable.'

'There are things so hard to be seen, my friend, that let us do
what we will we cannot see clearly into the middle of them. Perhaps
I could have explained to you better all this about the depreciation
of money, and the nominal rise in the value of everything else, if
I had understood it better myself.'

'I am sure you understand all about it – which a poor woman
can't ever do.'

'But this at any rate ought to give you confidence, that that
which you purpose to do is being done by everybody around you.
You were talking to me about the Weisses. Herr Weiss, I hear, had
his salary raised last spring.'

'Had he?' asked the Frau with energy and a little start. For
this piece of news had not reached her before.

'Somebody was saying so the other day. No doubt it was found
that he must be paid more because he had to pay more for everything he wanted. Therefore he ought to expect to have to pay you
more.'

This piece of information gave the Frau more comfort than anything she had yet heard. That gold should be common, what people
call a drug in the market, did not come quite within the scope of her
comprehension. Gold to her was gold, and a zwansiger a zwansiger.
But if Herr Weiss got more for his services from the community,
she ought to get more from him for her services. That did seem plain
to her. But then her triumph in that direction was immediately
diminished by a tender feeling as to other customers. 'But what
of those poor Fraulein Tendels?' she said.

'Ah, yes,' said Mr Cartwright. 'There you come to fixed incomes.'

'To what?'

'To people with fixed incomes. They must suffer, Frau Frohmann. There is an old saying that in making laws you cannot look
after all the little things. The people who work and earn their living
are the multitude, and to them these matters adjust themselves.
The few who live upon what they have saved or others have saved
for them must go to the wall.' Neither did the Frau understand this;
but she at once made up her mind, that, however necessary it might
be to raise her prices against the Weisses and the rest of the world,
she would never raise them against those two poor desolate frauleins.

So Herr Weiss had had his salary raised, and had said nothing
to her about it, no doubt prudently wishing to conceal the matter!
He had said nothing to her about it, although he had talked to her
about her own affairs, and had applauded her courage and her old

conservatism in that she would not demand that extra zwansiger and a half! This hardened her heart so much that she felt she would have a pleasure in sending a circular to him as to the new tariff. He might come or let it alone, as he pleased – certainly he ought to have told her that his own salary had been increased!

But there was more to do than sending out the new circular to her customers. How was she to send a circular round the valley to the old women and the others concerned? How was she to make Seppel, and Anton, and Josephine Bull understand that they should be forgiven, and have their old prices and their increased wages if they would come back to their allegiance, and never say a word again as to the sad affairs of the past summer? This circular must be of a nature very different from that which would serve for her customers. Thinking over it, she came to the opinion that Suse Krapp would be the best circular. A day or two after the Cartwrights were gone, she sent for Suse.

Suse was by no means a bad diplomate. When gaining her point she had no desire to triumph outwardly. When feeling herself a conqueror, she was quite ready to flatter the conquered one. She had never been more gracious, more submissive, or more ready to declare that in all matters the Frau's will was the law of the valley than now, when she was given to understand that everything should be bought on the same terms as heretofore, that the dairy should be discontinued during the next season, and that the wild fruits of the woods and mountains should be made welcome at the Peacock as had heretofore always been the case.

'Tomorrow will be the happiest day that ever was in the valley,' said Suse in her enthusiasm. 'And as for Seppel, he was telling me only yesterday that he would never be a happy man again till he could find himself once more at work in the old shed behind the chapel.'

Then Suse was told that Seppel might come as soon as he pleased.

'He'll be there the morning after next if I'm a living woman,' continued Suse energetically; and then she said another word, 'Oh, meine liebe Frau Frohmann, it broke my heart when they told me you were going away.'

'Going away!' said the Frau, as though she had been stung. 'Who said that I was going away?'

'I did hear it.'

'Psha! it was that stupid priest.' She had never before been heard to say a word against the kaplan; but now she could hardly restrain herself. 'Why should I go away?'

'No, indeed!'

'I am not thinking of going away. It would be a bad thing if I were to be driven out of my house by a little trouble as to the price of eggs and butter! No, Suse Krapp, I am not going away.'

'It will be the best word we have all of us heard this many a day, Frau Frohmann. When it came to that, we were all as though we would have broken our hearts.' Then she was sent upon her mission, not, upon this occasion, without a full glass of kirsch-wasser.

On the very day following Seppel was back. There was nothing said between him and his mistress, but he waited about the front of the house till he had an opportunity of putting his hand up to his cap and smiling at her as she stood upon the doorstep. And then, before the week was over, all the old women and all the young girls were crowding round the place with little presents which, on this first return to their allegiance, they brought to the Frau as peace-offerings.

The season was nearly over when she signified to Malchen her desire that Fritz Schlessen should come out to the valley. This she did with much good humour, explaining frankly that Fritz would have to prepare the new circulars, and that she must discuss with him the nature of the altered propositions which were to be made to the public. Fritz of course came, and was closeted with her for a full hour, during which he absolutely prepared the document for the Innsbruck printer. It was a simple announcement that for the future the charge made at the Brunnenthal Peacock would be seven and a half zwansigers per head per day. It then went on to declare that, as heretofore, the Frau Frohmann would endeavour to give satisfaction to all those who would do her the honour of visiting her establishment. And instructions were given to Schlessen as to sending the circulars out to the public. 'But whatever you do,' said the Frau, 'don't send one to those Tendel ladies.'

And something else was settled at this conference. As soon as it was over Fritz Schlessen was encountered by Malchen, who on such occasions would never be far away. Though the spot on which they met was one which might not have been altogether secure from intrusive eyes, he took her fondly by the waist and whispered a word in her ear.

'And will that do?' asked Malchen anxiously; to which question his reply was made by a kiss. In that whisper he had conveyed to her the amount now fixed for the *mitgift*.

8: IT DOESN'T MAKE ANY DIFFERENCE
TO ANY OF THEM

And so Frau Frohmann had raised her prices, and had acknowledged herself to all the world to have been beaten in her enterprise.
There are, however, certain misfortunes which are infinitely worse
in their anticipation than in their reality; and this, which had been
looked forward to as a terrible humiliation, was soon found to be
one of them. No note of triumph was sounded; none at least reached
her ear. Indeed, it so fell out that those with whom she had quarrelled for awhile seemed now to be more friendly with her than ever.
Between her and Hoff things were so sweet that no mention was
ever made of money. The meat was sent and the bills were paid with
a reticence which almost implied that it was not trade, but an
amiable giving and taking of the good things of the world. There
had never been a word of explanation with Seppel; but he was late
and early about the carts and the furniture, and innumerable little
acts of kindnesses made their way up to the mother and her many
children. Suse and Josephine had never been so brisk, and the eggs
had never been so fresh or the vegetables so good. Except from the
working of her own mind, she received no wounds.

But the real commencement of the matter did not take place
till the following summer – the commencement as regarded the
public. The circulars were sent out, but to such letters no answers
are returned; and up to the following June the Frau was ignorant
what effect the charge would have upon the coming of her customers.
There were times at which she thought that her house would be left
desolate, that the extra charge would turn away from her the hearts
of her visitors, and that in this way she would be compelled to
retire to Schwatz.

'Suppose they don't come at all,' she said to Peter one
day.

'That would be very bad,' said Peter, who also had his fears in
the same direction.

'Fritz Schlessen thinks it won't make any difference,' said the
Frau.

'A zwansiger and a half a day does make a difference to most men,'
replied Peter uncomfortably.

This was uncomfortable; but when Schlessen came out he raised
her spirits.

'Perhaps old Weiss won't come,' he said, 'but then there will be
plenty in his place. There are houses like the Peacock all over the

country now, in the Engadine and the Bregenz, and the Salzkammergut; and it seems to me the more they charge the fuller they are.'

'But they are for the grand folk.'

'For anybody that chooses. It has come to that, that the more money people are charged the better they like it. Money has become so plentiful with the rich, that they don't know what to do with it.'

This was a repetition of Mr Cartwright's barn full of gold. There was something in the assertion that money could be plentiful, in the idea that gold could be a drug, which savoured to her of innovation, and was therefore unpleasant. She still felt that the old times were good, and that no other times could be so good as the old times. But if the people would come and fill her house, and pay her the zwansiger and a half extra without grumbling, there would be some consolation in it.

Early in June Malchen made a call at the house of the Frauleins Tendel. Malchen at this time was known to all Innsbruck as the handsome Frau Schlessen who had been brought home in the winter to her husband's house with so very comfortable a *mitgift* in her hand. That was now quite an old story, and there were people in the town who said that the young wife already knew quite as much about her husband's business as she had ever done about her mother's. But at this moment she was obeying one of her mother's commands.

'Mother hopes you are both coming out to the Brunnenthal this year,' said Malchen. The elder fraulein shook her head sadly.

'Because –' Then Malchen paused, and the younger of the two ladies shook her head. 'Because you always have been there.'

'Yes, we have.'

'Mother means this. The change in the price won't have anything to do with you if you will come.'

'We couldn't think of that, Malchen.'

'Then mother will be very unhappy – that's all. The new circular was not sent to you.'

'Of course we heard of it.'

'If you don't come mother will take it very bad.' Then of course the ladies said they would come, and so that little difficulty was overcome.

This took place in June. But at that time the young wife was staying out in the valley with her mother, and had only gone into Innsbruck on a visit. She was with her mother preparing for the guests; but perhaps as the Frau too often thought, preparing for guests who would never arrive. From day to day, however, there came letters bespeaking rooms as usual, and when the 21st of June came there was Herr Weiss with all his family.

She taught herself to regard the coming of the Weisses as a kind of touchstone by which she might judge of the success of what she had done. If he remained away it would be because in spite of the increase in his salary, he could not encounter the higher cost of this recreation for his wife and family. He was himself too fond of the good living of the Peacock not to come if he could afford it. But if he could not pay so much, then neither could others in his rank of life; and it would be sad indeed to the Frau if her house were to be closed to her neighbour Germans, even though she might succeed in filling it with foreigners from a distance. But now the Weisses had come, not having given their usual notice, but having sent a message for rooms only two days before their arrival. And at once there was a little sparring match between Herr Weiss and the Frau.

'I didn't suppose that there would be much trouble as to finding rooms,' said Herr Weiss.

'Why shouldn't there be as much trouble as usual?' asked the Frau in return. She had felt that there was some slight in this arrival of the whole family without the usual preliminary inquiries – as though there would never again be competition for rooms at the Peacock.

'Well, my friend, I suppose that that little letter which was sent about the country will make a difference.'

'That's as people like to take it. It hasn't made any difference with you, it seems.'

'I had to think a good deal about it, Frau Frohmann; and I suppose we shall have to make our stay shorter. I own I am a little surprised to see the Tendel women here. A zwansiger and a half a day comes to a deal of money at the end of a month, when there are two or three.'

'I am happy to think it won't hurt you, Herr Weiss, as you have had your salary raised.'

'That is neither here nor there, Frau Frohmann,' said the magistrate, almost with a touch of anger. All the world knew, or ought to know, how very insufficient was his stipend when compared with the invaluable public services which he rendered. Such at least was the light in which he looked at the question.

'At any rate,' said the Frau as he stalked away, 'the house is like to be as full as ever.'

'I am glad to hear it. I am glad to hear it.' These were his last words on the occasion. But before the day was over he told his wife that he thought the place was not as comfortable as usual, and that the Frau with her high prices was more upsetting than ever.

His wife, who took delight in being called Madame Weiss at Brixen, and who considered herself to be in some degree a lady of fashion, had nevertheless been very much disturbed in her mind by the increased prices, and had suggested that the place should be abandoned. A raising of prices was in her eyes extortion – though a small raising of salary was simply justice, and, as she thought, inadequate justice. But the living at the Peacock was good. Nobody could deny that. And when a middle-aged man is taken away from the comforts of his home, how is he to console himself in the midst of his idleness unless he has a good dinner? Herr Weiss had therefore determined to endure the injury, and as usual to pass his holiday in the Brunnenthal. But when Madame Weiss saw those two frauleins from Innsbruck in the house, whose means she knew down to the last kreutzer, and who certainly could not afford the increased demand, she thought that there must be something not apparent to view. Could it be possible that the Frau should be so unjust, so dishonest, so extortious as to have different prices for different neighbours! That an Englishman, or even a German from Berlin, should be charged something extra, might not perhaps be unjust or extortionate. But among friends of the same district, to put a zwansiger and a half on to one and not to another seemed to Madame Weiss to be a sin for which there should be no pardon. 'I am so glad to see you here,' she said to the younger fraulein.

'That is so kind of you. But we always are here, you know.'

'Yes – yes. But I feared that perhaps –. I know that with us we had to think more than once about it before we could make up our minds to pay the increased charges. The Magistrat felt a little hurt about it.' To this the fraulein at first answered nothing, thinking that perhaps she ought not to make public the special benevolence shown by the Frau to herself and her sister. 'A zwansiger and a half each is a great deal of money to add on,' said Madame Weiss.

'It is, indeed.'

'We might have got it cheaper elsewhere. And then I thought that perhaps you might have done so too.'

'She has made no increase to us,' said the poor lady, who at last was forced to tell the truth, as by not doing so she would have been guilty of a direct falsehood in allowing it to be supposed that she and her sister paid the increased price.

'Soh – oh – oh!' exclaimed Madame Weiss, clasping her hands together and bobbing her head up and down. 'Soh – oh – oh!' She had found it all out.

Then, shortly after that – the next day – there was an uncomfortable perturbation of affairs at the Peacock, which was not known indeed to all the guests, but which to those who heard it, or heard of it, seemed for the time to be terrible. Madame Weiss and the Frau had – what is commonly called – a few words together.

'Frau Frohmann,' said Madame Weiss, 'I was quite astonished to hear from Agatha Tendel that you were only charging them the old prices.'

'Why shouldn't I charge them just what I please – or nothing at all, if I pleased?' asked the Frau sharply.

'Of course you can. But I do think, among neighbours, there shouldn't be one price to one and one to another.'

'Would it do you any good, Frau Weiss, if I were to charge those ladies more than they can pay? Does it do you any harm if they live here at a cheap rate?'

'Surely there should be one price – among neighbours!'

'Herr Weiss got my circular, no doubt. He knew. I don't suppose he wants to live here at a rate less than it costs me to keep him. You and he can do what you like about coming. And you and he can do what you like about staying away. You knew my prices. I have not made any secret about the change. But as for interference between me and my other customers, it is what I won't put up with. So now you know all about it.'

By the end of her speech the Frau had worked herself up into a grand passion, and spoke aloud, so that all near her heard her. Then there was a great commotion in the Peacock, and it was thought that the Weisses would go away. But they remained for their allotted time.

This was the only disturbance which took place, and it passed off altogether to the credit of the Frau. Something in a vague way came to be understood about fixed incomes – so that Peter and Malchen, with the kaplan, even down to Seppel and Suse Krapp, were aware that the two frauleins ought not to be made to pay as much as the prosperous magistrate who had had his salary raised. And then it was quite understood that the difference made in favour of those two poor ladies was a kindness shown to them, and could not therefore be an injury to any one else.

Later in the year, when the establishment was full and everything was going on briskly, when the two puddings were at the very height of their glory, and the wild fruits were brought up on the supper-table in huge bowls, when the Brunnenthal was at its loveliest, and the Frau was appearing on holidays in her gayest costume, the Cartwrights returned to the valley. Of course they had ordered their rooms much beforehand; and the Frau, trusting altogether to the wisdom of those counsels which she did not even yet quite understand, had kept her very best apartments for them. The greeting between them was most friendly – the Frau condescending to put on something of her holiday costume to add honour to their arrival – a thing which she had never been known to do before on behalf of any guests. Of course there was not then time for conversation; but a day or two had not passed before she made known to Mr Cartwright her later experience.

'The people have come, sir, just the same,' she said.

'So I perceive.'

'It don't seem to make any difference to any of them.'

'I didn't think it would. And I don't suppose anybody has complained.'

'Well – there was a little said by one lady, Mr Cartwright. But that was not because I charged her more, but because another old friend was allowed to pay less.'

'She didn't do you any harm, I dare say.'

'Harm – oh dear no! She couldn't do me any harm if she tried. But I thought I'd tell you, sir, because you said it would be so. The people don't seem to think any more of seven zwansigers and a half than they do of six! It's very odd – very odd, indeed. I suppose it's all right, sir?' This she asked, still thinking that there must be something wrong in the world when so monstrous a condition of things seemed to prevail.

'They'd think a great deal of it if you charged them more than they believed sufficient to give you a fair profit for your outlay and trouble.'

'How can they know anything about it, Mr Cartwright?'

'Ah – indeed. How do they? But they do. You and I, Frau Frohmann, must study these matters very closely before we can find out how they adjust themselves. But we may be sure of this, that the world will never complain of fair prices, will never long endure unfair prices, and will give no thanks at all to those who sell their goods at a loss.'

The Frau curtseyed and retired – quite satisfied that she had done the right thing in raising her prices; but still feeling that she had many a struggle to make before she could understand the matter.

JOHN BULL ON THE
GUADALQUIVIR

I am an Englishman, living, as all Englishmen should do, in England, and my wife would not, I think, be well pleased were anyone to insinuate that she were other than an Englishwoman; but in the circumstances of my marriage I became connected with the south of Spain, and the narrative which I am to tell requires that I should refer to some of those details.

The Pomfrets and Daguilars have long been in trade together in this country, and one of the partners has usually resided at Seville for the sake of the works which the firm there possesses. My father, James Pomfret, lived there for ten years before his marriage; and since that and up to the present period, old Mr Daguilar has always been on the spot. He was, I believe, born in Spain, but he came very early to England; he married an English wife, and his sons had been educated exclusively in England. His only daughter, Maria Daguilar, did not pass so large a proportion of her early life in this country, but she came to us for a visit at the age of seventeen, and when she returned I made up my mind that I most assuredly would go after her. So I did, and she is now sitting on the other side of the fireplace with a legion of small linen habiliments in a huge basket by her side.

I felt, at the first, that there was something lacking to make my cup of love perfectly delightful. It was very sweet, but there was wanting that flower of romance which is generally added to the heavenly draught by a slight admixture of opposition. I feared that the path of my true love would run too smooth. When Maria came to our house, my mother and elder sister seemed to be quite willing that I should be continually alone with her; and she had not been there ten days before my father, by chance, remarked that there was nothing old Mr Daguilar valued so highly as a thorough feeling of intimate alliance between the two families which had been so long connected in trade. I was never told that Maria was to be my wife, but I felt that the same thing was done without words; and when, after six weeks of somewhat elaborate attendance upon

her, I asked her to be Mrs John Pomfret, I had no more fear of a
refusal, or even of hesitation on her part, than I now have when
I suggest to my partner some commercial transaction of undoubted
advantage.

But Maria, even at that age, had about her a quiet sustained
decision of character quite unlike anything I had seen in English
girls. I used to hear, and do still hear, how much more flippant is
the education of girls in France and Spain than in England; and
I know that this is shown to be the result of many causes – the
Roman Catholic religion being, perhaps, the chief offender; but,
nevertheless, I rarely see in one of our young women the same power
of a self-sustained demeanour as I meet on the Continent. It goes
no deeper than the demeanour, people say. I can only answer that
I have not found that shallowness in my own wife.

Miss Daguilar replied to me that she was not prepared with an
answer; she had only known me six weeks and wanted more time
to think about it; besides, there was one in her own country with
whom she would wish to consult. I knew she had no mother; and
as for consulting old Mr Daguilar on such a subject, that idea, I
knew, could not have troubled her. Besides, as I afterwards learned,
Mr Daguilar had already proposed a division of assets. My mother
declared that Maria was a foolish chit – in which, by-the-by, she
showed her entire ignorance of Miss Daguilar's character; my eldest
sister begged that no constraint might be put on the young lady's
inclinations – which provoked me to assert that the young lady's
inclinations were by no means opposed to my own; and my father,
in the coolest manner, suggested that the matter might stand over
for twelve months, and that I might then go to Seville, and see
about it! Stand over for twelve months! Would not Maria, long
before that time, have been snapped up and carried off by one of
those inordinately rich Spanish grandees who are still to be met
with occasionally in Andalucia?

My father's dictum, however, had gone forth; and Maria, in the
calmest voice, protested that she thought it very wise. I should be
less of a boy by that time, she said, smiling at me, but driving
wedges between every fibre of my body as she spoke. 'Be it so,' I
said, proudly. 'At any rate, I am not so much of a boy that I shall
forget you.' 'And, John, you still have the trade to learn,' she
added, with her deliciously foreign intonation – speaking very
slowly, but with perfect pronunciation. The trade to learn! However, I said not a word, but stalked out of the room, meaning to see
her no more before she went. But I could not resist attending on
her in the hall as she started; and when she took leave of us, she

put her face up to be kissed by me, as she did by my father, and seemed to receive as much emotion from one embrace as from the other. 'He'll go out by the packet of the 1st April,' said my father, speaking of me as though I were a bale of goods. 'Ah! that will be so nice,' said Maria, settling her dress in the carriage; 'the oranges will be ripe for him then!'

On the 17th April I did sail, and felt still very like a bale of goods. I had received one letter from her, in which she merely stated that her papa would have a room ready for me on my arrival; and, in answer to that, I had sent an epistle somewhat longer, and, as I then thought, a little more to the purpose. Her turn of mind was more practical than mine, and I must confess my belief that she did not appreciate my poetry.

I landed at Cadiz, and was there joined by an old family friend, one of the very best fellows that ever lived. He was to accompany me up as far as Seville; and, as he had lived for a year or two at Xeres, was supposed to be more Spanish almost than a Spaniard. His name was Johnson, and he was in the wine trade; and whether for travelling or whether for staying at home – whether for paying you a visit in your own house, or whether for entertaining you in his – there never was (and I am prepared to maintain there never will be) a stancher friend, a choicer companion, or a safer guide than Thomas Johnson. Words cannot produce a eulogium sufficient for his merits. But, as I have since learned, he was not quite so Spanish as I had imagined. Three years among the *bodegas* of Xeres had taught him, no doubt, to appreciate the exact twang of a good, dry sherry; but not as I now conceive, the exactest flavour of the true Spanish character. I was very lucky, however, in meeting such a friend, and now reckon him as one of the stanchest allies of the house of Pomfret, Daguilar, and Pomfret.

He met me at Cadiz, took me about the town, which appeared to me to be of no very great interest – though the young ladies were all very well. But, in this respect, I was then a Stoic, till such time as I might be able to throw myself at the feet of her whom I was ready to proclaim the most lovely of all the Dulcineas of Andalucia. He carried me up by boat and railway to Xeres; gave me a most terrific headache, by dragging me out into the glare of the sun, after I had tasted some half a dozen different wines, and went through all the ordinary hospitalities. On the next day we returned to Puerto, and from thence getting across to St Lucar and Bonanza, found ourselves on the banks of the Guadalquivir, and took our places in the boat for Seville. I need say but little to my readers respecting that far-famed river. Thirty years ago we in England generally believed that on its banks was to be found a pure elysium of pastoral beauty; that picturesque shepherds and lovely maidens here fed their flocks in fields of asphodel; that the limpid stream ran cool and crystal over bright stones and beneath perennial shade; and that everything on the Guadalquivir was as lovely and as poetical as its name. Now, it is pretty widely known that no uglier river oozes down to its bourn in the sea through unwhole-some banks of low mud. It is brown and dirty; ungifted by any scenic advantage; margined for miles upon miles by huge, flat, expansive fields, in which cattle are reared – the bulls wanted for the bull-fights among other; and birds of prey sit constant on the shore, watching for the carcases of such as die. Such are the charms of the golden Guadalquivir.

At first we were very dull on board that steamer. I never found myself in a position in which there was less to do. There was a nasty smell about the little boat which made me almost ill; every turn in the river was so exactly like the last that we might have been stand-ing still; there was no amusement except eating, and that, when once done, was not of a kind to make an early repetition desirable. Even Johnson was becoming dull, and I began to doubt whether I was so desirous as I once had been to travel the length and breadth of all Spain. But about noon a little incident occurred which did for a time remove some of our tedium. The boat had stopped to take in passengers on the river; and among others, a man had come on board dressed in a fashion that, to my eyes, was equally strange and picturesque. Indeed, his appearance was so singular that I could not but regard him with care, though I felt at first averse to stare at a fellow-passenger on account of his clothes. He was a man of about fifty, but as active apparently as though not more than twenty-five; he was of low stature, but of admirable make; his hair was just becoming grizzled, but was short and crisp and well cared for; his face was prepossessing, having a look of good humour added to courtesy, and there was a pleasant, soft smile round his mouth which ingratiated one at the first sight. But it was his dress rather than his person which attracted attention. He wore the ordinary Andalucian cap – of which such hideous parodies are now making themselves common in England – but was not con-tented with the usual ornament of the double tuft. The cap was small, and jaunty; trimmed with silk velvet – as is common here with men careful to adorn their persons; but this man's cap was finished off with a jewelled button and golden filigree work. He was dressed in a short jacket with a stand-up collar; and that also was covered with golden buttons and with golden button-holes.

It was all gilt down the front, and all lace down the back; the rows of buttons were double; and those of the more backward row hung down in heavy pendules. His waistcoat was of coloured silk – very pretty to look at – and ornamented with a small sash, through which gold threads were worked. All the buttons of his breeches also were of gold; and there were gold tags to all the button-holes. His stockings were of the finest silk, and clocked with gold from the knee to the ankle.

Dress any Englishman in such a garb and he will at once give you the idea of a hog in armour. In the first place, he will lack the proper spirit to carry it off, and in the next place the motion of his limbs will disgrace the ornaments they bear. 'And so best,' most Englishmen will say. Very likely; and, therefore, let no English-man try it. But my Spaniard did not look at all like a hog in armour. He walked slowly down the plank into the boat, whistling lowly, but very clearly, a few bars from an opera tune. It was plain to see that he was master of himself, of his ornaments, and of his limbs. He had no appearance of thinking that men were looking at him, or of feeling that he was beauteous in his attire; nothing could be more natural than his footfall, or the quiet glance of his cheery eye. He walked up to the captain who held the helm, and lightly raised his hand to his cap. The captain, taking one hand from the wheel, did the same, and then the stranger, turning his back to the stern of the vessel, and fronting down the river with his face, continued to whistle slowly, clearly, and in excellent time. Grand as were his clothes they were no burden on his mind.

'What is he?' said I, going up to my friend Johnson, with a whisper.

'Well, I've been looking at him,' said Johnson – which was true enough; 'he's a – an uncommonly good-looking fellow, isn't he?'

'Particularly so,' said I; 'and got up quite irrespective of expense. Is he a – a – a gentleman, now, do you think?'

'Well, those things are so different in Spain that it's almost impossible to make an Englishman understand them. One learns to know all this sort of people by being with them in the country, but one can't explain.'

'No; exactly. Are they real gold?'

'Yes, yes; I dare say they are. They sometimes have them silver gilt.'

'It is quite a common thing, then, isn't it?' asked I.

'Well, not exactly; that – Ah! yes; I see of course. He is a *torero*.'

'A what?'

'A *mayo*. I will explain it all to you. You will see them about in all places, and you will get used to them.'

'But I haven't seen one other as yet.'

'No, and they are not all so gay as this, nor so new in their finery, you know.'

'And what is a *torero*?'

'Well, a *torero* is a man engaged in bull-fighting.'

'Oh! he is a matador, is he?' said I, looking at him with more than all my eyes.

'No, not exactly that; not of necessity. He is probably a *mayo*. A fellow that dresses himself smart for fairs, and will be seen hanging about with the bull-fighters. What would be a sporting fellow in England – only he won't drink and curse like a low man on the turf there. Come, shall we go and speak to him?'

'I can't talk to him,' said I, diffident of my Spanish. I had received lessons in England from Maria Daguilar, but six weeks is little enough for making love, let alone the learning of a foreign language.

'Oh! I'll do the talking. You'll find the language easy enough before long. It soon becomes the same as English to you, when you live among them.' And then Johnson, walking up to the stranger, accosted him with that good-natured familiarity with which a thoroughly nice fellow always opens a conversation with his inferior. Of course I could not understand the words which were exchanged; but it was clear enough that the *mayo* took the address in good part, and was inclined to be communicative and social.

'They are all of pure gold,' said Johnson, turning to me after a minute, making as he spoke a motion with his head to show the importance of the information.

'Are they indeed?' said I. 'Where on earth did a fellow like that get them?' Whereupon Johnson again returned to his conversation with the man. After another minute he raised his hand, and began to finger the button on the shoulder; and to aid him in doing so the man of the bull-ring turned a little on one side.

'They are wonderfully well made,' said Johnson, talking to me, and still fingering the button. 'They are manufactured, he says, at Osuna, and he tells me that they make them better there than anywhere else.'

'I wonder what the whole set would cost?' said I. 'An enormous deal of money for a fellow like him, I should think!'

'Over twelve ounces,' said Johnson, having asked the question: 'and that will be more than forty pounds.'

'What an uncommon ass he must be!' said I.

As Johnson by this time was very closely scrutinising the whole set of ornaments I thought I might do so also, and going up close to our friend, I too began to handle the buttons and tags on the other side. Nothing could have been more good-humoured than he was – so much so that I was emboldened to hold up his arm that I might see the cut of his coat, to take off his cap and examine the make, to stuff my finger in beneath his sash, and at last to kneel down while I persuaded him to hold up his legs that I might look to the clocking. The fellow was thoroughly good-natured, and why should I not indulge my curiosity?

'You'll upset him if you don't take care,' said Johnson; for I got fast hold of him by one ankle, and was determined to finish the survey completely.

'Oh no, I shan't,' said I; 'a bull-fighting chap can surely stand on one leg. But what I wonder at is, how on earth he can afford it!' Whereupon Johnson again began to interrogate him in Spanish.

'He says he has got no children,' said Johnson, having received a reply, 'and that as he has nobody but himself to look after he is able to allow himself such little luxuries.'

'Tell him that I say he would be better with a wife and couple of babies,' said I – and Johnson interpreted.

'He says that he'll think of it some of these days, when he finds that the supply of fools in the world is becoming short,' said Johnson.

We had nearly done with him now, but after regaining my feet I addressed myself once more to the heavy *pendules*, which hung down almost under his arm. I lifted one of these, meaning to feel its weight between my fingers; but unfortunately I gave a lurch, probably through the motion of the boat, and still holding by the button, tore it almost off from our friend's coat.

'Oh, I am so sorry,' I said, in broad English.

'It do not matter at all,' he said, bowing, and speaking with equal plainness. And then, taking a knife from his pocket, he cut the *pendule* off, leaving a bit of torn cloth on the side of his jacket.

'Upon my word, I am quite unhappy,' said I; 'but I always am so awkward.' Whereupon he bowed low.

'Couldn't I make it right?' said I, bringing out my purse.

He lifted his hand, and I saw that it was small and white; he lifted it, and gently put it upon my purse, smiling sweetly as he did so. 'Thank you, no, señor; thank you, no.' And then, bowing to us both, he walked away down into the cabin.

'Upon my word he is a deuced well-mannered fellow,' said I.

'You shouldn't have offered him money,' said Johnson; 'a Spaniard does not like it.'

'Why, I thought you could do nothing without money in this country. Doesn't every one take bribes?'

'Ah! yes; that is a different thing; but not the price of a button. By jove! he understood English, too. Did you see that?'

'Yes; and I called him an ass! I hope he doesn't mind it.'

'Oh! no; he won't think anything about it,' said Johnson. 'That sort of fellows don't. I dare say we shall see him in the bull-ring next Sunday, and then we'll make all right with a glass of lemonade.'

And so our adventure ended with the man of the gold ornaments. I was sorry that I had spoken English before him so heedlessly, and resolved that I would never be guilty of such gaucherie again. But, then, who would think that a Spanish bull-fighter would talk a foreign language? I was sorry, also, that I had torn his coat; it had looked so awkward; and sorry again that I had offered the man money. Altogether I was a little ashamed of myself; but I had too much to look forward to at Seville to allow any heaviness to remain long at my heart; and before I had arrived at the marvellous city I had forgotten both him and his buttons.

Nothing could be nicer than the way in which I was welcomed at Mr Daguilar's house, or more kind – I may almost say affectionate – than Maria's manner to me. But it was too affectionate; and I am not sure that I should not have liked my reception better had she been more diffident in her tone, and less inclined to greet me with open warmth. As it was, she again gave me her cheek to kiss, in her father's presence, and called me dear John, and asked me specially after some rabbits which I had kept at home merely for a younger sister; and then it seemed as though she were in no way embarrassed by the peculiar circumstances of our position. Twelve months since I had asked her to be my wife, and now she was to give me an answer; and yet she was as assured in her gait, and as serenely joyous in her tone, as though I were a brother just returned from college. It could not be that she meant to refuse me, or she would not smile on me and be so loving; but I could almost have found it in my heart to wish that she would. 'It is quite possible,' said I to myself, 'that I may not be found so ready for this family bargain. A love that is to be had like a bale of goods is not exactly the love to suit my taste.' But then, when I met her again in the morning, I could no more have quarrelled with her than I could have flown.

I was inexpressibly charmed with the whole city, and especially with the house in which Mr Daguilar lived. It opened from the corner of a narrow, unfrequented street – a corner like an elbow – and, as seen from the exterior, there was nothing prepossessing to recommend it; but the outer door led by a short hall or passage to an inner door or grille, made of open ornamental iron-work, and through that we entered a court, or patio, as they called it. Nothing could be more lovely or deliciously cool than was this small court. The building on each side was covered by trellis-work; and beautiful creepers, vines, and parasite flowers, now in the full magnificence

of the early summer, grew up and clustered round the windows. Every inch of wall was covered, so that none of the glaring white-wash wounded the eye. In the four corners of the patio were four large orange-trees, covered with fruit. I would not say a word in special praise of these, remembering that childish promise she had made on my behalf. In the middle of the court there was a fountain, and round about on the marble floor there were chairs, and here and there a small table, as though the space were really a portion of the house. It was here that we used to take our cup of coffee and smoke our cigarettes, I and old Mr Daguilar, while Maria sat by, not only approving, but occasionally rolling for me the thin paper round the fragrant weed with her taper fingers. Beyond the patio was an open passage or gallery, filled also with flowers in pots; and then, beyond this, one entered the drawing-room of the house. It was by no means a princely palace or mansion, fit for the owner of untold wealth. The rooms were not over large nor very numerous; but the most had been made of a small space, and everything had been done to relieve the heat of an almost tropical sun.

'It is pretty, is it not?' she said, as she took me through it.

'Very pretty,' I said. 'I wish we could live in such houses.'

'Oh, they would not do at all for dear old fat, cold, cozy England. You are quite different, you know, in everything from us in the south; more phlegmatic, but then so much steadier. The men and the houses are all the same.'

I can hardly tell why, but even this wounded me. It seemed to me as though she were inclined to put into one and the same category things English, dull, useful, and solid; and that she was disposed to show a sufficient appreciation for such necessaries of life, though she herself had another and inner sense – a sense keenly alive to the poetry of her own southern clime; and that I, as being English, was to have no participation in this latter charm. An English husband might do very well, the interests of the firm might make such an arrangement desirable, such a *mariage de convenance* – so I argued to myself – might be quite compatible with – with heaven only knows what delights of super-terrestrial romance, from which I, as being an English thick-headed lump of useful coarse mortality, was to be altogether debarred. She had spoken to me of oranges, and having finished the survey of the house, she offered me some sweet little cakes. It could not be that of such things were the thoughts which lay undivulged beneath the clear waters of those deep black eyes – undivulged to me, though no one else could have so good a right to read those thoughts! It could not be that that noble brow gave index of a mind intent on the trade of which she had spoken! Words of other sort than any that had been vouchsafed to me must fall at times from the rich curves of that perfect mouth.

So felt I then, pining for something to make me unhappy. Ah, me! I know all about it now, and am content. But I wish that some learned pundit would give us a good definition of romance, would describe in words that feeling with which our hearts are so pestered when we are young, which makes us sigh for we know not what, and forbids us to be contented with what God sends us. We invest female beauty with impossible attributes, and are angry because our women have not the spiritualised souls of angels, anxious as we are that they should also be human in the flesh. A man looks at her he would love as a distant landscape in a mountainous land. The peaks are glorious with more than the beauty of earth and rock and vegetation.

He dreams of some mysterious grandeur of design which tempts him on under the hot sun, and over the sharp rock, till he has reached the mountain goal which he had set before him. But when there, he finds that the beauty is well-nigh gone, and as for that delicious mystery, on which his soul had fed, it has vanished for ever.

I know all about it now, and am, as I said, content. Beneath those deep black eyes there lay a well of love, good, honest, homely love, love of father and husband and children that were to come – of that love which loves to see the loved ones prospering in honesty. That noble brow – for it is noble; I am unchanged in that opinion, and will go unchanged to my grave – covers thoughts as to the welfare of many, and an intellect fitted to the management of a household, of servants, namely, and children, and perchance a husband. That mouth can speak words of wisdom, of very useful wisdom – though of poetry it has latterly uttered little that was original. Poetry and romance! They are splendid mountain views seen in the distance. So let men be content to see them, and not attempt to tread upon the fallacious heather of the mystic hills.

In the first week of my sojourn in Seville I spoke no word of overt love to Maria, thinking, as I confess, to induce her thereby to alter her mode of conduct to myself. 'She knows that I have come here to make love to her – to repeat my offer; and she will at any rate be chagrined if I am slow to do so.' But it had no effect. At home my mother was rather particular about her table, and Maria's greatest efforts seemed to be used in giving me as nice dinners as we gave her. In those days I did not care a straw about my dinner, and I took an opportunity of telling her. 'Dear me,' said she, looking at me almost with grief, 'do you not? What a pity! And do you not like music either?' 'Oh, yes, I adore it,' I replied. I felt sure at the time that had I been born in her own sunny clime, she would never have talked to me about eating. But that was my mistake.

I used to walk out with her about the city, seeing all that is there of beauty and magnificence. And in what city is there more that is worth the seeing? At first this was very delightful to me, for I felt that I was blessed with a privilege that would not be granted to any other man. But its value soon fell in my eyes, for others would accost her, and walk on the other side, talking to her in Spanish, as though I hardly existed, or were a servant there for her protection. And I was not allowed to take her arm, and thus to appropriate her, as I should have done in England. 'No, John,' she said, with the sweetest, prettiest smile, 'we don't do that here; only when people are married,' and she made this allusion to married life out, openly, with no slightest tremor on her tongue.

'Oh, I beg pardon,' said I, drawing back my hand, and feeling angry with myself for not being fully acquainted with all the customs of a foreign country.

'You need not beg pardon,' said she; 'when we were in England we always walked so. It is just a custom, you know.' And then I saw her drop her large dark eyes to the ground, and bow gracefully in answer to some salute.

I looked round, and saw that we had been joined by a young cavalier – a Spanish nobleman, as I saw at once; a man with jet black hair, and a straight nose, and a black moustache, and patent leather boots, very slim and very tall, and – though I would not confess it then – uncommonly handsome. I myself am inclined to be stout, my hair is light, my nose broad, I have no hair on my upper lip, and my whiskers are rough and uneven. 'I could punch your head through, my fine fellow,' said I to myself, when I saw that he placed himself at Maria's side, 'and think very little of the achievement.'

The wretch went on with us round the plaza for some quarter of an hour talking Spanish with the greatest fluency, and she was every whit as fluent. Of course, I could not understand a word that they said. Of all positions that a man can occupy, I think that that is about the most uncomfortable; and I cannot say that, even up to this day, I have quite forgiven her for that quarter of an hour.

'I shall go in,' said I, unable to bear my feelings, and preparing to leave her. ' The heat is unendurable.'

'Oh dear, John, why did you not speak before?' she answered. 'You cannot leave me here, you know, as I am in your charge; but I will go with you almost directly.' And then she finished her conversation with the Spaniard, speaking with an animation she had never displayed in her conversations with me.

It had been agreed between us for two or three days before this that we were to rise early on the following morning for the sake of ascending the tower of the cathedral, and visiting the Giralda, as the iron figure is called, which turns upon a pivot on the extreme summit. We had often wandered together up and down the long dark gloomy aisle of the stupendous building, and had together seen its treasury of art; but as yet we had not performed the task which has to be achieved by all visitors to Seville; and in order that we might have a clear view over the surrounding country, and not be tormented by the heat of an advanced sun, we had settled that we would ascend the Giralda before breakfast.

And now, as I walked away from the plaza towards Mr Daguilar's house, with Maria by my side, I made up my mind that I would settle my business during this visit to the cathedral. Yes, and I would so manage the settlement that there should be no doubt left as to my intentions and my own ideas. I would not be guilty of shilly-shally conduct; I would tell her frankly what I felt and what I thought, and would make her understand that I did not desire her hand if I could not have her heart. I did not value the kindness of her manner, seeing that that kindness sprung from indifference rather than passion; and so I would declare to her. And I would ask her, also, who was this young man with whom she was intimate – for whom all her volubility and energy of tone seemed to be employed? She had told me once that it behoved her to consult a friend in Seville as to the expediency of her marriage to me. Was this the friend whom she had wished to consult? If so, she need not trouble herself. Under such circumstances I should decline the connection! And I resolved that I would find out how this might be. A man who proposes to take a woman to his bosom as his wife, has a right to ask for information – ay, and to receive it too. It flashed upon my mind at this moment that Donna Maria was well enough inclined to come to me as my wife, but – I could hardly

define the 'buts' to myself, for there were three or four of them.
Why did she always speak to me in a tone of childish affection, as
though I were a schoolboy home for the holidays? I would have all
this out with her on the tower on the following morning, standing
under the Giralda.

On that morning we met together in the patio, soon after five
o'clock, and started for the cathedral. She looked beautiful, with
her black mantilla over her head, and with black gloves on, and
her black morning silk dress – beautiful, composed, and at her ease
as though she were well satisfied to undertake this early morning
walk from feelings of good nature – sustained, probably, by some
under-current of a deeper sentiment. Well, I would know all about
it before I returned to her father's house.

There hardly stands, as I think, on the earth, a building more
remarkable than the cathedral of Seville, and hardly one more
grand. Its enormous size; its gloom and darkness; the richness of
ornamentation in the details, contrasted with the severe simplicity
of the large outlines; the variety of its architecture; the glory of its
paintings; and the wondrous splendour of its metallic decoration,
its altar-friezes, screens, rails, gates, and the like, render it, to my
mind, the first in interest among churches. It has not the coloured
glass of Chartres, or the marble glory of Milan, or such a forest of
aisles as Antwerp, or so perfect a hue in stone as Westminster, nor
in mixed beauty of form and colour does it possess anything equal
to the choir of Cologne; but, for combined magnificence and awe-
compelling grandeur, I regard it as superior to all other ecclesiastical
edifices.

It is its deep gloom with which the stranger is so greatly struck
on his first entrance. In a region so hot as the south of Spain, a cool
interior is a main object with the architect, and this it has been
necessary to effect by the exclusion of light; consequently the church
is dark, mysterious, and almost cold. On the morning in question,
as we entered, it seemed to be filled with gloom, and the distant
sound of a slow footstep here and there beyond the transept inspired one almost with awe. Maria, when she first met me, had begun
to talk with her usual smile, offering me coffee and a biscuit before
I started. 'I never eat biscuit,' I said, with almost a severe tone, as
I turned from her. That dark, horrid man of the plaza – would she
have offered him a cake had she been going to walk with him in the
gloom of the morning? After that little had been spoken between us.
She walked by my side with her accustomed smile; but she had, as I
flattered myself, begun to learn that I was not to be won by a mean-
ingless good nature. 'We are lucky in our morning for the view!'

That was all she said, speaking with that peculiarly clear, but slow pronunciation which she had assumed in learning our language.

We entered the cathedral, and, walking the whole length of the aisle, left it again at the porter's porch at the farther end. Here we passed through a low door on to the stone flight of steps, and at once began to ascend. 'There are a party of your countrymen up before us,' said Maria; 'the porter says that they went through the lodge half an hour since.' 'I hope they will return before we are on the top,' said I, bethinking myself of the task that was before me. And indeed my heart was hardly at ease within me, for that which I had to say would require all the spirit of which I was master.

The ascent to the Giralda is very long and very fatiguing; and we had to pause on the various landings and in the singular belfry in order that Miss Daguilar might recruit her strength and breath.

As we rested on one of these occasions, in a gallery which runs round the tower below the belfry, we heard a great noise of shouting and a clattering of sticks among the bells. 'It is the party of your countrymen who went up before us,' said she. 'What a pity that Englishmen should always make so much noise!' And then she spoke in Spanish to the custodian of the bells, who is usually to be found in a little cabin up there within the tower. 'He says that they went up shouting like demons,' continued Maria; and it seemed to me that she looked as though I ought to be ashamed of the name of an Englishman. 'They may not be so solemn in their demeanour as Spaniards,' I answered; 'but, for all that, there may be quite as much in them.'

We then again began to mount, and before we had ascended much farther we passed my three countrymen. They were young men, with grey coats and grey trousers, with slouched hats, and without gloves. They had fair faces and fair hair, and swung big sticks in their hands, with crooked handles. They laughed and talked loud, and, when we met them, seemed to be racing with each other; but nevertheless they were gentlemen. No one who knows by sight what an English gentleman is could have doubted that; but I did acknowledge to myself that they should have remembered that the edifice they were treading was a church, and that the silence they were invading was the cherished property of a courteous people.

'They are all just the same as big boys,' said Maria. The colour instantly flew into my face, and I felt that it was my duty to speak up for my own countrymen. The word 'boys' especially wounded my ears. It was as a boy that she treated me; but, on looking at that befringed young Spanish Don – who was not, apparently, my

elder in age – she had recognised a man. However, I said nothing
further till I reached the summit. One cannot speak with manly
dignity while one is out of breath on a staircase.

'There, John,' she said, stretching her hands away over the fair
plain of the Guadalquivir, as soon as we stood against the parapet,
'is not that lovely?'

I would not deign to notice this. 'Maria,' I said, 'I think that
you are too hard upon my countrymen.'

'Too hard! No; for I love them. They are so good and industrious;
and they come home to their wives, and take care of their children.
But why do they make themselves so – so – what the French call
gauche?'

'Good and industrious, and come home to their wives!' thought
I. 'I believe you hardly understand us as yet,' I answered. 'Our
domestic virtues are not always so very prominent; but, I believe,
we know how to conduct ourselves as gentlemen; at any rate, as
well as Spaniards.' I was very angry – not at the faults, but at the
good qualities imputed to us.

'In affairs of business, yes,' said Maria, with a look of firm confidence in her own opinion – that look of confidence which she has
never lost, and I pray that she may never lose it while I remain
with her – 'but in the little intercourses of the world, no! A Spaniard
never forgets what is personally due either to himself or his neighbours. If he is eating an onion, he eats it as an onion should be
eaten.'

'In such matters as that he is very grand, no doubt,' said I,
angrily.

'And why should you not eat an onion properly, John? Now, I
heard a story yesterday from Don – about two Englishmen, which
annoyed me very much.' I did not exactly catch the name of the
Don in question, but I felt through every nerve in my body that it
was the man who had been talking to her on the plaza.

'And what have they done?' said I. 'But it is the same everywhere. We are always abused; but, nevertheless, no people are so
welcome. At any rate, we pay for the mischief we do.' I was angry
with myself the moment the words were out of my mouth, for, after
all, there is no feeling more mean than that pocket-confidence
with which an Englishman sometimes swaggers.

'There was no mischief done in this case,' she answered. 'It was
simply that two men have made themselves ridiculous for ever.
The story is all about Seville, and, of course, it annoys me that they
should be Englishmen.'

'And what did they do?'

'The Marquis D'Almavivas was coming up to Seville in the boat, and they behaved to him in the most outrageous manner. He is here now, and is going to give a series of fêtes. Of course, he will not ask a single Englishman.'

'We shall manage to live, even though the Marquis D'Almavivas may frown upon us,' said I, proudly.

'He is the richest, and also the best of our noblemen,' continued Maria; 'and I never heard of anything so absurd as what they did to him. It made me blush when Don – told me.' Don Tomás, I thought she said.

'If he be the best of your noblemen, how comes it that he is angry because he has met two vulgar men? It is not to be supposed that every Englishman is a gentleman.'

'Angry! Oh, no! he was not angry; he enjoyed the joke too much for that. He got completely the best of them, though they did not know it; poor fools! How would your Lord John Russell behave if two Spaniards in an English railway carriage were to pull him about and tear his clothes?'

'He would give them in charge to a policeman, of course,' said I, speaking of such a matter with the contempt it deserved.

'If that were done here your ambassador would be demanding national explanations. But Almavivas did much better – he laughed at them without letting them know it.'

'But do you mean that they took hold of him violently, without any provocation? They must have been drunk.'

'Oh, no, they were sober enough. I did not see it, so I do not quite know exactly how it was, but I understand that they committed themselves most absurdly, absolutely took hold of his coat and tore it, and – but they did such ridiculous things that I cannot tell you.' And yet Don Tomás, if that was the man's name, had been able to tell her, and she had been able to listen to him.

'What made them take hold of the marquis?' said I.

'Curiosity, I suppose,' she answered. 'He dresses somewhat fancifully, and they could not understand that anyone should wear garments different from their own.' But even then the blow did not strike home upon me.

'Is it not pretty to look down upon the quiet town?' she said, coming close up to me, so that the skirt of her dress pressed me, and her elbow touched my arm. Now was the moment I should have asked her how her heart stood towards me; but I was sore and uncomfortable, and my destiny was before me. She was willing enough to let these English faults pass by without further notice, but I would not allow the subject to drop.

'I will find out who these men were,' said I, 'and learn the truth of it. When did it occur?'

'Last Thursday, I think he said.'

'Why, that was the day we came up in the boat, Johnson and myself. There was no marquis there then, and we were the only Englishmen on board.'

'It was on Thursday, certainly, because it was well known in Seville that he arrived on that day. You must have remarked him because he talks English perfectly – though, by-the-bye, these men would go on chatting before him about himself as though it were impossible that a Spaniard should know their language. They are ignorant of Spanish, and they cannot bring themselves to believe that anyone should be better educated than themselves.'

Now the blow had fallen, and I straightway appreciated the necessity of returning immediately to Clapham, where my family resided, and giving up for ever all idea of Spanish connections. I had resolved to assert the full strength of my manhood on that tower, and now words had been spoken which left me weak as a child. I felt that I was shivering, and did not dare to pronounce the trust which must be made known. As to speaking of love, and signifying my pleasure that Don Tomás should for the future be kept at a distance, any such effort was quite beyond me. Had Don Tomás been there, he might have walked off with her from before my face without a struggle on my part. 'Now I remember about it,' she continued, 'I think he must have been in the boat on Thursday.'

'And now that I remember,' I replied, turning away to hide my embarrassment, 'he was there. Your friend down below in the plaza seems to have made out a grand story. No doubt he is not fond of the English. There was such a man there, and I did take hold –'

'Oh, John, was it you?'

'Yes, Donna Maria, it was I; and if Lord John Russell were to dress himself in the same way –' But I had no time to complete my description of what might occur under so extravagantly impossible a combination of circumstances, for as I was yet speaking the little door leading out on to the leads of the tower was opened, and my friend, the *mayo* of the boat, still bearing all his gew-gaws on his back, stepped up on to the platform. My eye instantly perceived that the one *pendule* was still missing from his jacket. He did not come alone, but three other gentlemen followed him, who, however, had no peculiarities in their dress. He saw me at once, and bowed and smiled; and then observing Donna Maria, he lifted his cap from his head, and addressing himself to her in Spanish, began to converse with her as though she were an old friend.

'Señor,' said Maria, after the first words of greeting had been spoken between them; 'you must permit me to present to you my father's most particular friend, and my own – Mr Pomfret; John, this is the Marquis D'Almavivas.'

I cannot now describe the grace with which this introduction was effected, or the beauty of her face as she uttered the word. There was a boldness about her as though she had said, 'I know it all – the whole story. But, in spite of that you must take him on my representation, and be gracious to him in spite of what he has done. You must be content to do that; or in quarrelling with him you must quarrel with me also.' And it was done at the spur of the moment – without delay. She, who not five minutes since had been loudly condemning the unknown Englishman for his rudeness, had already pardoned him, now that he was known to be her friend; and had determined that he should be pardoned by others also or that she would share his disgrace. I recognised the nobleness of this at the moment; but, nevertheless, I was so sore that I would almost have preferred that she should have disowned me.

The marquis immediately lifted his cap with his left hand while he gave me his right. 'I have already had the pleasure of meeting this gentleman,' he said; 'we had some conversation in the boat together.'

'Yes,' said I, pointing to his rent, 'and you still bear the marks of our encounter.'

'Was it not delightful, Donna Maria,' he continued, turning to her; 'your friend's friend took me for a *torero*?'

'And it served you properly, señor,' said Donna Maria, laughing; 'you have no right to go about with all those rich ornaments upon you.'

'Oh! quite properly; indeed, I make no complaint; and I must beg your friend to understand, and his friend also, how grateful I am for their solicitude as to my pecuniary welfare. They were inclined to be severe on me for being so extravagant in such trifles. I was obliged to explain that I had no wife at home kept without her proper allowance of dresses in order that I might be gay.'

'They are foreigners, and you should forgive their error,' she said.

'And in token that I do so,' said the marquis, 'I beg your friend to accept the little ornament which attracted his attention.' And so saying, he pulled the identical button out of his pocket, and gracefully proffered it to me.

'I shall carry it about with me always,' said I, accepting it, 'as a memento of humiliation. When I look at it I shall ever remember the folly of an Englishman and the courtesy of a Spaniard,' and as I made the speech I could not but reflect whether it might, under any circumstances, be possible that Lord John Russell should be induced to give a button off his coat to a Spaniard.

There were other civil speeches made, and before we left the tower the marquis had asked me to his parties, and exacted from me an unwilling promise that I would attend them. 'The señora,' he said, bowing again to Maria, 'would he was sure, grace them. She had done so on the previous year; and as I had accepted his little present I was bound to acknowledge him as my friend.'

All this was very pretty, and, of course, I said that I would go, but I had not at that time the slightest intention of doing so. Maria had behaved admirably; she had covered my confusion, and shown herself not ashamed to own me, delinquent as I was; but, not the less, had she expressed her opinion, in language terribly strong, of the awkwardness of which I had been guilty, and had shown almost an aversion to my English character. I should leave Seville as quickly as I could, and should certainly not again put myself in the way of the Marquis D'Almavivas. Indeed, I dreaded the moment that I should be first alone with her, and should find myself forced to say something indicative of my feelings – to hear something also indicative of her feelings. I had come out this morning resolved to demand my rights and to exercise them – and now my only wish was to run away. I hated the marquis, and longed to be alone that I might cast his button from me. To think that a man should be so ruined by such a trifle!

We descended that prodigious flight without a word upon the subject, and almost without a word at all. She had carried herself well in the presence of Almavivas, and had been too proud to seem ashamed of her companion; but now, as I could well see, her feelings of disgust and contempt had returned. When I begged her not to hurry herself, she would hardly answer me; and when she did speak her voice was constrained and unlike herself. And yet how beautiful she was! Well, my dream of Spanish love must be over. But I was sure of this: that having known her, and given her my heart, I could never afterwards share it with another.

We came out at last on the dark, gloomy aisle of the cathedral, and walked together without a word up along the side of the choir, till we came to the transept. There was not a soul near us, and not a sound was to be heard but the distant, low pattering of a mass, then in course of celebration at some far-off chapel in the cathedral. When we got to the transept Maria turned a little, as though she was going to the transept door, and then stopped herself. She stood still; and when I stood also, she made two steps towards me, and put her hand on my arm. 'Oh, John!' she said.

'Well,' said I; 'after all it does not signify. You can make a joke of it when my back is turned.'

'Dearest John!' – she had never spoken to me in that way before – 'you must not be angry with me. It is better that we should explain to each other, is it not?'

'Oh, much better. I am very glad you heard of it at once. I do not look at it quite in the same light that you do; but nevertheless –'

'What do you mean? But I know you are angry with me. And yet you cannot think that I intended those words for you. Of course, I know now that there was nothing rude in what passed.'

'Oh, but there was.'

'No, I am sure there was not. You could not be rude though you are so free hearted. I see it all now, and so does the marquis. You will like him so much when you come to know him. Tell me that you won't be cross with me for what I have said. Sometimes I think that I have displeased you, and yet my whole wish has been to welcome you to Seville, and to make you comfortable as an old friend. Promise me that you will not be cross with me.'

Cross with her! I certainly had no intention of being cross, but I had begun to think that she would not care what my humour might be. 'Maria,' I said, taking hold of her hand.

'No, John, do not do that. It is in the church, you know.'

'Maria, will you answer me a question?'

'Yes,' she said, very slowly, looking down upon the stone slabs beneath our feet.

'Do you love me?'

'Love you!'

'Yes, do you love me? You were to give me an answer here, in Seville, and now I ask for it. I have almost taught myself to think that it is needless to ask; and now this horrid mischance –'

'What do you mean?' said she, speaking very quickly.

'Why this miserable blunder about the marquis's button! After that I suppose –'

'The marquis! Oh, John, is that to make a difference between you and me? – a little joke like that?'

'But does it not?'

'Make a change between us? – such a thing as that! Oh, John!'

'But tell me, Maria, what am I to hope? If you will say that you can love me, I shall care nothing for the marquis. In that case I can bear to be laughed at.'

'Who will dare to laugh at you? Not the marquis, whom I am sure you will like.'

'Your friend in the plaza, who told you of all this.'

'What, poor Tomás!'

'I do not know about his being poor. I mean the gentleman who was with you last night.'

'Yes, Tomás. You do not know who he is?'

'Not in the least.'

'How droll! He is your own clerk – partly your own, now that you are one of the firm. And, John, I mean to make you do something for him; he is such a good fellow; and last year he married a young girl whom I love – oh, almost like a sister.'

Do something for him! Of course I would. I promised, then and there, that I would raise his salary to any conceivable amount that a Spanish clerk could desire; which promise I have since kept, if not absolutely to the letter, at any rate, to an extent which has been considered satisfactory by the gentleman's wife.

'But, Maria – dearest Maria –'

'Remember, John, we are in the church; and poor papa will be waiting breakfast.'

I need hardly continue the story further. It will be known to all that my love-suit throve in spite of my unfortunate raid on the button of the Marquis D'Almavivas, at whose series of fêtes through that month I was, I may boast, an honoured guest. I have since that had the pleasure of entertaining him in my own poor house in England, and one of our boys bears his Christian name.

From that day in which I ascended the Giralda to this present day in which I write, I have never once had occasion to complain of a deficiency of romance either in Maria Daguilar or in Maria Pomfret.

MALACHI'S COVE

On the northern coast of Cornwall, between Tintagel and Bossiney, down on the very margin of the sea, there lived not long since an old man who got his living by saving seaweed 'from the waves, and selling it for manure. The cliffs there are bold and fine, and the sea beats in upon them from the north with a grand violence. I doubt whether it be not the finest morsel of cliff scenery in England, though it is beaten by many portions of the west coast of Ireland, and perhaps also by spots in Wales and Scotland. Cliffs should be nearly precipitous, they should be broken in their outlines, and should barely admit here and there of an insecure passage from their summit to the sand at their feet. The sea should come, if not up to them, at least very near to them, and then, above all things, the water below them should be blue, and not of that dead leaden colour which is so familiar to us in England. At Tintagel all these requisites are there, except that bright blue colour which is so lovely. But the cliffs themselves are bold and well broken, and the margin of sand at high water is very narrow – so narrow that at spring tides there is barely a footing there.

Close upon this margin was the cottage or hovel of Malachi Trenglos, the old man of whom I have spoken. But Malachi, or old Glos, as he was commonly called by the people around him, had not built his house absolutely upon the sand. There was a fissure in the rock so great that at the top it formed a narrow ravine, and so complete from the summit to the base that it afforded an opening for a steep and ragged track from the top of the rock to the bottom. This fissure was so wide at the bottom that it had afforded space for Trenglos to fix his habitation on a foundation of rock, and here he had lived for many years. It was told of him that in the early days of his trade he had always carried the weed in a basket on his back to the top, but latterly he had been possessed of a donkey which had been trained to go up and down the steep track with a single pannier over his loins, for the rocks would not admit of panniers hanging by his side; and for this assistant he had built a shed adjoining his own, and almost as large as that in which he himself resided.

But, as years went on, old Glos procured other assistance than that of the donkey, or, as I should rather say, Providence supplied him with other help; and, indeed, had it not been so, the old man must have given up his cabin and his independence and gone into the workhouse at Camelford. For rheumatism had afflicted him, old age had bowed him till he was nearly double, and by degrees he became unable to attend the donkey on its upward passage to the world above, or even to assist in rescuing the coveted weed from the waves.

At the time to which our story refers Trenglos had not been up the cliff for twelve months, and for the last six months he had done nothing towards the furtherance of his trade, except to take the money and keep it, if any of it was kept, and occasionally to shake down a bundle of fodder for the donkey. The real work of the business was done altogether by Mahala Trenglos, his grand-daughter.

Mally Trenglos was known to all the farmers round the coast, and to all the small tradespeople in Camelford. She was a wild-looking, almost unearthly creature, with wild-flowing, black, uncombed hair, small in stature, with small hands and bright black eyes; but people said that she was very strong, and the children around declared that she worked day and night, and knew nothing of fatigue. As to her age there were many doubts. Some said she was ten, and others five-and-twenty, but the reader may be allowed to know that at this time she had in truth passed her twentieth birthday. The old people spoke well of Mally, because she was so good to her grandfather; and it was said of her that though she carried to him a little gin and tobacco almost daily, she bought nothing for herself – and as to the gin, no one who looked at her would accuse her of meddling with that. But she had no friends, and but few acquaintances among people of her own age. They said that she was fierce and ill-natured, that she had not a good word for anyone, and that she was, complete at all points, a thorough little vixen.

The young men did not care for her; for, as regarded dress, all days were alike with her. She never made herself smart on Sundays. She was generally without stockings, and seemed to care not at all to exercise any of those feminine attractions which might have been hers had she studied to attain them. All days were the same to her in regard to dress; and, indeed, till lately, all days had, I fear, been the same to her in other respects. Old Malachi had never been seen inside a place of worship since he had taken to live under the cliff.

But within the last two years Mally had submitted herself to the teaching of the clergyman at Tintagel, and had appeared at church on Sundays, if not absolutely with punctuality, at any rate so often that no one who knew the peculiarity of her residence was disposed

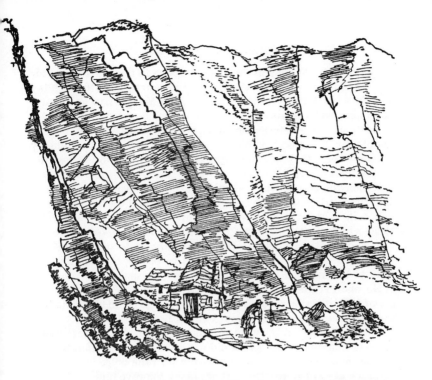

to quarrel with her on that subject. But she made no difference in her dress on these occasions. She took her place in a low stone seat just inside the church door, clothed as usual in her thick red serge petticoat and loose brown serge jacket, such being the apparel which she had found to be best adapted for her hard and perilous work among the waters. She had pleaded to the clergyman when he attacked her on the subject of church attendance with vigour that she had got no church-going clothes. He had explained to her that she would be received there without distinction to her clothing. Mally had taken him at his word, and had gone, with a courage which certainly deserved admiration, though I doubt whether there was not mingled with it an obstinacy which was less admirable.

For people said that old Glos was rich, and that Mally might have proper clothes if she chose to buy them. Mr Polwarth, the clergyman, who, as the old man could not come to him, went down the rocks to the old man, did make some hint on the matter in Mally's absence. But old Glos, who had been patient with him on other matters, turned upon him so angrily when he made an allusion to money, that Mr Polwarth found himself obliged to give that matter up, and Mally continued to sit upon the stone bench in her short serge petticoat, with her long hair streaming down her face. She did so far sacrifice to decency as on such occasions to tie up her back hair with an old shoe-string. So tied it would remain through the Monday and Tuesday, but by Wednesday afternoon Mally's hair had generally managed to escape.

As to Mally's indefatigable industry there could be no manner of doubt, for the quantity of seaweed which she and the donkey amassed between them was very surprising. Old Glos, it was declared, had never collected half what Mally gathered together; but then the article was becoming cheaper, and it was necessary that the exertion should be greater. So Mally and the donkey toiled and toiled, and the seaweed came up in heaps which surprised those who looked at her little hands and light form. Was there not someone who helped her at nights, some fairy, or demon, or the like? Mally was so snappish in her answers to people that she had no right to be surprised if ill-natured things were said of her.

No one ever heard Mally Trenglos complain of her work, but about this time she was heard to make great and loud complaints of the treatment she received from some of her neighbours.

It was known that she went with her plaints to Mr Polwarth; and when he could not help her, or did not give her such instant help as she needed, she went – ah, so foolishly – to the office of a certain attorney at Camelford, who was not likely to prove himself a better friend than Mr Polwarth.

Now the nature of her injury was as follows. The place in which she collected her seaweed was a little cove; the people had come to call it Malachi's Cove, from the name of the old man who lived there – which was so formed that the margin of the sea therein could only be reached by the passage from the top down to Trenglos's hut. The breadth of the cove when the sea was out might perhaps be two hundred yards, and on each side the rocks ran out in such a way that both from north and south the domain of Trenglos was guarded from intruders. And this locality had been well chosen for its intended purpose.

There was a rush of the sea into the cove, which carried there large, drifting masses of seaweed, leaving them among the rocks when the tide was out. During the equinoctial winds of the spring and autumn the supply would never fail; and even when the sea was calm the long, soft, salt-bedewed, trailing masses of the weed could be gathered there when they could not be found elsewhere for miles along the coast. The task of getting the weed from the breakers was often difficult and dangerous – so difficult that much of it was left to be carried away by the next incoming tide.

Mally doubtless did not gather half the crop that was there at her feet. What was taken by the returning waves she did not regret; but when interlopers came upon her cove, and gathered her wealth – her grandfather's wealth – beneath her eyes, then her heart was broken. It was this interloping, this intrusion, that drove poor Mally to the Camelford attorney. But, alas, though the Camelford attorney took Mally's money, he could do nothing for her, and her heart was broken!

She had an idea, in which no doubt her grandfather shared, that the path to the cove was, at any rate, their property. When she was told that the cove, and sea running into the cove, were not the freeholds of her grandfather, she understood that the statement might be true. But what then as to the use of the path? Who had made the path what it was? Had she not painfully, wearily, with exceeding toil, carried up bits of rock with her own little hands, that her grandfather's donkey might have footing for his feet? Had she not scraped together crumbs of earth along the face of the cliff that she might make easier to the animal the track of that rugged way? And now, when she saw big farmers' lads coming down with other donkeys – and, indeed, there was one who came with a pony; no boy, but a young man, old enough to know better than rob a poor old man and a young girl – she reviled the whole human race, and swore that the Camelford attorney was a fool.

Any attempt to explain to her that there was still weed enough for her was worse than useless. Was it not all hers and his, or, at any rate, was not the sole way to it his and hers? And was not her trade stopped and impeded? Had she not been forced to back her laden donkey down, twenty yards, she said, but it had, in truth, been five, because Farmer Gunliffe's son had been in the way with his thieving pony? Farmer Gunliffe had wanted to buy her weed at his own price, and because she had refused he had set on his thieving son to destroy her in this wicked way.

'I'll hamstring the beast the next time as he's down here!' said Mally to old Glos, while the angry fire literally streamed from her eyes.

Farmer Gunliffe's small homestead – he held about fifty acres of land – was close by the village of Tintagel, and not a mile from the cliff. The sea-wrack, as they call it, was pretty well the only manure within his reach, and no doubt he thought it hard that he should be kept from using it by Mally Trenglos and her obstinacy.

'There's heaps of other coves, Barty,' said Mally to Barty Gunliffe, the farmer's son.

'But none so nigh, Mally, nor yet none that fills 'emselves as this place.'

Then he explained to her that he would not take the weed that came up close to hand. He was bigger than she was, and stronger, and would get it from the outer rocks, with which she never meddled. Then, with scorn in her eye, she swore that she could get it where he durst not venture, and repeated her threat of hamstringing the pony. Barty laughed at her wrath, jeered her because of her wild hair, and called her a mermaid.

'I'll mermaid you!' she cried. 'Mermaid, indeed! I wouldn't be a man to come and rob a poor girl and an old cripple. But you're no man, Barty Gunliffe! You're not half a man.'

Nevertheless, Bartholomew Gunliffe was a very fine young fellow, as far as the eye went. He was about five feet eight inches high, with strong arms and legs, with light curly brown hair and blue eyes. His father was but in a small way as a farmer, but, nevertheless, Barty Gunliffe was well thought of among the girls around. Everybody liked Barty – excepting only Mally Trenglos, and she hated him like poison.

Barty, when he was asked why so good-natured a lad as he persecuted a poor girl and an old man, threw himself upon the justice of the thing. It wouldn't do at all, according to his view, that any single person should take upon himself to own that which God Almighty sent as the common property of all. He would do Mally no harm, and so he had told her. But Mally was a vixen – a wicked little vixen; and she must be taught to have a civil tongue in her head. When once Mally would speak him civil as he went for weed, he would get his father to pay the old man some sort of toll for the use of the path.

'Speak him civil!' said Mally. 'Never; not while I have a tongue in my mouth!' And I fear old Glos encouraged her rather than otherwise in her view of the matter.

But her grandfather did not encourage her to hamstring the pony. Hamstringing a pony would be a serious thing, and old Glos thought it might be very awkward for both of them if Mally were put into prison. He suggested, therefore, that all manner of impediments should be put in the way of the pony's feet, surmising that the well-trained donkey might be able to work in spite of them. And Barty Gunliffe, on his next descent, did find the passage very awkward when he came near to Malachi's hut, but he made his way down, and poor Mally saw the lumps of rock at which she had laboured so hard pushed on one side or rolled out of the way with a steady persistency of injury towards herself that almost drove her frantic.

'Well, Barty, you're a nice boy,' said old Glos, sitting in the doorway of the hut, as he watched the intruder.

'I ain't a doing no harm to none as doesn't harm me,' said Barty. 'The sea's free to all, Malachi.'

'And the sky's free to all, but I mustn't get up on the top of your big barn to look at it,' said Mally, who was standing among the rocks with a long hook in her hand. The long hook was the tool with which she worked in dragging the weed from the waves. 'But you ain't got no justice nor yet no sperrit, or you wouldn't come here to vex an old man like he.'

'I didn't want to vex him, nor yet to vex you, Mally. You let me be for a while, and we'll be friends yet.'

'Friends!' exclaimed Mally. 'Who'd have the likes of you for a friend? What are you moving them stones for? Them stones belongs to grandfather.' And in her wrath she made a movement as though she were going to fly at him.

'Let him be, Mally,' said the old man; 'let him be. He'll get his punishment. He'll come to be drowned some day if he comes down here when the wind is in shore.'

'That he may be drowned then!' said Mally, in her anger. 'If he was in the big hole there among the rocks, and the sea running in at half tide, I wouldn't lift a hand to help him out.'

'Yes, you would, Mally; you'd fish me up with your hook like a big stock of seaweed.'

She turned from him with scorn as he said this, and went into the hut. It was time for her to get ready for her work, and one of the great injuries done her lay in this – that such a one as Barty Gunliffe should come and look at her during her toil among the breakers.

It was an afternoon in April, and the hour was something after four o'clock. There had been a heavy wind from the north-west all the morning, with gusts of rain, and the seagulls had been in and out of the cove all the day, which was a sure sign to Mally that the incoming tide would cover the rocks with weed. The quick waves were now returning with wonderful celerity over the low reefs, and the time had come at which the treasure must be seized if it was to be garnered on that day. By seven o'clock it would be growing dark, at nine it would be high water, and before daylight the crop would be carried out again if not collected. All this Mally understood very well, and some of this Barty was beginning to understand also.

As Mally came down with her bare feet, bearing her long hook in her hand, she saw Barty's pony standing patiently on the sand, and in her heart she longed to attack the brute. Barty at this moment, with a common three-pronged fork in his hand, was standing down on a large rock, gazing forth towards the waters. He had declared that he would gather the weed only at places

which were inaccessible to Mally, and he was looking out that he
might settle where he would begin.

'Let 'un be, let 'un be,' shouted the old man to Mally, as he saw
her take a step towards the beast, which she hated almost as much
as she hated the man.

Hearing her grandfather's voice through the wind, she desisted
from her purpose, if any purpose she had had, and went forth to

her work. As she passed down the cove, and scrambled in among
the rocks, she saw Barty still standing on his perch; out beyond, the
white-curling waves were cresting and breaking themselves with
violence, and the wind was howling among the caverns and abut-
ments of the cliff.

Every now and then there came a squall of rain, and though
there was sufficient light, the heavens were black with clouds. A
scene more beautiful might hardly be found by those who love
the glories of the coast. The light for such objects was perfect.
Nothing could exceed the grandeur of the colours – the blue of the
open sea, the white of the breaking waves, the yellow sands, or
the streaks of red and brown which gave such richness to the cliff.

But neither Mally nor Barty were thinking of such things as

these. Indeed, they were hardly thinking of their trade after its ordinary forms. Barty was meditating how he might best accomplish his purpose of working beyond the reach of Mally's feminine powers, and Mally was resolving that wherever Barty went she would go farther.

And, in many respects, Mally had the advantage. She knew every rock in the spot, and was sure of those which gave a good foothold, and sure also of those which did not. And then her activity had been made perfect by practice for the purpose to which it was to be devoted. Barty, no doubt, was stronger than she, and quite as active. But Barty could not jump among the waves from one stone to another as she could do, nor was he as yet able to get aid in his work from the very force of the water as she could get it. She had been hunting seaweed in that cove since she had been an urchin of six years old, and she knew every hole and corner and every spot of vantage. The waves were her friends, and she could use them. She could measure their strength, and knew when and where it would cease.

Mally was great down in the salt pools of her own cove – great and very fearless. As she watched Barty make his way forward from rock to rock, she told herself, gleefully, that he was going astray. The curl of the wind as it blew into the cove would not carry the weed up to the northern buttresses of the cove; and then there was the great hole just there – the great hole of which she had spoken when she wished him evil.

And now she went to work, hooking up the dishevelled hairs of the ocean, and landing many a cargo on the extreme margin of the sand, from whence she would be able in the evening to drag it back before the invading waters would return to reclaim the spoil.

And on his side also Barty made his heap up against the northern buttresses of which I have spoken. Barty's heap became big and still bigger, so that he knew, let the pony work as he might, he could not take it all up that evening. But still it was not as large as Mally's heap. Mally's hook was better than his fork, and Mally's skill was better than his strength. And when he failed in some haul Mally would jeer him with a wild, weird laughter, and shriek to him through the wind that he was not half a man. At first he answered her with laughing words, but before long, as she boasted of her success and pointed to his failure, he became angry, and then he answered her no more. He became angry with himself, in that he missed so much of the plunder before him.

The broken sea was full of the long straggling growth which the waves had torn up from the bottom of the ocean, but the masses

were carried past him, away from him – nay, once or twice over
him; and then Mally's weird voice would sound in his ear, jeering
him. The gloom among the rocks was now becoming thicker and
thicker, the tide was beating in with increased strength, and the
gusts of wind came with quicker and greater violence. But still
he worked on. While Mally worked he would work, and he would
work for some time after she was driven in. He would not be beaten
by a girl.

The great hole was now full of water, but of water which seemed
to be boiling as though in a pot. And the pot was full of floating
masses – large treasures of seaweed which were thrown to and fro
upon its surface, but lying there so thick that one would seem almost
to rest upon it without sinking.

Mally knew well how useless it was to attempt to rescue aught
from the fury of that boiling caldron. The hole went in under the
rocks, and the side of it towards the shore lay high, slippery and
steep. The hole, even at low water, was never empty; and Mally
believed that there was no bottom to it. Fish thrown in there could
escape out to the ocean, miles away – so Mally in her softer moods
would tell the visitors to the cove. She knew the hole well. Poul-
nadioul she was accustomed to call it; which was supposed, when
translated, to mean that this was the hole of the Evil One. Never
did Mally attempt to make her own of weed which had found its
way into that pot.

But Barty Gunliffe knew no better, and she watched him as he
endeavoured to steady himself on the treacherously slippery edge
of the pool. He fixed himself there and made a haul, with some small
success. How he managed it she hardly knew, but she stood still
for a while watching him anxiously, and then she saw him slip.
He slipped, and recovered himself – slipped again, and again recovered himself.

'Barty, you fool!' she screamed; 'if you get yourself pitched in
there, you'll never come out no more.'

Whether she simply wished to frighten him, or whether her heart
relented and she had thought of his danger with dismay, who shall
say? She could not have told herself. She hated him as much as
ever – but she could hardly have wished to see him drowned before
her eyes.

'You go on, and don't mind me,' said he, speaking in a hoarse,
angry tone.

'Mind you! – Who minds you?' retorted the girl. And then she
again prepared herself for her work.

But as she went down over the rocks with her long hook balanced in her hands she suddenly heard a splash, and, turning quickly round, saw the body of her enemy tumbling amidst the eddying waves in the pool. The tide had now come up so far that every succeeding wave washed into it and over it from the side nearest to the sea, and then ran down again back from the rocks, as the rolling wave receded, with a noise like the fall of a cataract. And then, when the surplus water had retreated for a moment, the surface of the pool would be partly calm, though the fretting bubbles would still boil up and down, and there was ever a simmer on the surface, as though, in truth, the caldron were heated. But this time of comparative rest was but a moment, for the succeeding breaker would come up almost as soon as the foam of the preceding one had gone, and then again the waters would be dashed upon the rocks, and the sides would echo with the roar of the angry wave.

Instantly Mally hurried across to the edge of the pool, crouching down upon her hands and knees for security as she did so. As a wave receded, Barty's head and face was carried near to her, and she could see that his forehead was covered with blood. Whether he were alive or dead she did not know. She had seen nothing but his blood, and the light-coloured hair of his head lying amidst the foam. Then his body was drawn along by the suction of the retreating wave; but the mass of water that escaped was not on this occasion large enough to carry the man out with it.

Instantly Mally was at work with her hook, and getting it fixed into his coat, dragged him towards the spot on which she was kneeling. During the half minute of repose she got him so close that she could touch his shoulder. Straining herself down, laying herself over the long bending handle of the hook, she strove to grasp him with her right hand. But she could not do it; she could only touch him.

Then came the next breaker, forcing itself on with a roar, looking to Mally as though it must certainly knock her from her resting-place and destroy them both. But she had nothing for it but to kneel and hold by her hook.

What prayer passed through her mind at that moment for herself or for him, or for that old man who was sitting unconsciously up at the cabin, who can say? The great wave came and rushed over her as she lay almost prostrate, and when the water was gone from her eyes, and the tumult of the foam, and the violence of the roaring breaker had passed by her, she found herself at her length upon the rock, while his body had been lifted up, free from her hook, and was lying upon the slippery ledge, half in the water and half out of it. As she looked at him, in that instant, she could see that his eyes were open and that he was struggling with his hands.

'Hold by the hook, Barty,' she cried, pushing the stick of it before him, while she seized the collar of his coat in her hands.

Had he been her brother, her lover, her father, she could not have clung to him with more of the energy of despair. He did contrive to hold by the stick which she had given him, and when the succeeding wave had passed by he was still on the ledge. In the next moment she was seated a yard or two above the hole, in comparative safety, while Barty lay upon the rocks with his still bleeding head resting upon her lap.

What could she do now? She could not carry him; and in fifteen minutes the sea would be up where she was sitting. He was quite insensible and very pale, and the blood was coming slowly – very slowly – from the wound on his forehead. Ever so gently she put her hand upon his hair to move it back from his face; and then she bent over his mouth to see if he breathed, and as she looked at him she knew that he was beautiful.

What would she not give that he might live? Nothing now was so precious to her as his life – as this life which she had so far rescued from the waters. But what could she do? Her grandfather could scarcely get himself down over the rocks, if indeed he could succeed in doing so much as that. Could she drag the wounded man backwards, if it were only a few feet, that he might lie above the reach of the waves till further assistance could be procured?

She set herself to work and she moved him, almost lifting him. As she did so she wondered at her own strength, but she was very strong at that moment. Slowly, tenderly, falling on the rocks herself so that he might fall on her, she got him back to the margin of the sand, to a spot which the waters would not reach for the next two hours.

Here her grandfather met them, having seen at last what had happened from the door.

'Dada,' she said, 'he fell into the pool yonder, and was battered against the rocks. See there at his forehead.'

'Mally, I'm thinking that he's dead already,' said old Glos, peering down over the body.

'No, Dada, he is not dead; but mayhap he's dying. But I'll go at once up to the farm.'

'Mally,' said the old man, 'look at his head. They'll say we murdered him.'

'Who'll say so? Who'll lie like that? Didn't I pull him out of the hole?'

'What matters that? His father'll say we killed him.'

It was manifest to Mally that whatever anyone might say

hereafter her present course was plain before her. She must run up the path to Gunliffe's farm and get necessary assistance. If the world were as bad as her grandfather said, it would be so bad that she would not care to live longer in it. But be that as it might, there was no doubt as to what she must do now.

So away she went as fast as her naked feet could carry her up the cliff. When at the top she looked round to see if any person might be within ken, but she saw no one. So she ran with all her speed along the headland of the cornfield which led in the direction of old Gunliffe's house, and as she drew near to the homestead she saw that Barty's mother was leaning on the gate. As she approached she attempted to call, but her breath failed her for any purpose of loud speech, so she ran on till she was able to grasp Mrs Gunliffe by the arm.

'Where's himself?' she said, holding her hand upon her beating heart that she might husband her breath.

'Who is it you mean?' said Mrs Gunliffe, who participated in the family feud against Trenglos and his grand-daughter. 'What does the girl clutch me for in that way?'

'He's dying then, that's all.'

'Who is dying? Is it old Malachi? If the old man's bad, we'll send some one down.'

'It ain't Dada, it's Barty! Where's himself? Where's the master?'

But by this time Mrs Gunliffe was in an agony of despair and was calling out for assistance lustily. Happily Gunliffe, the father, was at hand, and with him a man from the neighbouring village.

'Will you not send for the doctor?' said Mally. 'Oh man, you should send for the doctor!'

Whether any orders were given for the doctor she did not know, but in a very few minutes she was hurrying across the field again towards the path to the cove, and Gunliffe with the other man and his wife were following her.

As Mally went along she recovered her voice, for their step was not so quick as hers, and that which to them was a hurried movement allowed her to get her breath again. And as she went, she tried to explain to the father what had happened, saying but little, however, of her own doings in the matter. The wife hung behind listening, exclaiming every now and again that her boy was killed, and then asking wild questions as to his being yet alive. The father, as he went, said little. He was known as a silent, sober man, well spoken of for diligence, and general conduct, but supposed to be stern and very hard when angered.

As they drew near to the top of the path the other man whispered something to him, and then he turned round upon Mally and stopped her.

'If he has come by his death between you, your blood shall be taken for his,' said he.

Then the wife shrieked out that her child had been murdered, and Mally, looking round into the faces of the three, saw that her grandfather's words had come true. They suspected her of having taken the life in saving which she had nearly lost her own.

She looked round at them with awe in her face, and then, without saying a word, preceded them down the path. What had she to answer when such a charge as that was made against her? If they chose to say that she pushed him into the pool, and hit him with her hook as he lay amidst the water, how could she show that it was not?

Poor Mally knew little of the law of evidence, and it seemed to her that she was in their hands. But as she went down the steep track with a hurried step – a step so quick that they could not keep up with her – her heart was very full – very full and very high. She had striven for the man's life as though he had been her brother. The blood was yet not dry on her own legs and arms, where she had torn them in his service. At one moment she had felt sure that she would die with him in that pool. And now they said that she had murdered him! It may be that he was not dead, and what would he say if ever he should speak again? Then she thought of that moment when his eyes had opened, and he had seemed to see her. She had no fear for herself, for her heart was very high. But it was full also – full of scorn, disdain, and wrath.

When she had reached the bottom she stood close to the door of the hut waiting for them, so that they might precede her to the other group, which was there in front of them, at a little distance on the sand.

'He is there, and Dada is with him. Go and look at him,' said Mally.

The father and mother ran on stumbling over the stones, but Mally remained behind by the door of the hut.

Barty Gunliffe was lying on the sand where Mally had left him, and old Malachi Trenglos was standing over him, resting himself with difficulty upon a stick.

'Not a move he's moved since she left him,' said he, 'not a move. I put his head on the old rug as you see, and I tried 'un with a drop of gin, but he wouldn't take it – he wouldn't take it.'

'Oh, my boy! my boy!' said the mother, throwing herself beside her son upon the sand.

'Haud your tongue, woman,' said the father, kneeling down slowly by the lad's head, 'whimpering that way will do 'un no good.'

Then having gazed for a minute or two upon the pale face beneath him, he looked up sternly into that of Malachi Trenglos.

The old man hardly knew how to bear this terrible inquisition. 'He would come,' said Malachi; 'he brought it all upon hisself.'

'Who was it struck him?' said the father.

'Sure he struck hisself, as he fell among the breakers.'

'Liar!' said the father, looking up at the old man.

'They have murdered him! – They have murdered him!' shrieked the mother.

'Haud your peace, woman!' said the husband again. 'They shall give us blood for blood.'

Mally, leaning against the corner of the hovel, heard it all, but did not stir. They might say what they liked. They might make it out to be murder. They might drag her and her grandfather to Camelford gaol, and then to Bodmin, and the gallows; but they could not take from her the conscious feeling that was her own. She had done her best to save him – her very best. And she had saved him!

She remembered her threat to him before they had gone down on the rocks together, and her evil wish. Those words had been very wicked; but since that she had risked her life to save his. They might say what they pleased of her, and do what they pleased. She knew what she knew!

Then the father raised his son's head and shoulders in his arms, and called on the others to assist him in carrying Barty towards the path. They raised him between them carefully and tenderly, and lifted their burden on towards the spot at which Mally was standing. She never moved, but watched them at their work; and the old man followed them, hobbling after them with his crutch.

When they had reached the end of the hut she looked upon Barty's face, and saw that it was very pale. There was no longer blood upon the forehead, but the great gash was to be seen there plainly, with its jagged cut, and the skin livid and blue round the orifice. His light brown hair was hanging back, as she had made it to hang when she had gathered it with her hand after the big wave had passed over them. Ah, how beautiful he was in Mally's eyes with that pale face, and the sad scar upon his brow! She turned her face away, that they might not see her tears; but she did not move, nor did she speak.

But now, when they had passed the end of the hut, shuffling along with their burden, she heard a sound which stirred her. She roused herself quickly from her leaning posture, and stretched forth her head as though to listen; then she moved to follow them. Yes, they had stopped at the bottom of the path, and had again laid the body on the rocks. She heard that sound again, as of a long, long sigh, and then, regardless of any of them, she ran to the wounded man's head.

'He is not dead,' she said. 'There; he is not dead.'

As she spoke Barty's eyes opened, and he looked about him.

'Barty, my boy, speak to me,' said the mother.

Barty turned his face upon his mother, smiled, and then stared about him wildly.

'How is it with thee, lad?' said his father. Then Barty turned his face again to the latter voice, and as he did so his eyes fell upon Mally.

'Mally!' he said, 'Mally!'

It could have wanted nothing further to any of those present to teach them that, according to Barty's own view of the case, Mally had not been his enemy; and in truth, Mally herself wanted no further triumph. That word had vindicated her, and she withdrew back to the hut.

'Dada,' she said, 'Barty is not dead, and I'm thinking they won't say anything more about our hurting him.'

Old Glos shook his head. He was glad the lad hadn't met his death there; he didn't want the young man's blood, but he knew what folk would say. The poorer he was the more sure the world would be to trample on him. Mally said what she could to comfort him, being full of comfort herself.

She would have crept up to the farm if she dared, to ask how Barty was. But her courage failed her when she thought of that, so she went to work again, dragging back the weed she had saved to the spot at which on the morrow she would load the donkey. As she did this she saw Barty's pony still standing patiently under the rock, so she got a lock of fodder and threw it down before the beast.

It had become dark down in the cove, but she was still dragging back the seaweed when she saw the glimmer of a lantern coming down the pathway. It was a most unusual sight, for lanterns were not common down in Malachi's Cove. Down came the lantern rather slowly – much more slowly than she was in the habit of descending; and then through the gloom she saw the figure of a man standing at the bottom of the path. She went up to him, and saw that it was Mr Gunliffe, the father.

'Is that Mally?' said Gunliffe.

'Yes, it is Mally; and how is Barty, Mr Gunliffe?'

'You must come to 'un yourself, now at once,' said the farmer. 'He won't sleep a wink till he's seed you. You must not say but you'll come.'

'Sure I'll come if I'm wanted,' said Mally.

Gunliffe waited a moment, thinking that Mally might have to prepare herself, but Mally needed no preparation. She was dripping with salt water from the weed which she had been dragging, and her elfin locks were streaming wildly from her head; but, such as she was, she was ready.

'Dada's in bed,' she said, 'and I can go now, if you please.'

Then Gunliffe turned round and followed her up the path, wondering at the life which this girl led so far away from all her sex. It was now dark night, and he had found her working at the very edge of the rolling waves by herself, in the darkness, while the only human being who might seem to be her protector had already gone to his bed.

When they were at the top of the cliff, Gunliffe took her by her hand and led her along. She did not comprehend this, but she made no attempt to take her hand from his. Something he said about falling on the cliffs, but it was muttered so lowly that Mally hardly understood him. But, in truth, the man knew that she had saved his boy's life, and that he had injured her instead of thanking her. He was now taking her to his heart, and as words were wanting to him, he was showing his love after this silent fashion. He held her by the hand as though she were a child, and Mally tripped along at his side asking him no questions.

When they were at the farmyard gate he stopped there for a moment.

'Mally, my girl,' he said, 'he'll not be content till he sees thee, but thou must not stay long wi' him, lass. Doctor says he's weak like, and wants sleep badly.'

Mally merely nodded her head, and then they entered the house. Mally had never been within it before, and looked about with wondering eyes at the furniture of the big kitchen. Did any idea of future destiny flash upon her then, I wonder? But she did not pause here a moment, but was led up to the bedroom above stairs, where Barty was lying on his mother's bed.

'Is it Mally herself?' said the voice of the weak youth.

'It's Mally herself,' said the mother, ' so now you can say what you please.'

'Mally,' said he, 'Mally, it's along of you that I'm alive this moment.'

'I'll not forget it on her,' said the father, with his eyes turned away from her. 'I'll never forget it on her.'

'We hadn't a one but only him,' said the mother, with her apron up to her face.

'Mally, you'll be friends with me now?' said Barty.

To have been made lady of the manor of the cove for ever, Mally couldn't have spoken a word now. It was not only that the words and presence of the people there cowed her and made her speechless, but the big bed, and the looking-glass, and the unheard-of wonders of the chamber, made her feel her own insignificance. But she crept up to Barty's side, and put her hand upon his.

'I'll come and get the weed, Mally; but it shall all be for you,' said Barty.

'Indeed, you won't then, Barty dear,' said the mother; 'you'll never go near the awesome place again. What would we do if you were took from us?'

'He mustn't go near the hole if he does,' said Mally, speaking at last in a solemn voice, and imparting the knowledge which she had kept to herself while Barty was her enemy; ''specially not if the wind's any way from the nor'ard.'

'She'd better go down now,' said the father.

Barty kissed the hand which he held, and Mally, looking at him as he did so, thought that he was like an angel.

'You'll come and see us tomorrow, Mally,' said he.

To this she made no answer, but followed Mrs Gunliffe out of the room. When they were down in the kitchen the mother had tea for her, and thick milk, and a hot cake – all the delicacies which the farm could afford. I don't know that Mally cared much for the eating and drinking that night, but she began to think that the Gunliffes were good people – very good people. It was better thus, at any rate, than being accused of murder and carried off to Camelford prison.

'I'll never forget it on her – never,' the father had said.

Those words stuck to her from that moment, and seemed to sound in her ears all the night. How glad she was that Barty had come down to the cove – oh, yes, how glad! There was no question of his dying now, and as for the blow on his forehead, what harm was that to a lad like him?

'But father shall go with you,' said Mrs Gunliffe, when Mally prepared to start for the cove by herself. Mally, however, would not hear of this. She could find her way to the cove whether it was light or dark.

'Mally, thou art my child now, and I shall think of thee so,' said the mother, as the girl went off by herself.

Mally thought of this, too, as she walked home. How could she become Mrs Gunliffe's child; ah, how?

I need not, I think, tell the tale any further. That Mally did become Mrs Gunliffe's child, and how she became so the reader will understand; and in process of time the big kitchen and all the wonders of the farmhouse were her own. The people said that Barty Gunliffe had married a mermaid out of the sea; but when it was said in Mally's hearing, I doubt whether she liked it; and when Barty himself would call her a mermaid, she would frown at him, and throw about her black hair, and pretend to cuff him with her little hand.

Old Glos was brought up to the top of the cliff, and lived his few remaining days under the roof of Mr Gunliffe's house; and as for the cove and the right of seaweed, from that time forth all that has been supposed to attach itself to Gunliffe's farm, and I do not know that any of the neighbours are prepared to dispute the right.

AARON TROW

I would wish to declare at the beginning of this story, that I shall never regard that cluster of islets which we call Bermuda as the Fortunate Islands of the Ancients. Do not let professional geographers take me up, and say that no one has so accounted them, and that the ancients have never been supposed to have gotten themselves so far westwards. What I mean to assert is this – that, had any ancient been carried thither by enterprise or stress of weather, he would not have given those islands so good a name. That the Neapolitan sailors of King Alonzo should have been wrecked here, I consider to be more likely. The vexed Bermoothes is a good name for them. There is no getting in or out of them without the greatest difficulty, and a patient, slow navigation, which is very heart-rending. That Caliban should have lived here I can imagine; that Ariel would have been sick of the place is certain; and that Governor Prospero should have been willing to abandon his governorship, I conceive to have been only natural. When one regards the present state of the place, one is tempted to doubt whether any of the governors have been conjurors since his days.

Bermuda, as all the world knows, is a British colony at which we maintain a convict establishment. Most of our outlying convict establishments have been sent back upon our hands from our colonies, but here one is still maintained. There is also in the islands a strong military fortress, though not a fortress looking magnificent to the eyes of civilians as do Malta and Gibraltar. There are also here some six thousand white people and some six thousand black people, eating, drinking, sleeping, and dying.

The convict establishment is the most notable feature of Bermuda to a stranger, but it does not seem to attract much attention from the regular inhabitants of the place. There is no intercourse between the prisoners and the Bermudians. The convicts are rarely visited. As to the prisoners themselves, of course it is not open to them – or should not be open to them – to have intercourse with any but the prison authorities.

There have, however, been instances in which convicts have escaped from their confinement, and made their way out among the islands. Poor wretches! As a rule, there is but little chance for any that can so escape. The whole length of the cluster is but twenty miles, and the breadth is under four. The prisoners are, of course, white men, and the lower orders of Bermuda, among whom alone could a runaway have any chance of hiding himself, are all negroes; so that such a one would be known at once. Their clothes are all marked. Their only chance of a permanent escape would be in the hold of an American ship; but what captain of an American or other ship would willingly encumber himself with an escaped convict? But, nevertheless, men have escaped; and in one instance, I believe, a convict got away, so that of him no further tidings were ever heard.

For the truth of the following tale I will not by any means vouch. If one were to inquire on the spot one might probably find that the ladies all believe it, and the old men; that all the young men know exactly how much of it is false and how much true; and that the steady, middle-aged, well-to-do islanders are quite convinced that it is romance from beginning to end. My readers may range themselves with the ladies, the young men, or the steady, well-to-do, middle-aged islanders, as they please.

Some years ago, soon after the prison was first established on its present footing, three men did escape from it, and among them a certain notorious prisoner named Aaron Trow. Trow's antecedents in England had not been so villanously bad as those of many of his fellow-convicts, though the one offence for which he was punished had been of a deep dye: he had shed man's blood. At a period of great distress in a manufacturing town he had led men on to riot, and with his own hands had slain the first constable who had endeavoured to do his duty against him. There had been courage in the doing of the deed, and probably no malice; but the deed, let its moral blackness have been what it might, had sent him to Bermuda, with a sentence against him of penal servitude for life. Had he been then amenable to prison discipline – even then, with such a sentence against him as that – he might have won his way back, after the lapse of years, to the children, and perhaps, to the wife, that he had left behind him; but he was amenable to no rules – to no discipline. His heart was sore to death with an idea of injury, and he lashed himself against the bars of his cage with a feeling that it would be well if he could so lash himself till he might perish in his fury.

And then a day came in which an attempt was made by a large body of convicts, under his leadership, to get the better of the officers of the prison. It is hardly necessary to say that the attempt failed. Such attempts always fail. It failed on this occasion signally, and Trow, with two other men, were condemned to be scourged terribly, and then kept in solitary confinement for some lengthened term of months. Before, however, the day of scourging came, Trow and his two associates had escaped.

I have not the space to tell how this was effected, nor the power to describe the manner. They did escape from the establishment into the islands, and though two of them were taken after a single day's run at liberty, Aaron Trow had not been yet retaken even when a week was over. When a month was over he had not been retaken, and the officers of the prison began to say that he had got away from them in a vessel to the States. It was impossible, they said, that he should have remained in the islands and not been discovered. It was not impossible that he might have destroyed himself, leaving his body where it had not yet been found. But he could not have lived on in Bermuda during that month's search. So, at least, said the officers of the prison. There was, however, a report through the islands that he had been seen from time to time; that he had gotten bread from the negroes at night, threatening them with death if they told of his whereabouts; and that all the clothes of the mate of a vessel had been stolen while the man was bathing, including a suit of dark blue cloth, in which suit of clothes, or in one of such a nature, a stranger had been seen skulking about the rocks near St George. All this the governor of the prison affected to disbelieve, but the opinion was becoming rife in the islands that Aaron Trow was still there.

A vigilant search, however, is a task of great labour, and cannot be kept up for ever. By degrees it was relaxed. The warders and gaolers ceased to patrol the island roads by night, and it was agreed that Aaron Trow was gone, or that he would be starved to death, or that he would in time be driven to leave such traces of his whereabouts as must lead to his discovery; and this at last did turn out to be the fact.

There is a sort of prettiness about these islands which, though it never rises to the loveliness of romantic scenery, is nevertheless attractive in its way. The land breaks itself into little knolls, and the sea runs up, hither and thither, in a thousand creeks and inlets; and then, too, when the oleanders are in bloom, they give a wonderfully bright colour to the landscape. Oleanders seem to be the roses of Bermuda, and are cultivated round all the villages of the better class through the islands. There are two towns, St George and Hamilton, and one main high road, which connects them; but even this high road is broken by a ferry, over which every vehicle going from St George to Hamilton must be conveyed. Most of the locomotion in these parts is done by boats, and the residents look to the sea with its narrow creeks, as their best highway from their farms to their best market. In those days – and those days were not very long since – the building of small ships was their chief trade, and they valued their land mostly for the small scrubby cedar-trees with which this trade was carried on.

As one goes from St George to Hamilton the road runs between two seas; that to the right is the ocean; that on the left is an inland creek, which runs up through a large portion of the islands, so that the land on the other side of it is near to the traveller. For a considerable portion of the way there are no houses lying near the road, and there is one residence, some way from the road, so secluded that no other house lies within a mile of it by land. By water it might probably be reached within half a mile. This place was called Crump Island, and here lived, and had lived for many years, an old gentleman, a native of Bermuda, whose business it had been to buy up cedar wood and sell it to the ship-builders at Hamilton. In our story we shall not have very much to do with old Mr Bergen, but it will be necessary to say a word or two about his house.

It stood on what would have been an island in the creek, had not a narrow causeway, barely broad enough for a road, joined it to that large island on which stands the town of St George. As the main road approaches the ferry it runs through some rough, hilly open ground, which on the right side towards the ocean has never been cultivated. The distance from the ocean here may, perhaps, be a quarter of a mile, and the ground is for the most part covered with low furze. On the left of the road the land is cultivated in patches, and here, some half mile or more from the ferry, a path turns away to Crump Island. The house cannot be seen from the road, and, indeed, can hardly be seen at all, except from the sea. It lies, perhaps, three furlongs from the high road, and the path to it is but little used, as the passage to and from it is chiefly made by water.

Here, at the time of our story, lived Mr Bergen, and here lived Mr Bergen's daughter. Miss Bergen was well known at St George as a steady, good girl, who spent her time in looking after her father's household matters, in managing his two black maidservants and the black gardener, and who did her duty in that sphere of life to which she had been called. She was a comely, well-shaped young woman, with a sweet countenance, rather large in size, and very quiet in demeanour. In her earlier years, when young girls usually first bud forth into womanly beauty, the neighbours had not thought much of Anastasia Bergen, nor had the young men of St George been wont to stay their boats under the window of Crump Cottage in order that they might listen to her voice or feel the light of her eye; but slowly as years went by, Anastasia Bergen became a woman that a man might well love; and a man learned to love her who was well worthy of a woman's heart. This was Caleb Morton, the Presbyterian minister of St George; and Caleb Morton had been engaged to marry Miss Bergen for the last two years past, at the period of Aaron Trow's escape from prison.

Caleb Morton was not a native of Bermuda, but had been sent thither by the synod of his church from Nova Scotia. He was a tall, handsome man, at this time of some thirty years of age, of a presence which might almost have been called commanding. He was very strong, but of a temperament which did not often give him opportunity to put forth his strength; and his life had been such that neither he nor others knew of what nature might be his courage. The greater part of his life was spent in preaching to some few of the white people around him, and in teaching as many of the blacks as he could get to hear him. His days were very quiet, and had been altogether without excitement until he had met with Anastasia Bergen. It will suffice for us to say that he did meet her, and that now, for two years past, they had been engaged as man and wife.

Old Mr Bergen, when he heard of the engagement, was not well pleased at the information. In the first place, his daughter was very necessary to him, and the idea of her marrying and going away had hardly as yet occurred to him; and then he was by no means inclined to part with any of his money. It must not be presumed that he had amassed a fortune by his trade in cedar wood. Few tradesmen in Bermuda do, as I imagine, amass fortunes. Of some few hundred pounds he was possessed, and these, in the course of nature, would go to his daughter when he died; but he had no inclination to hand any portion of them over to his daughter before they did go to her in the course of nature. Now, the income which Caleb Morton earned as a Presbyterian clergyman was not large, and, therefore, no day had been fixed as yet for his marriage with Anastasia.

But, though the old man had been from the first averse to the match, his hostility had not been active. He had not forbidden Mr Morton his house, or affected to be in any degree angry because his daughter had a lover. He had merely grumbled forth an intimation that those who marry in haste repent at leisure – that love kept nobody warm if the pot did not boil; and that, as for him, it was as much as he could do to keep his own pot boiling at Crump Cottage.

In answer to this Anastasia said nothing. She asked him for no money, but still kept his accounts, managed his household, and looked patiently forward for better days.

Old Mr Bergen himself spent much of his time at Hamilton, where he had a woodyard with a couple of rooms attached to it. It was his custom to remain here three nights of the week, during which Anastasia was left alone at the cottage; and it happened by no means seldom that she was altogether alone, for the negro whom they called the gardener would go to her father's place at Hamilton, and the two black girls would crawl away up to the road, tired with the monotony of the sea at the cottage. Caleb had more than once told her that she was too much alone, but she had laughed at him, saying that solitude in Bermuda was not dangerous. Nor, indeed, was it; for the people are quiet and well-mannered, lacking much energy, but being, in the same degree, free from any propensity to violence.

'So you are going,' she said to her lover, one evening, as he rose from the chair on which he had been swinging himself at the door of the cottage which looks down over the creek of the sea. He had sat there for an hour talking to her as she worked, or watching her as she moved about the place. It was a beautiful evening, and the sun had been falling to rest with almost tropical glory before his feet. The bright oleanders were red with their blossoms all around him, and he had thoroughly enjoyed his hour of easy rest. 'So you are going,' she said to him, not putting her work out of her hand as he rose to depart.

'Yes; and it is time for me to go. I have still work to do before I can get to bed. Ah, well; I suppose the day will come at last when I need not leave you as soon as my hour of rest is over.'

'Come; of course it will come. That is, if your reverence should choose to wait for it another ten years or so.'

'I believe you would not mind waiting twenty years.'

'Not if a certain friend of mine would come down and see me of evenings when I'm alone after the day. It seems to me that I shouldn't mind waiting as long as I had that to look for.'

'You are right not to be impatient,' he said to her, after a pause, as he held her hand before he went. 'Quite right. I only wish I could school myself to be as easy about it.'

'I did not say I was easy,' said Anastasia. 'People are seldom easy in this world, I take it. I said I could be patient. Do not look in that way, as though you pretended that you were dissatisfied with me. You know that I am true to you, and you ought to be very proud of me.'

'I am proud of you, Anastasia – ' on hearing which she got up and curtseyed to him. 'I am proud of you; so proud of you that I feel you should not be left here all alone, with no one to help you if you were in trouble.'

'Women don't get into trouble as men do, and do not want any one to help them. If you were alone in the house you would have to go to bed without your supper, because you could not make a basin of boiled milk ready for your own meal. Now, when your reverence has gone, I shall go to work and have my tea comfortably.' And then he did go, bidding God bless her as he left her. Three hours after that he was disturbed in his own lodgings by one of the negro girls from the cottage rushing to his door, and begging him in Heaven's name to come down to the assistance of her mistress.

When Morton left her, Anastasia did not proceed to do as she had said, and seemed to have forgotten her evening meal. She had been working sedulously with her needle during all that last conversation; but when her lover was gone, she allowed the work to fall from her hands, and sat motionless for awhile, gazing at the last streak of colour left by the setting sun; but there was no longer a sign of its glory to be traced in the heavens around her. The twilight in Bermuda is not long and enduring as it is with us, though the daylight does not depart suddenly, leaving the darkness of night behind it without any intermediate time of warning, as is the case farther south, down among the islands of the tropics. But the soft, sweet light of the evening had waned and gone, and night had absolutely come upon her, while Anastasia was still seated before the cottage with her eyes fixed upon the white streak of motionless sea which was still visible through the gloom. She was thinking of him, of his ways of life, of his happiness, and of her duty towards him. She had told him, with her pretty feminine falseness, that she could wait without impatience; but now she said to herself that it would not be good for him to wait longer. He lived alone and without comfort, working very hard for his poor pittance, and she could see and feel and understand that a companion in his life was to him almost a necessity. She would tell her father that all this must be brought to an end. She would not ask him for money, but she would make him understand that her services must, at any rate in part, be transferred. Why should not she and Morton still live at the cottage when they were married? And so thinking, and at last resolving, she sat there till the dark night fell upon her.

She was at last disturbed by feeling a man's hand upon her shoulder. She jumped from her chair and faced him – not screaming, for it was especially within her power to control herself, and to make no utterance except with forethought. Perhaps it might have been better for her had she screamed, and sent a shrill shriek down the shore of that inland sea. She was silent, however, and with awe-struck face and outstretched hands gazed into the face of him who still held her by the shoulder. The night was dark; but her eyes were now accustomed to the darkness, and she could see indistinctly something of his features. He was a low-sized man, dressed in a suit of sailor's blue clothing, with a rough cap of hair on his head, and a beard that had not been clipped for many weeks. His eyes were large, and hollow, and frightfully bright, so that she seemed to see nothing else of him; but she felt the strength of his fingers as he grasped her tighter and more tightly by the arm.

'Who are you?' she said, after a moment's pause.

'Do you know me?' he asked.

'Know you! No.' But the words were hardly out of her mouth before it struck her that the man was Aaron Trow, of whom every one in Bermuda had been talking.

'Come into the house,' he said, 'and give me food.' And he still held her with his hand as though he would compel her to follow him.

She stood for a moment thinking what she would say to him; for even then, with that terrible man standing close to her in the darkness, her presence of mind did not desert her, 'Surely,' she said, 'I will give you food if you are hungry. But take your hand from me. No man would lay his hands on a woman.'

'A woman!' said the stranger. 'What does the starved wolf care for that? A woman's blood is as sweet to him as that of a man. Come into the house, I tell you.' And then she preceded him through the open door into the narrow passage, and thence to the kitchen. There she saw that the back door, leading out on to the other side of the house, was open, and she knew that he had come down from the road and entered on that side. She threw her eyes round, looking for the negro girls; but they were away, and she remembered that there was no human being within sound of her voice but this man who had told her that he was as a wolf thirsty after her blood!

'Give me food at once,' he said.

'And will you go if I give it you?' she asked.

'I will knock out your brains if you do not,' he replied, lifting from the grate a short, thick poker which lay there. 'Do as I bid you at once. You also would be like a tiger if you had fasted for two days, as I have done.'

She could see, as she moved across the kitchen, that he had already searched there for something that he might eat, but that he had searched in vain. With the close economy common among his class in the islands, all comestibles were kept under close lock and key in the house of Mr Bergen. Their daily allowance was given day by day to the negro servants, and even the fragments were then gathered up and locked away in safety. She moved across the kitchen to the accustomed cupboard, taking the keys from her pocket, and he followed close upon her. There was a small oil lamp hanging from the low ceiling which just gave them light to see each other. She lifted her hand to this to take it from its hook, but he prevented her. 'No, by Heaven!' he said, 'you don't touch that till I've done with it. There's light enough for you to drag out your scraps.'

She did drag out her scraps and a bowl of milk, which might hold perhaps a quart. There was a fragment of bread, a morsel of cold potato-cake, and the bone of a leg of kid. 'And is that all?' said he. But as he spoke he fleshed his teeth against the bone as a dog would have done.

'It is the best I have,' she said; 'I wish it were better, and you should have had it without violence, as you have suffered so long from hunger.'

'Bah! Better; yes! You would give the best no doubt, and set the hell hounds on my track the moment I am gone. I know how much I might expect from your charity.'

'I would have fed you for pity's sake,' she answered.

'Pity! Who are you, that you should dare to pity me! By—my young woman, it is I that pity you. I must cut your throat unless you give me money. Do you know that?'

'Money! I have got no money.'

'I'll make you have some before I go. Come; don't move till I have done.' And as he spoke to her he went on tugging at the bone, and swallowing the lumps of stale bread. He had already finished the bowl of milk. 'And, now,' said he, 'tell me who I am.'

'I suppose you are Aaron Trow,' she answered very slowly.

He said nothing on hearing this, but continued his meal, standing close to her so that she might not possibly escape from him out into the darkness. Twice or thrice in those few minutes she made up her mind to make such an attempt, feeling that it would be better to leave him in possession of the house, and make sure, if possible, of her own life. There was no money there; not a dollar! What money her father kept in his possession was locked up in his safe at Hamilton. And might he not keep to his threat, and murder her, when he found that she could give him nothing? She did not tremble outwardly, as she stood there watching him as he ate, but she thought how probable it might be that her last moments were very near. And yet she could scrutinise his features, form, and garments, so as to carry away in her mind a perfect picture of them. Aaron Trow – for of course it was the escaped convict – was not a man of frightful, hideous aspect. Had the world used him well, giving him when he was young ample wages and separating him from turbulent spirits, he also might have used the world well; and then women would have praised the brightness of his eye and the manly vigour of his brow. But things had not gone well with him. He had been separated from the wife he had loved, and the children who had been raised at his knee – separated by his own violence; and now, as he had said of himself, he was a wolf rather than a man. As he stood there satisfying the craving of his appetite, breaking up the large morsels of food, he was an object very sad to be seen. Hunger had made him gaunt and yellow, he was squalid with the dirt of his hidden lair, and he had the look of a beast – that look to which men fall when they live like the brutes of prey, as outcasts from their brethren. But still there was that about his brow which might have redeemed him – which might have turned her horror into pity, had he been willing that it should be so.

'And now give me some brandy,' he said.

There was brandy in the house – in the sitting-room which was close at their hand, and the key of the little press which held it was in her pocket. It was useless, she thought, to refuse him; and so she told him that there was a bottle partly full, but that she must go to the next room to fetch it him.

'We'll go together, my darling,' he said. 'There's nothing like good company.' And he again put his hand upon her arm as they passed into the family sitting-room.

'I must take the light,' she said. But he unhooked it himself, and carried it in his own hand.

Again she went to work without trembling. She found the key of the side cupboard, and unlocking the door, handed him a bottle which might contain about half-a-pint of spirits. 'And is that all?' he said.

'There is a full bottle here,' she answered, handing him another; 'but if you drink it, you will be drunk, and they will catch you.'

'By Heavens, yes; and you would be the first to help them; would you not?'

'Look here,' she answered. 'If you will go now, I will not say a word to any one of your coming, nor set them on your track to follow you. There, take the full bottle with you. If you will go, you shall be safe from me.'

'What, and go without money!'

'I have none to give you. You may believe me when I say so. I have not a dollar in the house.'

Before he spoke again he raised the half empty bottle to his mouth, and drank as long as there was a drop to drink. 'There,' said he, putting the bottle down, 'I am better after that. As to the other you are right, and I will take it with me. And now, young woman, about the money?'

'I tell you that I have not a dollar.'

'Look here,' said he, and he spoke now in a softer voice, as though he would be on friendly terms with her. 'Give me ten sovereigns, and I will go, I know you have it, and with ten sovereigns it is possible that I may save my life. You are good, and would not wish that a man should die so horrid a death. I know you are good. Come, give me the money.' And he put his hands up, beseeching her, and looked into her face with imploring eyes.

'On the word of a Christian woman I have not got money to give you,' she replied.

'Nonsense!' And as he spoke he took her by the arm and shook her. He shook her violently so that he hurt her, and her breath for a moment was all but gone from her. 'I tell you you must make dollars before I leave you, or I will so handle you that it would have been better for you to coin your very blood.'

'May God help me at my need,' she said, 'as I have not above a few penny pieces in the house.'

'And you expect me to believe that! Look here! I will shake the teeth out of your head, but I will have it from you.' And he did shake her again, using both his hands and striking her against the wall.

'Would you – murder me?' she said, hardly able now to utter the words.

'Murder you, yes; why not? I cannot be worse than I am, were I to murder you ten times over. But with money I may possibly be better.'

'I have it not.'

'Then I will do worse than murder you. I will make you such an object that all the world shall loathe to look on you.' And so saying he took her by the arm and dragged her forth from the wall against which she had stood.

Then there came from her a shriek that was heard far down the shore of that silent sea, and away across to the solitary houses of

those living on the other side – a shriek very sad, sharp, and prolonged – which told plainly to those who heard it of woman's woe
when in her extremest peril. That sound was spoken of in Bermuda
for many a day after that, as something which had been terrible

to hear. But then, at that moment, as it came wailing through the
dark, it sounded as though it were not human. Of those who heard
it, not one guessed from whence it came, nor was the hand of any
brother put forward to help that woman at her need.

'Did you hear that?' said the young wife to her husband, from
the far side of the arm of the sea.

'Hear it! Oh Heaven, yes! Whence did it come?' The young wife
could not say from whence it came, but clung close to her husband's
breast, comforting herself with the knowledge that that terrible
sorrow was not hers.

But aid did come at last, or rather that which seemed as aid.
Long and terrible was the fight between that human beast of prey
and the poor victim which had fallen into his talons. Anastasia
Bergen was a strong, well-built woman, and now that the time had
come to her when a struggle was necessary, a struggle for life, for
honour, for the happiness of him who was more to her than herself,
she fought like a tigress attacked in her own lair. At such a moment as
this she also could become wild and savage as the beast of the forest.
When he pinioned her arms with one of his, as he pressed her down

upon the floor, she caught the first joint of the forefinger of his other hand between her teeth till he yelled in agony, and another sound was heard across the silent water. And then, when one hand was loosed in the struggle, she twisted it through his long hair, and dragged back his head till his eyes were nearly starting from their sockets. Anastasia Bergen had hitherto been a sheer woman, all feminine in her nature. But now the foam came to her mouth, and fire sprang from her eyes, and the muscles of her body worked as though she had been trained to deeds of violence. Of violence, Aaron Trow had known much in his rough life, but never had he combated with harder antagonist than her whom he now held beneath his breast.

'By – I will put an end to you,' he exclaimed, in his wrath, as he struck her violently across the face with his elbow. His hand was occupied, and he could not use it for a blow, but nevertheless, the violence was so great that the blood gushed from her nostrils, while the back of her head was driven with violence against the floor. But yet she did not lose her hold of him. Her hand was still twined closely through his thick hair, and in every move he made she clung to him with all her might. 'Leave go my hair,' he shouted at her, but she still kept her hold, though he again dashed her head against the floor.

There was still light in the room, for when he first grasped her with both his hands, he had put the lamp down on a small table. Now they were rolling on the floor together, and twice he had essayed to kneel on her that he might crush the breath from her body, and deprive her altogether of her strength; but she had been too active for him, moving herself along the ground, though in doing so she dragged him with her. But by degrees he got one hand at liberty, and with that he pulled a clasp knife out of his pocket and opened it. 'I will cut your head off, if you do not let go my hair,' he said. But still she held fast by him. He then stabbed at her arm, using his left hand and making short ineffectual blows. Her dress partly saved her, and partly also the continual movement of all her limbs; but, nevertheless, the knife wounded her. It wounded her in several places about the arm, covering them both with blood – but still she hung on. So close was her grasp in her agony, that, as she afterwards found, she cut the skin of her own hand with her own nails. Had the man's hair been less thick or strong, or her own tenacity less steadfast, he would have murdered her before any interruption could have saved her.

And yet he had not purposed to murder her, or even, in the first instance, to inflict on her any bodily harm. But he had been determined to get money. With such a sum of money as he had named, it might, he thought, be possible for him to win his way across to America. He might bribe men to hide him in the hold of a ship, and thus there might be for him, at any rate, a possibility of escape. That there must be money in the house, he had still thought when first he laid hands on the poor woman; and then, when the struggle had once begun, when he had felt her muscles contending with his, the passion of the beast was aroused within him, and he strove against her as he would have striven against a dog. But yet, when the knife was in his hand, he had not driven it against her heart.

Then suddenly, while they were yet rolling on the floor, there was a sound of footsteps in the passage. Aaron Trow instantly leaped to his feet, leaving his victim on the ground, with huge lumps of his thick clotted hair in her hand. Thus, and thus only, could he have liberated himself from her grasp. He rushed at the door with the open knife still in his hand, and there he came against the two negro servant-girls who had returned down to their kitchen from the road on which they had been straying. Trow, as he half saw them in the dark, not knowing how many there might be, or whether there was a man among them, rushed through them, upsetting one scared girl in his passage. With the instinct and with the timidity of a beast, his impulse now was to escape, and he hurried away back to the road and to his lair, leaving the three women together in the cottage. Poor wretch! As he crossed the road, not skulking in his impotent haste, but running at his best, another pair of eyes saw him, and when the search became hot after him, it was known that his hiding-place was not distant.

It was some time before any of the women were able to act, and when some step was taken, Anastasia was the first to take it. She had not absolutely swooned, but the reaction, after the violence of her efforts, was so great, that for some minutes she had been unable to speak. She had risen from the floor when Trow left her, and had even followed him to the door; but since that she had fallen back into her father's old armchair, and there she sat gasping not only for words, but for breath also. At last she bade one of the girls to run into St George, and beg Mr Morton to come to her aid. The girl would not stir without her companion; and even then, Anastasia, covered as she was with blood, with dishevelled hair and her clothes half torn from her body, accompanied them as far as the road. There they found a negro lad still hanging about the place, and he told them that he had seen the man cross the road, and run down over the open ground towards the rocks of the sea-coast. 'He must be there,' said the lad, pointing in the direction of a corner of the rocks;

'unless he swim across the mouth of the ferry.' But the mouth of
that ferry is an arm of the sea, and it was not probable that a man
would do that when he might have taken the narrow water by
keeping on the other side of the road.

At about one that night Caleb Morton reached the cottage breath-
less with running, and before a word was spoken between them,
Anastasia had fallen on his shoulder and had fainted. As soon as
she was in the arms of her lover, all her power had gone from her.
The spirit and passion of the tiger had gone, and she was again a
weak woman shuddering at the thought of what she had suffered.
She remembered that she had had the man's hand between her
teeth, and by degrees she found his hair still clinging to her fingers;
but even then she could hardly call to mind the nature of the struggle
she had undergone. His hot breath close to her own cheek she did
remember, and his glaring eyes, and even the roughness of his beard
as he pressed his face against her own; but she could not say whence
had come the blood, nor till her arm became stiff and motionless
did she know that she had been wounded.

It was all joy with her now, as she sat motionless without speaking,
while he administered to her wants and spoke words of love into
her ears. She remembered the man's horrid threat, and knew that by
God's mercy she had been saved. And *he* was there caressing her,
loving her, comforting her! As she thought of the fate that had
threatened her, of the evil that had been so imminent, she fell
forward on her knees, and with incoherent sobs uttered her thanks-
givings, while her head was still supported on his arms.

It was almost morning before she could induce herself to leave
him and lie down. With him she seemed to be perfectly safe; but
the moment he was away she could see Aaron Trow's eyes gleaming
at her across the room. At last, however, she slept; and when he
saw that she was at rest, he told himself that his work must then
begin. Hitherto Caleb Morton had lived in all respects the life of a
man of peace; but now, asking himself no questions as to the propriety of what he would do, using no inward arguments as to this or
that line of conduct, he girded the sword on his loins, and prepared
himself for war. The wretch who had thus treated the woman whom
he loved should be hunted down like a wild beast, as long as he had
arms and legs with which to carry on the hunt. He would pursue
the miscreant with any weapons that might come to his hands; and
might Heaven help him at his need, as he dealt forth punishment
to that man, if he caught him within his grasp. Those who had
hitherto known Morton in the island, could not recognise the man
as he came forth on that day, thirsty after blood, and desirous to

thrust himself into personal conflict with the wild ruffian who had injured him. The meek Presbyterian minister had been a preacher, preaching ways of peace, and living in accordance with his own doctrines. The world had been very quiet for him, and he had walked quietly in his appointed path. But now the world was quiet no longer, nor was there any preaching of peace. His cry was for blood; for the blood of the untamed savage brute who had come upon his young doe in her solitude, and striven with such brutal violence to tear her heart from her bosom.

He got to his assistance early in the morning some of the constables from St George, and before the day was over, he was joined by two or three of the warders from the convict establishment. There was with him also a friend or two, and thus a party was formed, numbering together ten or twelve persons. They were of course all armed, and therefore it might be thought that there would be but small chance for the wretched man if they should come upon his track. At first they all searched together, thinking, from the tidings which had reached them, that he must be near to them; but gradually they spread themselves along the rocks between St George and the ferry, keeping watchmen on the road, so that he should not escape unnoticed into the island.

Ten times during the day did Anastasia send from the cottage up to Morton, begging him to leave the search to others, and come down to her. But not for a moment would he lose the scent of his prey. What! should it be said that she had been so treated, and that others had avenged her? He sent back to say that her father was with her now, and that he would come when his work was over. And in that job of work the life-blood of Aaron Trow was counted up.

Towards evening they were all congregated on the road near to the spot at which the path turns off towards the cottage, when a voice was heard hallooing to them from the summit of a little hill which lies between the road and the sea on the side towards the ferry, and presently a boy came running down to them full of news. 'Danny Lund has seen him,' said the boy, 'he has seen him plainly in among the rocks.' And then came Danny Lund himself, a small negro lad about fourteen years of age, who was known in those parts as the idlest, most dishonest, and most useless of his race. On this occasion, however, Danny Lund became important, and every one listened to him. He had seen, he said, a pair of eyes moving down in a cave of the rocks which he well knew. He had been in the cave often, he said, and could get there again. But not now; not whilst that pair of eyes was moving at the bottom of it. And so they all went up over the hill, Morton leading the way with hot haste. In his waistband he held a pistol, and his hand grasped a short iron bar with which he had armed himself. They ascended the top of the hill, and when there, the open sea was before them on two sides, and on the third was the narrow creek over which the ferry passed. Immediately beneath their feet were the broken rocks; for on that side, towards the sea, the earth and grass of the hill descended but a little way towards the water. Down among the rocks they all went, silently, Caleb Morton leading the way, and Danny Lund directing him from behind.

'Mr Morton,' said an elderly man from St George, 'had you not better let the warders of the gaol go first; he is a desperate man, and they will best understand his ways?'

In answer to this Morton said nothing, but he would let no one put a foot before him. He still pressed forward among the rocks, and at last came to a spot from whence he might have sprung at one leap into the ocean. It was a broken cranny on the sea-shore into which the sea beat, and surrounded on every side but the one by huge broken fragments of stone, which at first sight seemed as though they would have admitted of a path down among them to the water's edge; but which, when scanned more closely, were seen to be so large in size, that no man could climb from one to another. It was a singularly romantic spot, but now well known to them all there, for they had visited it over and over again that morning.

'In there,' said Danny Lund, keeping well behind Morton's body, and pointing at the same time to a cavern high up among the rocks, but quite on the opposite side of the little inlet of the sea. The mouth of the cavern was not twenty yards from them where they stood, but at the first sight it seemed as though it must be impossible to reach it. The precipice on the brink of which they all now stood, ran down sheer into the sea, and the fall from the mouth of the cavern on the other side was as steep. But Danny solved the mystery by pointing upwards and showing them how he had been used to climb to a projecting rock over their heads, and from thence creep round by certain vantages of the stone till he was able to let himself down into the aperture. But now, at the present moment, he was unwilling to make essay of his prowess as a cragsman. He had, he said, been up on that projecting rock thrice, and there had seen the eyes moving in the cavern. He was quite sure of that fact of the pair of eyes, and declined to ascend the rock again.

Traces soon became visible to them by which they knew that some one had passed in and out of the cavern recently. The stone, when examined, bore those marks of friction which passage and

repassage over it will always give. At the spot from whence the climber left the platform and commenced his ascent, the side of the stone had been rubbed by the close friction of a man's body. A light boy like Danny Lund might find his way in and out without leaving such marks behind him, but no heavy man could do so. Thus before long they all were satisfied that Aaron Trow was in the cavern before them.

Then there was a long consultation as to what they would do to carry on the hunt, and how they would drive the tiger from his lair. That he should not again come out, except to fall into their hands, was to all of them a matter of course. They would keep watch and ward there, though it might be for days and nights. But that was a process which did not satisfy Morton, and did not indeed well satisfy any of them. It was not only that they desired to inflict punishment on the miscreant in accordance with the law, but also that they did not desire that the miserable man should die in a hole like a starved dog, and that then they should go after him to take out his wretched skeleton. There was something in that idea so horrid in every way, that all agreed that active steps must be taken. The warders of the prison felt that they would all be disgraced if they could not take their prisoner alive. Yet who would get round that perilous ledge in the face of such an adversary? A touch to any man while climbing there would send him headlong down among the waves! And then his fancy told to each what might be the nature of an embrace with such an animal as that, driven to despair, hopeless of life, armed, as they knew, at any rate, with a knife! If the first adventurous spirit should succeed in crawling round that ledge, what would be the reception which he might expect in the terrible depth of that cavern?

They called to their prisoner, bidding him come out, and telling him that they would fire in upon him if he did not show himself; but not a sound was heard. It was indeed possible that they should send their bullets to, perhaps, every corner of the cavern; and if so, in that way they might slaughter him; but even of this they were not sure. Who could tell that there might not be some protected nook in which he could lay secure? And who could tell when the man was struck, or whether he were wounded?

'I will get to him,' said Morton, speaking with a low dogged voice, and so saying he clambered up to the rock to which Danny Lund had pointed. Many voices at once attempted to restrain him, and one or two put their hands upon him to keep him back, but he was too quick for them, and now stood upon the ledge of rock. 'Can you see him?' they asked below.

'I can see nothing within the cavern,' said Morton.

'Look down very hard, Massa,' said Danny, 'very hard indeed down in deep dark hole, and then see him big eyes moving!'

Morton now crept along the ledge, or rather he was beginning to do so, having put forward his shoulders and arms to make a first step in advance from the spot on which he was resting, when a hand was put forth from one corner of the cavern's mouth – a hand armed with a pistol; – and a shot was fired. There could be no doubt now but that Danny Lund was right, and no doubt now as to the whereabouts of Aaron Trow.

A hand was put forth, a pistol fired, and Caleb Morton still clinging to a corner of the rock with both his arms, was seen to falter. 'He is wounded,' said one of the voices from below; and then they all expected to see him fall into the sea. But he did not fall, and after a moment or two, he proceeded carefully to pick his steps along the ledge. The ball had touched him, grazing his cheek and cutting through the light whiskers that he wore; but he had not felt it, though the blow had nearly knocked him from his perch.

And then four or five shots were fired from the rocks into the mouth of the cavern. The man's arm had been seen, and indeed one or two declared that they had traced the dim outline of his figure. But no sound was heard to come from the cavern, except the sharp crack of the bullets against the rock, and the echo of the gunpowder. There had been no groan as of a man wounded, no sound of a body falling, no voice wailing in despair. For a few seconds all was dark with the smoke of the gunpowder, and then the empty mouth of the cave was again yawning before their eyes. Morton was now near it, still cautiously creeping. The first danger to which he was exposed was this; that his enemy within the recess might push him down from the rocks with a touch. But on the other hand, there were three or four men ready to fire, the moment that a hand should be put forth; and then Morton could swim – was known to be a strong swimmer – whereas of Aaron Trow it was already declared by the gaolers that he could not swim. Two of the warders had now followed Morton on the rocks, so that in the event of his making good his entrance into the cavern, and holding his enemy at bay for a minute, he would be joined by aid.

It was strange to see how those different men conducted themselves as they stood on the opposite platform watching the attack. The officers from the prison had no other thought but of their prisoner, and were intent on taking him alive or dead. To them it was little or nothing what became of Morton. It was their business to encounter peril, and they were ready to do so – feeling, however, by no means sorry to have such a man as Morton in advance of them. Very little was said by them. They had their wits about them, and remembered that every word spoken for the guidance of their ally would be heard also by the escaped convict. Their prey was sure, sooner or later, and had not Morton been so eager in his pursuit, they would have waited till some plan had been devised of trapping him without danger. But the townsmen from St George, of whom some dozen were now standing there, were quick and eager and loud in their counsels. 'Stay where you are, Mr Morton – stay awhile for the love of God – or he'll have you down.' 'Now's your time, Caleb; in on him now, and you'll have him.' 'Close with him, Morton, close with him at once; it's your only chance.' 'There's four of us here; we'll fire on him if he as much as shows a limb.' All of which words as they were heard by that poor wretch within, must have sounded to him as the barking of a pack of hounds thirsting for his blood. For him at any rate there was no longer any hope in this world.

My reader, when chance has taken you into the hunting-field, has

it ever been your lot to sit by on horseback, and watch the digging
out of a fox? The operation is not an uncommon one, and in some
countries it is held to be in accordance with the rules of fair sport.
For myself, I think that when the brute has so far saved himself,
he should be entitled to the benefit of his cunning; but I will not
now discuss the propriety or impropriety of that practice in venery.
I can never, however, watch the doing of that work without thinking
much of the agonising struggles of the poor beast whose last refuge
is being torn from over his head. There he lies within a few yards
of his arch enemy, the huntsman. The thick breath of the hounds
make hot the air within his hole. The sound of their voices is close
upon his ears. His breast is nearly bursting with the violence of
that effort which at last has brought him to his retreat. And then
pickaxe and mattock are plied above his head, and nearer and more
near to him press his foes – his double foes, human and canine – till
at last a huge hand grasps him, and he is dragged forth among his
enemies. Almost as soon as his eyes have seen the light the eager
noses of a dozen hounds have moistened themselves in his entrails.
Ah me! I know that he is vermin, the vermin after whom I have
been risking my neck, with a bold ambition that I might ultimately
witness his death-struggles; but, nevertheless, I would fain have
saved him that last half hour of gradually diminished hope.

And Aaron Trow was now like a hunted fox, doomed to be dug
out from his last refuge, with this addition to his misery, that these
hounds when they caught their prey, would not put him at once out
of his misery. When first he saw that throng of men coming down
from the hill top and resting on the platform, he knew that his
fate was come. When they called to him to surrender himself he was
silent, but he knew that his silence was of no avail. To them who
were eager to be his captors the matter seemed to be still one of
considerable difficulty; but, to his thinking, there was no difficulty.
There were there some score of men, fully armed, within twenty
yards of him. If he but showed a trace of his limbs he would become
a mark for their bullets. And then if he were wounded, and no one
would come to him! If they allowed him to lie there without food
till he perished! Would it not be well for him to yield himself? Then
they called again and he was still silent. That idea of yielding is
very terrible to the heart of a man. And when the worst had come
to the worst, did not the ocean run deep beneath his cavern's mouth?

But as they yelled at him and halloa-ed, making their prepara-
tions for his death, his presence of mind deserted the poor wretch.
He had stolen an old pistol on one of his marauding expeditions, of
which one barrel had been loaded. That in his mad despair he had

fired; and now, as he lay near the mouth of the cavern, under the cover of the projecting stone, he had no weapon with him but his hands. He had had a knife, but that had dropped from him during the struggle on the floor of the cottage. He had now nothing but his hands, and was considering how he might best use them in ridding himself of the first of his pursuers. The man was near him, armed with all the power and majesty of right on his side; whereas on his side, Aaron Trow had nothing – not a hope. He raised his head that he might look forth, and a dozen voices shouted as his face appeared above the aperture. A dozen weapons were levelled at him, and he could see the gleaming of the muzzles of the guns. And then the foot of his pursuer was already on the corner stone at the cavern's mouth. 'Now, Caleb, on him at once!' shouted a voice. Ah me! it was a moment in which to pity even such a man as Aaron Trow.

'Now, Caleb, at him at once!' shouted the voice. No, by heavens; not so, even yet! The sound of triumph in those words roused the last burst of energy in the breast of that wretched man; and he sprang forth, head foremost, from his prison house. Forth he came, manifest enough before the eyes of them all, and with head well down, and hands outstretched but with his wide glaring eyes still turned towards his pursuers as he fell, he plunged down into the waves beneath him. Two of those who stood by, almost unconscious of what they did, fired at his body as it made its rapid way to the water; but, as they afterwards found, neither of the bullets struck him. Morton, when his prey thus leaped forth, escaping him for awhile, was already on the verge of the cavern – had even then prepared his foot for that onward spring which should bring him to the throat of his foe. But he arrested himself, and for a moment stood there, watching the body as it struck the water, and hid itself at once beneath the ripple. He stood there for a moment watching the deed and its effect, and then, leaving his hold upon the rock, he once again followed his quarry. Down he went, head foremost, right on to the track in the waves which the other had made; and when the two rose to the surface together, each was struggling in the grasp of the other.

It was a foolish, nay, a mad deed to do. The poor wretch who had first fallen could not have escaped. He could not even swim, and had therefore flung himself to certain destruction when he took that leap from out of the cavern's mouth. It would have been sad to see him perish beneath the waves – to watch him as he rose gasping for breath, and then to see him sinking again, to rise again and then to go for ever. But his life had been fairly forfeit – and why should one so much more precious have been flung after it? It was surely with no view of saving that pitiful life that Caleb Morton had leaped after his enemy. But the hound, hot with the chase, will follow the stag over the precipice and dash himself to pieces against the rocks. The beast, thirsting for blood, will rush in even among the weapons of men. Morton in his fury had felt but one desire, burned with but one passion. If the Fates would but grant him to fix his clutches in the throat of the man who had ill-used his love – for the rest it might all go as it would!

In the earlier part of the morning, while they were all searching for their victim, they had brought a boat up into this very inlet among the rocks; and the same boat had been at hand during the whole day. Unluckily, before they had come hither, it had been taken round the headland to a place among the rocks, at which a government skiff is always moored. The sea was still so quiet that there was hardly a ripple on it, and the boat had been again sent for when first it was supposed that they had at last traced Aaron Trow to his hiding-place. Anxiously now were all eyes turned to the headland, but as yet no boat was there.

The two men rose to the surface, each struggling in the arms of the other. Trow, though he was in an element to which he was not used, though he had sprung thither as another suicide might spring to certain death beneath a railway engine, did not altogether lose his presence of mind. Prompted by a double instinct, he had clutched hold of Morton's body when he encountered it beneath the waters. He held on to it, as to his only protection, and he held on to him also as to his only enemy. If there was a chance for a life struggle, they would share that chance together; and if not, then together would they meet that other fate.

Caleb Morton was a very strong man, and though one of his arms was altogether encumbered by his antagonist, his other arm and his legs were free. With these he seemed to succeed in keeping his head above water, weighted as he was with the body of his foe. But Trow's efforts were also used with the view of keeping himself above the water. Though he had purposed to destroy himself in taking that leap, and now hoped for nothing better than that they might both perish together, he yet struggled to keep his head above the waves. Bodily power he had none left to him, except that of holding on to Morton's arm and plunging with his legs; but he did hold on, and thus both heads remained above the surface.

But this could not last long. It was easy to see that Trow's strength was nearly spent, and that when he went down Morton must go with him. If indeed they could be separated – if Morton could once make himself free from that embrace into which he had been so anxious to leap – then indeed there might be a hope. All round that little inlet the rock fell sheer down into the deep sea, so that there was no resting place for a foot; but round the headlands on either side, even within forty or fifty yards of that spot, Morton might rest on the rocks, till a boat should come to his assistance. To him that distance would have been nothing, if only his limbs had been at liberty.

Upon the platform of rock they were all at their wit's ends. Many were anxious to fire at Trow; but even if they hit him, would Morton's position have been better? Would not the wounded man have still clung to him who was not wounded? And then there could be no certainty that any one of them would hit the right man. The ripple of the waves, though it was very slight, nevertheless sufficed to keep the bodies in motion; and then, too, there was not among them any marksman peculiar for his skill.

Morton's efforts in the water were too severe to admit of his speaking, but he could hear and understand the words which were addressed to him. 'Shake him off, Caleb.' 'Strike him from you with your foot.' 'Swim to the right shore; swim for it, even if you take him with you.' Yes; he could hear them all; but hearing and obeying were very different. It was not easy to shake off that dying man; and as for swimming with him, that was clearly impossible. It was as much as he could do to keep his head above water, let alone any attempt to move in one settled direction.

For some four or five minutes they lay thus battling on the waves before the head of either of them went down. Trow had been twice below the surface, but it was before he had succeeded in supporting himself by Morton's arm. Now it seemed as though he must sink again – as though both must sink. His mouth was barely kept above the water, and as Morton shook him with his arm, the tide would pass over him. It was horrid to watch from the shore the glaring upturned eyes of the dying wretch, as his long streaming hair lay back upon the wave. 'Now, Caleb, hold him down. Hold him under,' was shouted in the voice of some eager friend. Rising up on the water, Morton made a last effort to do as he was bid. He did press the man's head down – well down below the surface – but still the hand clung to him, and as he struck out against the water, he was powerless against that grasp.

Then there came a loud shout along the shore, and all those on the platform, whose eyes had been fixed so closely on that terrible struggle beneath them, rushed towards the rocks on the other coast. The sound of oars was heard close to them – an eager pressing stroke, as of men who knew well that they were rowing for the salvation of a life. On they came, close under the rocks, obeying with every muscle of their bodies the behests of those who called to them from the shore. The boat came with such rapidity – was so recklessly urged – that it was driven somewhat beyond the inlet; but in passing, a blow was struck which made Caleb Morton once more the master of his own life. The two men had been carried out in their struggle towards the open sea; and as the boat curved in, so as to be as close as the rocks would allow, the bodies of the men were brought within the sweep of the oars. He in the bow – for there were four pulling in the boat – had raised his oar as he neared the rocks – had raised it high above the water; and now, as they passed close by the struggling men, he let it fall with all its force on the upturned face of the wretched convict. It was a terrible, frightful thing to do – thus striking one who was so stricken; but who shall say that the blow was not good and just? Methinks, however, that the eyes and face of that dying man will haunt for ever the dreams of him who carried that oar.

Trow never rose again to the surface. Three days afterwards his body was found at the ferry, and then they carried him to the convict island and buried him. Morton was picked up and taken into the boat. His life was saved; but it may be a question how the battle might have gone had not that friendly oar been raised in his behalf. As it was, he lay at the cottage for days before he was able to be moved, so as to receive the congratulations of those who had watched that terrible conflict from the shore. Nor did he feel that there had been anything in that day's work of which he could be proud – much rather of which it behoved him to be thoroughly ashamed. Some six months after that he obtained the hand of Anastasia Bergen, but they did not remain long in Bermuda. 'He went away, back to his own country,' my informant told me; 'because he could not endure to meet the ghost of Aaron Trow, at that point of the road which passes near the cottage.' That the ghost of Aaron Trow may be seen there and round the little rocky inlet of the sea, is part of the creed of every young woman in Bermuda.

THE MAN WHO KEPT HIS
MONEY IN A BOX

I first saw the man who kept his money in a box in the midst of the ravine of the Via Mala. I interchanged a few words with him or with his wife at the hospice at the top of the Splugen; and I became acquainted with him in the courtyard of Conradi's hotel at Chiavenna. It was, however, afterwards at Bellaggio, on the lake of Como, that that acquaintance ripened into intimacy. A good many years have rolled by since then, and I believe this little episode in his life may be told without pain to the feelings of anyone.

His name was – let us for the present say that his name was Greene. How he learned that my name was Robinson I do not know, but I remember well that he addressed me by my name at Chiavenna. To go back, however, for a moment to the Via Mala – I had been staying for a few days at the Golden Eagle at Tusis – which, by-the-bye, I hold to be the best small inn in all Switzerland, and its hostess to be, or to have been, certainly the prettiest landlady – and on the day of my departure southwards I had walked on, into the Via Mala, so that the diligence might pick me up in the gorge. This pass I regard as one of the grandest spots to which my wandering steps have ever carried me, and though I had already lingered about it for many hours, I now walked thither again to take my last farewell of its dark, towering rocks, its narrow causeway and roaring river, trusting to my friend the landlady to see that my luggage was duly packed upon the diligence. I need hardly say that my friend did not betray her trust.

As one goes out from Switzerland towards Italy, the road through the Via Mala ascends somewhat steeply, and passengers by the diligence may walk from the inn at Tusis into the gorge, and make their way through the greater part of the ravine before the vehicle will overtake them. This, however, Mr Greene with his wife and daughter had omitted to do. When the diligence passed me in the defile, the horses trotting for a few yards over some level portion of the road, I saw a man's nose pressed close against the glass of the *coupé* window. I saw more of his nose than of any other part of

his face, but yet I could perceive that his neck was twisted and his
eye upturned, and that he was making a painful effort to look upwards to the summit of the rocks from his position inside the carriage.

There was such a roar of wind and waters at the spot that it was
not practicable to speak to him, but I beckoned with my finger
and then pointed to the road, indicating that he should have walked.
He understood me, though I did not at the moment understand his
answering gesture. It was subsequently, when I knew somewhat of
his habits, that he explained to me that on pointing to his open
mouth, he had intended to signify that he would be afraid of sore
throat in exposing himself to the air of that damp and narrow
passage.

I got up into the conductor's covered seat at the back of the
diligence, and in this position encountered the drifting snow of the
Splugen. I think it is coldest of all the passes. Near the top of the
pass the diligence stops for a while, and it is here, if I remember, that
the Austrian officials demand the travellers' passports. At least
in those days they did so. These officials have now retreated behind
the Quadrilatère, – soon, as we hope, to make a further retreat, – and
the district belongs to the kingdom of United Italy. There is a place
of refreshment or hospice here, into which we all went for a few
moments, and I then saw that my friend with the weak throat
was accompanied by two ladies.

'You should not have missed the Via Mala,' I said to him, as he
stood warming his toes at the huge covered stove.

'We miss everything,' said the elder of the two ladies, who,
however, was very much younger than the gentleman, and not very
much older than her companion.

'I saw it beautifully, mamma,' said the younger one; whereupon
mamma gave her head a toss, and made up her mind, as I thought,
to take some little vengeance before long upon her step-daughter.
I observed that Miss Greene always called her step-mother mamma
on the first approach of any stranger, so that the nature of the
connection between them might be understood. And I observed
also that the elder lady always gave her head a toss when she was
so addressed.

'We don't mean to enjoy ourselves till we get down to the lake
of Como,' said Mr Greene. As I looked at him cowering over the
stove, and saw how oppressed he was with greatcoats and warm
wrappings for his throat, I quite agreed with him that he had not
begun to enjoy himself as yet. Then we all got into our places again,
and I saw no more of the Greenes till we were standing huddled
together in the large courtyard of Conradi's hotel at Chiavenna.

Chiavenna is the first Italian town which the tourist reaches by this route, and I know no town in the north of Italy which is so closely surrounded by beautiful scenery. The traveller as he falls down to it from the Splugen road is bewildered by the loveliness of the valleys – that is to say, if he so arranges that he can see them without pressing his nose against the glass of a coach window. And then from the town itself there are walks of two, three, and four hours, which I think are unsurpassed for wild and sometimes startling beauties. One gets into little valleys, green as emeralds, and surrounded on all sides by grey broken rocks, in which Italian Rasselases might have lived in perfect bliss; and then again one comes upon distant views up the river courses, bounded far away by the spurs of the Alps, which are perfect – to which the fancy can add no additional charm. Conradi's hotel also is by no means bad; or was not in those days. For my part I am inclined to think that Italian hotels have received a worse name than they deserve; and I must profess that, looking merely to creature comforts, I would much sooner stay a week at the Golden Key at Chiavenna, than with mine host of the King's Head in the thriving commercial town of Muddleboro, on the borders of Yorkshire and Lancashire.

I am always rather keen about my room in travelling, and having secured a chamber looking out upon the mountains, had returned to the courtyard to collect my baggage before Mr Greene had succeeded in realising his position, or understanding that he had to take upon himself the duties of settling his family for the night in the hotel by which he was surrounded. When I descended he was stripping off the outermost of three great coats, and four waiters around him were beseeching him to tell them what accommodation he would require. Mr Greene was giving sundry very urgent instructions to the conductor respecting his boxes; but as these were given in English I was not surprised to find that they were not accurately followed. The man, however, was much too courteous to say in any language that he did not understand every word that was said to him. Miss Greene was standing apart, doing nothing. As she was only eighteen years of age, it was, of course, her business to do nothing; and a very pretty little girl she was, by no means ignorant of her own beauty, and possessed of quite sufficient wit to enable her to make the most of it.

Mr Greene was very leisurely in his proceedings, and the four waiters were almost reduced to despair.

'I want two bedrooms, a dressing-room, and some dinner,' he said at last, speaking very slowly and in his own vernacular. I could not in the least assist him by translating it into Italian, for I

did not speak a word of the language myself, but I suggested that
the man would understand French. The waiter, however, had
understood English. Waiters do understand all languages with a
facility that is marvellous; and this one now suggested that Mrs
Greene should follow him upstairs. Mrs Greene, however, would not
move till she had seen that her boxes were all right; and as Mrs
Greene was also a pretty woman, I found myself bound to apply
myself to her assistance.

'Oh, thank you,' said she. 'The people are so stupid that one
can really do nothing with them. And as for Mr Greene, he is of no
use at all. You see that box, the smaller one. I have four hundred
pounds' worth of jewellery in that, and therefore I am obliged to
look after it.'

'Indeed,' said I, rather startled at this amount of confidence on
rather a short acquaintance. 'In that case I do not wonder at your
being careful. But is it not rather rash, perhaps –'

'I know what you are going to say. Well, perhaps it is rash. But
when you are going to foreign parts, what are you to do? If you
have got those sort of things you must wear them.'

As I was not myself possessed of anything of that sort, and had no
intention of going to any foreign court, I could not argue the matter
with her. But I assisted her in getting together an enormous pile
of luggage, among which there were seven large boxes covered with
canvas, such as ladies not uncommonly carry with them when
travelling. That one which she represented as being smaller than
the others, and as holding jewellery, might be about a yard long
by a foot and a half deep. Being ignorant in those matters, I should
have thought it sufficient to carry all a lady's wardrobe for twelve
months. When the boxes were collected together, she sat down
upon the jewel-case and looked up into my face. She was a pretty
woman, perhaps thirty years of age, with long light yellow hair,
which she allowed to escape from her bonnet, knowing, perhaps, that
it was not unbecoming to her when thus dishevelled. Her skin was
very delicate, and her complexion good. Indeed, her face would have
been altogether prepossessing had there not been a want of gentle-
ness in her eyes. Her hands, too, were soft and small, and, on
the whole, she may be said to have been possessed of a strong
battery of feminine attractions. She also well knew how to use
them.

'Whisper,' she said to me, with a peculiar but very proper aspiration on the h – 'Whisper,' and both by the aspiration and the use
of the word I knew at once from what island she had come. 'Mr
Greene keeps all his money in this box also; so I never let it go out

of my sight for a moment. But whatever you do, don't tell him that I told you so.'

I laid my hand on my heart, and made a solemn asseveration that I would not divulge her secret. I need not, however, have troubled myself much on that head, for, as I walked upstairs, keeping my eye upon the precious trunk, Mr Greene addressed me.

'You are an Englishman, Mr Robinson,' said he. I acknowledged that I was.

'I am another. My wife, however, is Irish. My daughter – by a former marriage – is English also. You see that box there.'

'Oh, yes,' said I, 'I see it.' I began to be so fascinated by the box that I could not keep my eyes off it.

'I don't know whether or no it is prudent, but I keep all my money there; my money for travelling, I mean.'

'If I were you, then,' I answered, 'I would not say anything about it to anyone.'

'Oh, no, of course not,' said he; 'I should not think of mentioning it. But those brigands in Italy always take away what you have about your person, but they don't meddle with the heavy luggage.'

'Bills of exchange, or circular notes,' I suggested.

'Ah, yes; and if you can't identify yourself, or happen to have a headache, you can't get them changed. I asked an old friend of mine, who has been connected with the Bank of England for the

last fifty years, and he assured me that there was nothing like sovereigns.'

'But you never get the value for them.'

'Well, not quite. One loses a franc, or a franc and a half. But still, there's the certainty, and that's the great matter. An English sovereign will go anywhere,' and he spoke these words with considerable triumph.

'Undoubtedly, if you consent to lose a shilling on each sovereign.'

'At any rate, I have got three hundred and fifty in that box,' he said. 'I have them done up in rolls of twenty-five pounds each.'

I again recommended him to keep this arrangement of his as private as possible – a piece of counsel which I confess seemed to me to be much needed – and then I went away to my own room, having first accepted an invitation from Mrs Greene to join their party at dinner. 'Do,' said she, 'we have been so dull, and it will be so pleasant.'

I did not require to be much pressed to join myself to a party in which there was so pretty a girl as Miss Greene, and so attractive a woman as Mrs Greene. I therefore accepted the invitation readily, and went away to make my toilet. As I did so I passed the door of Mr Greene's room, and saw the long file of boxes being borne into the centre of it.

I spent a pleasant evening, with, however, one or two slight drawbacks. As to old Greene himself, he was all that was amiable; but then he was nervous, full of cares, and somewhat apt to be a bore. He wanted information on a thousand points, and did not seem to understand that a young man might prefer the conversation of his daughter to his own. Not that he showed any solicitude to prevent conversation on the part of his daughter. I should have been perfectly at liberty to talk to either of the ladies had he not wished to engross all my attention to himself. He also had found it dull to be alone with his wife and daughter for the last six weeks.

He was a small spare man, probably over fifty years of age, who gave me to understand that he had lived in London all his life, and had made his own fortune in the city. What he had done in the city to make his fortune he did not say. Had I come across him there I should no doubt have found him to be a sharp man of business, quite competent to teach me many a useful lesson of which I was as ignorant as an infant. Had he caught me on the Exchange, or at Lloyd's, or in the big room of the Bank of England, I should have been compelled to ask him everything. Now, in this little town under the Alps, he was as much lost as I should have been in Lombard Street, and was ready enough to look to me for information.

I was by no means chary in giving him my counsel, and imparting to him my ideas on things in general in that part of the world – only I should have preferred to be allowed to make myself civil to his daughter.

In the course of conversation it was mentioned by him that they intended to stay a few days at Bellaggio, which, as all the world knows, is a central spot on the lake of Como, and a favourite resting-place for travellers. There are three lakes, which all meet here, and to all of which we give the name of Como. They are properly called the lakes of Como, Colico and Lecco; and Bellaggio is the spot at which their waters join each other. I had half made up my mind to sleep there one night on my road into Italy, and now, on hearing their purpose, I declared that such was my intention.

'How very pleasant,' said Mrs Greene. 'It will be quite delightful to have some one to show us how to settle ourselves, for really –'

'My dear, I'm sure you can't say that you ever have much trouble.'

'And who does then, Mr Greene? I am sure Sophonisba does not do much to help me.'

'You won't let me,' said Sophonisba, whose name I had not before heard. Her papa had called her Sophy in the yard of the inn. Sophonisba Greene! Sophonisba Robinson did not sound so badly in my ears, and I confess that I had tried the names together. Her papa had mentioned to me that he had no other child, and had mentioned also that he had made his fortune.

And then there was a little family contest as to the amount of travelling labour which fell to the lot of each of the party, during which I retired to one of the windows of the big front room in which we were sitting. And how much of this labour there is incidental to a tourist's pursuits! And how often these little contests do arise upon a journey! Who has ever travelled and not known them? I had taken up such a position at the window as might, I thought, have removed me out of hearing; but, nevertheless, from time to time a word would catch my ear about that precious box. 'I have never taken my eyes off it since I left England,' said Mrs Greene, speaking quick, and with a considerable brogue superinduced by her energy. 'Where would it have been at Basle if I had not been looking after it?' 'Quite safe,' said Sophonisba; 'those large things always are safe.' 'Are they, miss? That's all you know about it. I suppose your bonnet-box was quite safe when I found it on the platform at – at – I forget the name of the place?'

'Freidrichshafen,' said Sophonisba, with almost an unnecessary amount of Teutonic skill in her pronunciation. 'Well, mamma, you

have told me of that at least twenty times.' Soon after that, the ladies took them to their own rooms, weary with the travelling of two days and a night, and Mr Greene went fast asleep in the very comfortless chair in which he was seated.

At four o'clock on the next morning we started on our journey.

> *Early to bed, and early to rise,*
> *Is the way to be healthy, and wealthy, and wise.*

We all know that lesson, and many of us believe in it; but if the lesson be true, the Italians ought to be the healthiest and wealthiest and wisest of all men and women. Three or four o'clock seems to them quite a natural hour for commencing the day's work. Why we should have started from Chiavenna at four o'clock in order that we might be kept waiting for the boat an hour and a half on the little quay at Colico, I don't know; but such was our destiny. There we remained an hour and a half, Mrs Greene sitting pertinaciously on the one important box. She had designated it as being smaller than the others, and, as all the seven were now ranged in a row, I had an opportunity of comparing them. It was something smaller – perhaps an inch less high, and an inch and a half shorter. She was a sharp woman, and observed my scrutiny. 'I always know it,' she said in a loud whisper, 'by this little hole in the canvas,' and she put her finger on a slight rent on one of the ends. 'As for Greene, if one of those Italian brigands were to walk off with it on his shoulders, before his eyes, he wouldn't be the wiser. How helpless you men are, Mr Robinson!'

'It is well for us that we have women to look after us.'

'But you have got no one to look after you; – or perhaps you have left her behind?'

'No, indeed. I'm all alone in the world as yet. But it's not my own fault. I have asked half a dozen.'

'Now, Mr Robinson!' And in this way the time passed on the quay at Colico, till the boat came and took us away. I should have preferred to pass my time in making myself agreeable to the younger lady; but the younger lady stood aloof, turning up her nose, as I thought, at her mamma.

I will not attempt to describe the scenery about Colico. The little town itself is one of the vilest places under the sun, having no accommodation for travellers, and being excessively unhealthy; but there is very little either north or south of the Alps – and, perhaps, I may add, very little elsewhere – to beat the beauty of the mountains which cluster round the head of the lake. When we had sat upon those boxes that hour and a half we were taken on board the steamer, which had been lying off a little way from the shore, and then we commenced our journey. Of course, there was a good deal of exertion and care necessary in getting the packages off from the shore on to the boat, and I observed that anyone with half an eye in his head might have seen that the mental anxiety expended on that one box which was marked by the small hole in the canvas far exceeded that which was extended to all the other six boxes. 'They deserve that it should be stolen,' I said to myself, 'for being such fools.' And then we went down to breakfast in the cabin.

'I suppose it must be safe,' said Mrs Greene to me, ignoring the fact that the cabin waiter understood English, although she had just ordered some veal cutlets in that language.

'As safe as a church,' I replied, not wishing to give much apparent importance to the subject.

'They can't carry it off here,' said Mr Greene. But he was innocent of any attempt at a joke, and was looking at me with all his eyes.

'They might throw it overboard,' said Sophonisba. I at once made up my mind that she could not be a good-natured girl. The moment that breakfast was over, Mrs Greene returned again upstairs, and I found her seated on one of the benches near the funnel, from which she could keep her eyes fixed upon the box. 'When one is obliged to carry about one's jewels with one, one must be careful,

Mr Robinson,' she said to me apologetically. But I was becoming tired of the box, and the funnel was hot and unpleasant, therefore I left her.

I had made up my mind that Sophonisba was ill-natured; but, nevertheless, she was pretty, and I now went through some little manoeuvres with the object of getting into conversation with her. This I soon did, and was surprised by her frankness. 'How tired you must be of mamma and her box,' she said to me. To this I made some answer, declaring that I was rather interested than otherwise in the safety of the precious trunk. 'It makes me sick,' said Sophonisba, 'to hear her go on in that way to a perfect stranger. I heard what she said about her jewellery.'

'It is natural she should be anxious,' I said, 'seeing that it contains so much that is valuable.'

'Why did she bring them?' said Sophonisba. 'She managed to live very well without jewels till papa married her, about a year since; and now she can't travel about for a month without lugging them with her everywhere. I should be so glad if some one would steal them.'

'But all Mr Greene's money is there also.'

'I don't want papa to be bothered, but I declare I wish the box might be lost for a day or so. She is such a fool; don't you think so, Mr Robinson?'

At this time it was just fourteen hours since I first had made their acquaintance in the yard of Conradi's hotel, and of those fourteen hours more than half had been passed in bed. I must confess that I looked upon Sophonisba, as being almost more indiscreet than her mother-in-law. Nevertheless, she was not stupid, and I continued my conversation with her the greatest part of the way down the lake towards Bellaggio.

These steamers which run up and down the lake of Como and the Lago Maggiore put out their passengers at the towns on the banks of the water by means of small rowing-boats, and the persons who are about to disembark generally have their own articles ready to their hands when their turn comes for leaving the steamer. As we came near to Bellaggio, I looked up my own portmanteau, and, pointing to the beautiful wood-covered hill that stands at the fork of the waters, told my friend Greene that he was near his destination. 'I am very glad to hear it,' said he, complacently, but he did not at the moment busy himself about the boxes. Then the small boat ran up alongside the steamer, and the passengers for Como and Milan crowded up the side.

'We have to go in that boat,' I said to Greene.

'Nonsense!' he exclaimed.

'Oh, but we have.'

'What! put our boxes into that boat,' said Mrs Greene. 'Oh dear! Here, boatman! there are seven of these boxes, all in white like this,' and she pointed to the one that had the hole in the canvas. 'Make haste. And there are two bags, and my dressing case, and Mr Greene's portmanteau. Mr Greene, where is your portmanteau?'

The boatman whom she addressed no doubt did not understand a word of English, but nevertheless he knew what she meant, and, being well accustomed to the work, got all the luggage together in an incredibly small number of movements.

'If you will get down into the boat,' I said, 'I will see that the luggage follows you before I leave the deck.'

'I won't stir,' she said, 'till I see that box lifted down. Take care; you'll let it fall into the lake. I know you will.'

'I wish they would,' Sophonisba whispered into my ear.

Mr Greene said nothing, but I could see that his eyes were as anxiously fixed on what was going on as were those of his wife. At last, however, the three Greenes were in the boat, as also were all the packages. Then I followed them, my portmanteau having gone down before me, and we pushed off for Bellaggio. Up to this period most of the attendants around us had understood a word or two of English, but now it would be well if we could find some one to whose ears French would not be unfamiliar. As regarded Mr Greene and his wife, they, I found, must give up all conversation, as they knew nothing of any language but their own. Sophonisba could make herself understood in French, and was quite at home, as she assured me, in German. And then the boat was beached on the shore at Bellaggio, and we all had to go again to work with the object of getting ourselves lodged at the hotel which overlooks the water.

I had learned before that the Greenes were quite free from any trouble in this respect, for their rooms had been taken for them before they left England. Trusting to this, Mrs Greene gave herself no inconsiderable airs the moment her foot was on the shore, and ordered the people about as though she were the Lady Paramount of Bellaggio. Italians, however, are used to this from travellers of a certain description. They never resent such conduct, but simply put it down in the bill with the other articles. Mrs Greene's words on this occasion were innocent enough, seeing that they were English; but had I been that head waiter who came down to the beach with his nice black shiny hair, and his napkin under his arm, I should have thought her manner very insolent.

Indeed, as it was, I did think so, and was inclined to be angry with her. She was to remain for some time at Bellaggio, and therefore it behoved her, as she thought, to assume the character of the grand lady at once. Hitherto she had been willing enough to do the work, but now she began to order about Mr Greene and Sophonisba, and, as it appeared to me, to order me about also. I did not quite enjoy this; so, leaving her still among her luggage and satellites, I walked up to the hotel to see about my own bedroom. I had some seltzer water, stood at the window for three or four minutes, and then walked up and down the room. But still the Greenes were not there. As I had put in at Bellaggio solely with the object of seeing something more of Sophonisba, it would not do for me to quarrel with them, or to allow them so to settle themselves in their private sitting-room that I should be excluded. Therefore I returned again to the road by which they must come up, and met the procession near the house.

Mrs Greene was leading it with great majesty, the waiter with the shiny hair walking by her side to point out to her the way. Then came all the luggage – each porter carrying a white canvas-covered box. That which was so valuable no doubt was carried next to Mrs Greene, so that she might at a moment's notice put her eye upon the well-known valuable rent. I confess that I did not observe the hole as the train passed by me, nor did I count the number of the boxes. Seven boxes, all alike, are very many; and then they were followed by three other men with the inferior articles – Mr Greene's portmanteau, the carpet-bag, etc., etc. At the tail of the line, I found Mr Greene, and behind him Sophonisba. 'All your fatigues will be over now,' I said to the gentleman, thinking it well not to be too particular in my attentions to his daughter. He was panting beneath a terrible greatcoat, having forgotten that the shores of an Italian lake are not so cold as the summits of the Alps, and did not answer me. 'I'm sure I hope so,' said Sophonisba. 'And I shall advise Papa not to go any farther unless he can persuade Mrs Greene to send her jewels home.' 'Sophy, my dear,' he said, 'for Heaven's sake let us have a little peace since we are here.' From all which I gathered that Mr Greene had not been fortunate in his second matrimonial adventure. We then made our way slowly up to the hotel, having been altogether distanced by the porters, and when we reached the house we found that the different packages were already being carried away through the house, some this way and some that. Mrs Greene, the meanwhile, was talking loudly at the door of her own sitting-room.

'Mr Greene,' she said, as soon as she saw her heavily oppressed spouse - for the noon-day sun was up - 'Mr Greene, where are you?'

'Here, my dear,' and Mr Greene threw himself panting into the corner of a sofa.

'A little seltzer water and brandy,' I suggested. Mr Greene's inmost heart leaped at the hint, and nothing that his remonstrant wife could say would induce him to move until he had enjoyed the delicious draught. In the meantime the box with the hole in the canvas had been lost.

Yes, when we came to look into matters, to count the packages, and to find out where we were, the box with the hole in the canvas was not there. Or, at any rate, Mrs Greene said it was not there. I worked hard to look it up, and even went into Sophonisba's bedroom in my search. In Sophonisba's bedroom there was but one canvas-covered box. 'That is my own,' said she, 'and it is all that I have, except this bag.'

'Where on earth can it be?' said I, sitting down on the trunk in question. At the moment I almost thought that she had been instrumental in hiding it.

'How am I to know?' she answered; and I fancied that even she was dismayed. 'What a fool that woman is!'

'The box must be in the house,' I said.

'Do find it, for papa's sake, there's a good fellow. He will be so wretched without his money. I heard him say that he had only two pounds in his purse.'

'Oh, I can let him have money to go on with,' I answered grandly. And then I went off to prove that I was a good fellow, and searched throughout the house. Two white boxes had by order been left downstairs, as they would not be needed, and these two were in a large cupboard of the hall, which was used expressly for stowing away luggage. And then there were three in Mrs Greene's bedroom, which had been taken there as containing the wardrobe which she would require while remaining at Bellaggio. I searched every one of these myself to see if I could find the hole in the canvas. But the hole in the canvas was not there. And, let me count as I would, I could make out only six. Now there certainly had been seven on board the steamer, though I could not swear that I had seen seven put into the small boat.

'Mr Greene,' said the lady standing in the middle of her remaining treasures, all of which were now open, 'you are worth nothing when travelling. Were you not behind?' But Mr Greene's mind was full, and he did not answer.

'It has been stolen before your very eyes,' she continued.

'Nonsense, mamma,' said Sophonisba. 'If ever it came out of the steamer it certainly came into the house.'

'I saw it out of the steamer,' said Mrs Greene, 'and it certainly is not in the house. Mr Robinson, may I trouble you to send for the police? – At once, if you please, sir.'

I had been at Bellaggio twice before, but nevertheless I was ignorant of their system of police. And then, again, I did not know what was the Italian for the word.

'I will speak to the landlord,' I said.

'If you will have the goodness to send for the police at once, I will be obliged to you.' And as she thus reiterated her command she stamped with her foot upon the floor.

'There are no police at Bellaggio,' said Sophonisba.

'What on earth shall I do for money to go on with?' said Mr Greene, looking piteously up to the ceiling, and shaking both his hands.

And now the whole house was in an uproar, including not only the landlord, his wife and daughters, and all the servants, but also every other visitor at the hotel. Mrs Greene was not a lady who hid either her glories or her griefs under a bushel, and, though she spoke only in English, she soon made her protestations sufficiently audible. She protested loudly that she had been robbed, and that she had been robbed since she left the steamer. The box had come on shore; of that she was certain. If the landlord had any regard either for his own character, or for that of his house, he would ascertain before an hour was over where it was, and who had been the thief. She would give him an hour. And then she sat down; but in two minutes she was up again, vociferating her wrongs as loudly as ever. All this was filtered through me and Sophonisba to the waiter in French, and from the waiter to the landlord; but the lady's gestures required no translation to make them intelligible, and the state of her mind on the matter was, I believe, perfectly well understood.

Mr Greene I really did pity. His feelings of dismay seemed to be quite as deep, but his sorrow and solicitude were repressed into more decorum. 'What am I to do for money?' he said. 'I have not a shilling to go on with!' and he still looked up at the ceiling.

'You must send to England,' said Sophonisba.

'It will take a month,' he replied.

'Mr Robinson will let you have what you want at present,' added Sophonisba. Now I certainly had said so, and had meant it at the time. But my whole travelling store did not exceed forty or fifty pounds, with which I was going on to Venice, and then back to England through the Tyrol. Waiting a month for Mr Greene's money from England might be even more inconvenient to me than to him. Then it occurred to me that the wants of the Greene family would be numerous and expensive, and that my small stock would go but a little way among so many. And what also if there had been no money and no jewels in that accursed box! I confess that at the moment such an idea did strike my mind. One hears of sharpers on every side committing depredations by means of most singular intrigues and contrivances. Might it not be possible that the whole batch of Greenes belonged to this order of society. It was a base idea, I own, but I confess that I entertained it for a moment.

I retired to my own room for a while that I might think over all the circumstances. There certainly had been seven boxes, and one had had a hole in the canvas. All the seven had certainly been on board the steamer. To so much I felt that I might safely swear. I had not counted the seven into the small boat, but on leaving the larger vessel I had looked about the deck to see that none of the Greene trappings were forgotten. If left on the steamer, it had been so left through an intent on the part of some one there employed. It was quite possible that the contents of the box had been ascertained through the imprudence of Mrs Greene, and that it had been conveyed away so that it might be rifled at Como. As to Mrs Greene's assertion that all the boxes had been put into the small boat, I thought nothing of it. The people at Bellaggio could not have known which box to steal, nor had there been time to concoct a plan in carrying the boxes up to the hotel. I came at last to this conclusion, that the missing trunk had either been purloined and carried on to Como – in which case it would be necessary to lose no time in going after it; or that it had been put out of sight in some uncommonly clever way, by the Greenes themselves, as an excuse for borrowing as much money as they could raise and living without payment of their bills. With reference to the latter hypothesis, I declared to myself that Greene did not look like a swindler; but as to Mrs Greene – I confess that I did not feel so confident in regard to her.

Charity begins at home, so I proceeded to make myself comfortable in my room, feeling almost certain that I should not be able to leave Bellaggio on the following morning. I had opened my portmanteau when I first arrived, leaving it open on the floor as is my wont. Some people are always being robbed, and are always locking up everything; while others wander safe over the world and never lock up anything. For myself, I never turn a key anywhere, and no one ever purloins from me even a handkerchief. *Cantabit vacuus* –, and I am always sufficiently *vacuus*. Perhaps it is that I have not a handkerchief worth the stealing. It is your heavy-laden, suspicious, maladroit Greenes that the thieves attack. I now found out that the accommodating Boots, who already knew my ways, had taken my travelling gear into a dark recess which was intended to do for a dressing-room, and had there spread my portmanteau open upon some table or stool in the corner. It was a convenient arrangement, and there I left it during the whole period of my sojourn.

Mrs Greene had given the landlord an hour to find the box, and during that time the landlord, the landlady, their three daughters, and all the servants in the house certainly did exert themselves to the utmost. Half a dozen times they came to my door, but I was luxuriating in a washing-tub, making up for that four-o'clock start from Chiavenna. I assured them, however, that the box was not there, and so the search passed by. At the end of the hour I went back to the Greenes according to promise, having resolved that some one must be sent on to Como to look after the missing article.

There was no necessity to knock at their sitting-room door, for it was wide open. I walked in, and found Mrs Greene still engaged in attacking the landlord, while all the porters who had carried the luggage up to the house were standing round. Her voice was loud above the others, but, luckily for them all, she was speaking English. The landlord, I saw, was becoming sulky. He spoke in Italian, and we none of us understood him, but I gathered that he was declining to do anything further. The box, he was certain, had never come out of the steamer. The Boots stood by interpreting into French, and, acting as second interpreter, I put it into English.

Mr Greene, who was seated on the sofa, groaned audibly, but said nothing. Sophonisba, who was sitting by him, beat upon the floor with both her feet.

'Do you hear, Mr Greene?' said Mrs Greene, turning to him. 'Do you mean to allow that vast amount of property to be lost without an effort? Are you prepared to replace my jewels?'

'Her jewels!' said Sophonisba, looking up into my face. 'Papa had to pay the bill for every stitch she had when he married her.' These last words were so spoken as to be audible only by me, but her first exclamation was loud enough. Were they people for whom it would be worth my while to delay my journey, and put myself to serious inconvenience with reference to money?

A few minutes afterwards I found myself with Greene on the terrace before the house, 'What ought I to do?' said he.

'Go to Como,' said I, 'and look after your box. I will remain here and go on board the return steamer. It may perhaps be there.'

'But I can't speak a word of Italian,' said he.

'Take the Boots,' said I.

'But I can't speak a word of French.' And then it ended in my undertaking to go to Como. I swear that the thought struck me that I might as well take my portmanteau with me, and cut and run when I got there. The Greenes were nothing to me.

I did not, however, do this. I made the poor man a promise, and I kept it. I took merely a dressing-bag, for I knew that I must sleep at Como, and, thus resolving to disarrange all my plans, I started. I was in the midst of beautiful scenery, but I found it quite impossible to draw any enjoyment from it – from that or from anything around me. My whole mind was given up to anathemas against this odious box, as to which I had undoubtedly heavy cause of complaint. What was the box to me? I went to Como by the afternoon steamer, and spent a long dreary evening down on the steamboat quays searching everywhere, and searching in vain. The boat by which we had left Colico had gone back to Colico, but the people swore that nothing had been left on board it. It was just possible that such a box might have gone on to Milan with the luggage of other passengers.

I slept at Como, and on the following morning I went on to Milan. There was no trace of the box to be found in that city. I went round to every hotel and travelling office, but could hear nothing of it. Parties had gone to Venice, and Florence, and Bologna, and any of them might have taken the box. No one, however, remembered it, and I returned back to Como, and thence to Bellaggio, reaching the latter place at nine in the evening, disappointed, weary, and cross.

'Has Monsieur found the accursed trunk?' said the Bellaggio Boots, meeting me on the quay.

'In the name of the –, no. Has it not turned up here?'

'Monsieur,' said the Boots, 'we shall all be mad soon. The poor master, he is mad already.' And then I went up to the house.

'My jewels!' shouted Mrs Greene, rushing to me with her arms stretched out as soon as she heard my step in the corridor. I am sure that she would have embraced me had I found the box. I had not, however, earned any such reward. 'I can hear nothing of the box either at Como or Milan,' I said.

'Then what on earth am I to do for my money?' said Mr Greene.

I had had neither dinner nor supper, but the elder Greenes did not care for that. Mr Greene sat silent in despair, and Mrs Greene stormed about the room in her anger. 'I am afraid you are very tired,' said Sophonisba.

'I am tired, and hungry, and thirsty,' said I. I was beginning to get angry, and to think myself ill-used. And that idea as to a family of swindlers became strong again. Greene had borrowed ten napoleons from me before I started for Como, and I had spent above four in my fruitless journey to that place and Milan. I was beginning to fear that my whole purpose as to Venice and the Tyrol would be destroyed; and I had promised to meet friends at Innsbruck, who, – who were very much preferable to the Greenes. As events turned out, I did meet them. Had I failed in this, the present Mrs Robinson would not have been sitting opposite to me.

I went to my room and dressed myself, and then Sophonisba presided over the tea-table for me. 'What are we to do?' she asked me in a confidential whisper.

'Wait for money from England.'

'But they will think we are all sharpers,' she said, 'and upon my word I do not wonder at it from the way in which that woman goes on.' She then leaned forward, resting her elbow on the table and her face on her hand, and told me a long history of all their family discomforts. Her papa was a very good sort of man, only he had been made a fool of by that intriguing woman, who had been left without a sixpence with which to bless herself. And now they had nothing but quarrels and misery. Papa did not always get the worst of it – Papa could rouse himself sometimes; only now he was beaten down and cowed by the loss of his money. This whispering confidence was very nice in its way, seeing that Sophonisba was a pretty girl; but the whole matter seemed to be full of suspicion.

'If they did not want to take you in in one way, they did in another,' said the present Mrs Robinson, when I told the story to her at Innsbruck. I beg that it may be understood that at the time of my meeting the Greenes I was not engaged to the present Mrs Robinson, and was open to make any matrimonial engagement that might have been pleasing to me.

On the next morning, after breakfast, we held a council of war. I had been informed that Mr Greene had made a fortune, and was justified in presuming him to be a rich man. It seemed to me, therefore, that his course was easy. Let him wait at Bellaggio for more money, and when he returned home, let him buy Mrs Greene more jewels. A poor man always presumes that a rich man is indifferent about his money. But in truth a rich man never is indifferent about his money, and poor Greene looked very blank at my proposition.

'Do you mean to say that it's gone for ever?' he asked.

'I'll not leave the country without knowing more about it,' said Mrs Greene.

'It certainly is very odd,' said Sophonisba. Even Sophonisba seemed to think that I was too off-hand.

'It will be a month before I can get money, and my bill here will be something tremendous,' said Greene.

'I wouldn't pay them a farthing till I got my box,' said Mrs Greene.

'That's nonsense,' said Sophonisba. And so it was.

'Hold your tongue, miss!' said the step-mother.

'Indeed, I shall not hold my tongue,' said the step-daughter.

Poor Greene! He had lost more than his box within the last twelve months, for, as I had learned in that whispered conversation over the tea-table with Sophonisba, this was in reality her papa's marriage trip.

Another day was now gone, and we all went to bed. Had I not been very foolish I should have had myself called at five in the morning, and have gone away by the early boat, leaving my ten napoleons behind me. But, unfortunately, Sophonisba had extracted a promise from me that I would not do this, and thus all chance of spending a day or two in Venice was lost to me. Moreover, I was thoroughly fatigued, and almost glad of any excuse which would allow me to lie in bed on the following morning. I did lie in bed till nine o'clock, and then found the Greenes at breakfast.

'Let us go and look at the Serbelloni Gardens,' said I, as soon as the silent meal was over; 'or take a boat over to the Sommariva Villa.'

'I should like it so much,' said Sophonisba.

'We will do nothing of the kind till I have found my property,' said Mrs Greene. 'Mr Robinson, what arrangement did you make yesterday with the police at Como?'

'The police at Como?' I said. 'I did not go to the police.'

'Not go to the police? And do you mean to say that I am to be robbed of my jewels and no efforts made for redress? Is there no such thing as a constable in this wretched country? Mr Greene, I do insist upon it that you at once go to the nearest British consul.'

'I suppose I had better write home for money,' said he.

'And do you mean to say that you haven't written yet?' said I, probably with some acrimony in my voice.

'You needn't scold papa,' said Sophonisba.

'I don't know what I am to do,' said Mr Greene, and he began walking up and down the room; but still he did not call for pen and ink, and I began again to feel that he was a swindler. Was it possible that a man of business, who had made his fortune in London, should allow his wife to keep all her jewels in a box, and carry about his own money in the same?

'I don't see why you need be so very unhappy, papa,' said Sophonisba. 'Mr Robinson, I'm sure, will let you have whatever money you may want at present.' This was pleasant!

'And will Mr Robinson return me my jewels which were lost? I must say, in a great measure, through his carelessness,' said Mrs Greene. This was pleasanter!

'Upon my word, Mrs Greene, I must deny that,' said I, jumping up. 'What on earth could I have done more than I did do? I have been to Milan and nearly fagged myself to death.'

'Why didn't you bring a policeman back with you?'

'You would tell everybody on board the boat what there was in it,' said I.

'I told nobody but you,' she answered.

'I suppose you mean to imply that I've taken the box,' I rejoined. So that on this, the third or fourth day of our acquaintance, we did not go on together quite pleasantly.

But what annoyed me, perhaps, the most, was the confidence with which it seemed to be Mr Greene's intention to lean upon my resources. He certainly had not written home yet, and had taken my ten napoleons, as one friend may take a few shillings from another when he finds that he has left his own silver on his dressing-table. What could he have wanted of ten napoleons? He had alleged the necessity of paying the porters, but the few francs he had had in his pocket would have been enough for that. And now Sophonisba was ever and again prompt in her assurances that he need not annoy himself about money, because I was at his right hand. I went upstairs into my own room, and counting all my treasures, found that thirty-six pounds and some odd silver was the extent of my wealth. With that I had to go, at any rate, as far as Innsbruck, and from thence back to London. It was quite impossible that I should make myself responsible for the Greenes' bill at Bellaggio.

We dined early, and, after dinner, according to a promise made in the morning, Sophonisba ascended with me into the Serbelloni Gardens, and walked round the terraces on that beautiful hill which commands the view of the three lakes. When we started I confess that I would sooner have gone alone, for I was sick of the Greenes in my very soul. We had had a terrible day. The landlord had been sent for so often that he refused to show himself again. The landlady – though Italians of that class are always courteous - had been so driven that she snapped her fingers in Mrs Greene's face. The three girls would not show themselves. The waiters kept out of the way as much as possible; and the Boots, in confidence, abused them to me behind their back. 'Monsieur,' said the Boots, 'do you think there ever was such a box?' 'Perhaps not,' said I; and yet I knew that I had seen it.

I would, therefore, have preferred to walk without Sophonisba, but that now was impossible. So I determined that I would utilise the occasion by telling her of my present purpose. I had resolved to start on the following day, and it was now necessary to make my friends understand that it was not in my power to extend to them any further pecuniary assistance.

Sophonisba, when we were on the hill, seemed to have forgotten the box, and to be willing that I should forget it also. But this was impossible. When, therefore, she told me how sweet it was to escape from that terrible woman, and leaned on my arm with all the freedom of old acquaintance, I was obliged to cut short the pleasure of the moment.

'I hope your father has written that letter,' said I.

'He means to write it from Milan. We know you want to get on, so we purpose to leave here the day after tomorrow.'

'Oh!' said I, thinking of the bill immediately and remembering that Mrs Greene had insisted on having champagne for dinner.

'And if anything more is to be done about the nasty box, it may be done there,' continued Sophonisba.

'But I must go tomorrow,' said I, 'at 5 am.'

'Nonsense,' said Sophonisba. 'Go tomorrow, when I - I mean we - are going on the next day!'

'And I might as well explain,' said I, gently dropping the hand that was on my arm, 'that I find - I find it will be impossible for me - to - to -'

'To what?'

'To advance Mr Greene any more money just at present.' Then Sophonisba's arm dropped all at once, and she exclaimed, 'Oh, Mr Robinson!'

After all, there was a certain hard good sense about Miss Greene which would have protected her from my evil thoughts had I known all the truth. I found out afterwards that she was a considerable heiress, and, in spite of the opinion expressed by the present Mrs Robinson when Miss Walker, I do not for a moment think she would have accepted me had I offered to her.

'You are quite right not to embarrass yourself,' she said, when I explained to her my immediate circumstances; 'but why did you make Papa an offer which you cannot perform? He must remain here till he hears from England. Had you explained it all at first, the ten napoleons would have carried us to Milan.' This was all true, and yet I thought it hard upon me.

It was evident to me now that Sophonisba was prepared to join her stepmother in thinking that I had ill-treated them, and I had not much doubt that I should find Mr Greene to be of the same opinion. There was very little more said between us during the walk, and when we reached the hotel at seven or half-past seven o'clock, I merely remarked that I would go in and wish her father and mother goodbye. 'I suppose you will drink tea with us,' said Sophonisba, and to this I assented.

I went into my own room, and put all my things into my portmanteau, for according to the custom, which is invariable in Italy when an early start is premeditated, the Boots was imperative in his demand that the luggage should be ready overnight. I then went to the Greenes' sitting-room, and found that the whole party was now aware of my intentions.

'So you are going to desert us,' said Mrs Greene.

'I must go on upon my journey,' I pleaded in a weak apologetic voice.

'Go on upon your journey, sir!' said Mrs Greene. 'I would not for a moment have you put yourself to inconvenience on our account.' And yet I had already lost fourteen napoleons, and given up all prospect of going to Venice!

'Mr Robinson is certainly right not to break his engagement with Miss Walker,' said Sophonisba. Now I had said not a word about an engagement with Miss Walker, having only mentioned incidentally that she would be one of the party at Innsbruck. 'But,' continued she, 'I think he should not have misled us.' And in this way we enjoyed our evening meal.

I was just about to shake hands with them all, previous to my final departure from their presence, when the Boots came into the room.

'I'll leave the portmanteau till tomorrow morning,' said he.

'All right,' said I.

'Because,' said he, 'there will be such a crowd of things in the hall. The big trunk I will take away now.'

'Big trunk – what big trunk?'

'The trunk with your rug over it, on which your portmanteau stood.'

I looked round at Mr, Mrs, and Miss Greene, and saw that they were all looking at me. I looked round at them, and as their eyes met mine I felt that I turned as red as fire. I immediately jumped up and rushed away to my own room, hearing as I went that all their steps were following me. I rushed to the inner recess, pulled down the portmanteau, which still remained in its old place, tore away my own carpet rug which covered the support beneath it, and there saw – a white canvas-covered box, with a hole in the canvas on the next side to me!

'It is my box,' said Mrs Greene, pushing me away, as she hurried up and put her finger within the rent.

'It certainly does look like it,' said Mr Greene, peering over his wife's shoulder.

'There's no doubt about the box,' said Sophonisba.

'Not the least in life,' said I, trying to assume an indifferent look.

'*Mon Dieu!*' said the Boots.

'*Corpo di Baccho!*' exclaimed the landlord, who had now joined the party.

'Oh-h-h-h –!' screamed Mrs Greene, and then she threw herself back on to my bed, and shrieked hysterically.

There was no doubt whatsoever about the fact. There was the lost box, and there it had been during all those tedious hours of unavailing search. While I was suffering all that fatigue in Milan, spending all my precious zwanzigers in driving about from one hotel to another, the box had been safe, standing in my own room at Bellaggio, hidden by my own rug. And now that it was found everybody looked at me as though it were all my fault. Mrs Greene's eyes, when she had done being hysterical, were terrible, and Sophonisba looked at me as though I were a convicted thief.

'Who put the box here?' I said, turning fiercely upon the Boots.

'I did,' said the Boots, 'by Monsieur's express order.'

'By my order?' I exclaimed.

'Certainly,' said the Boots.

'*Corpo di Baccho!*' said the landlord, and he also looked at me as though I were a thief. In the meantime the landlady and the three daughters had clustered round Mrs Greene, administering to her all manner of Italian consolation. The box, and the money, and the jewels were after all a reality, and much incivility can be forgiven to a lady who has really lost her jewels, and has really found them again.

There and then there arose a hurly-burly among us as to the manner in which the odious trunk found its way into my room. Had anybody been just enough to consider the matter coolly, it must have been quite clear that I could not have ordered it there. When I entered the hotel, the boxes were already being lugged about, and I had spoken a word to no one concerning them. That traitorous

Boots had done it – no doubt without *malice prepense*; but he had done it; and now that the Greenes were once more known as moneyed people, he turned upon me and told me to my face that I had desired that box to be taken to my own room as part of my own luggage!

'My dear,' said Mr Greene, turning to his wife, 'you should never mention the contents of your luggage to anyone.'

'I never will again,' said Mrs Greene, with a mock repentant air, 'but I really thought –'

'One never can be sure of sharpers,' said Mr Greene.

'That's true,' said Mrs Greene.

'After all, it may have been accidental,' said Sophonisba, on hearing which good-natured surmise both Papa and Mamma Greene shook their suspicious heads.

I was resolved to say nothing then. It was all but impossible that they should really think that I had intended to steal their box; nor, if they did think so, would it have become me to vindicate myself before the landlord and all his servants. I stood by therefore in silence, while two of the men raised the trunk and joined the procession which followed it as it was carried out of my room into that of the legitimate owner. Everybody in the house was there by that time, and Mrs Greene, enjoying the triumph, by no means grudged them the entrance into her sitting-room. She had felt that she was suspected, and now she was determined that the world of Bellaggio should know how much she was above suspicion. The box was put down upon two chairs, the supporters who had borne it retiring a pace each. Mrs Greene then advanced proudly with the selected key, and Mr Greene stood by at her right shoulder, ready to receive his portion of the hidden treasure. Sophonisba was now indifferent, and threw herself on the sofa, while I walked up and down the room thoughtfully – meditating what words I should say when I took my last farewell of the Greenes.

But as I walked I could see what occurred. Mrs Greene opened the box, and displayed to view the ample folds of a huge yellow woollen dressing-gown. I could fancy that she would not willingly have exhibited this article of her toilet, had she not felt that its existence would speedily be merged in the presence of the glories which were to follow. This had merely been the padding at the top of the box. Under that lay a long *papier-mâché* case, and in that were all her treasures. 'Ah, they are safe,' she said, opening the lid and looking upon her tawdry pearls and carbuncles.

Mr Greene, in the meantime, well knowing the passage for his hand, had dived down to the very bottom of the box, and seized hold of a small canvas bag. 'It is here,' said he, dragging it up, 'and as far as I can tell, as yet, the knot has not been untied.' Whereupon he sat himself down by Sophonisba, and employing her to assist him in holding them, began to count his rolls. 'They are all right,' said he; and he wiped the perspiration from his brow.

I had not yet made up my mind in what manner I might best utter my last words among them so as to maintain the dignity of my character, and now I was standing over against Mr Greene with my arms folded on my breast. I had on my face a frown of displeasure, which I am able to assume upon occasions, but I had not yet determined what words I would use. After all, perhaps, it might be as well that I should leave them without any last words.

'Greene, my dear,' said the lady, 'pay the gentleman his ten napoleons.'

'Oh yes, certainly'; whereupon Mr Greene undid one of the rolls and extracted eight sovereigns. 'I believe that will make it right, sir,' said he, holding them to me.

I took the gold, slipped it with an indifferent air into my waistcoat pocket, and then refolded my arms across my breast.

'Papa,' said Sophonisba, in a very audible whisper, 'Mr Robinson went for you to Como. Indeed, I believe he says he went to Milan.'

'Do not let that be mentioned,' said I.

'By all means pay him his expenses,' said Mrs Greene; 'I would not owe him anything for worlds.'

'He should be paid,' said Sophonisba.

'Oh, certainly,' said Mr Greene. And he at once extracted another sovereign, and tended it to me in the face of the assembled multitude.

This was too much! 'Mr Greene,' said I, 'I intended to be of service to you when I went to Milan, and you are very welcome to the benefit of my intentions. The expense of that journey, whatever may be its amount, is my own affair.' And I remained standing with my closed arms.

'We will be under no obligation to him,' said Mrs Greene; 'and I shall insist on his taking the money.'

'The servant will put it on his dressing-table,' said Sophonisba. And she handed the sovereign to the Boots, giving him instructions.

'Keep it yourself, Antonio,' I said. Whereupon the man chucked it to the ceiling with his thumb, caught it as it fell, and with a well-satisfied air, dropped it into the recesses of his pocket. The air of the Greenes was also well satisfied, for they felt that they had paid me in full for all my services.

And now, with many obsequious bows and assurances of deep

respect, the landlord and his family withdrew from the room. 'Was there anything else they could do for Mrs Greene?' Mrs Greene was all affability. She had shown her jewels to the girls, and allowed them to express their admiration in pretty Italian superlatives. There was nothing else she wanted tonight. She was very happy and liked Bellaggio. She would stay yet a week, and would make herself quite happy. And, though none of them understood a word that the other said, each understood that things were now rose-coloured, and so with scrapings, bows, and grinning smiles, the landlord and all his myrmidons withdrew. Mr Greene was still counting his money, sovereign by sovereign, and I was still standing with my folded arms upon my bosom.

'I believe I may now go,' said I.

'Good night,' said Mrs Greene.

'*Adieu,*' said Sophonisba.

'I have the pleasure of wishing you goodbye,' said Mr Greene.

And then I walked out of the room. After all, what was the use of saying anything? And what could I say that would have done me any service? If they were capable of thinking me a thief – which they certainly did – nothing that I could say would remove the impression. Nor, as I thought, was it suitable that I should defend myself from such an imputation. What were the Greenes to me? So I walked slowly out of the room, and never again saw one of the family from that day to this.

As I stood upon the beach the next morning, while my portmanteau was being handed into the boat, I gave the Boots five zwanzigers. I was determined to show him that I did not condescend to feel anger against him.

He took the money, looked into my face, and then whispered to me, 'Why did you not give me a word of notice beforehand?' he said, and winked one eye. He was evidently a thief, and took me to be another – but what did it matter?

I went thence to Milan, in which city I had no heart to look at anything; thence to Verona, and so over the pass of the Brenner to Innsbruck. When I once found myself near to my dear friends the Walkers I was again a happy man; and I may safely declare that, though a portion of my journey was so troublesome and unfortunate, I look back upon that tour as the happiest and the luckiest epoch of my life.

LOTTA SCHMIDT

As all the world knows, the old fortifications of Vienna have been pulled down – the fortifications which used to surround the centre or kernel of the city; and the vast spaces thus thrown open and forming a broad ring in the middle of the town have not as yet been completely filled up with those new buildings and gardens which are to be there, and which, when there, will join the outside city and the inside city together, so as to make them into one homogeneous whole.

The work, however, is going on, and if the war which has come and passed has not swallowed everything appertaining to Austria into its maw, the ugly remnants of destruction will be soon carted away, and the old glacis will be made bright with broad pavements, and gilded railings, and well-built lofty mansions, and gardens beautiful with shrubs – and beautiful with turf also, if Austrian patience can make turf to grow beneath an Austrian sky.

On an evening of September, when there was still something left of daylight, at eight o'clock, two girls were walking together in the Burgplatz, or large open space which lies between the city palace of the emperor and the gate which passes thence from the old town out to the new town. Here at present stand two bronze equestrian statues, one of the Archduke Charles, and the other of Prince Eugene. And they were standing there also, both of them, when these two girls were walking round them; but that of the prince had not as yet been uncovered for the public.

There was coming a great gala day in the city. Emperors and empresses, archdukes and grand-dukes, with their archduchesses and grand-duchesses, and princes and ministers, were to be there, and the new statue of Prince Eugene was to be submitted to the art-critics of the world. There was very much thought at Vienna of the statue in those days. Well; since that, the statue has been submitted to the art-critics, and henceforward it will be thought of as little as any other huge bronze figure of a prince on horseback. A very ponderous prince is poised in an impossible position, on an enormous dray horse. But yet the thing is grand, and Vienna is so far a finer city in that it possesses the new equestrian statue of Prince Eugene.

'There will be such a crowd, Lotta,' said the elder of the two girls, 'that I will not attempt it. Besides, we shall have plenty of time for seeing it afterwards.'

'Oh, yes,' said the younger girl, whose name was Lotta Schmidt; 'of course we shall all have enough of the old prince for the rest of our lives; but I should like to see the grand people sitting up there on the benches; and there will be something nice in seeing the canopy drawn up. I think I will come. Herr Crippel has said that he would bring me, and get me a place.'

'I thought, Lotta, you had determined to have nothing more to say to Herr Crippel.'

'I don't know what you mean by that. I like Herr Crippel very much, and he plays beautifully. Surely a girl may know a man old enough to be her father without having him thrown in her teeth as her lover.'

'Not when the man old enough to be her father has asked her to be his wife twenty times, as Herr Crippel has asked you. Herr Crippel would not give up his holiday afternoon to you if he thought it was to be for nothing.'

'There I think you are wrong, Marie. I believe Herr Crippel likes to have me with him simply because every gentleman likes to have a lady on such a day as that. Of course it is better than being alone. I don't suppose he will say a word to me except to tell me who the people are, and to give me a glass of beer when it is over.'

It may be as well to explain at once, before we go any further, that Herr Crippel was a player on the violin, and that he led the musicians in the orchestra of the great beer-hall in the Volksgarten. Let it not be thought that because Herr Crippel exercised his art in a beer-hall therefore he was a musician of no account. No one will think so who has once gone to a Vienna beer-hall, and listened to such music as is there provided for the visitors.

The two girls, Marie Weber and Lotta Schmidt, belonged to an establishment in which gloves were sold in the Graben, and now, having completed their work for the day – and indeed their work for the week, for it was Saturday evening – had come out for such recreation as the evening might afford them. And on behalf of these two girls, as to one of whom at least I am much interested, I must beg my English readers to remember that manners and customs differ much in Vienna from those which prevail in London.

Were I to tell of two London shop girls going out into the streets after their day's work, to see what friends and what amusement the fortune of the evening might send to them, I should be supposed to be speaking of young women as to whom it would be better that I should be silent; but these girls in Vienna were doing simply that which all their friends would expect and wish them to do. That they should have some amusement to soften the rigours of long days of work was recognised to be necessary; and music, beer, dancing, with the conversation of young men, are thought in Vienna to be the natural amusements of young women, and in Vienna are believed to be innocent.

The Viennese girls are almost always attractive in their appearance, without often coming up to our English ideas of prettiness. Sometimes they do fully come up to our English idea of beauty. They are generally dark, tall, light in figure, with bright eyes, which are however very unlike the bright eyes of Italy, and which constantly remind the traveller that his feet are carrying him eastward in Europe. But perhaps the peculiar characteristic in their faces which most strikes a stranger is a certain look of almost fierce independence, as though they had recognised the necessity, and also acquired the power, of standing alone, and of protecting themselves. I know no young women by whom the assistance of a man's arm seems to be so seldom required as the young women of Vienna. They almost invariably dress well, generally preferring black, or colours that are very dark; and they wear hats that are, I believe, of Hungarian origin, very graceful in form, but which are peculiarly calculated to add something to that assumed savageness of independence of which I have spoken.

Both the girls who were walking in the Burgplatz were of the kind that I have attempted to describe. Marie Weber was older, and not so tall, and less attractive than her friend; but as her position in life was fixed, and as she was engaged to marry a cutter of diamonds, I will not endeavour to interest the reader specially in her personal appearance. Lotta Schmidt was essentially a Viennese pretty girl of the special Viennese type. She was tall and slender, but still had none of that appearance of feminine weakness which is so common among us with girls who are tall and slim. She walked as though she had plenty both of strength and courage for all purposes of life without the assistance of any extraneous aid. Her hair was jet-black, and very plentiful, and was worn in long curls which were brought round from the back of her head over her shoulders. Her eyes were blue – dark blue – and were clear and deep rather than bright. Her nose was well formed, but somewhat prominent, and made you think at the first glance of the tribes of Israel. But yet no observer of the physiognomy of races would believe for half a moment that Lotta Schmidt was a Jewess. Indeed, the type of form which I am endeavouring to describe is in truth as far removed from the Jewish type as it is from the Italian; and it has no connexion whatever with that which we ordinarily conceive to be the German type. But, overriding everything in her personal appearance, in her form, countenance, and gait, was that singular fierceness of independence, as though she were constantly asserting that she would never submit herself to the inconvenience of feminine softness. And yet Lotta Schmidt was a simple girl, with a girl's heart, looking forward to find all that she was to have of human happiness in the love of some man, and expecting and hoping to do her duty as a married woman and the mother of a family. Nor would she have been at all coy in saying as much had the subject of her life's prospects become matter of conversation in any company; no more than one lad would be coy in saying that he hoped to be a doctor, or another in declaring a wish for the army.

When the two girls had walked twice round the hoarding within which stood all those tons of bronze which were intended to represent Prince Eugene, they crossed over the centre of the Burgplatz, passed under the other equestrian statue, and came to the gate leading into the Volksgarten. There, just at the entrance, they were overtaken by a man with a fiddle-case under his arm, who raised his hat to them, and then shook hands with both of them.

'Ladies,' he said, 'are you coming in to hear a little music? We will do our best.'

'Herr Crippel always does well,' said Marie Weber. 'There is never any doubt when one comes to hear him.'

'Marie, why do you flatter him?' said Lotta.

'I do not say half to his face that you said just now behind his back,' said Marie.

'And what did she say of me behind my back?' said Herr Crippel. He smiled as he asked the question, or attempted to smile, but it was easy to see that he was too much in earnest. He blushed up to his eyes, and there was a slight trembling motion in his hands as he stood with one of them pressed upon the other.

As Marie did not answer at the moment, Lotta replied for her.

'I will tell you what I said behind your back. I said that Herr Crippel had the firmest hand upon a bow, and the surest fingers among the strings, in all Vienna – when his mind was not woolgathering. Marie, is not that true?'

'I do not remember anything about the wool-gathering,' said Marie.

'I hope I shall not be wool-gathering tonight; but I shall doubtless – I shall doubtless – for I shall be thinking of your judgment. Shall I get you seats at once? There; you are just before me. You see I am not coward enough to fly from my critics.' And he placed them to sit at a little marble table, not far from the front of the low orchestra in the foremost place in which he would have to take his stand.

'Many thanks, Herr Crippel,' said Lotta. 'I will make sure of a third chair, as a friend is coming.'

'Oh, a friend!' said he; and he looked sad, and all his sprightliness was gone.

'Marie's friend,' said Lotta, laughing. 'Do not you know Carl Stobel?'

Then the musician became bright and happy again. 'I would have got two more chairs if you would have let me; one for the fraulein's sake, and one for his own. And I will come down presently, and you shall present me, if you will be so very kind.'

Marie Weber smiled and thanked him, and declared that she should be very proud – and the leader of the band went up into his place.

'I wish he had not placed us here,' said Lotta.

'And why not?'

'Because Fritz is coming.'

'No!'

'But he is.'

'And why did you not tell me?'

'Because I did not wish to be speaking of him. Of course you understand why I did not tell you. I would rather it should seem that he came of his own account – with Carl. Ha, ha!' Carl Stobel was the diamond-cutter to whom Marie Weber was betrothed. 'I should not have told you now – only that I am disarranged by what Herr Crippel has done.'

'Had we not better go – or at least move our seats? We can make any excuse afterwards.'

'No,' said Lotta. 'I will not seem to run away from him. I have nothing to be ashamed of. If I choose to keep company with Fritz Planken, that should be nothing to Herr Crippel.'

'But you might have told him.'

'No; I could not tell him. And I am not sure Fritz is coming either. He said he would come with Carl if he had time. Never mind; let us be happy now. If a bad time comes by-and-bye, we must make the best of it.'

Then the music began, and, suddenly, as the first note of a fiddle was heard, every voice in the great beer-hall of the Volksgarten became silent. Men sat smoking, with their long beer-glasses before them, and women sat knitting, with their long beer-glasses also before them, but not a word was spoken. The waiters went about with silent feet, but even orders for beer were not given, and money was not received. Herr Crippel did his best, working with his wand as carefully – and I may say as accurately – as a leader in a fashionable opera-house in London or Paris. But every now and then, in the course of the piece, he would place his fiddle to his shoulder and join in the performance. There was hardly one there in the hall, man or woman, boy or girl, who did not know, from personal knowledge and judgment, that Herr Crippel was doing his work very well.

'Excellent, was it not?' said Marie.

'Yes; he is a musician. Is it not a pity he should be so bald?' said Lotta.

'He is not so very bald,' said Marie.

'I should not mind his being bald so much, if he did not try to cover his old head with the side hairs. If he would cut off those loose straggling locks, and declare himself to be bald at once, he would be ever so much better. He would look to be fifty then. He looks sixty now.'

'What matters his age? He is forty-five, just; for I know. And he is a good man.'

'What has his goodness to do with it?'

'A great deal. His old mother wants for nothing, and he makes two hundred florins a month. He has two shares in the summer theatre. I know it.'

'Bah! what is all that when he will plaster his hair over his old bald head?'

'Lotta, I am ashamed of you.' But at this moment the further expression of Marie's anger was stopped by the entrance of the diamond-cutter; and as he was alone, both the girls received him very pleasantly. We must give Lotta her due, and declare that, as things had gone, she would much prefer now that Fritz should stay away, though Fritz Planken was as handsome a young fellow as there was in Vienna, and one who dressed with the best taste, and danced so that no one could surpass him, and could speak French, and was confidential clerk at one of the largest hotels in Vienna, and was a young man acknowledged to be of much general importance – and had, moreover, in plain language declared his love for Lotta Schmidt. But Lotta would not willingly give unnecessary pain to Herr Crippel, and she was generously glad when Carl Stobel, the diamond-cutter, came by himself. Then there was a second and third piece played, and after that Herr Crippel came down, according to promise, and was presented to Marie's lover.

'Ladies,' said he, 'I hope I have not gathered wool.'

'You have surpassed yourself,' said Lotta.

'At wool-gathering?' said Herr Crippel.

'At sending us out of this world into another,' said Lotta.

'Ah! go into no other world but this,' said Herr Crippel, 'lest I should not be able to follow you.' And then he went away again to his post.

Before another piece had been commenced, Lotta saw Fritz Planken enter the door. He stood for a moment gazing round the hall, with his cane in his hand and his hat on his head, looking for the party which he intended to join. Lotta did not say a word, nor would she turn her eyes towards him. She would not recognise him if it were possible to avoid it. But he soon saw her, and came up to the table at which they were sitting. When Lotta was getting the third chair for Marie's lover, Herr Crippel, in his gallantry, had brought a fourth, and now Fritz occupied the chair which the musician had placed there. Lotta, as she perceived this, was sorry that it should be so. She could not even dare to look up to see what effect this new arrival would have upon the leader of the band.

The new comer was certainly a handsome young man – such a one as inflicts unutterable agonies on the hearts of the Herr Crippels of the world. His boots shone like mirrors, and fitted his feet like gloves. There was something in the make and set of his trousers which Herr Crippel, looking at them, as he could not help looking at them, was quite unable to understand. Even twenty years ago, Herr Crippel's trousers, as Herr Crippel very well knew, had never looked like that. And Fritz Planken wore a blue frock coat with silk lining to the breast, which seemed to have come from some tailor among the gods. And he had on primrose gloves, and round his neck a bright pink satin handkerchief, joined by a ring, which gave a richness of colouring to the whole thing which nearly killed Herr Crippel, because he could not but acknowledge that the colouring was good. And then the hat! And when the hat was taken off for a moment, then the hair – perfectly black, and silky as a raven's wing, just waving with one curl! And when Fritz put up his hand, and ran his fingers through his locks, their richness and plenty and beauty were conspicuous to all beholders. Herr Crippel, as he saw it, involuntarily dashed his hand up to his own pate, and scratched his straggling, lanky hairs from off his head.

'You are coming to Sperl's tomorrow, of course?' said Fritz to Lotta. Now Sperl's is a great establishment for dancing in the Leopoldstadt, which is always open of a Sunday evening, and which Lotta Schmidt was in the habit of attending with much regularity. It was here she had become acquainted with Fritz. And certainly to dance with Fritz was to dance indeed! Lotta, too, was a beautiful dancer. To a Viennese such as Lotta Schmidt, dancing is a thing of serious importance. It was a misfortune to her to have to dance with a bad dancer, as it is to a great whist-player among us to sit down with a bad partner. Oh, what she had suffered more than once when Herr Crippel had induced her to stand up with him!

'Yes; I shall go. Marie, you will go?'

'I do not know,' said Marie.

'You will make her go, Carl; will you not?' said Lotta.

'She promised me yesterday, as I understood,' said Carl.

'Of course we will all be there,' said Fritz, somewhat grandly; 'and I will give a supper for four.'

Then the music began again, and the eyes of all of them became fixed upon Herr Crippel. It was unfortunate that they should have been placed so fully before him, as it was impossible that he should avoid seeing them. As he stood up with his violin to his shoulder, his eyes were fixed on Fritz Planken and Fritz Planken's boots, and coat, and hat, and hair. And as he drew his bow over the strings he was thinking of his own boots and of his own hair. Fritz was sitting, leaning forward in his chair, so that he could look up into Lotta's face, and he was playing with a little amber-headed cane, and every now and then he whispered a word. Herr Crippel could hardly play a

note. In very truth he was wool-gathering. His hand became un-
steady, and every instrument was more or less astray.

'Your old friend is making a mess of it tonight,' said Fritz to Lotta.
'I hope he has not taken a glass too much of schnapps.'

'He never does anything of the kind,' said Lotta, angrily. 'He
never did such a thing in his life.'

'He is playing awfully bad,' said Fritz.

'I never heard him play better in my life than he has played tonight,' said Lotta.

'His hand is tired. He is getting old,' said Fritz. Then Lotta moved
her chair and drew herself back, and was determined that Marie and
Carl should see that she was angry with her young lover. In the
meantime the piece of music had been finished, and the audience
had shown their sense of the performers' inferiority by withdrawing
those plaudits which they were so ready to give when they were
pleased.

After this some other musician led for a while, and then Herr
Crippel had to come forward to play a solo. And on this occasion the
violin was not to be his instrument. He was a great favourite among
the lovers of music in Vienna, not only because he was good at the
fiddle and because with his bow in his hand he could keep a band of
musicians together, but also as a player on the zither. It was not
often now-a-days that he would take his zither to the music-hall in
the Volksgarten; for he would say that he had given up that instrument; that he now played it only in private; that it was not fit for a
large hall, as a single voice, the scraping of a foot, would destroy its
music. And Herr Crippel was a man who had his fancies and his
fantasies, and would not always yield to entreaty. But occasionally
he would send his zither down to the public hall; and in the pro-
gramme for this evening there had been put forth that Herr Crippel's
zither would be there and that Herr Crippel would perform. And
now the zither was brought forward, and a chair was put for the
zitherist, and Herr Crippel stood for a moment behind his chair and
bowed. Lotta glanced up at him, and could see that he was very pale.
She could even see that the perspiration stood upon his brow. She
knew that he was trembling, and that he would have given almost
his zither itself to be quit of his promised performance for that night.
But she knew also that he would make the attempt.

'What! the zither?' said Fritz. 'He will break down as sure as he is
a living man.'

'Let us hope not,' said Carl Stobel.

'I love to hear him play the zither better than anything,' said
Lotta.

'It used to be very good,' said Fritz; 'but everybody says he has lost his touch. When a man has the slightest feeling of nervousness he is done for the zither.'

'H – sh; let him have his chance at any rate,' said Marie.

Reader, did you ever hear the zither? When played, as it is sometimes played in Vienna, it combines all the softest notes of the human voice. It sings to you of love, and then wails to you of disappointed love, till it fills you with a melancholy from which there is no escaping – from which you never wish to escape. It speaks to you as no other instrument ever speaks, and reveals to you with wonderful eloquence the sadness in which it delights. It produces a luxury of anguish, a fulness of the satisfaction of imaginary woe, a realisation of the mysterious delights of romance, which no words can ever thoroughly supply. While the notes are living, while the music is still in the air, the ear comes to covet greedily every atom of tone which the instrument will produce, so that the slightest extraneous sound becomes an offence. The notes sink and sink so low and low, with their soft sad wail of delicious woe, that the listener dreads that something will be lost in the struggle of listening. There seems to come some lethargy on his sense of hearing, which he fears will shut out from his brain the last, lowest, sweetest strain, the very pearl of the music, for which he has been watching with all the intensity of prolonged desire. And then the zither is silent, and there remains a fond memory together with a deep regret.

Herr Crippel seated himself on his stool and looked once or twice round about upon the room almost with dismay. Then he struck his zither, uncertainly, weakly, and commenced the prelude of his piece. But Lotta thought that she had never heard so sweet a sound. When he paused after a few strokes there was a noise of applause in the room – of applause intended to encourage by commemorating past triumphs. The musician looked again away from his music to his audience, and his eyes caught the eyes of the girl he loved; and his gaze fell also upon the face of the handsome, well-dressed, young Adonis who was by her side.

He, Herr Crippel the musician, could never make himself look like that; he could make no slightest approach to that outward triumph. But then, he could play the zither, and Fritz Planken could only play with his cane! He would do what he could! He would play his best! He had once almost resolved to get up and declare that he was too tired that evening to do justice to his instrument. But there was an insolence of success about his rival's hat and trousers which spirited him on to the fight. He struck his zither again, and they who understood him and his zither knew that he was in earnest.

The old men who had listened to him for the last twenty years declared that he had never played as he played on that night. At first he was somewhat bolder, somewhat louder than was his wont; as though he were resolved to go out of his accustomed track; but, after a while, he gave that up; that was simply the effect of nervousness, and was continued only while the timidity remained present with him. But he soon forgot everything but his zither and his desire to do it justice. The attention of all present soon became so close that you might have heard a pin fall. Even Fritz sat perfectly still, with his mouth open, and forgot to play with his cane. Lotta's eyes were quickly full of tears, and before long they were rolling down her cheeks. Herr Crippel, though he did not know that he looked at her, was aware that it was so. Then came upon them all there an ecstasy of delicious sadness. As I have said before, every ear was struggling that no softest sound might escape unheard. And then at last the zither was silent, and no one could have marked the moment when it had ceased to sing.

For a few moments there was perfect silence in the room, and the musician still kept his seat with his face turned upon his instrument. He knew well that he had succeeded, that his triumph had been complete, and every moment that the applause was suspended was an added jewel to his crown. But it soon came, the loud shouts of praise, the ringing bravos, the striking of glasses, his own name repeated from all parts of the hall, the clapping of hands, the sweet sound of women's voices, and the waving of white handkerchiefs. Herr Crippel stood up, bowed thrice, wiped his face with a handkerchief, and then sat down on a stool in the corner of the orchestra.

'I don't know much about his being too old,' said Carl Stobel.

'Nor I either,' said Lotta.

'That is what I call music,' said Marie Weber.

'He can play the zither, certainly,' said Fritz; 'but as to the violin, it is more doubtful.'

'He is excellent with both, – with both,' said Lotta, angrily.

Soon after that the party got up to leave the hall, and as they went out they encountered Herr Crippel.

'You have gone beyond yourself tonight,' said Marie, 'and we wish you joy.'

'Oh, no. It was pretty good, was it? With the zither it depends mostly on the atmosphere; whether it is hot, or cold, or wet, or dry, or on I know not what. It is an accident if one plays well. Goodnight to you. Goodnight, Lotta. Goodnight, sir.' And he took off his hat, and bowed – bowed, as it were, expressly to Fritz Planken.

'Herr Crippel,' said Lotta, 'one word with you.' And she dropped behind from Fritz, and returned to the musician. 'Herr Crippel, will you meet me at Sperl's tomorrow night?'

'At Sperl's? No. I do not go to Sperl's any longer, Lotta. You told me that Marie's friend was coming tonight, but you did not tell me of your own.'

'Never mind what I told you, or did not tell you. Herr Crippel, will you come to Sperl's tomorrow?'

'No; you would not dance with me, and I should not care to see you dance with any one else.'

'But I will dance with you.'

'And Planken will be there?'

'Yes, Fritz will be there. He is always there; I cannot help that.'

'No, Lotta; I will not go to Sperl's. I will tell you a little secret. At forty-five one is too old for Sperl's.'

'There are men there every Sunday over fifty – over sixty, I am sure.'

'They are men different in their ways of life from me, my dear. No, I will not go to Sperl's. When will you come and see my mother?'

Lotta promised that she would go and see the Frau Crippel before long, and then tripped off and joined her party.

Stobel and Marie had walked on, while Fritz remained a little behind for Lotta.

'Did you ask him to come to Sperl's tomorrow?' he said.

'To be sure I did.'

'Was that nice of you, Lotta?'

'Why not nice? Nice or not, I did it. Why should not I ask him, if I please?'

'Because I thought I was to have the pleasure of entertaining you; that it was a little party of my own.'

'Very well, Herr Planken,' said Lotta, drawing herself a little away from him: 'if a friend of mine is not welcome at your little party, I certainly shall not join it myself.'

'But, Lotta, does not everyone know what it is that Crippel wishes of you?'

'There is no harm in his wishing. My friends tell me that I am very foolish not to give him what he wishes. But I still have the chance.'

'O yes, no doubt you still have the chance.'

'Herr Crippel is a very good man. He is the best son in the world, and he makes two hundred florins a month.'

'Oh, if that is to count!'

'Of course it is to count. Why should it not count? Would the

Princess Theresa have married the other day if the young prince had had no income to support her?'

'You can do as you please, Lotta.'

'Yes, I can do as I please, certainly. I suppose Adela Bruhl will be at Sperl's tomorrow?'

'I should say so, certainly. I hardly ever knew her to miss her Sunday evening.'

'Nor I. I, too, am fond of dancing – very. I delight in dancing. But I am not a slave to Sperl's, and then I do not care to dance with every one.'

'Adela Bruhl dances very well,' said Fritz.

'That is as one may think. She ought to; for she begins at ten, and goes on till two, always. If there is no one nice for dancing she puts up with some one that is not nice. But all that is nothing to me.'

'Nothing, I should say, Lotta.'

'Nothing in the world. But this is something; last Sunday you danced three times with Adela.'

'Did I? I did not count.'

'I counted. It is my business to watch those things, if you are to be ever anything to me, Fritz. I will not pretend that I am indifferent. I am not indifferent. I care very much about it. Fritz, if you dance tomorrow with Adela you will not dance with me again – either then or ever.' And having uttered this threat she ran on and found Marie, who had just reached the door of the house in which they both lived.

Fritz, as he walked home by himself, was in doubt as to the course which it would be his duty as a man to pursue in reference to the lady whom he loved. He had distinctly heard that lady ask an old admirer of hers to go to Sperl's and dance with her; and yet, within ten minutes afterwards, she had peremptorily commanded him not to dance with another girl! Now, Fritz Planken had a very good opinion of himself, as he was well entitled to have, and was quite aware that other pretty girls besides Lotta Schmidt were within his reach. He did not receive two hundred florins a month, as did Herr Crippel, but then he was five-and-twenty instead of five-and-forty; and, in the matter of money, too, he was doing pretty well. He did love Lotta Schmidt. It would not be easy for him to part with her. But she, too, loved him, as he told himself, and she would hardly push matters to extremities. At any rate, he would not submit to a threat. He would dance with Adela Bruhl, at Sperl's. He thought, at least, that when the time should come he would find it well to dance with her.

Sperl's dancing saloon, in the Tabor Strasse, is a great institution at Vienna. It is open always of a Sunday evening, and dancing there commences at ten, and is continued till two or three o'clock in the morning. There are two large rooms, in one of which the dancers dance, and in the other the dancers and visitors who do not dance, eat, and drink, and smoke continually. But the most wonderful part of Sperl's establishment is this, that there is nothing there to offend any one. Girls dance and men smoke, and there is eating and drinking, and everybody is as well behaved as though there was a protecting phalanx of dowagers sitting round the walls of the saloon. There are no dowagers, though there may probably be a policeman somewhere about the place. To a stranger it is very remarkable that there is so little of what we call flirting – almost none of it. It would seem that to the girls dancing is so much a matter of business, that here at Sperl's they can think of nothing else. To mind their steps, and at the same time their dresses, lest they should be trod upon, to keep full pace with the music, to make all the proper turns at every proper time, and to have the foot fall on the floor at the exact instant; all this is enough, without further excitement. You will see a girl dancing with a man as though the man were a chair, or a stick, or some necessary piece of furniture. She condescends to use his services, but as soon as the dance is over she sends him away. She hardly speaks a word to him, if a word! She has come there to dance, and not to talk; unless, indeed, like Marie Weber and Lotta Schmidt, she has a recognised lover there of her very own.

At about half-past ten Marie and Lotta entered the saloon, and paid their kreutzers and sat themselves down on seats in the further saloon, from which through open archways they could see the dancers. Neither Carl nor Fritz had come as yet, and the girls were quite content to wait. It was to be presumed that they would be there before the men, and they both understood that the real dancing was not commenced early in the evening. It might be all very well for such as Adela Bruhl to dance with any one who came at ten o'clock, but Lotta Schmidt would not care to amuse herself after that fashion. As to Marie, she was to be married after another week, and of course she would dance with no one but Carl Stobel.

'Look at her,' said Lotta, pointing with her foot to a fair girl, very pretty, but with hair somewhat untidy, who at this moment was waltzing in the other room. 'That lad is a waiter from the Minden hotel. I know him. She would dance with any one.'

'I suppose she likes dancing, and there is no harm in the boy,' said Marie.

'No, there is no harm, and if she likes it I do not begrudge it her. See what red hands she has.'

'She is of that complexion,' said Marie.

'Yes, she is of that complexion all over; look at her face. At any rate she might have better shoes on. Did you ever see anybody so untidy?'

'She is very pretty,' said Marie.

'Yes, she is pretty. There is no doubt she is pretty. She is not a native here. Her people are from Munich. Do you know, Marie, I think girls are always thought more of in other countries than in their own.'

Soon after this Carl and Fritz came in together, and Fritz, as he passed across the end of the first saloon, spoke a word or two to Adela. Lotta saw this, but determined that she would take no offence at so small a matter. Fritz need not have stopped to speak, but his doing so might be all very well. At any rate, if she did quarrel with him she would quarrel on a plain, intelligible ground. Within two minutes Carl and Marie were dancing, and Fritz had asked Lotta to stand up. 'I will wait a little,' said she, 'I never like to begin much before eleven.'

'As you please,' said Fritz; and he sat down in the chair which Marie had occupied. Then he played with his cane, and as he did so his eyes followed the steps of Adela Bruhl.

'She dances very well,' said Lotta.

'H – m – m, yes.' Fritz did not choose to bestow any strong praise on Adela's dancing.

'Yes, Fritz, she does dance well, – very well, indeed. And she is never tired. If you ask me whether I like her style, I cannot quite say that I do. It is not what we do here – not exactly.'

'She has lived in Vienna since she was a child.'

'It is in the blood then, I suppose. Look at her fair hair, all blowing about. She is not like one of us.'

'Oh no, she is not.'

'That she is very pretty, I quite admit,' said Lotta. 'Those soft grey eyes are delicious. Is it not a pity she has no eyebrows?'

'But she has eyebrows.'

'Ah! you have been closer than I, and you have seen them. I have never danced with her, and I cannot see them. Of course they are there – more or less.'

After a while the dancing ceased, and Adela Bruhl came up into the supper-room, passing the seats on which Fritz and Lotta were sitting.

'Are you not going to dance, Fritz?' she said, with a smile, as she passed them.

'Go, go,' said Lotta; 'why do you not go? She has invited you.'

'No; she has not invited me. She spoke to us both.'

'She did not speak to me, for my name is not Fritz. I do not see how you can help going, when she asked you so prettily.'

'I shall be in plenty of time presently. Will you dance now, Lotta? They are going to begin a waltz, and we will have a quadrille afterwards.'

'No, Herr Planken, I will not dance just now.'

'Herr Planken, is it? You want to quarrel with me then, Lotta.'

'I do not want to be one of two. I will not be one of two. Adela Bruhl is very pretty, and I advise you to go to her. I was told only yesterday her father can give her fifteen hundred florins of fortune! For me – I have no father.'

'But you may have a husband tomorrow.'

'Yes, that is true, and a good one. Oh, such a good one!'

'What do you mean by that?'

'You go and dance with Adela Bruhl, and you shall see what I mean.'

Fritz had some idea in his own mind, more or less clearly developed, that his fate, as regarded Lotta Schmidt, now lay in his own hands. He undoubtedly desired to have Lotta for his own. He would have married her there and then – at that moment, had it been possible. He had quite made up his mind that he preferred her much to Adela Bruhl, though Adela Bruhl had fifteen hundred florins. But he did not like to endure tyranny, even from Lotta, and he did not know how to escape the tyranny otherwise than by dancing with Adela. He paused a moment, swinging his cane, endeavouring to think how he might best assert his manhood and yet not offend the girl he loved. But he found that to assert his manhood was now his first duty.

'Well, Lotta,' he said, 'since you are so cross with me, I will ask Adela to dance.' And in two minutes he was spinning round the room with Adela Bruhl in his arms.

'Certainly she dances very well,' said Lotta, smiling, to Marie, who had now come back to her seat.

'Very well,' said Marie, who was out of breath.

'And so does he.'

'Beautifully,' said Marie.

'Is it not a pity that I should have lost such a partner for ever?'

'Lotta!'

'It is true. Look here, Marie, there is my hand upon it. I will never dance with him again – never – never – never. Why was he so hard upon Herr Crippel last night?'

'Was he hard upon Herr Crippel?'

'He said that Herr Crippel was too old to play the zither; too old! Some people are too young to understand. I shall go home, I shall not stay to sup with you tonight.'

'Lotta, you must stay for supper.'

'I will not sup at his table. I have quarrelled with him. It is all over. Fritz Planken is as free as the air for me.'

'Lotta, do not say anything in a hurry. At any rate do not do anything in a hurry.'

'I do not mean to do anything at all. It is simply this – I do not care very much for Fritz, after all. I don't think I ever did. It is all very well to wear your clothes nicely, but if that is all, what does it come to? If he could play the zither, now!'

'There are other things except playing the zither. They say he is a good book-keeper.'

'I don't like book-keeping. He has to be at his hotel from eight in the morning till eleven at night.'

'You know best.'

'I am not so sure of that. I wish I did know best. But I never saw such a girl as you are. How you change! It was only yesterday you scolded me because I did not wish to be the wife of your dear friend Crippel.'

'Herr Crippel is a very good man.'

'You go away with your good man! You have got a good man of your own. He is standing there waiting for you, like a gander on one leg. He wants you to dance; go away.' Then Marie did go away, and Lotta was left alone by herself. She certainly had behaved badly to Fritz, and she was aware of it. She excused herself to herself by remembering that she had never yet given Fritz a promise. She was her own mistress, and had, as yet, a right to do what she pleased with herself. He had asked her for her love, and she had not told him that he should not have it. That was all. Herr Crippel had asked her a dozen times, and she had at last told him definitely, positively, that there was no hope for him. Herr Crippel, of course, would not ask her again – so she told herself. But if there was no such person as Herr Crippel in all the world, she would have nothing more to do with Fritz Planken – nothing more to do with him as a lover. He had given her fair ground for a quarrel, and she would take advantage of it. Then as she sat still while they were dancing, she closed her eyes and thought of the zither and of the zitherist. She remained alone for a long time. The musicians in Vienna will play a waltz for twenty minutes, and the same dancers will continue to dance almost without a pause; and then, almost immediately afterwards, there was a quadrille. Fritz, who was resolved to put down tyranny, stood up with Adela for the quadrille also. 'I am so glad,' said Lotta to herself. 'I will wait till this is over, and then I will say goodnight to Marie, and will go home.' Three or four men had asked her to dance, but she had

refused. She would not dance tonight at all. She was inclined, she
thought, to be a little serious, and would go home. At last Fritz returned to her, and bade her come to supper. He was resolved to see
how far his mode of casting off tyranny might be successful, so he
approached her with a smile, and offered to take her to his table as
though nothing had happened.

'My friend,' she said, 'your table is laid for four, and the places
will all be filled.'

'The table is laid for five,' said Fritz.

'It is one too many. I shall sup with my friend, Herr Crippel.'

'Herr Crippel is not here.'

'Is he not? Ah me! then I shall be alone, and I must go to bed
supperless. Thank you, no, Herr Planken.'

'And what will Marie say?'

'I hope she will enjoy the nice dainties you will give her. Marie is all
right. Marie's fortune is made. Woe is me! my fortune is to seek.
There is one thing certain, it is not to be found here in this room.'

Then Fritz turned on his heel and went away; and as he went
Lotta saw the figure of a man, as he made his way slowly and hesi-
tatingly into the saloon from the outer passage. He was dressed in a
close frock-coat, and had on a hat of which she knew the shape as

well as she did the make of her own gloves. 'If he has not come after all!' she said to herself. Then she turned herself a little round, and drew her chair somewhat into an archway, so that Herr Crippel should not see her readily.

The other four had settled themselves at their table, Marie having said a word of reproach to Lotta as she passed. Now, on a sudden, she got up from her seat and crossed to her friend.

'Herr Crippel is here,' she said.

'Of course he is here,' said Lotta.

'But you did not expect him?'

'Ask Fritz if I did not say I would sup with Herr Crippel. You ask him. But I shall not, all the same. Do not say a word. I shall steal away when nobody is looking.'

The musician came wandering up the room, and had looked into every corner before he had even found the supper-table at which the four were sitting. And then he did not see Lotta. He took off his hat as he addressed Marie, and asked some questions as to the absent one.

'She is waiting for you somewhere, Herr Crippel,' said Fritz, as he filled Adela's glass with wine.

'For me?' said Herr Crippel as he looked round. 'No, she does not expect me.' And in the meantime Lotta had left her seat, and was hurrying away to the door.

'There! there!' said Marie; 'you will be too late if you do not run.'

Then Herr Crippel did run, and caught Lotta as she was taking her hat from the old woman, who had the girls' hats and shawls in charge near the door.

'What! Herr Crippel, you at Sperl's? When you told me expressly, in so many words, that you would not come! That is not behaving well to me, certainly.'

'What, my coming? Is that behaving bad?'

'No; but why did you say you would not come when I asked you? You have come to meet some one. Who is it?'

'You, Lotta; you.'

'And yet you refused me when I asked you! Well, and now you are here, what are you going to do? You will not dance.'

'I will dance with you, if you will put up with me.'

'No, I will not dance. I am too old. I have given it up. I shall come to Sperl's no more after this. Dancing is a folly.'

'Lotta, you are laughing at me now.'

'Very well; if you like, you may have it so.' By this time he had brought her back into the room, and was walking up and down the length of the saloon with her. 'But it is no use our walking about here,' she said. 'I was just going home, and now, if you please, I will go.'

'Not yet, Lotta.'

'Yes; now, if you please.'

'But why are you not supping with them?'

'Because it did not suit me. You see there are four. Five is a foolish number for a supper party.'

'Will you sup with me, Lotta?' She did not answer him at once. 'Lotta,' he said, 'if you sup with me now you must sup with me always. How shall it be?'

'Always? No. I am very hungry now, but I do not want supper always. I cannot sup with you always, Herr Crippel.'

'But you will tonight?'

'Yes, tonight.'

'Then it shall be always.'

And the musician marched up to a table, and threw his hat down, and ordered such a supper that Lotta Schmidt was frightened. And when presently Carl Stobel and Marie Weber came up to their table – for Fritz Planken did not come near them again that evening – Herr Crippel bowed courteously to the diamond-cutter, and asked him when he was to be married. 'Marie says it shall be next Sunday,' said Carl.

'And I will be married the Sunday afterwards,' said Herr Crippel. 'Yes; and there is my wife.'

And he pointed across the table with both his hands to Lotta Schmidt.

'Herr Crippel, how can you say that?' said Lotta.

'Is it not true, my dear?'

'In fourteen days! No, certainly not. It is out of the question.'

But, nevertheless, what Herr Crippel said came true, and on the next Sunday but one he took Lotta Schmidt home to his house as his wife.

'It was all because of the zither,' Lotta said to her old mother-in-law. 'If he had not played the zither that night I should not have been here now.'

CHRISTMAS AT THOMPSON HALL

1: MRS BROWN'S SUCCESS

Everyone remembers the severity of the Christmas of 187–. I will
not designate the year more closely, lest I should enable those who
are too curious to investigate the circumstances of this story, and
inquire into details which I do not intend to make known. That
winter, however, was especially severe, and the cold of the last ten
days of December was more felt, I think, in Paris than in any part of
England. It may, indeed, be doubted whether there is any town in
any country in which thoroughly bad weather is more afflicting
than in the French capital. Snow and hail seem to be colder there,
and fires certainly are less warm, than in London. And then there is
a feeling among visitors to Paris that Paris ought to be gay; that
gaiety, prettiness, and liveliness are its aims, as money, commerce,
and general business are the aims of London – which with its outside sombre darkness does often seem to want an excuse for its
ugliness. But on this occasion, at this Christmas of 187–, Paris was
neither gay nor pretty nor lively. You could not walk the streets
without being ankle deep, not in snow, but in snow that had just
become slush; and there was falling throughout the day and night of
the 23rd of December a succession of damp half-frozen abomina-
tions from the sky which made it almost impossible for men and
women to go about their business.

It was at ten o'clock on that evening that an English lady and
gentleman arrived at the Grand Hotel on the Boulevard des Italiens.
As I have reasons for concealing the names of this married couple I
will call them Mr and Mrs Brown. Now I wish it to be understood
that in all the general affairs of life this gentleman and this lady
lived happily together, with all the amenities which should bind a
husband and a wife. Mrs Brown was one of a wealthy family, and
Mr Brown, when he married her, had been relieved from the necessity
of earning his bread. Nevertheless she had at once yielded to him
when he expressed a desire to spend the winters of their life in the
south of France; and he, though he was by disposition somewhat
idle, and but little prone to the energetic occupations of life, would

generally allow himself, at other periods of the year, to be carried hither and thither by her, whose more robust nature delighted in the excitement of travelling. But on this occasion there had been a little difference between them.

Early in December an intimation had reached Mrs Brown at Pau that on the coming Christmas there was to be a great gathering of all the Thompsons in the Thompson family hall at Stratford-le-Bow, and that she who had been a Thompson was desired to join the party with her husband. On this occasion her only sister was desirous of introducing to the family generally a most excellent young man to whom she had recently become engaged. The Thompsons – the real name, however, is in fact concealed – were a numerous and a thriving people. There were uncles and cousins and brothers who had all done well in the world, and who were all likely to do better still. One had lately been returned to Parliament for the Essex Flats, and was at the time of which I am writing a conspicuous member of the gallant Conservative majority. It was partly in triumph at this success that the great Christmas gathering of the Thompsons was to be held, and an opinion had been expressed by the legislator himself that should Mrs Brown, with her husband, fail to join the family on this happy occasion she and he would be regarded as being but *fainéant* Thompsons.

Since her marriage, which was an affair now nearly eight years old, Mrs Brown had never passed a Christmas in England. The desirability of doing so had often been mooted by her. Her very soul craved the festivities of holly and mince-pies. There had ever been meetings of the Thompsons at Thompson Hall, though meetings not so significant, not so important to the family, as this one which was now to be collected. More than once had she expressed a wish to see old Christmas again in the old house among the old faces. But her husband had always pleaded a certain weakness about his throat and chest as a reason for remaining among the delights of Pau. Year after year she had yielded, and now this loud summons had come.

It was not without considerable trouble that she had induced Mr Brown to come as far as Paris. Most unwillingly had he left Pau; and then, twice on his journey – both at Bordeaux and Tours – he had made an attempt to return. From the first moment he had pleaded his throat, and when at last he had consented to make the journey he had stipulated for sleeping at those two towns and at Paris. Mrs Brown, who, without the slightest feeling of fatigue, could have made the journey from Pau to Stratford without stopping, had assented to everything – so that they might be at Thompson Hall on

Christmas Eve. When Mr Brown uttered his unavailing complaints
at the two first towns at which they stayed, she did not perhaps
quite believe all that he said of his own condition. We know how
prone the strong are to suspect the weakness of the weak – as the
weak are to be disgusted by the strength of the strong. There were
perhaps a few words between them on the journey, but the result
had hitherto been in favour of the lady. She had succeeded in bringing Mr Brown as far as Paris.

Had the occasion been less important, no doubt she would have
yielded. The weather had been bad even when they left Pau, but as
they had made their way northwards it had become worse and still
worse. As they left Tours Mr Brown, in a hoarse whisper, had declared his conviction that the journey would kill him. Mrs Brown,
however, had unfortunately noticed half an hour before that he had
scolded the waiter on the score of an overcharged franc or two
with a loud and clear voice. Had she really believed that there was
danger, or even suffering, she would have yielded – but no woman is
satisfied in such a matter to be taken in by false pretences. She observed that he ate a good dinner on his way to Paris, and that he took
a small glass of cognac with complete relish – which a man really
suffering from bronchitis surely would not do. So she persevered, and
brought him into Paris, late in the evening, in the midst of all that
slush and snow. Then, as they sat down to supper, she thought that
he did speak hoarsely, and her loving feminine heart began to mis-
give her.

But this now was at any rate clear to her – that he could not be
worse off by going on to London than he would be should he remain
in Paris. If a man is to be ill he had better be ill in the bosom of his
family than at an hotel. What comfort could he have, what relief in
that huge barrack? As for the cruelty of the weather, London could
not be worse than Paris, and then she thought she had heard that
sea air is good for a sore throat. In that bedroom which had been
allotted to them *au quatrième*, they could not even get a decent fire.
It would in every way be wrong now to forego the great Christmas
gathering when nothing could be gained by staying in Paris.

She had perceived that as her husband became really ill he became also more tractable and less disputatious. Immediately after
that little glass of cognac he had declared that he would be —— if he
would go beyond Paris, and she began to fear that, after all, everything would have been done in vain. But as they went down to
supper between ten and eleven he was more subdued, and merely
remarked that this journey would, he was sure, be the death of him.
It was half-past eleven when they got back to their bedroom, and

then he seemed to speak with good sense – and also with much real apprehension. 'If I can't get something to relieve me I know I shall never make my way on,' he said. It was intended that they should leave the hotel at half-past five the next morning, so as to arrive at Stratford, travelling by the tidal train, at half-past seven on Christmas Eve. The early hour, the long journey, the infamous weather, the prospect of that horrid gulf between Boulogne and Folkestone, would have been as nothing to Mrs Brown, had it not been for that settled look of anguish which had now pervaded her husband's face. 'If you don't find something to relieve me I shall never live through

it,' he said again, sinking back into the questionable comfort of a Parisian hotel arm-chair.

'But, my dear, what can I do?' she asked, almost in tears, standing over him and caressing him. He was a thin, genteel-looking man, with a fine long, soft brown beard, a little bald at the top of the head, but certainly a genteel-looking man. She loved him dearly, and in her softer moods was apt to spoil him with her caresses. 'What can I do, my dearie? You know I would do anything if I could. Get into bed, my pet, and be warm, and then tomorrow morning you will be all right.' At this moment he was preparing himself for his bed, and she was assisting him. Then she tied a piece of flannel round his throat, and kissed him, and put him in beneath the bed-clothes.

'I'll tell you what you can do,' he said very hoarsely. His voice was so bad now that she could hardly hear him. So she crept close to him, and bent over him. She would do anything if he would only say what.

Then he told her what was his plan. Down in the salon he had seen a large jar of mustard standing on a sideboard. As he left the room he had observed that this had not been withdrawn with the other appurtenances of the meal. If she could manage to find her way down there, taking with her a handkerchief folded for the purpose, and if she could then appropriate a part of the contents of that jar, and, returning with her prize, apply it to his throat, he thought that he could get some relief, so that he might be able to leave his bed the next morning at five. 'But I am afraid it will be very disagreeable for you to go down all alone at this time of night,' he croaked out in a piteous whisper.

'Of course I'll go,' said she. 'I don't mind going in the least. Nobody will bite me,' and she at once began to fold a clean handkerchief. 'I won't be two minutes, my darling, and if there is a grain of mustard in the house I'll have it on your chest immediately.' She was a woman not easily cowed, and the journey down into the salon was nothing to her. Before she went she tucked the clothes carefully up to his ears, and then she started.

To run along the first corridor till she came to a flight of stairs was easy enough, and easy enough to descend them. Then there was another corridor, and another flight, and a third corridor, and a third flight, and she began to think that she was wrong. She found herself in a part of the hotel which she had not hitherto visited, and soon discovered by looking through an open door or two that she had found her way among a set of private sitting-rooms which she had not seen before. Then she tried to make her way back, up the same stairs and through the same passages, so that she might start again. She was beginning to think that she had lost herself altogether, and that she would be able to find neither the salon nor her bedroom, when she happily met the night-porter. She was dressed in a loose white dressing-gown, with a white net over her loose hair, and with white worsted slippers. I ought perhaps to have described her personal appearance sooner. She was a large woman, with a commanding bust, thought by some to be handsome, after the manner of Juno. But with strangers there was a certain severity of manner about her – a fortification, as it were, of her virtue against all possible attacks – a declared determination to maintain, at all points, the beautiful character of a British matron, which, much as it had been appreciated at Thompson Hall, had met with some ill-natured criticism among French men and women. At Pau she had been called La Fière Anglaise. The name had reached her own ears and those of her husband. He had been much annoyed, but she had taken it in good part – had, indeed, been somewhat proud of the title – and had endeavoured to live up to it. With her husband she could, on occasion, be soft, but she was of opinion that with other men a British matron should be stern. She was now greatly in want of assistance; but, nevertheless, when she met the porter she remembered her character. 'I have lost my way wandering through these horrid passages,' she said, in her severest tone. This was in answer to some question from him – some question to which her reply was given very slowly. Then when he asked where Madame wished to go, she paused, again thinking what destination she would announce. No doubt the man could take her back to her bedroom, but if so, the mustard must be renounced, and with the mustard, as she now feared, all hope of reaching Thompson Hall on Christmas Eve. But she, though she was in many respects a brave woman, did not dare to tell the man that she was prowling about the hotel in order that she might make a midnight raid upon the mustard pot. She paused, therefore, for a moment, that she might collect her thoughts, erecting her head as she did so in her best Juno fashion, till the porter was lost in admiration. Thus she gained time to fabricate a tale. She had, she said, dropped her handkerchief under the supper-table; would he show her the way to the salon, in order that she might pick it up? But the porter did more than that, and accompanied her to the room in which she had supped.

Here, of course, there was a prolonged, and, it need hardly be said, a vain search. The good-natured man insisted on emptying an enormous receptacle of soiled table-napkins, and on turning them over one by one, in order that the lady's property might be found. The lady stood by unhappy, but still patient, and, as the man was stooping to his work, her eye was on the mustard pot. There it was, capable of containing enough to blister the throats of a score of sufferers. She edged off a little towards it while the man was busy, trying to persuade herself that he would surely forgive her if she took the mustard, and told him her whole story. But the descent from her Juno bearing would have been so great! She must have owned, not only to the quest for mustard, but also to a fib – and she could not do it. The porter was at last of opinion that Madame must have made a mistake, and Madame acknowledged that she was afraid it was so.

With a longing, lingering eye, with an eye turned back, oh! so sadly, to the great jar, she left the room, the porter leading the way. She assured him that she could find it by herself, but he would not leave her till he had put her on to the proper passage. The journey seemed to be longer now even than before, but as she ascended the many stairs she swore to herself that she would not even yet be baulked of her object. Should her husband want comfort for his poor throat, and the comfort be there within her reach, and he not have it? She counted every stair as she went up, and marked every turn well. She was sure now that she would know the way, and that she could return to the room without fault. She would go back to the salon. Even though the man should encounter her again, she would go boldly forward and seize the remedy which her poor husband so grievously required.

'Ah, yes,' she said, when the porter told her that her room, No. 333, was in the corridor which they had then reached, 'I know it all now. I am so much obliged. Do not come a step further.' He was anxious to accompany her up to the very door, but she stood in the passage and prevailed. He lingered awhile – naturally. Unluckily she had brought no money with her, and could not give him the two-franc piece which he had earned. Nor could she fetch it from her room, feeling that were she to return to her husband without the mustard no second attempt would be possible. The disappointed man turned on his heel at last, and made his way down the stairs and along the passage. It seemed to her to be almost an eternity while she listened to his still audible footsteps. She had gone on, creeping noiselessly up to the very door of her room, and there she stood, shading the candle in her hand, till she thought that the man must have wandered away into some furthest corner of that endless building. Then she turned once more and retraced her steps.

There was no difficulty now as to the way. She knew it, every stair. At the head of each flight she stood and listened, but not a sound was to be heard, and then she went on again. Her heart beat high with anxious desire to achieve her object, and at the same time with fear. What might have been explained so easily at first would now be as difficult of explanation. At last she was in the great public vestibule, which she was now visiting for the third time, and of which, at her last visit, she had taken the bearings accurately. The door was there – closed, indeed, but it opened easily to the hand. In the hall, and on the stairs, and along the passages, there had been gas, but here there was no light beyond that given by the little taper which she carried. When accompanied by the porter she had not feared the darkness, but now there was something in the obscurity which made her dread to walk the length of the room up to the mustard jar. She paused, and listened, and trembled. Then she thought of the glories of Thompson Hall, of the genial warmth of a British Christmas, of that proud legislator who was her first cousin, and with a rush she made good the distance, and laid her hand upon the copious delf. She looked round, but there was no one there; no sound was heard; not the distant creak of a shoe, not a rattle from one of those thousand doors. As she paused with her fair hand upon the top of the jar, while the other held the white cloth on which the medicinal compound was to be placed, she looked like Lady Macbeth as she listened at Duncan's chamber door.

There was no doubt as to the sufficiency of the contents. The jar was full nearly up to the lips. The mixture was, no doubt, very different from that good wholesome English mustard which your cook makes fresh for you, with a little water, in two minutes. It was impregnated with a sour odour, and was, to English eyes, unwholesome of colour. But still it was mustard. She seized the horn spoon, and without further delay spread an ample sufficiency on the folded square of the handkerchief. Then she commenced to hurry her return.

But still there was a difficulty, no thought of which had occurred to her before. The candle occupied one hand, so that she had but the other for the sustenance of her treasure. Had she brought a plate or saucer from the salon, it would have been all well. As it was she was obliged to keep her eye intent on her right hand, and to proceed very slowly on her return journey. She was surprised to find what an aptitude the thing had to slip from her grasp. But still she progressed slowly, and was careful not to miss a turning. At last she was safe at her chamber door. There it was, No. 333.

2: MRS BROWN'S FAILURE

With her eye still fixed upon her burden, she glanced up at the number of the door – 333. She had been determined all through not to forget that. Then she turned the latch and crept in. The chamber also was dark after the gaslight on the stairs, but that was so much the better. She herself had put out the two candles on the dressing-table before she had left her husband. As she was closing the door behind her she paused, and could hear that he was sleeping. She was well aware that she had been long absent – quite long enough for a man to fall into slumber who was given that way. She must have been gone, she thought, fully an hour. There had been no end to that turning over of napkins which she had so well known to be altogether vain. She paused at the centre table of the room, still looking at the mustard, which she now delicately dried from off her hand. She had had no idea that it would have been so difficult to carry so light and so small an affair. But there it was, and nothing had been lost. She took some small instrument from the washing-stand, and with the handle collected the flowing fragments into the centre. Then the question occurred to her whether, as her husband was sleeping so sweetly, it would be well to disturb him. She listened again, and felt that the slight murmur of a snore with which her ears were regaled was altogether free from any real malady in the throat. Then it occurred to her, that after all, fatigue perhaps had only made him cross. She bethought herself how, during the whole journey, she had failed to believe in his illness. What meals he had eaten! How thoroughly he had been able to enjoy his full complement of cigars! And then that glass of brandy, against which she had raised her voice slightly in feminine opposition. And now he was sleeping there like an infant, with full, round, perfected, almost sonorous workings of the throat. Who does not know that sound, almost of two rusty bits of iron scratching against each other, which comes from a suffering windpipe? There was no semblance of that here. Why disturb him when he was so thoroughly enjoying that rest which, more certainly than anything else, would fit him for the fatigue of the morrow's journey?

I think that, after all her labour, she would have left the pungent cataplasm on the table, and have crept gently into bed beside him, had not a thought suddenly struck her of the great injury he had been doing her if he were not really ill. To send her down there, in a strange hotel, wandering among the passages, in the middle of the night, subject to the contumely of anyone who might meet her, on a commission which, if it were not sanctified by absolute necessity, would be so thoroughly objectionable! At this moment she hardly did believe that he had ever really been ill. Let him have the cataplasm; if not as a remedy, then as a punishment. It could, at any rate, do him no harm. It was with an idea of avenging rather than of justifying the past labours of the night that she proceeded at once to quick action.

Leaving the candle on the table so that she might steady her right hand with the left, she hurried stealthily to the bedside. Even though he was behaving badly to her, she would not cause him discomfort by waking him roughly. She would do a wife's duty to him as a British matron should. She would not only put the warm mixture on his neck, but would sit carefully by him for twenty minutes, so that she might relieve him from it when the proper period should have come for removing the counter irritation from his throat. There would doubtless be some little difficulty in this – in collecting the mustard after it had served her purpose. Had she been at home, surrounded by her own comforts, the application would have been made with some delicate linen bag, through which the pungency of the spice would have penetrated with strength sufficient for the purpose. But the circumstance of the occasion had not admitted this. She had, she felt, done wonders in achieving so much success as this which she had obtained. If there should be anything disagreeable in the operation he must submit to it. He had asked for mustard for his throat, and mustard he should have.

As these thoughts passed quickly through her mind, leaning over him in the dark, with her eye fixed on the mixture lest it should slip, she gently raised his flowing beard with her left hand, and with her other inverted rapidly, steadily but very softly fixed the handkerchief on his throat. From the bottom of his chin to the spot at which the collar bones meeting together form the orifice of the chest it covered the whole noble expanse. There was barely time for a glance, but never had she been more conscious of the grand proportions of that manly throat. A sweet feeling of pity came upon her, causing her to determine to relieve his sufferings in the shorter space of fifteen minutes. He had been lying on his back, with his lips apart, and, as she held back his beard, that and her hand nearly covered the features of his face. But he made no violent effort to free himself from the encounter. He did not even move an arm or a leg. He simply emitted a snore louder than any that had come before. She was aware that it was not his wont to be so loud – that there was generally something more delicate and perhaps more querulous in his nocturnal voice, but then the present circumstances were exceptional. She dropped the beard very softly – and there on the pillow before her lay the face of a stranger. She had put the mustard plaster on the wrong man.

Not Priam wakened in the dead of night, not Dido when first she learned that Æneas had fled, not Othello when he learned that Desdemona had been chaste, not Medea when she became conscious of her slaughtered children, could have been more struck with horror than was this British matron as she stood for a moment gazing with awe on that stranger's bed. One vain, half-completed, snatching grasp she made at the handkerchief, and then drew back her hand. If she were to touch him would he not wake at once, and find her standing there in his bedroom? And then how could she explain it? By what words could she so quickly make him know the circumstances of that strange occurrence that he should accept it all before he had said a word that might offend her? For a moment she stood all but paralyzed after that faint ineffectual movement of her arm. Then he stirred his head uneasily on the pillow, opened wider his lips, and twice in rapid succession snored louder than before. She started back a couple of paces, and with her body placed between him and the candle, with her face averted, but with her hand still resting on the foot of the bed, she endeavoured to think what duty required of her.

She had injured the man. Though she had done it most unwittingly, there could be no doubt but that she had injured him. If for a moment she could be brave, the injury might in truth be little; but how disastrous might be the consequences if she were now in her cowardice to leave him, who could tell? Applied for fifteen to twenty minutes a mustard plaster may be the salvation of a throat ill at ease, but if left there throughout the night upon the neck of a strong man, ailing nothing, only too prone in his strength to slumber soundly, how sad, how painful, for aught she knew how dangerous might be the effects! And surely it was an error which any man with a heart in his bosom would pardon! Judging from what little she had seen of him she thought that he must have a heart in his bosom. Was it not her duty to wake him, and then quietly to extricate him from the embarrassment which she had brought upon him?

But in doing this what words should she use? How should she wake him? How should she make him understand her goodness, her beneficence, her sense of duty, before he should have jumped from the bed and rushed to the bell, and have summoned all above and all below to the rescue? 'Sir, sir, do not move, do not stir, do not scream. I have put a mustard plaster on your throat, thinking that you were my husband. As yet no harm has been done. Let me take it off, and then hold your peace for ever.' Where is the man of such native constancy and grace of spirit that, at the first moment of waking with a shock, he could hear these words from the mouth of an unknown woman by his bedside, and at once obey them to the letter? Would he not surely jump from his bed, with that horrid compound falling about him – from which there could be no complete relief unless he would keep his present attitude without a motion? The picture which presented itself to her mind as to his probable conduct was so terrible that she found herself unable to incur the risk.

Then an idea presented itself to her mind. We all know how in a moment quick thoughts will course through the subtle brain. She would find that porter and send him to explain it all. There should be no concealment now. She would tell the story and would bid him to find the necessary aid. Alas! as she told herself that she would do so, she knew well that she was only running from the danger which it was her duty to encounter. Once again she put out her hand as though to return along the bed. Then thrice he snorted louder than before, and moved up his knee uneasily beneath the clothes as though the sharpness of the mustard were already working upon his skin. She watched him for a moment longer, and then, with the candle in her hand, she fled.

Poor human nature! Had he been an old man, even a middle-aged man, she would not have left him to his unmerited sufferings. As it was, though she completely recognised her duty, and knew what justice and goodness demanded of her, she could not do it. But there was still left to her that plan of sending the night-porter to him. It was not till she was out of the room and had gently closed the door behind her, that she began to bethink herself how she had made the mistake. With a glance of her eye she looked up, and then saw the number on the door: 353. Remarking to herself, with a Briton's natural criticism on things French, that those horrid foreigners do not know how to make their figures, she scudded rather than ran along the corridor, and then down some stairs and along another passage – so that she might not be found in the neighbourhood should the poor man in his agony rush rapidly from his bed.

In the confusion of her first escape she hardly ventured to look for her own passage – nor did she in the least know how she had lost her way when she came upstairs with the mustard in her hand. But at the present moment her chief object was the night-porter. She went on descending till she came again to that vestibule, and looking up at the clock saw that it was now past one. It was not yet midnight when she left her husband, but she was not at all astonished at the lapse of time. It seemed to her as though she had passed a night among these miseries. And, oh, what a night! But there was yet much to be done. She must find that porter, and then return to her own suffering husband. Ah – what now should she say to him? If he should really be ill, how should she assuage him? And yet how more than ever necessary was it that they should leave that hotel early in the morning – that they should leave Paris by the very earliest and quickest train that would take them as fugitives from their present dangers! The door of the salon was open, but she had no courage to go in search of a second supply. She would have lacked strength to carry it up the stairs. Where now, oh, where, was that man? From the vestibule she made her way into the hall, but everything seemed to be deserted. Through the glass she could see a light in the court beyond, but she could not bring herself to endeavour even to open the hall doors.

And now she was very cold – chilled to her very bones. All this had been done at Christmas, and during such severity of weather as had never before been experienced by living Parisians. A feeling of great pity for herself gradually came upon her. What wrong had she done that she should be so grievously punished? Why should she be driven to wander about in this way till her limbs were failing her? And then, so absolutely important as it was that her strength should support her in the morning! The man would not die even though he were left there without aid, to rid himself of the cataplasm as best he might. Was it absolutely necessary that she should disgrace herself?

But she could not even procure the means of disgracing herself, if that telling her story to the night-porter would have been a disgrace. She did not find him, and at last resolved to make her way back to her own room without further quest. She began to think that she had done all that she could do. No man was ever killed by a mustard plaster on his throat. His discomfort at the worst would not be worse than hers had been – or too probably than that of her poor husband. So she went back up the stairs and along the passages, and made her way on this occasion to the door of her room without any difficulty. The way was so well known to her that she could not but wonder that she had failed before. But now her hands had been empty, and her eyes had been at her full command. She looked up, and there was the number, very manifest on this occasion – 333. She opened the door most gently, thinking that her husband might be sleeping as soundly as that other man had slept, and she crept into the room.

3: MRS BROWN ATTEMPTS TO ESCAPE

But her husband was not sleeping. He was not even in bed, as she had left him. She found him sitting there before the fire-place, on which one half-burned log still retained a spark of what had once pretended to be a fire. Nothing more wretched than his appearance could be imagined. There was a single lighted candle on the table, on which he was leaning with his two elbows, while his head rested between his hands. He had on a dressing-gown over his night-shirt, but otherwise was not clothed. He shivered audibly, or rather shook himself with the cold, and made the table to chatter as she entered the room. Then he groaned, and let his head fall from his hands on to the table. It occurred to her at the moment as she recognised the tone of his querulous voice, and as she saw the form of his neck, that she must have been deaf and blind when she had mistaken that stalwart stranger for her husband. 'Oh, my dear,' she said, 'why are you not in bed?' He answered nothing in words, but only groaned again. 'Why did you get up? I left you warm and comfortable.'

'Where have you been all night?' he half whispered, half croaked, with an agonising effort.

'I have been looking for the mustard.'

'Have been looking all night and haven't found it? Where have you been?'

She refused to speak a word to him till she had got him into bed, and then she told her story! But, alas, that which she told was not the true story! As she was persuading him to go back to his rest, and while she arranged the clothes again around him, she with difficulty made up her mind as to what she would do and what she would say. Living or dying he must be made to start for Thompson Hall at half-past five on the next morning. It was no longer a question of the amenities of Christmas, no longer a mere desire to satisfy the family ambition of her own people, no longer an anxiety to see her new brother-in-law. She was conscious that there was in that house one whom she had deeply injured, and from whose vengeance, even from whose aspect, she must fly. How could she endure to see that face which she was so well sure that she would recognise, or to hear the slightest sound of that voice which would be quite familiar to her ears, though it had never spoken a word in her hearing? She must certainly fly on the wings of the earliest train which would carry her towards the old house; but in order that she might do so she must propitiate her husband.

So she told her story. She had gone forth, as he had bade her, in search of the mustard, and then had suddenly lost her way. Up and down the house she had wandered, perhaps nearly a dozen times. 'Had she met no one?' he asked in that raspy, husky whisper. 'Surely there must have been some one about the hotel! Nor was it possible that she could have been roaming about all those hours.' 'Only one hour, my dear,' she said. Then there was a question about the duration of time, in which both of them waxed angry, and as she became angry her husband waxed stronger, and as he became violent beneath the clothes the comfortable idea returned to her that he was not perhaps so ill as he would seem to be. She found herself driven to tell him something about the porter, having to account for that lapse of time by explaining how she had driven the poor man to search for the handkerchief which she had never lost.

'Why did you not tell him you wanted the mustard?'

'My dear!'

'Why not? There is nothing to be ashamed of in wanting mustard.'

'At one o'clock in the morning! I couldn't do it. To tell you the truth, he wasn't very civil, and I thought that he was, – perhaps a little tipsy. Now, my dear, do go to sleep.'

'Why didn't you get the mustard?'

'There was none there – nowhere at all about the room. I went down again and searched everywhere. That's what took me so long. They always lock up those kind of things at these French hotels. They are too close-fisted to leave anything out. When you first spoke of it I knew that it would be gone when I got there. Now, my dear, do go to sleep, because we positively must start in the morning.'

'That is impossible,' said he, jumping up in bed.

'We must go, my dear. I say that we must go. After all that has passed I wouldn't not be with Uncle John and my cousin Robert tomorrow evening for more – more – more than I would venture to say.'

'Bother!' he exclaimed.

'It's all very well for you to say that, Charles, but you don't know. I say that we must go tomorrow, and we will.'

'I do believe you want to kill me, Mary.'

'That is very cruel, Charles, and most false, and most unjust. As for making you ill, nothing could be so bad for you as this wretched place, where nobody can get warm either day or night. If anything will cure your throat for you at once it will be the sea air. And only think how much more comfortable they can make you at Thompson Hall than anywhere in this country. I have so set my heart upon it, Charles, that I will do it. If we are not there tomorrow night Uncle John won't consider us as belonging to the family.'

'I don't believe a word of it.'

'Jane told me so in her letter. I wouldn't let you know before because I thought it so unjust. But that has been the reason why I've been so earnest about it all through.'

It was a thousand pities that so good a woman should have been driven by the sad stress of circumstances to tell so many fibs. One after another she was compelled to invent them, that there might be a way open to her of escaping the horrors of a prolonged sojourn in that hotel. At length, after much grumbling, he became silent, and she trusted that he was sleeping. He had not as yet said that he would start at the required hour in the morning, but she was perfectly determined in her own mind that he should be made to do so. As he lay there motionless, and as she wandered about the room pretending to pack her things, she more than once almost resolved that she would tell him everything. Surely then he would be ready to make any effort. But there came upon her an idea that he might perhaps fail to see all the circumstances, and that, so failing, he would insist on remaining that he might tender some apology to the injured gentleman. An apology might have been very well had she not left him there in his misery – but what apology would be possible now? She would have to see him and speak to him, and everyone in the hotel would know every detail of the story. Every-one in France would know that it was she who had gone to the strange man's bedside, and put the mustard plaster on the strange man's throat in the dead of night! She could not tell the story even to her husband, lest even her husband should betray her.

Her own sufferings at the present moment were not light. In her perturbation of mind she had foolishly resolved that she would not herself go to bed. The tragedy of the night had seemed to her too deep for personal comfort. And then how would it be were she to sleep, and have no one to call her? It was imperative that she should have all her powers ready for thoroughly arousing him. It occurred to her that the servant of the hotel would certainly run her too short of time. She had to work for herself and for him too, and therefore she would not sleep. But she was very cold, and she put on first a shawl over her dressing-gown and then a cloak. She could not con-sume all the remaining hours of the night in packing one bag and one portmanteau, so that at last she sat down on the narrow red cotton velvet sofa, and, looking at her watch, perceived that as yet it was not much past two o'clock. How was she to get through those other three long, tedious, chilly hours?

Then there came a voice from the bed – 'Ain't you coming?'

'I hoped you were asleep, my dear.'

'I haven't been asleep at all. You'd better come, if you don't mean to make yourself as ill as I am.'

'You are not so very bad, are you, darling?'

'I don't know what you call bad. I never felt my throat so choked in my life before!' Still as she listened she thought that she remem-bered his throat to have been more choked. If the husband of her bosom could play with her feelings and deceive her on such an occasion as this – then, then – then she thought that she would rather not have any husband of her bosom at all. But she did creep into bed, and lay down beside him without saying another word.

Of course she slept, but her sleep was not the sleep of the blest. At every striking of the clock in the quadrangle she would start up in alarm, fearing that she had let the time go by. Though the night was so short it was very long to her. But he slept like an infant. She could hear from his breathing that he was not quite so well as she could wish him to be, but still he was resting in beautiful tranquillity. Not once did he move when she started up, as she did so frequently. Orders had been given and repeated over and over again that they should be called at five. The man in the office had almost been angry as he assured Mrs Brown for the fourth time that Monsieur and Madame would most assuredly be wakened at the appointed time.

through a side door that very night-porter whom she dreaded, with a soiled pocket-handkerchief in his hand.

Even before the sound of her own name met her ears Mrs Brown knew it all. She understood the full horror of her position from that man's hostile face, and from the little article which he held in his hand. If during the watches of the night she had had money in her pocket, if she had made a friend of this greedy fellow by well-timed liberality, all might have been so different! But she reflected that she had allowed him to go unfee'd after all his trouble, and she knew that he was her enemy. It was the handkerchief that she feared. She thought that she might have brazened out anything but that. No one had seen her enter or leave that strange man's room. No one had seen her dip her hands in that jar. She had, no doubt, been found wandering about the house while the slumberer had been made to suffer so strangely, and there might have been suspicion, and perhaps accusation. But she would have been ready with frequent protestations to deny all charges made against her, and, though no one might have believed her, no one could have convicted her. Here, however, was evidence against which she would be unable to stand for a moment. At the first glance she acknowledged the potency of that damning morsel of linen.

During all the horrors of the night she had never given a thought to the handkerchief, and yet she ought to have known that the evidence it would bring against her was palpable and certain. Her name, 'M. Brown,' was plainly written on the corner. What a fool she had been not to have thought of this! Had she but remembered the plain marking which she, as a careful, well-conducted British matron, had put upon all her clothes, she would at any hazard have recovered the article. Oh that she had waked the man, or bribed the porter, or even told her husband! But now she was, as it were, friendless, without support, without a word that she could say in her own defence, convicted of having committed this assault upon a strange man in his own bedroom, and then of having left him! The thing must be explained by the truth; but how to explain such truth, how to tell such story in a way to satisfy injured folk, and she with only barely time sufficient to catch the train! Then it occurred to her that they could have no legal right to stop her because the pocket-handkerchief had been found in a strange gentleman's bedroom. 'Yes, it is mine,' she said, turning to her husband, as the porter, with a loud voice, asked if she were not Madame Brown. 'Take it, Charles, and come on.' Mr Brown naturally stood still in astonishment. He did put out his hand, but the porter would not allow the evidence to pass readily out of his custody.

But still she would trust to no one, and was up and about the room before the clock had struck half-past four.

In her heart of hearts she was very tender towards her husband. Now, in order that he might feel a gleam of warmth while he was dressing himself, she collected together the fragments of half-burned wood, and endeavoured to make a little fire. Then she took out from her bag a small pot, and a patent lamp, and some chocolate, and prepared for him a warm drink, so that he might have it instantly as he was awakened. She would do anything for him in the way of ministering to his comfort – only he must go! Yes, he certainly must go!

And then she wondered how that strange man was bearing himself at the present moment. She would fain have ministered to him too had it been possible; but ah! – it was so impossible! Probably before this he would have been aroused from his troubled slumbers. But then – how aroused? At what time in the night would the burning heat upon his chest have awakened him to a sense of torture which must have been so altogether incomprehensible to him? Her strong imagination showed to her a clear picture of the scene – clear, though it must have been done in the dark. How he must have tossed and hurled himself under the clothes; how those strong knees must have worked themselves up and down before the potent god of sleep would allow him to return to perfect consciousness; how his fingers, restrained by no reason, would have trampled over his feverish throat, scattering everywhere that unhappy poultice! Then when he should have sat up wide awake, but still in the dark – with her mind's eye she saw it all – feeling that some fire as from the infernal regions had fallen upon him, but whence he would know not, how fiercely wild would be the working of his spirit! Ah, now she knew, now she felt, now she acknowledged how bound she had been to awaken him at the moment, whatever might have been the personal inconvenience to herself! In such a position what would he do – or rather what had he done? She could follow much of it in her own thoughts – how he would scramble madly from his bed, and, with one hand still on his throat, would snatch hurriedly at the matches with the other. How the light would come, and how then he would rush to the mirror. Ah, what a sight he would behold! She could see it all to the last widespread daub.

But she could not see, she could not tell herself, what in such a position a man would do – at any rate, not what that man would do. Her husband, she thought, would tell his wife, and then the two of them, between them, would – put up with it. There are misfortunes which, if they be published, are simply aggravated by ridicule. But she remembered the features of the stranger as she had seen them at that instant in which she had dropped his beard, and she thought that there was a ferocity in them, a certain tenacity of self-import-ance, which would not permit their owner to endure such treatment in silence. Would he not storm and rage, and ring the bell, and call all Paris to witness his revenge?

But the storming and the raging had not reached her yet, and now it wanted but a quarter to five. In three-quarters of an hour they would be in that demi-omnibus which they had ordered for them-selves, and in half an hour after that they would be flying towards Thompson Hall. Then she allowed herself to think of the coming comforts – of those comforts so sweet, if only they would come! That very day now present to her was the 24th December, and on that very evening she would be sitting in Christmas joy among all her uncles and cousins, holding her new brother-in-law affectionately by the hand. Oh, what a change from Pandemonium to Paradise – from that wretched room, from that miserable house in which there was such ample cause for fear, to all the domestic Christmas bliss of the home of the Thompsons! She resolved that she would not, at any rate, be deterred by any light opposition on the part of her husband. 'It wants just a quarter to five,' she said, putting her hand steadily upon his shoulder, 'and I'll get a cup of chocolate for you, so that you may get up comfortably.'

'I've been thinking about it,' he said, rubbing his eyes with the back of his hands. 'It will be so much better to go over by the mail train tonight. We should be in time for Christmas just the same.'

'That will not do at all,' she answered, energetically. 'Come, Charles, after all the trouble do not disappoint me.'

'It is such a horrid grind.'

'Think what I have gone through – what I have done for you! In twelve hours we shall be there, among them all. You won't be so little like a man as not to go on now.' He threw himself back upon the bed, and tried to readjust the clothes round his neck. 'No, Charles, no,' she continued; 'not if I know it. Take your chocolate and get up. There is not a moment to be lost.' With that she laid her hand upon his shoulder, and made him clearly understand that he would not be allowed to take further rest in that bed.

Grumbling, sulky, coughing continually, and declaring that life under such circumstances was not worth having, he did at last get up and dress himself. When once she knew that he was obeying her she became again tender to him, and certainly took much more than her own share of the trouble of the proceedings. Long before the time was up she was ready, and the porter had been summoned to

take the luggage downstairs. When the man came she was rejoiced to see that it was not he whom she had met among the passages during her nocturnal rambles. He shouldered the box, and told them that they would find coffee and bread and butter in the small salle à-manger below.

'I told you that it would be so, when you would boil that stu said the ungrateful man, who had nevertheless swallowed the chocolate when it was given to him.

They followed their luggage down into the hall; but as she w at every step, the lady looked around her. She dreaded the sig that porter of the night; she feared lest some potential author the hotel should come to her and ask her some horrid questio of all her fears her greatest fear was that there should arise bef an apparition of that face which she had seen recumbent pillow.

As they passed the door of the great salon, Mr Brown lo 'Why, there it is still!' said he.

'What?' said she, trembling in every limb.

'The mustard-pot!'

'They have put it in there since,' she exclaimed energ her despair. 'But never mind. The omnibus is here. C And she absolutely took him by the arm.

But at that moment a door behind them opened, and heard herself called by her name. And there was the n with a handkerchief in his hand. But the further d morning must be told in a further chapter.

4: MRS BROWN DOES ESCA

It had been visible to Mrs Brown from the first arrival on the ground floor that 'something was may be allowed to use such a phrase; and she felt that this something had reference to her. She fanc of the hotel were looking at her as she swallowed, her coffee. When her husband was paying the thing disagreeable in the eye of the man who w Her sufferings were very great, and no one sy Her husband was quite at his ease, except tha of the cold. When she was anxious to get him he still stood there leisurely, arranging shawl throat. 'You can do that quite as well in an said to him very crossly, when there ap

'What does it all mean?' asked Mr Brown.

'A gentleman has been – eh – eh –. Something has been done to a gentleman in his bedroom,' said the clerk.

'Something done to a gentleman!' repeated Mr Brown.

'Something very bad indeed,' said the porter. 'Look here,' and he showed the condition of the handkerchief.

'Charles, we shall lose the train,' said the affrighted wife.

'What the mischief does it all mean?' demanded the husband.

'Did Madame go into the gentleman's room?' asked the clerk. Then there was an awful silence, and all eyes were fixed upon the lady.

'What does it all mean?' demanded the husband. 'Did you go into anybody's room?'

'I did,' said Mrs Brown with much dignity, looking round upon her enemies as a stag at bay will look upon the hounds which are attacking him. 'Give me the handkerchief.' But the night-porter quickly put it behind his back. 'Charles, we cannot allow ourselves to be delayed. You shall write a letter to the keeper of the hotel, explaining it all.' Then she essayed to swim out, through the front door, into the courtyard in which the vehicle was waiting for them. But three or four men and women interposed themselves, and even her husband did not seem quite ready to continue his journey. 'Tonight is Christmas Eve,' said Mrs Brown, 'and we shall not be at Thompson Hall! Think of my sister!'

'Why did you go into the man's bedroom, my dear?' whispered Mr Brown in English.

But the porter heard the whisper, and understood the language – the porter who had not been 'tipped'. 'Ye'es; – vy?' asked the porter.

'It was a mistake, Charles; there is not a moment to lose. I can explain it all to you in the carriage.' Then the clerk suggested that Madame had better postpone her journey a little. The gentleman upstairs had certainly been very badly treated, and had demanded to know why so great an outrage had been perpetrated. The clerk said that he did not wish to send for the police – here Mrs Brown gasped terribly and threw herself on her husband's shoulder – but he did not think he could allow the party to go till the gentleman upstairs had received some satisfaction. It had now become clearly impossible that the journey could be made by the early train. Even Mrs Brown gave it up herself, and demanded of her husband that she should be taken back to her own bedroom.

'But what is to be said to the gentleman?' asked the porter.

Of course it was impossible that Mrs Brown should be made to tell her story there in the presence of them all. The clerk, when he found he had succeeded in preventing her from leaving the house, was satisfied with a promise from Mr Brown that he would inquire from his wife what were these mysterious circumstances, and would then come down to the office and give some explanation. If it were necessary, he would see the strange gentleman – whom he now ascertained to be a certain Mr Jones returning from the east of Europe. He learned also that this Mr Jones had been most anxious to travel by that very morning train which he and his wife had intended to use – that Mr Jones had been most particular in giving his orders accordingly, but that at the last moment he had declared himself to be unable even to dress himself, because of the injury which had been done him during the night. When Mr Brown heard this from the clerk just before he was allowed to take his wife upstairs, while she was sitting on a sofa in a corner with her face hidden, a look of awful gloom came over his own countenance. What could it be that his wife had done to the man of so terrible a nature? 'You had better come up with me,' he said to her with marital severity, and the poor cowed woman went with him tamely as might have done some patient Grizel. Not a word was spoken till they were in the room and the door was locked. 'Now,' said he, 'what does it all mean?'

It was not till nearly two hours had passed that Mr Brown came down the stairs very slowly – turning it all over in his mind. He had now gradually heard the absolute and exact truth, and had very gradually learned to believe it. It was first necessary that he should understand that his wife had told him many fibs during the night; but as she constantly alleged to him when he complained of her conduct in this respect, they had all been told on his behalf. Had she not struggled to get the mustard for his comfort, and when she had secured the prize had she not hurried to put it on – so she had fondly thought – his throat? And though she had fibbed to him afterwards, had she not done so in order that he might not be troubled? 'You are not angry with me because I was in that man's room?' she asked, looking full into his eyes, but not quite without a sob. He paused a moment and then declared, with something of a true husband's confidence in his wife, that he was not in the least angry with her on that account. Then she kissed him, and bade him remember that after all no one could really injure them. 'What harm has been done, Charles? The gentleman won't die because he has had a mustard plaster on his throat. The worst is about Uncle John and dear Jane. They do think so much of Christmas Eve at Thompson Hall!'

Mr Brown, when he again found himself in the clerk's office, requested that his card might be taken up to Mr Jones. Mr Jones had sent down his own card, which was handed to Mr Brown: 'Mr Barnaby Jones.' 'And how was it all, sir?' asked the clerk, in a whisper – a whisper which had at the same time something of authoritative demand and something also of submissive respect. The clerk of course was anxious to know the mystery. It is hardly too much to say that everyone in that vast hotel was by this time anxious to have the mystery unravelled. But Mr Brown would tell nothing to anyone. 'It is merely a matter to be explained between me and Mr Jones,' he said. The card was taken upstairs, and after awhile he was ushered into Mr Jones' room. It was, of course, that very 353 with which the reader is already acquainted. There was a fire burning, and the remains of Mr Jones' breakfast were on the table. He was sitting in his dressing-gown and slippers, with his shirt open in the front, and a silk handkerchief very loosely covering his throat. Mr Brown, as he entered the room, of course looked with considerable anxiety at the gentleman of whose condition he had heard so sad an account; but he could only observe some considerable stiffness of movement and demeanour as Mr Jones turned his head round to greet him.

'This has been a very disagreeable accident, Mr Jones,' said the husband of the lady.

'Accident! I don't know how it could have been an accident. It has been a most – most – most – a most monstrous, – er – er – I must say, interference with a gentleman's privacy, and personal comfort.'

'Quite so, Mr Jones, but, – on the part of the lady, who is my wife –'

'So I understand. I myself am about to become a married man, and I can understand what your feelings must be. I wish to say as little as possible to harrow them.' Here Mr Brown bowed. 'But – there's the fact. She did do it.'

'She thought it was – me!'

'What!'

'I give you my word as a gentleman, Mr Jones. When she was putting that mess upon you she thought it was me! She did, indeed.'

Mr Jones looked at his new acquaintance and shook his head. He did not think it possible that any woman would make such a mistake as that.

'I had a very bad sore throat,' continued Mr Brown, 'and indeed you may perceive it still' – in saying this, he perhaps aggravated a little the sign of his distemper, 'and I asked Mrs Brown to go down and get one – just what she put on you.'

'I wish you'd had it,' said Mr Jones, putting his hand up to his neck.

'I wish I had – for your sake as well as mine – and for hers, poor woman. I don't know when she will get over the shock.'

'I don't know when I shall. And it has stopped me on my journey. I was to have been tonight, this very night, this Christmas Eve, with the young lady I am engaged to marry. Of course I couldn't travel. The extent of the injury done nobody can imagine at present.'

'It has been just as bad to me, sir. We were to have been with our family this Christmas Eve. There were particular reasons – most particular. We were only hindered from going by hearing of your condition.'

'Why did she come into my room at all? I can't understand that. A lady always knows her own room at an hotel.'

'353 – that's yours; 333 – that's ours. Don't you see how easy it was? She had lost her way, and she was a little afraid lest the thing should fall down.'

'I wish it had, with all my heart.'

'That's how it was. Now I'm sure, Mr Jones, you'll take a lady's apology. It was a most unfortunate mistake – most unfortunate; but what more can be said?'

Mr Jones gave himself up to reflection for a few moments before he replied to this. He supposed that he was bound to believe the story as far as it went. At any rate, he did not know how he could say that he did not believe it. It seemed to him to be almost incredible – especially incredible in regard to that personal mistake, for, except that they both had long beards and brown beards, Mr Jones thought that there was no point of resemblance between himself and Mr Brown. But still, even that, he felt, must be accepted. But then why had he been left, deserted, to undergo all those torments? 'She found out her mistake at last, I suppose?'

'Oh, yes.'

'Why didn't she wake a fellow and take it off again?'

'Ah!'

'She can't have cared very much for a man's comfort when she went away and left him like that.'

'Ah! there was the difficulty, Mr Jones.'

'Difficulty! Who was it that had done it? To come to me, in my bedroom, in the middle of the night, and put that thing on me, and then leave it there and say nothing about it! It seems to me deuced like a practical joke.'

'No, Mr Jones!'

'That's the way I look at it,' said Mr Jones, plucking up his courage.

'There isn't a woman in all England, or in all France, less likely to do such a thing than my wife. She's as steady as a rock, Mr Jones, and would no more go into another gentleman's bedroom in joke than — Oh dear no! You're going to be a married man yourself.'

'Unless all this makes a difference,' said Mr Jones, almost in tears. 'I had sworn that I would be with her this Christmas Eve.'

'Oh, Mr Jones, I cannot believe that will interfere with your happiness. How could you think that your wife, as is to be, would do such a thing as that in joke?'

'She wouldn't do it at all – joke or anyway.'

'How can you tell what accident might happen to anyone?'

'She'd have wakened the man then afterwards. I'm sure she would. She would never have left him to suffer in that way. Her heart is too soft. Why didn't she send you to wake me, and explain it all? That's what my Jane would have done; and I should have gone and wakened him. But the whole thing is impossible,' he said, shaking his head as he remembered that he and his Jane were not in a condition as yet to undergo any such mutual trouble. At last Mr Jones was brought to acknowledge that nothing more could be done. The lady had sent her apology, and told her story, and he must bear the trouble and inconvenience to which she had subjected him. He still, however, had his own opinion about her conduct generally, and could not be brought to give any sign of amity. He simply bowed when Mr Brown was hoping to induce him to shake hands, and sent no word of pardon to the great offender.

The matter, however, was so far concluded that there was no
further question of police interference, nor any doubt but that the
lady with her husband was to be allowed to leave Paris by the night
train. The nature of the accident probably became known to all.
Mr Brown was interrogated by many, and though he professed to
declare that he would answer no question, nevertheless he found it
better to tell the clerk something of the truth than to allow the matter to be shrouded in mystery. It is to be feared that Mr Jones, who
did not once show himself through the day, but who employed the
hours in endeavouring to assuage the injury done him, still lived in
the conviction that the lady had played a practical joke on him. But
the subject of such a joke never talks about it, and Mr Jones could
not be induced to speak even by the friendly adherence of the night-
porter.

Mrs Brown also clung to the seclusion of her own bedroom, never
once stirring from it till the time came in which she was to be taken
down to the omnibus. Upstairs she ate her meals, and upstairs she
passed her time in packing and unpacking, and in requesting that
telegrams might be sent repeatedly to Thompson Hall. In the course
of the day two such telegrams were sent, in the latter of which the
Thompson family were assured that the Browns would arrive,
probably in time for breakfast on Christmas Day, certainly in time
for church. She asked more than once tenderly after Mr Jones' welfare, but could obtain no information. 'He was very cross, and that's
all I know about it,' said Mr Brown. Then she made a remark as to
the gentleman's Christian name, which appeared on the card as
'Barnaby'. 'My sister's husband's name will be Burnaby,' she said.
'And this man's Christian name is Barnaby; that's all the difference,'
said her husband, with ill-timed jocularity.

We all know how people under a cloud are apt to fail in asserting
their personal dignity. On the former day a separate vehicle had
been ordered by Mr Brown to take himself and his wife to the station,
but now, after his misfortunes, he contented himself with such pro-
vision as the people at the hotel might make for him. At the appointed hour he brought his wife down, thickly veiled. There were many
strangers as she passed through the hall, ready to look at the lady
who had done that wonderful thing in the dead of night, but none
could see a feature of her face as she stepped across the hall, and was
hurried into the omnibus. And there were many eyes also on Mr
Jones, who followed very quickly, for he also, in spite of his sufferings, was leaving Paris on the evening in order that he might be with
his English friends on Christmas Day. He, as he went through the
crowd, assumed an air of great dignity, to which, perhaps, something

was added by his endeavours, as he walked, to save his poor throat from irritation. He, too, got into the same omnibus, stumbling over the feet of his enemy in the dark. At the station they got their tickets, one close after the other, and then were brought into each other's presence in the waiting-room. I think it must be acknowledged that here Mr Jones was conscious, not only of her presence, but of her consciousness of his presence, and that he assumed an attitude, as though he should have said, 'Now do you think it possible for me to believe that you mistook me for your husband?' She was perfectly quiet, but sat through that quarter of an hour with her face continually veiled. Mr Brown made some little overture of conversation to Mr Jones, but Mr Jones, though he did mutter some reply, showed plainly enough that he had no desire for further intercourse. Then came the accustomed stampede, the awful rush, the internecine struggle in which seats had to be found. Seats, I fancy, are regularly found, even by the most tardy, but it always appears that every British father and every British husband is actuated at these stormy moments by a conviction that unless he proves himself a very Hercules he and his daughters and his wife will be left desolate in Paris. Mr Brown was quite Herculean, carrying two bags and a hat-box in his own hands, besides the cloaks, the coats, the rugs, the sticks, and the umbrellas. But when he had got himself and his wife well seated, with their faces to the engine, with a corner seat for her – there was Mr Jones immediately opposite to her. Mr Jones, as soon as he perceived the inconvenience of his position, made a scramble for another place, but he was too late. In that contiguity the journey as far as Calais had to be made. She, poor woman, never once took up her veil. There he sat, without closing an eye, stiff as a ramrod, sometimes showing by little uneasy gestures that the trouble at his neck was still there, but never speaking a word, and hardly moving a limb.

Crossing from Calais to Dover the lady was, of course, separated from her victim. The passage was very bad, and she more than once reminded her husband how well it would have been with them now had they pursued their journey as she had intended – as though they had been detained in Paris by his fault! Mr Jones, as he laid himself down on his back, gave himself up to wondering whether any man before him had ever been made subject to such absolute injustice. Now and again he put his hand up to his own beard, and began to doubt whether it could have been moved, as it must have been moved, without waking him. What if chloroform had been used? Many such suspicions crossed his mind during the misery of that passage.

They were again together in the same railway carriage from Dover to London. They had now got used to the close neighbourhood, and knew how to endure each the presence of the other. But as yet Mr Jones had never seen the lady's face. He longed to know what were the features of the woman who had been so blind – if indeed that story were true. Or if it were not true, of what like was the woman who would dare in the middle of the night to play such a trick as that?

From Cannon Street the Browns took their departure in a cab for the Liverpool Street Station, whence they would be conveyed by the Eastern Counties Railway to Stratford. Now at any rate their troubles were over. They would be in ample time, not only for Christmas Day church, but for Christmas Day breakfast. 'It will be just the same as getting in there last night,' said Mr Brown, as he walked across the platform to place his wife in the carriage for Stratford. She entered it the first, and as she did so there she saw Mr Jones seated in the corner! Hitherto she had borne his presence well, but now she could not restrain herself from a little start and a little scream. He bowed his head very slightly, as though acknowledging the compliment, and then down she dropped her veil. When they arrived at Stratford, the journey being over in a quarter of an hour, Jones was out of the carriage even before the Browns.

'There is Uncle John's carriage,' said Mrs Brown, thinking that now, at any rate, she would be able to free herself from the presence of this terrible stranger. No doubt he was a handsome man to look at, but on no face so sternly hostile had she ever before fixed her eyes. She did not, perhaps, reflect that the owner of no other face had ever been so deeply injured by herself.

5: MRS BROWN AT THOMPSON HALL

'Please, sir, we were to ask for Mr Jones,' said the servant, putting his head into the carriage after both Mr and Mrs Brown had seated themselves.

'Mr Jones!' exclaimed the husband.

'Why ask for Mr Jones?' demanded the wife. The servant was about to tender some explanation when Mr Jones stepped up and said that he was Mr Jones. 'We are going to Thompson Hall,' said the lady with great vigour.

'So am I,' said Mr Jones, with much dignity. It was, however, arranged that he should sit with the coachman, as there was a rumble behind for the other servant. The luggage was put into a cart, and away all went for Thompson Hall.

'What do you think about it, Mary?' whispered Mr Brown, after a pause. He was evidently awestruck by the horror of the occasion.

'I cannot make it out at all. What do you think?'

'I don't know what to think. Jones going to Thompson Hall?'

'He's a very good-looking young man,' said Mrs Brown.

'Well; – that's as people think. A stiff, stuck-up fellow, I should say. Up to this moment he has never forgiven you for what you did to him.'

'Would you have forgiven his wife, Charles, if she'd done it to you?'

'He hasn't got a wife – yet.'

'How do you know?'

'He is coming home now to be married,' said Mr Brown. 'He expects to meet the young lady this very Christmas Day. He told me so. That was one of the reasons why he was so angry at being stopped by what you did last night.'

'I suppose he knows Uncle John, or he wouldn't be going to the Hall,' said Mrs Brown.

'I can't make it out,' said Mr Brown, shaking his head.

'He looks quite like a gentleman,' said Mrs Brown, 'though he has been so stiff. Jones! Barnaby Jones! You're sure it was Barnaby?'

'That was the name on the card.'

'Not Burnaby?' asked Mrs Brown.

'It was Barnaby Jones on the card – just the same as "Barnaby Rudge", and as for looking like a gentleman, I'm by no means quite so sure. A gentleman takes an apology when it's offered.'

'Perhaps, my dear, that depends on the condition of his throat. If you had had a mustard plaster on all night, you might not have liked it. But here we are at Thompson Hall at last.'

Thompson Hall was an old brick mansion, standing within a huge iron gate, with a gravel sweep before it. It had stood there before Stratford was a town, or even a suburb, and had then been known by the name of Box Place. But it had been in the hands of the present family for the last thirty years, and was now known far and wide as Thompson Hall – a comfortable, roomy, old-fashioned place, perhaps a little dark and dull to look at, but much more substantially built than most of our modern villas. Mrs Brown jumped with alacrity from the carriage, and with a quick step entered the home of her forefathers. Her husband followed her more leisurely, but he, too, felt that he was at home at Thompson Hall. Then Mr Jones walked in also – but he looked as though he were not at all at home. It was still very early, and no one of the family was as yet down. In these circumstances it was almost necessary that something should be said to Mr Jones.

'Do you know Mr Thompson?' asked Mr Brown.

'I never had the pleasure of seeing him – as yet,' answered Mr Jones, very stiffly.

'Oh, – I didn't know; – because you said you were coming here.'

'And I have come here. Are you friends of Mr Thompson?'

'Oh, dear, yes,' said Mrs Brown. 'I was a Thompson myself before I married.'

'Oh, – indeed!' said Mr Jones. 'How very odd, – very odd, indeed.'

During this time the luggage was being brought into the house, and two old family servants were offering them assistance. Would the new comers like to go up to their bedrooms? Then the house-keeper, Mrs Green, intimated with a wink that Miss Jane would, she was sure, be down quite immediately. The present moment, how-ever, was still very unpleasant. The lady probably had made her guess as to the mystery; but the two gentlemen were still altogether in the dark. Mrs Brown had no doubt declared her parentage, but Mr Jones, with such a multitude of strange facts crowding on his mind, had been slow to understand her. Being somewhat suspicious by nature, he was beginning to think whether possibly the mustard had been put by this lady on his throat with some reference to his connexion with Thompson Hall. Could it be that she, for some reason of her own, had wished to prevent his coming, and had con-trived this untoward stratagem out of her brain? or had she wished to make him ridiculous to the Thompson family, – to whom, as a family, he was at present unknown? It was becoming more and more improbable to him that the whole thing should have been an acci-dent. When, after the first horrid moments of that morning in which he had in his agony invoked the assistance of the night-porter, he had begun to reflect on his situation, he had determined that it would be better that nothing further should be said about it. What would life be worth to him if he were to be known wherever he went as the man who had been mustard-plastered in the middle of the night by a strange lady? The worst of a practical joke is that the remembrance of the absurd condition sticks so long to the sufferer! At the hotel that night-porter, who had possessed himself of the handkerchief and had read the name, and had connected that name with the occupant of 333 whom he had found wandering about the house with some strange purpose, had not permitted the thing to sleep. The porter had pressed the matter home against the Browns, and had produced the interview which has been recorded. But during the whole of that day Mr Jones had been resolving that he would never again think of the Browns or speak of them. A great injury had been done to him – a most outrageous injustice – but it was a thing which had to be endured. A horrid woman had come across him like a nightmare. All he could do was to endeavour to forget the terrible visitation. Such had been his resolve – in making which he had passed that long day in Paris. And now the Browns had stuck to him from the moment of his leaving his room! he had been forced to travel with them, but had travelled with them as a stranger. He had tried to comfort himself with the reflection that at every fresh stage he would shake them off. In one railway after another the vicinity had been bad – but still they were strangers. Now he found himself in the same house with them – where of course the story would be told. Had not the thing been done on purpose that the story might be told there at Thompson Hall?

Mrs Brown had acceded to the proposition of the housekeeper, and was about to be taken to her room when there was heard a sound of footsteps along the passage above and on the stairs, and a young lady came bounding on to the scene. 'You have all of you come a quarter of an hour earlier than we thought possible,' said the young lady. 'I did so mean to be up to receive you!' With that she passed her sister on the stairs – for the young lady was Miss Jane Thompson, sister to our Mrs Brown – and hurried down into the hall. Here Mr Brown, who had ever been on affectionate terms with his sister-in-law, put himself forward to receive her embraces; but she, apparently not noticing him in her ardour, rushed on and threw herself on to the breast of the other gentleman. 'This is my Charles,' she said. 'Oh, Charles, I thought you never would be here.'

Mr Charles Burnaby Jones, for such was his name since he had inherited the Jones property in Pembrokeshire, received into his arms the ardent girl of his heart with all that love and devotion to which she was entitled, but could not do so without some external shrinking from her embrace. 'Oh, Charles, what is it?' she said.

'Nothing, dearest – only – only –.' Then he looked piteously up into Mrs Brown's face, as though imploring her not to tell the story.

'Perhaps, Jane, you had better introduce us,' said Mrs Brown.

'Introduce you! I thought you had been travelling together, and staying at the same hotel – and all that.'

'So we have; but people may be in the same hotel without knowing each other. And we have travelled all the way home with Mr Jones without in the least knowing who he was.'

'How very odd! Do you mean you have never spoken?'

'Not a word,' said Mrs Brown.

'I do so hope you'll love each other,' said Jane.

'It shan't be my fault if we don't,' said Mrs Brown.

'I'm sure it shan't be mine,' said Mr Brown, tendering his hand to the other gentleman. The various feelings of the moment were too much for Mr Jones, and he could not respond quite as he should have done. But as he was taken upstairs to his room he determined that he would make the best of it.

The owner of the house was old Uncle John. He was a bachelor, and with him lived various members of the family. There was the great Thompson of them all, Cousin Robert, who was now member of Parliament for the Essex Flats, and young John, as a certain enterprising Thompson of the age of forty was usually called, and then there was old Aunt Bess, and among other young branches there was Miss Jane Thompson, who was now engaged to marry Mr Charles Burnaby Jones. As it happened, no other member of the family had as yet seen Mr Burnaby Jones, and he, being by nature of a retiring disposition, felt himself to be ill at ease when he came into the breakfast parlour among all the Thompsons. He was known to be a gentleman of good family and ample means, and all the Thompsons had approved of the match, but during the first Christmas breakfast he did not seem to accept his condition jovially. His own Jane sat beside him, but then on the other side sat Mrs Brown. She assumed an immediate intimacy, – as women know how to do on such occasions – being determined from the very first to regard her sister's husband as a brother; but he still feared her. She was still to him the woman who had come to him in the dead of night with that horrid mixture – and had then left him.

'It was so odd that both of you should have been detained on the very same day,' said Jane.

'Yes, it was odd,' said Mrs Brown, with a smile looking round upon her neighbour.

'It was abominably bad weather, you know,' said Brown.

'But you were both so determined to come,' said the old gentleman. 'When we got the two telegrams at the same moment, we were sure that there had been some agreement between you.'

'Not exactly an agreement,' said Mrs Brown; whereupon Mr Jones looked as grim as death.

'I'm sure there is something more than we understand yet,' said the member of Parliament.

Then they all went to church, as a united family ought to do on Christmas Day, and came home to a fine old English early dinner at three o'clock – a sirloin of beef a foot-and-a-half broad, a turkey as big as an ostrich, a plum-pudding bigger than the turkey, and two or three dozen mince-pies. 'That's a very large bit of beef,' said Mr Jones, who had not lived much in England latterly. 'It won't look so large,' said the old gentleman, 'when all our friends downstairs have had their say to it.' 'A plum-pudding on Christmas Day can't be too big,' he said again, 'if the cook will but take time enough over it. I never knew a bit go to waste yet.'

By this time there had been some explanation as to past events between the two sisters. Mrs Brown had indeed told Jane all about it, how ill her husband had been, how she had been forced to go down and look for the mustard, and then what she had done with the mustard. 'I don't think they are a bit alike you know, Mary, if you mean that,' said Jane.

'Well, no; perhaps not quite alike. I only saw his beard, you know. No doubt it was stupid, but I did it.'

'Why didn't you take it off again?' asked the sister.

'Oh, Jane, if you'd only think of it! Could you?' Then of course all that occurred was explained, how they had been stopped on their journey, how Brown had made the best apology in his power, and how Jones had travelled with them and had never spoken a word. The gentleman had only taken his new name a week since, but of course had had his new card printed immediately. 'I'm sure I should have thought of it if they hadn't made a mistake with the first name. Charles said it was like Barnaby Rudge.'

'Not at all like Barnaby Rudge,' said Jane; 'Charles Burnaby Jones is a very good name.'

'Very good indeed, – and I'm sure that after a little bit he won't be at all the worse for the accident.'

Before dinner the secret had been told no further, but still there had crept about among the Thompsons, and, indeed, downstairs also, among the retainers, a feeling that there was a secret. The old housekeeper was sure that Miss Mary, as she still called Mrs Brown, had something to tell if she could only be induced to tell it, and that this something had reference to Mr Jones' personal comfort. The head of the family, who was a sharp old gentleman, felt this also, and the member of Parliament, who had an idea that he specially should never be kept in the dark, was almost angry. Mr Jones, suffering from some kindred feeling throughout the dinner, remained silent and unhappy. When two or three toasts had been drunk – the Queen's health, the old gentleman's health, the young couple's health, Brown's health, and the general health of all the Thompsons, then tongues were loosened and a question was asked, 'I know that there has been something doing in Paris between these young people that we haven't heard as yet,' said the uncle. Then Mrs Brown laughed, and Jane, laughing too, gave Mr Jones to understand that she at any rate knew all about it.

'If there is a mystery I hope it will be told at once,' said the member of Parliament, angrily.

'Come, Brown, what is it?' asked another male cousin.

'Well, there was an accident. I'd rather Jones should tell,' said he.

Jones' brow became blacker than thunder, but he did not say a word. 'You mustn't be angry with Mary,' Jane whispered into her lover's ear.

'Come, Mary, you never were slow at talking,' said the uncle.

'I do hate this kind of thing,' said the member of Parliament.

'I will tell it all,' said Mrs Brown, very nearly in tears, or else pretending to be very nearly in tears. 'I know I was very wrong, and I do beg his pardon, and if he won't say that he forgives me I never shall be happy again.' Then she clasped her hands, and turning round, looked him piteously in the face.

'Oh yes; I do forgive you,' said Mr Jones.

'My brother,' said she, throwing her arms round him and kissing him. He recoiled from the embrace, but I think that he attempted to return the kiss. 'And now I will tell the whole story,' said Mrs Brown. And she told it, acknowledging her fault with true contrition, and swearing that she would atone for it by life-long sisterly devotion.

'And you mustard-plastered the wrong man!' said the old gentleman, almost rolling off his chair with delight.

'I did,' said Mrs Brown, sobbing, 'and I think that no woman ever suffered as I suffered.'

'And Jones wouldn't let you leave the hotel?'

'It was the handkerchief stopped us,' said Brown.

'If it had turned out to be anybody else,' said the member of Parliament, 'the results might have been most serious – not to say discreditable.'

'That's nonsense, Robert,' said Mrs Brown, who was disposed to resent the use of so severe a word, even from the legislator cousin.

'In a strange gentleman's bedroom!' he continued. 'It only shows that what I have always said is quite true. You should never go to bed in a strange house without locking your door.'

Nevertheless it was a very jovial meeting, and before the evening was over Mr Jones was happy, and had been brought to acknowledge that the mustard-plaster would probably not do him any permanent injury.